Bad Reputation

STEFANIE LONDON

sourcebooks
casablanca

Copyright © 2018 by Stefanie London
Cover and internal design © 2018 by Sourcebooks, Inc.
Cover design by John Kicksee
Cover images © PeoplesImages/Getty Images; © Fer Gregory/Shutterstock

Sourcebooks and the colophon are registered trademarks of Sourcebooks, Inc.

Published by Sourcebooks Casablanca, an imprint of Sourcebooks, Inc.
P.O. Box 4410, Naperville, Illinois 60567-4410
(630) 961-3900
Fax: (630) 961-2168
sourcebooks.com

Printed and bound in Canada.
MBP 10 9 8 7 6 5 4 3 2 1

*To my husband, who taught me to ruthlessly pursue
happiness and to never take life too seriously*

*And to all the Aussies who've terrified people
with stories about their "thongs"*

Wes,

I'm sure you're not enough of a douchebag to have a Google Alert set up for your own name (or if you are, no judgment. Okay…a little judgment), so you may not have seen this. But your junk is famous! No, that's not a typo.

I'm not the kind of woman to have a one-night stand, but after I saw a picture of him on holiday in Bora Bora with that Victoria's Secret model, Nadja Vasiliev, I HAD to know if it was real. And I can tell you, ladies, that bulge is not a product of Photoshop.

Let's just say that most guys are garden snakes. If you're lucky, you might get a king snake. But Wes is an anaconda…and he knows how to use it.

Oh. My. God.

I don't even know what to say. There's this app that allows New York women to rate men they've dated or something crazy like that. I was checking it out for a friend *cough-it-was-totally-me-cough* and I found you on there. Your reviews were enlightening, my friend. Maybe I should rescind my previous request that we never get in each other's pants. Because apparently, you've been hiding a predator in there.

Here's the link: badbachelors.com/reviews/
Wes-Evans/

Happy reading.
Sadie out.

Chapter 1

"Does size really matter? I think you know the answer to that."

—NoPicklesPlease

SOMETHING WASN'T RIGHT. EITHER IT WAS TOO LONG OR too…thick. Remi Drysdale tilted her head and stared. "I don't think it's going to fit."

"They all say that." The man in front of her flashed a brilliant smile, which was enhanced by yesterday's five o'clock shadow. Remi rolled her eyes. She was used to cocky guys talking a big game. But if online dating had taught her anything, it was that men grossly overestimated themselves.

Noting her unimpressed expression, he added, "It'll fit. Trust me."

"I don't know about that." She leaned forward, narrowing her eyes. "I'm assuming you've done this before."

His smile slipped. "Of *course* I've done this before."

Suddenly he didn't look so confident. Remi stepped forward and touched his arm, using her sweetest smile to keep him from leaving the job unfinished. "We don't want to damage anything. Just…go easy. Slow and steady, all right?"

"You wait and see. It'll slide right in and fit like a glove."

"If you say so."

She stepped back as the man and his partner carried the long piece of wood across the barre studio and set it in the glossy, black brackets they'd installed moments before. The barre fit…barely. The rounded edge was a hairbreadth from the wall, and her boss had insisted that the studio's fresh paint job remain scratch-free.

"See." He winked. "Told you."

"You were cutting it close." She inspected the barre, running her hand along the smoothly polished surface. "But I stand corrected."

"We'll bring the other one in along with the portable units," he said. "Then I'll need someone to sign. If your boss isn't here, it'll have to be you. I've got another delivery to make right after this."

Remi nodded. "I'll call her again."

She waited for the men to leave before her lips split into a wide grin. She punctuated her excitement with a pirouette, the rubber soles of her Converse sneakers squeaking against the polished floor.

The studio was *perfect*. Formerly an accounting office, it had been so run-down it could have been used for the set of a zombie apocalypse movie. But Remi's boss, Mish, had replaced the windows and flooring, painted the walls, and installed floor-to-ceiling mirrors on two sides— behind the barre and along the front of the room, where the instructors would stand. The mirrors made the room look enormous and gave the space a bright, airy feel.

Best of all, this new studio was a scant ten-minute walk from Remi's Park Slope apartment, which would mean no more getting up at the butt crack of dawn to haul ass to the Upper East Side.

Remi pulled her phone out of her bag and swiped her thumb across the screen. She was about to hit the Call button when Mish burst into the studio.

"Sorry, sorry, sorry!"

Remi laughed. "I know you're Canadian, but three sorrys seems a bit much. Even for you."

"Shut it, Aussie." Mish pulled a hair tie off her wrist and attempted to tame her mane of wild, blond frizz into a ponytail. "This looks amazing."

"It really does. The guys are bringing in the second barre now, and then they've got the portable ones too. Where were you thinking of putting those?"

"Probably in the storage room. I don't know how full the classes are going to be until we open, so we may not need them until business picks up."

Mish had opened Allongé Barre Fitness with a single tiny studio on the Upper East Side. When Remi started working there four years ago, she'd only taught two classes per week. But over the years she and Mish had grown close and Remi's schedule had expanded. Now Mish was about to open her third studio—the first in Brooklyn—and Remi was going to be the main instructor.

A quiet voice niggled in the back of her mind, like a tiny pinprick in her skull. Not big enough to cause any real pain, but she felt it nonetheless.

This isn't what you're supposed to be doing…

Shoving the feeling aside, Remi wrapped her arms around Mish and squeezed. "I can't believe you're opening studio number three. I'm *so* proud of you."

"I couldn't do it without you," she said. "Seriously. Owning a small business is tough, and I feel so much more confident knowing you have my back."

"Always. This is going to be a huge success, I know it."

The men returned with the second barre and installed it a foot below the first one. Remi could already see her little students in here—the parents and kids' classes were her favorite. She loved the wide-eyed wonder of children learning something new, the way they tackled things without the fear of embarrassment or failure that inhibited her older students.

Sure, this wasn't *real* ballet. Perhaps that was why it suited her.

"We're going to set up the rack for the hand weights here." Mish pointed to the back corner of the studio. "And the yoga mats can be rolled up and put into containers. They get too messy when they're stacked in a pile."

"Agreed."

Mish walked over to the deliverymen and apologized for being late. She directed them out to the studio's reception area, leaving Remi alone.

This place was exactly what she'd yearned for as a young girl—a bright space with a long barre. A room ripe with possibility. The floor waiting for the strike of her *frappé*, for the graceful *whoosh* of her toes as they left the floor in a *grand battement*. For the soundless landing of a perfect *pas de chat*. And the mirror was there to watch it all. To soak in her excitement and creativity and the little thrill she got whenever the wind rushed through her ponytail, fluttering the ribbon holding it in place, as she turned and turned and turned.

"Remi?"

She jumped at the sound of Mish's voice, startled by the sudden intrusion on her thoughts. "All done?"

"Yes." Mish shot her a rueful smile. "Thanks so much for coming here last minute to meet the delivery guys. You totally saved me."

"No worries." Remi hitched her bag higher up on her shoulder. "Hopefully the kitten doesn't have any more stomach troubles."

"Who knows? That's what I get for taking in strays, eh?" She shook her head. "We've got an appointment with the vet later today to get him checked out."

"You've got a good heart."

"And a deep disrespect for my carpet."

Remi laughed and checked her watch. "I've got to run. I promised Darcy I'd meet her for coffee this afternoon, and I want to walk, seeing as it's so lovely out."

"Go." Mish made a shooing motion. "I'll call you tomorrow so we can review the timetable."

Remi waved as she headed out of the studio. It was a perfect early fall day—sunny and pleasant but with a hint of crispness to the air—cool enough for a jacket if you felt so inclined. After a long, sticky summer, Remi craved this kind of weather. Not to mention fall was beautiful in New York—all those golden-amber and rich-red tones. They hardly got any of that back in Australia. Too many native evergreens.

"Speaking of home," she muttered to herself as she

turned onto Flatbush Avenue. She was due to Skype
with her parents soon.

They would be arriving back from their "retreat" any
day now. For most couples their age a relaxing getaway
probably included a cruise or a resort. Even touristy
holidays seeing the sights of another country. At the very
least, there'd be a caravan trip of some kind—or, what the
heck did they call them here? Winnebagos? Motor homes?

Anyhow, her parents weren't like most couples their
age. No siree.

For Opal and Dan Drysdale, a vacation was not
complete without some kind of enlightenment. In this
case, it was a tantric couple's retreat in Nimben, a.k.a.
the hippie capital of Australia.

Her parents were taking sex workshops.

Remi cringed. Undoubtedly, her mother would
want to tell her all about it too. And, as usual, she'd have
to listen to Opal complaining that Remi had turned into
one of those "conservative, middle-class prudes" who
got all squeamish about sex. Remi *wasn't* squeamish
about sex. Not even a little bit. She happened to quite
enjoy the occasional roll in the hay with a hot guy. In
fact, she'd *very* much enjoyed her sexy weekend with the
hottie from Texas who had asked her to strut around
his hotel room wearing only a pair of pink-rhinestone-
studded cowgirl boots. No, she was definitely *not* a prude.

But she didn't want to hear about her parents doing
it. Ever.

Remi pulled out her phone and set a reminder to
check in with her folks that weekend. They might be
New Age-this and artisanal-that, but Opal and Dan still

expected to talk to her once a month. *That* was where they clung to tradition.

Half an hour later, Remi turned onto Schermerhorn Street. For some reason, every time she headed to Darcy's new place in DUMBO, she'd take this detour. The street itself wasn't particularly interesting. At this time of year, it was clogged with the "prewinter" construction rush, which meant walking under scaffolding and dodging traffic cones.

But there was one thing that always drew her down this street.

"Excuse me." A small woman with inky hair pulled into a tight bun gracefully stepped around Remi. She wore a pair of black leggings that ended at the bottom of her calf, exposing a few inches of pink tights above her high-top sneakers.

She was one of a dozen people streaming in and out of the Brooklyn Ballet building. Mostly women, but a few young men as well. All with that strong yet willowy figure ballet dancers were known for.

Their movements were fluid, making everything seem perfectly choreographed, from the gentle wrist flick of a wave to how they darted across the street between traffic. Even something as simple as bending down to tie a shoelace embodied an otherworldly grace.

After she'd soaked it in, Remi hurried down the street, sliding her headphones over her ears to drown out the city.

Wes Evans was used to women checking him out. He exercised often and presented himself well, always living by his father's advice that he should dress like he was about to meet someone important. In New York City, a meeting like that could take place anywhere—riding in an elevator, sitting in the back of a cab, or lining up to order a coffee.

After a stint as a guest judge on *Dance Idol*, his face had garnered even more attention. Fans of the show wanted to gush over their front-runner picks, and wannabe performers tried to make an impression in the hopes he might remember them the next time he held an audition.

But this…this was different.

"What can I get you?" The barista devoured him with her eyes, the smooth dart of her tongue leaving behind a glossy sheen on her pink lips.

"Cold brew." He pulled his wallet out of the back pocket of his jeans. "Black."

She tilted her head slightly. Behind a set of thick-framed glasses, her gaze roamed down his body, lingering south of his belt. "Size?"

"Grande."

She reached for a clear plastic cup, sticking the cap of her Sharpie into her mouth and pulling the pen out with a pop. Another barista passed behind her, also checking him out. "I heard he was more of a Venti," she said in a not-so-quiet whisper.

The first barista wrinkled her nose as though trying to stifle a laugh while she marked the cup. "It's Wes, right?"

"Yeah."

He wanted to ask how she knew his name, but frankly, he wasn't about to subject himself to more assessment. He felt like a piece of steak being wheeled around on a cart at one of those fancy restaurants, just waiting for people to comment on his shape and size.

"Can I get you anything else?" she asked.

"No thanks." He handed over a ten-dollar bill and walked away before she had time to count his change.

He was ready to be done with today. And the quicker he got his caffeine fix, the better. Perhaps he should have chosen a place a little less public for this meeting. But when Sadie, his best friend and now business associate, had forwarded him the email about the Bad Bachelors website earlier that morning, he hadn't taken it too seriously. The second he'd stepped out of his Upper East Side apartment though, he'd realized that Sadie wasn't the only one using this tabloid cesspool of a website.

The barista placed his cold brew on the counter and winked at him. She'd written her phone number on his cup.

"Wes!" Sadie waved at him from a table in the back corner of the café. Her hair was cropped close on one side and left longer on the other, the blue and purple strands curving down around her jaw. "Or should I say, Mr. Anaconda?"

"Don't start," he said, dropping into the seat across from her. "I'm beginning to wonder if the human race suddenly developed X-ray vision with the way everyone is looking at me."

"I doubt they need it. Someone did a digital recreation

over that picture of you and…what was her name? The Russian chick. Natasha? Natalia?"

"Nadja."

"That's it." Sadie snapped her fingers. "Anyway, it's floating around online. They Photoshopped it to show what was going on underneath your board shorts, and I have to say—"

"You *really* don't."

Sadie grinned and waded her straw through a mound of whipped cream sitting on top of some caramel-mocha monstrosity. "You've been keeping things from me."

"I thought we had an agreement."

Wes and Sadie had been friends as long as anyone could remember. They'd grown up as neighbors in one of the most exclusive apartment buildings in Manhattan, traded lunches on the playground, and, after a disaster of a kiss around the time they were eighteen, had promptly agreed that they would always and forever be friends. Nothing more.

"We do. But that was *before* I knew you were packing more than the average salami." She couldn't keep a straight face and burst out laughing. "Ew. No, I can't even joke about it without feeling dirty."

"Gee, thanks."

"Nothing personal. Besides, you're going to have every other woman in this goddamn city chasing after you now. You don't need my attention too."

"Excellent." He clapped his hands. "Can we cut the locker room bullshit and get back to work, then?"

"No need to get snippy." Sadie looked too damn smug for her own good.

Wes opened the spreadsheet that had their production budget outlined to the very last detail, with a total that would make most people's eyes pop. Broadway productions were expensive. Even those classified as "Off-Off-Broadway," which were held in small theaters that seated fewer than a hundred people, cost a pretty penny. In this case, many of those involved were taking part for next to nothing, hoping the show would break out. But the theater still needed to be paid for, costumes needed to be created, and sets needed to be designed.

All of which required deep pockets.

"I got a final figure from the Attic," Wes said. "It's more than we budgeted for, but we can manage it. I'll push the investors harder, and I have wiggle room with my own funds."

"You're already pouring so much of your own money into this." Sadie frowned.

She didn't often show her stress, but Wes knew her well enough to detect the hint of concern in her voice. It wasn't exactly unwarranted. He *was* putting everything into this crazy idea.

Out of Bounds was his brainchild, a dance production with no separation between stage and seating. The cast was part of the audience and the audience part of the show. It was the antithesis of the world he'd grown up in, one fortified with rules and posture and tradition. With his big-picture view and Sadie's talent for turning his vague descriptions into something living and breathing, he *knew* they had something special. All they had to do was back themselves long enough to give the rest of New York a chance to agree.

"I can manage a bit more," he said. "I want this to work."

Sadie bit her lip and nodded. "I do too, but I'm worried you'll get cleaned out if this fails."

"It won't fail."

Even as he said the words, the stats danced in his head. Successful Broadway productions were in the minority, with less than 25 percent turning a profit. And those were the ones with big advertising budgets. Breakouts like *Hamilton* were rare, and most productions ended up in a financial graveyard littered with the bones of failed dreams.

Fact was, the numbers were against them. They were more likely to crash and burn and end up with bank accounts drier than the Sahara.

"Besides," he added, "I have the city's best choreographer working for me."

Sadie snorted. "Flattery won't get you anywhere, Wes. But I hope you're right. I burned a hell of a bridge leaving your parents' company to do this with you."

"You and me both," he muttered.

Out of Bounds was either going to make or break his future, and Wes wasn't the kind of guy who backed down from a challenge.

"Now all we need to do is secure the funding and find our perfect ballerina," he said with a grin. "No sweat at all."

Chapter 2

"All these women who say 'looks shouldn't matter' are deluding themselves. Physical attraction is part of what creates that first spark of chemistry. Deep down, everybody wants that jolt of lightning."

—JamieChoo

"IT'S A *TENDU*, DUH!" WES'S FIVE-YEAR-OLD NIECE, Frankie, did her best impression of a *tendu*, which looked more like a cross between a ninja kick and a Jack Russell peeing on a wall.

"Of course it is," Wes said, smothering a laugh. His mind was still full of ideas and plans from his meeting with Sadie earlier that day; however, Frankie made it tough to focus on anything but her. The kid was a whirlwind and a natural-born charmer.

"She's got my grace." Chantel laid a hand on his shoulder as she breezed past, a subtle cloud of perfume following her. "Can't you tell?"

Wes grinned at his twin sister. "What did Mom used to call you? A bull in a china shop?"

"A what?" Frankie cocked her head, but her foot continued to frantically "*tendu*" as if of its own accord.

"Nothing, darling." Chantel bent down and kissed Frankie on the cheek, swiping her thumb across the faint lipstick print she left behind.

The action made Wes smile. Their mother used to do the same thing on the rare occasions that she kissed them. Not that he would point it out. Comparing Chantel to their mother was an offense punishable by a withering death stare.

"Thanks for taking her to class." Chantel stood and smoothed her hands down the front of her all-black outfit. "I told Marnie weeks ago I'd cover for her today. But *someone* was quite determined not to have her schedule interrupted."

Apparently when she'd tried to explain to Frankie that they wouldn't be going to their "parents and kids" barre class today, there had been tears of the end-of-the-world kind. Since Wes's production wasn't yet under way, he could spare the hour to keep his niece happy. And he wanted to.

Once *Out of Bounds* launched, he'd be run off his feet for weeks, doing everything he could to ensure its success. And that would mean sacrificing things like playdates with Frankie and her baby sister, Daisy.

"Someone was being determined? Color me shocked." He winked at Frankie, who twirled, almost taking out a vase and their old cat, Nellie, with her flailing arms.

"The human tornado strikes again." Chantel shook her head.

Frankie leaned in close to Wes and whispered, "That's me."

"Go and grab your dance bag, Frankie," Chantel

said. The second her daughter raced from the room, she turned to Wes. "Last time I asked Mom for some advice on dealing with Frankie's 'spirited temperament,' she told me it was karma."

Wes snorted. "Sounds like something she would say."

"I guess I shouldn't complain. We *are* on speaking terms at the moment. That's got to count for something, right?" She rubbed her fingers against her temples. "And she agreed to take Daisy for the afternoon."

"She wasn't up for a barre class?" he teased, already knowing what the answer would be.

"Are you kidding me? She thinks bringing ballet 'to the masses' is an abomination. You know, because such things should only be available to those serious enough to pursue it properly."

Black or white—that was his mother in a nutshell. One should chase the prima ballerina dream until they soared, or until it burned them to the ground. If they weren't willing to push themselves to the limit for the sake of art, then they had no place standing at a barre. He'd heard those words over and over as a kid. Which was exactly why Chantel and his mother's relationship had barely survived her quitting the ballet world at eighteen. And it was precisely why he'd never wanted to be a performer. His place was behind the scenes, directing and creating. Bringing his visions to life.

"How's the show going?" Chantel asked.

"It's coming together." He bobbed his head. "We're almost ready to begin rehearsals and we've got a venue locked in."

"Fabulous." Chantel squinted at him. "You don't

look like someone who's escaped the clutches of the day job to follow some big, crazy dream. You should be bouncing off the walls."

Wes laughed and ran a hand through his hair. "I'll be bouncing off the walls when I know we've got a full cast."

"Still no perfect ballerina?"

He shook his head. The hunt for the centerpiece of the show had proven difficult, despite his industry connections. Last week, he'd lost the ballerina originally cast as the lead for *Out of Bounds*. Ashleigh had checked all the boxes—impeccable technique and training, she was also a gifted actress and had some musical theater experience, which gave her stage presence greater depth.

However, after signing, she'd asked if it was possible to meet with his mother for a mentoring opportunity and, of course, Wes had agreed. He'd hoped it might show Adele Evans how serious he was taking this work. But all it had done was prove people were out for number one. Ashleigh had used that connection to score herself a company role, thus dropping out of his show at the last minute, and his mother had lent her a helping hand.

And you're surprised people are using you as a stepping-stone? When has that not been the case?

"What about that 'diamond in the rough' Mom found in Detroit?"

"Oh, I thought of her. But she's the perfect little protégé now." Wes let out a humorless laugh. "I guess I *could* completely napalm my relationship with Mother Dearest."

"Not advised," Chantel said with a shake of her head. "Have you talked to her about what happened with Ashleigh?"

"I tried. But she fed me some bullshit about how she must do what's in the best interest of the dancer. I didn't even bother after that. It's like talking to a brick wall."

"Ah, so I take it she still isn't on board with your 'weird' idea?"

That was an understatement. "What did she say? I'm 'taking all she holds dear and bringing a hammer down on it.'"

For years Wes had fooled himself into thinking that drama was part of the Adele Evans charm, a persona of sorts. But the last six months had proven him wrong. His mother had acted like Wes's dream to create his own show was a personal attack on her, the family company, *and* the art form she adored.

"Are we going yet?" Frankie planted her hands on her hips. She wore a pink leotard and tights, and a pair of purple high-top sneakers. "It's rude to be late."

Wes raised a brow, and Chantel shrugged. "Hey, I'm not going to complain if she wants to be punctual."

"All right, human tornado. Let's go." He held his hand out, and Frankie shoved her chubby, little fist into his palm. "First, class. Then, we can go for gelato."

"I want peppermint." Frankie nodded as though giving it serious thought. "With chocolate sprinkles."

"You can have whatever you want, princess."

Remi eased herself into first position, rotating her turnout from the hips and resting both hands on the barre. Her touch was featherlight, as though her fingertips meant to graze the polished wood. She rose into a *relevé* and held the position for a second before pressing her heels back down into the floor.

This gentle up-down motion came as naturally as breathing. As naturally as being.

Despite all the tangled-up feelings in her heart when it came to dance, her body still knew what it wanted. What felt right.

She repeated the action a few times more, warming her ankles and calves in preparation for her class. Words swirled in her head, snippets of the Skype call she'd had with her parents last night.

Her mother hadn't bought the whole "great opportunity to support a local business" angle that Remi had pitched them when she'd described her work at the new barre fitness studio. Opal Drysdale might be all peace, love, and light, with her predilection for crystal healing and daily positivity mantras, but the woman knew bullshit when she smelled it. And Remi was no actress. As usual, her father hadn't said much and simply looked adoringly at his wife whenever she spoke.

But no amount of chiding from Opal was going to change things. And Remi certainly wasn't going to "meditate on it."

"Excuse me." A deep, smooth voice startled Remi out of her thoughts.

Remi turned, her heart thudding in her chest at the sight of the man in front of her. He was one of those "so hot he should come with a fire hazard warning" kind of guys. Wavy, dark hair. Piercing blue eyes. A touch of stubble coating a jaw sharp enough to slice butter, a.k.a.

the type of guy she usually avoided because they tended to be entitled douches who were selfish in and out of the bedroom.

And you're thinking about bedrooms now because...?

He walked toward her with a practiced roll of the hips that was halfway between a John Wayne movie and a wet dream. Remi sucked in a breath. "Can I help you?"

"I hope so." His gaze flicked over her like he wanted to look but was trying to retain a semblance of human decency.

That's right, buddy. Eyes up here.

"My niece is in your class." He thumbed the belt loops on his jeans. "Francesca Mancini."

Francesca. The name didn't ring a bell, and Remi prided herself on learning everyone's names, especially her young students. Shit, how could she have forgotten Francesca?

It's the hot-dude voodoo scrambling your brain.

"Frankie," he offered.

"Oh, yes, Frankie." She nodded. Rambunctious five-year-old, a bit of a handful due to her high energy levels. But she was adorable and charming. Must be a family trait. "Of course, Chantel's daughter."

"And I'm Chantel's brother." He smiled and Remi studiously ignored the ripple of attraction that shot through her, warming her insides like palms turned to an open flame. "I'm on Frankie duty today."

She found herself returning the smile. "Lucky you."

"Absolutely. I'd spend all day every day with that kid if I could."

Her heart melted into a puddle of marshmallow goo. Okay, so not a *total* douche then.

"What time does the class finish?" he asked, taking a step closer. A blue-and-white checked shirt hugged broad shoulders and strong arms, the cuffs folded back to reveal a heavy watch and strong hands. The kind of hands that looked incredibly…dexterous.

In fact, he looked familiar, now that she thought about it. But she couldn't place him.

Maybe in your nameless-hot-guy dreams?

"We say forty-five minutes, but it can run over depending on how many people we have."

"I'll be back in forty-five minutes on the dot then."

"Back?"

"Yeah." He nodded, his dark brows crinkling slightly. "To pick Frankie up."

"This is a parents-and-kids class," Remi said, stifling a smile. "Parents are required to accompany their kids for the duration of the class."

Her gaze skimmed down his body, over the tan belt highlighting his trim waist, to the faded denim hugging his thighs and… Oh. The soft-looking denim hugged *everything*.

Hey, no double standards here. Eyes up, soldier!

"And by accompany I assume you mean participate?" he said.

"That's right."

He shook his head, a rueful smile crossing his lips. "Funny how my sister didn't mention that bit."

The thought of this insanely hot man following her command was doing unspeakable things to her insides. Tingling things. The kind of things that were definitely "not safe for work." She'd been attracted to men who could dance ever since she'd first laid eyes on Paul Mercurio in *Strictly Ballroom*. And later on, her theory that skills on the dance floor translated to skills in the bedroom had been upheld on almost all occasions.

Instinct told her that this man would *not* disappoint.

"I'm sure you can keep up," Remi said, walking past him to greet the other students streaming into the room. "You look like you have a few moves in your arsenal."

"More than a few," he replied, his eyes tracking her as she breezed past.

"I look forward to seeing them."

Frankie raced into the studio and tugged on her uncle's hand. His intense, burning gaze dissolved into something softer and a whole lot sweeter as he bent down to fix the ribbon in her hair. The little girl waved frantically, almost knocking her uncle square in the face.

Remi waved back and began preparing for her class. It appeared she wasn't the only one interested in the handsome newcomer. Each Allongé Barre Fitness location had a slightly different clientele. They predicted more groups of girlfriends at the new Brooklyn studio, people who were looking for a fun and relaxed atmosphere. The Midtown location had a lot of office workers seeking a pre- or post-workday stress release. And the Upper East Side studio had a lot of well-dressed women wearing designer workout gear and perfectly styled hair. But overwhelmingly, their clients were female, regardless of location.

Which meant Mr. McHottie stood out like a sore thumb. Or would that be a sexy thumb?

Focus. Pretty sure Mish wouldn't want you fraternizing with the customers.

Her brain immediately refuted that thought. Technically, he wasn't a customer. He was simply helping his sister out. Brownie point number one. And Mish didn't actually have a no-fraternization policy for the studio that she was aware of.

Besides, indulging in a little eye candy was hardly cause for concern.

"If everyone can take their places at the barre, we'll get started." Remi waited for the class to settle. A few of the women tried to casually shuffle closer to Frankie's uncle.

"You're not supposed to wear shoes," Frankie said loudly. She pointed to the sneakers on her uncle's feet, and he looked at Remi.

The eye contact was like having a hole blown through her, and she sucked in a breath. Since when did a worldly woman like herself get all shaken up by a sexy, blue gaze? Never. Remi wasn't a blushing wallflower by any means, but it seemed like all her carefully curated composure had melted away.

"Shoes off," she confirmed with a nod, swallowing back the fizzing excitement that seemed determined to bubble over.

"See?" Frankie turned back to face the barre, her small feet immediately settling into a perfect first position. "Told you."

Rubber squeaked against the floor as the man toed off his sneakers. The air around Remi was thick as she waited until he was barefoot.

"We're going to start by warming up our ankles."

She positioned herself next to the teacher's barre to demonstrate the exercise. "Slide your right foot along the floor in front of you, keeping toes pointed. Then flex and point, flex and point."

The routine rolled off her tongue—she'd done it so many times now, she was quite sure she muttered "flex and point" in her sleep. To her surprise, the man had decent flexibility in his feet and ankles and didn't sickle his foot like a lot of people did when they were new to ballet.

"Bring your foot into first position and then out to the side. Flex and point…"

While the rest of the class concentrated—the little ones in varying positions, legs and arms akimbo—the man watched her. He moved surely, confidently. Like a tiger. Remi was sure any other man in his position would have been at least mildly mortified at having to take part in a barre fitness class without preparation. But he was unfazed.

When she instructed them to start the next exercise, his eyes never left her. It was like he could see through her clothes, through her perky smile and plump ballerina bun. Through the layers of pink Lycra she wore like armor.

This wasn't simple attraction. It was electric.

Stop it. You owe it to Mish to be professional.

Right, she had a job to do…but only for the next forty-five minutes.

Chapter 3

"On a scale of one to Jon Hamm, Wes Evans sits squarely at the 'two hands required' end of the spectrum."

—PlainSlice

WES IMMENSELY ENJOYED THE SUBTLE GAME OF CAT AND mouse he had going with the instructor of Frankie's class. Her smug expression had been a red, flapping cape when she'd told him that he would have to join the class—almost as though she thought it would make him squirm. Little did she know…

It'd been a heck of a long time since Wes had done anything close to dancing. These days, he favored going for a run through Central Park or chasing Frankie around until they were both huffing and puffing. But muscle memory was a fascinating thing, and his body knew exactly what was required. He'd retained some of his fluidity, some of that strong posture and confident, graceful movement. All the things that allowed him to enter a room with a bang.

Most guys his age were monster trucks—big and powerful but clunky. Lumbering. Despite merciless bullying about his dancing when he was a kid, Wes knew it had been the very thing that made him who he was today. A sports car—smooth, stylish. A head turner.

Did that make him cocky? Hell yeah. But modesty didn't get you anywhere. Not in this city, anyway.

Watching the instructor subtly raise a brow as he followed her steps had been enormously satisfying. She'd underestimated him.

"Great job, class. We've got a few final stretches and then we're done." Miss Perky Instructor grinned at the students, the bright expression turning smoky when her eyes landed on him. "Take a *port de bras* up over your heads and then hinge forward. Touch the floor if you can."

The first movement of her demonstration grabbed his attention, the gentle whisk of her hands above her head into that perfect *port de bras* shape. But when she bent forward, folding herself in half and thrusting her pert ass into the air, Wes's lungs almost gave out. The woman was wildfire.

The floor-to-ceiling mirrors behind her gave him a perfect view of her long, shapely legs and sweet, heart-shaped butt. But he wasn't only captivated by her gorgeous body—there was something about her movement too. A quiet musicality and grace that hinted at formal training. Perhaps not much, since Wes knew everyone in the New York ballet scene. Though she *did* have an accent.

"Uncle Wes," Frankie hissed. "You're supposed to be standing up."

He grunted when a small but sharp elbow landed hard against his rib cage. "Sorry, Frankie."

He righted himself, catching up to the group and enjoying the instructor's delightful smirk. Busted! She knew he'd been checking her out.

When the class finished, Frankie raced off to change into her sneakers, her distinctive voice rising above the more subdued murmur from the rest of the students.

"Thanks for being a good sport." The instructor walked over, her feet ever-so-slightly turned out and her hands brushing delicately by her sides. Yep, she'd definitely trained at some point. Talented too, he'd bet. "Even if you were unprepared."

"You certainly kept me on my toes."

"Was that a ballet pun?" She narrowed her eyes, the corner of her mouth fighting a smile.

"Definitely not," he said with a mock-serious expression.

"Because I really don't see the *pointe* of those. It's not that I have a bad *attitude*, but I need to set the *barre* higher than that." A mischievous twinkle lit her dark eyes.

"That's impressive."

"Don't even try to out-pun me. I'm like the Energizer Bunny of bad jokes."

He chuckled. "What else you got?"

"What animals are poor dancers?" She paused. "Four-legged ones, because they have two left feet."

"I'll have to tell Frankie that one."

"Actually, I'm pretty sure she told *me* that joke." Remi shook her head. "Your niece has a great sense of humor."

"It's a family gift." He pretended to brush something off his shoulder and was rewarded with the tinkling sound of her laughter. Damn, that sound was straight out of heaven. "Good turnout and a passion for lame jokes."

"That all?"

"Well, I have a few personal talents."

She raised an eyebrow. "Such as?"

"I make a mean stir-fry. And my *tendu* was pretty damn spectacular, in case you didn't notice." He winked, barely able to keep a straight face.

"Oh, I noticed." The words were fired back and forth lightning fast. Like fireflies zipping around them. "I'm Remi, by the way." She stuck her hand out.

"Wes." Her palm slid into his, and he closed his fingers around her hand. Judging by the quick flare of her nostrils, she felt the snap of electricity too. "I know all the ballerinas in New York, but I've never seen you before."

"How lucky for all the ballerinas in New York." Her voice was husky as she pulled her hand back, severing the crackling connection between them. "You got some kind of tutu fetish?"

"Yeah, I love that scratchy feeling." He shoved his hands into his back pockets. "And nice job dodging the question, by the way. That's some politician-level interview skills you got there."

"I wasn't aware I was being interviewed," she replied with a smirk. "And if you watch the replay I think you'll find you didn't actually ask me a question."

The exchange made him even more curious. "How come I haven't met you already?"

"I'm not from around here, if you couldn't tell."

"I want to say you're from New Zealand or Australia." He cocked his head. "But I won't claim to know the difference well enough to pick a side."

"Chicken," she teased.

He chuckled. "Don't you mean smart?"

She toyed with the neckline of her leotard, which had long sleeves and a funky cutout at the top, exposing just a hint of skin at her chest. Freckles peeked out between the gaps in the material, and he had an overwhelming desire to trace them with his fingertip.

"I'm an Aussie, born and bred." She narrowed her eyes as though trying to figure something out. "But I'm not a ballerina, which would explain why you don't know me."

Wes would bet his last dollar bill Remi was classically trained. He'd seen a lot of dancers come in and out of his parents' school over the years, and if there was one thing he could spot with ease, it was the way a ballerina moved.

"Why are you looking at me like that?" she asked.

"Just wondering why you're lying to me."

Remi blinked. "I'm not lying."

"You said you weren't a ballerina."

"I said I'm *not* a ballerina," she corrected, tucking a loose strand of hair behind her ear. It almost immediately curled back against her face, rebellious and soft. "Present tense."

Ah, that explained it. He was tempted to argue that one never stopped being a ballerina, even if they weren't training or performing anymore. But instinct told him it was a touchy subject. "Right."

"You've got a good eye, though."

He wasn't sure if she was wary or impressed. "Decided it wasn't for you?"

"Other way around." Darkness flickered across her face, casting a shadow over her rich brown eyes. "Ballet decided I wasn't right for it."

Cryptic. Color him intrigued.

"How do you know so much about ballerinas?" she asked as they turned and headed out of the studio.

"My mother was a principal dancer at the New York City Ballet. Now she and my father own a dance school."

"Wes Evans." Her mouth popped open. "I thought I recognized you!"

He tried not to cringe. This was the part he would never get used to—the way someone changed when they found out who he was. The way expectations and demands and motives shifted. In this industry, so much was *who* you knew. A foot in the door could be the difference between a career taking off or crumbling to dust. Which was exactly why he was having a hard time finding the lead for *Out of Bounds*.

Too many people knew how Adele Evans felt about it and so they were staying the hell away.

"I'm a huge *Dance Idol* fan, obviously. I thought you made a great judge." They reached the exit of the studio and she hovered by the door. "There's a real art to delivering a critique that will help someone grow without tearing apart their self-esteem. I think all the contestants will be better off in their careers having worked with you."

Wes blinked. Okay, so he hadn't been expecting *that*.

Usually the next thing that came after "I'm a huge fan of *insert thing here*" was a request of some kind—information, insight, or, for those who had brass balls, a favor.

"Have dinner with me," he blurted out.

Smooth, Evans. Like fucking sandpaper.

Remi laughed and looked at him for a moment as though she was seriously considering it. "No, I'm afraid I can't."

Without any further explanation, she touched his arm and sent electricity bolting through him. After a brief smile floated across her lips, she headed into the studio's reception area. He didn't even get a backward glance. Just a flat-out no.

You're losing your touch.

Or maybe there was something deeper at play. Regardless, all Remi had done was crank his curiosity up to maximum levels.

"Looks like you've got another barre fitness class to attend," he said under his breath as Frankie came running up to him.

Son of Broadway royalty and his new show are overshadowed by giant bulge...

By Peta McKinnis (*Spill the Tea* society and culture reporter)

Bigger is better, right? That certainly seems to be the case for a former *Dance Idol* judge who also happens to be the son of famed ballerina Adele Evans and her Broadway-legend husband, Rich Evans. The young bachelor celebrated his thirtieth birthday last year with a Victoria's Secret supermodel on his arm in Bora Bora, where shots were taken of the two frolicking on the beach and playing around on Jet Skis.

For once, eyes weren't on international supermodel Nadja Vasiliev, but rather on what was going on in Wes's pants.

Rumor has it that Wes is trying to get a new show off the ground, separate from his well-connected parents. At this stage, there hasn't been a lot of official talk about the show, but sources say it's a dance production slated for an Off-Off-Broadway run.

Spill the Tea reached out to a former staffer who happened to have a personal connection to Evans. Our anonymous source said: "I've never dated Wes, but I went to school with him and caught him changing backstage at our senior production. The man was genetically blessed beyond what should be legal for one person. He's physical perfection. It's intimidating."

The question remains though: Will Wes be able to get people talking about his work instead of his...well, you know?

Probably not, if the Bad Bachelors app has anything to do with it. The app—which allows New York women to rate their dates (or use it for possible post-breakup revenge, as *Spill the Tea* has previously speculated)—has been the cause of misery for some men and a source of notoriety for others. What will it be for Wes?

The app is the apparent source of his new nickname—"The Anaconda"—and features reviews from a handful of women who've been lucky enough to confirm the rumors.

"Wes Evans sits squarely at the 'two hands required' end of the spectrum." —PlainSlice

A representative from *Spill the Tea* reached out to Bad Bachelors to see what they think about the potential negative impact of the site's reviews, and received the following response:

"Bad Bachelors is committed to providing the women of New York a platform on which to empower themselves while dating. We encourage all members of the site to review in accordance with the Bad Bachelors terms and conditions."

There you have it. As your number-one source of gossip, *Spill the Tea* eagerly awaits the next installment of this David and his Goliath story.

"I am *seriously* concerned." Darcy pressed the back of her hand to Remi's forehead, her button nose wrinkled.

"Because I said no to a date?" Remi shoved her friend's hand aside and rolled her eyes. Remi, Annie, and Darcy usually made it a point to hang out at the end of every week. This week they were at a bowling alley, and Remi had filled her friends in on her encounter with Wes. "Do you think I'm a floozy who would say yes to anyone?"

"I wouldn't put it like *that* exactly." Darcy chuckled as she ducked away from Remi's swatting hand. "Just that you're more confident when it comes to dating."

"That's because you never dated. You went straight from being engaged to being a sexual hermit back to being engaged again."

Darcy looked at the giant rock glinting on her left hand, an uncharacteristically dreamy expression crossing her face. For as long as Remi had known her former roommate, Darcy was the opposite of dreamy. The girl was prickly, tattooed, and dressed like she'd never fully left her teenage goth phase behind. Which were precisely the things Remi loved about her—opposites attract, and all that.

Darcy was now engaged to Reed, a guy who used to be Manhattan's most notorious bachelor. They too were an unlikely pair.

Reed had also been a victim of Bad Bachelors. Being labeled their number-one worst bachelor had caused him serious problems, especially when he and Darcy had started working together. Eventually, the site had stopped posting articles about him, but not before creating a media shit storm that had resulted in his sick father being harassed by journalists and causing Reed to step away from his lucrative career as a PR consultant.

"Pshh!" Darcy waved her assessment away. "In any case, of all the people I thought would jump at the chance to go out with a guy called the Anaconda—"

"Don't you mean jump *on* the chance." Their other friend, Annie, chuckled to herself.

"—it would be you," Darcy finished.

Remi sighed. Okay, so they had a point. She liked to date—not seriously or with any end goal in mind—but she enjoyed being wined and dined, and, on occasion, she enjoyed taking a guy to bed. Sometimes the guys stuck around for a while if she liked them enough, but mostly they didn't. Keeping things light was the name of the game. And right up until the moment that she'd realized exactly who Wes Evans was, she would have happily accepted his offer.

Remi picked up her bowling ball and walked to the start of the lane. She swung her arm back and sent the ball sailing straight into the gutter.

"Bloody hell," she muttered.

"Don't bowl angry," Annie advised from where she sat, her legs dangling over the side of a chair as she brought a bottle of Coke to her lips.

"Super helpful, thanks." Remi waited for her ball to come rolling back into the return unit.

Her head had been all messed up ever since yesterday's class. It was like Wes had burrowed into her subconscious and kept popping into her thoughts like a jack-in-the-box. No matter how hard she tried, she couldn't shake him. Declining his invite went against everything she stood for, against all the rules that she'd put in place the second she'd boarded the plane on a one-way ticket to New York City:

Don't be scared.

Say yes to every opportunity.

Fun comes first.

But she *was* scared. Scared that a guy like Wes might unpick the careful stitches around her wounds, that he might summon all the doubts and regrets she'd tried so hard to bury and that were everything she'd run away from before.

"Uh, Remi?" Darcy's voice cut into her thoughts.

Remi's pink bowling ball sat in front of her, forced by the conveyer belt to spin on the spot. Like her brain.

"Got it." She picked the ball up and slid her fingers into the three slots. This time she wouldn't miss.

Letting a guy like Wes Evans into her head was dangerous. She knew enough about chemistry from years of trying to find it with her dancing partners to identify when something was stronger than the average attraction. Normally a good-looking guy would give her a *zing*, a pleasant little tingle that she might feel all the way down to her toes if he was particularly charming or witty.

But Wes's intense stare was like being hit from behind by a tidal wave.

"Yeah, and you don't want to get crushed like some sucker." She drew her arm back, calm and straight. "You're in control here."

When she released the ball, it sailed perfectly, hitting

the floor with a solid *thump* and racing toward the center front pin. *Strike!*

"Still got it." Remi wiggled her hips and sauntered back to her friends, a cocky grin on her lips. "How many strikes is that now?"

"Technically, it's a spare, since you had a gutter ball the first time," Annie said, smirking.

"If my math checks out…" Remi craned her head up to the screen above their lane. "Yep, still winning."

"Enough fighting, children." Darcy pushed up from her seat to retrieve her bowling ball. "Prepare to watch a miracle."

The girls cracked up. Darcy was so far behind there was no way she would catch up, not even if God himself sent her ball sailing down the lane. And she lacked the fierce competitive streak that Annie and Remi shared, priding herself on being able to score as little as possible with the utmost creativity.

"I'm still confused," Annie said. "Why did you say no?"

"She's worried his giant cock will eat her alive," Darcy said from the front of the lane.

"Darcy!" Annie shushed her as the people in the next lane whipped their heads around, suddenly interested in the sordid turn of conversation between the three women.

"Believe me, it's *not* that. All that online gossip stuff is bullshit anyway." Remi toyed with the strap on her top. "And who cares if he's well-endowed unless he can use it."

"So why turn him down?"

"He's part of the world I left behind…" She sighed. "I don't know exactly. I think I got scared about being tempted by all that stuff again."

"Does that mean you're really done with trying to get into a company?" Annie asked.

Remi knew what her answer should be: *yes, I'm done.* But no matter how much time passed, she couldn't force herself to say it aloud.

"I'm done with making a fool out of myself," she replied carefully. "Besides, Allongé is really starting to pick up. The new studio opens next week, and Mish has given me a good chunk of the schedule. I might even branch out on my own one day."

"You mean take the safe route." Annie bobbed her head.

"Going into business is *not* taking the safe route," Remi argued.

But even as she said the words, her thoughts contradicted her. It *did* feel like the safer option, because no one was going to point at her during class and tell her that she didn't deserve to be there. That she'd gotten her position through nefarious means.

No one would question whether she was good enough. She'd proven herself already, and *that* meant she was safe.

"If it's really what you want, you know we support you," Annie said. "But I remember the bright-eyed woman who walked into Darcy's apartment and proclaimed that she was going to be the best ballerina New York had ever seen."

God, she'd been so naive back then, thinking she could swan into this great big city and make something of herself.

"With age comes wisdom, I guess."

Annie wrinkled her nose. "Or settling."

Was that what she was doing by accepting more hours at the barre studio? By not going out with a guy whose chemistry grabbed her by the throat simply because he reminded her of her past? Maybe. But despite what her parents had always told her about aiming for the stars and all that bullshit, it was better to excel where she knew success was possible than open herself up to even more disappointment.

"In any case," Remi said. "If I was going to attempt to get back into a production or a company—which I am *not*—sleeping with the guy who has the ability to make or break my success wouldn't exactly be the smartest move on the earth, would it?"

Darcy made a *hmm* sound. "That's a very good point."

She didn't need the girls to confirm it. Her ex, Alex, had made damned sure she learned that lesson when he'd denied having any feelings for her or for the baby she'd told him she was carrying. Guys in that world were driven by their own needs; they put their careers before everything else. Before obligation, before responsibility, before any other living, breathing person.

"Why does it matter if you're not planning to go back into auditioning?" Annie asked.

"I don't want to be reminded," she said. "No amount of great sex is worth opening that old wound."

She'd moved on, healed. Mourned the loss of her career. Why would she ever put herself through that again? It was emotional sabotage, and Remi had learned the best way to avoid that was to keep things at a distance—her old dreams, her memories…and men.

Chapter 4

"Dating Wes is like riding a roller coaster in Disneyland. It's thrilling, but first you have to get in line."

—SohoHoney

DOUBT WAS A STUBBORN BITCH. IT BURROWED UNDER Remi's skin and forced her to question every life decision she'd ever made in an incessant loop. Replaying all the times she'd screwed up like some montage of failure, waking her at the crack of dawn and holding sleep firmly out of reach.

Seven a.m. Her alarm wouldn't go off for another hour and yet she was already out in the crisp, early-morning air. She burrowed her chin into her bomber jacket as she headed out of the Lexington Avenue subway station. The city had cooled over the past week, the mornings developing an edge. Especially at this hour.

And while she would have loved to cuddle up with her duvet and a coffee instead of heading out into the bracing wind, the apartment was too silent. *Way* too silent.

The quiet made her think. Remember. Doubt. All things she avoided. Keep life fun and light, that was her motto. But lately, it'd started to feel hollow and worn out.

On her way to the Upper East Side studio, Remi turned the corner and hurried down East Sixty-Sixth. The trees lining the street had commenced their annual change, turning from green to yellow and orange. This walk always felt so "New York" to her, with the cute apartment buildings and their zigzagged fire escapes, the yellow school buses and cabs, and the buildings with the awnings that stuck out onto the street to shelter people from the rain. It had all the things she'd seen on *Seinfeld*, *Friends*, and *Sex and the City* growing up in Australia.

According to the new schedule, the second studio would be free for a few more hours. That'd give her enough time to stretch out and unwind. To lose herself.

"You're early." Mish looked up from the reception desk, dark rings under her eyes. "I thought you were starting at nine."

"I needed to get out of the house." Remi shrugged out of her jacket and slung it over one arm. "Do you mind if I use studio B?"

"Of course not." Mish yawned.

"Late nights with the kitten again?"

As if on cue, a tiny *meow* cut through the quiet reception area. Remi had been so wrapped up in her thoughts she'd failed to notice Mish's feline companion, who was tucked neatly inside her sweater, a fluffy, gray head poking out where the zipper stopped midchest.

"Yeah. I think I'm going to call him Pukey."

"He's entirely too adorable for a name like that." Remi reached out to gently stroke his head, and the kitten shut his eyes contentedly.

"It's Pukey for short," Mish said. "His full name will

be Little Cat of House Mish. First of his name. King of the litter box. Shredder of curtains. Destroyer of carpets."

Remi grinned. "Rolls off the tongue, doesn't it?"

"Well, he certainly acts like a king when he's not curled up like this. I'm convinced he's only cute when other people are around." She chuckled and nuzzled the kitten's head. "My sister suggested I call him Runt."

"How about Mikhail?"

"As in Baryshnikov?"

"Yeah." Remi studied the kitten. He *was* a scrawny little thing, with hair that stuck out in all directions and a charming twinkle in his eye. "He might not have the stature of other cats, but there's something special about him." Just like the famed male ballet dancer.

"I'll call you over the next time he decides to revisit his meal and see if you still think he's special then," Mish grumbled, but Remi could plainly see that her friend was totally and utterly smitten.

"It'll get easier, mama cat." Remi paused for one more bit of kitten love and then headed into the smaller of the two studio spaces.

The empty room chilled Remi to her core. Somehow it felt colder inside than it was outside.

Remi rubbed her hands together as she walked the length of the room, the slap of her sneakers echoing off the walls. She pulled her phone out of her pocket and set it into the docking station. A second later, her warm-up playlist floated through the studio's speakers.

She took her time warming up, giving her muscles and joints an extra-long stretch. Lately, she'd found herself coming to the studio outside her scheduled classes, a certain piece of choreography tugging at her brain. Calling to her. It was the feeling she used to get back home when she danced regularly, a gnawing obsession to tweak and perfect. Which meant she'd been dancing more and more, no longer satisfied by simply conducting barre fitness classes.

It was a tough piece occupying her brain—a piece that could be magic in the hands (or was that feet?) of a talented ballerina but a hot mess if performed incorrectly.

Giselle.

Remi identified with the famous ballet, with the naïveté of the heroine in early act one. Unaware of her fate, unaware that things were about to fall apart in a way she could never have imagined. This piece was the blissful ignorance of a girl who incorrectly assumed she had everything before her.

Like Remi had in the past.

She slipped on her pointe shoes, a pair that was knocking on death's door. She couldn't bring herself to replace them, because that would be like admitting she might have a use for them beyond dancing alone in a studio, like admitting she wished that someone would watch her. That someone would see the spark she felt deep in her bones.

"No one is watching," she muttered to herself as she reached for the pale ribbons attached to her shoes.

There was something ritualistic about it. About the silky feel of the satin at her fingertips, the fluid way she crossed the ribbon in front and behind, tying the knot and tucking away the ends. She pointed and flexed her feet a few times, making sure the ribbons didn't cut in.

The music wound through her, notes seeped in hope and optimism. It was lively and upbeat. Remi could practically see the corps de ballet around her, dressed in their peasant costumes with puffy sleeves and knee-length skirts.

She tried to imagine she was Svetlana Zakharova, her career idol, prima ballerina with the Bolshoi Ballet. A prodigy. Widely considered one of the best ballerinas of modern times.

Remi rocked forward into first arabesque, her back leg extending behind her as high as it could go. *Try to touch the back wall.* Then her heel came down, and she pushed her opposite leg higher still, for just a second.

"Not good enough." She started the music again.

This time she pushed harder, stretching higher. Feeling the pull in her arms and back and hamstrings. Yes. Arabesque in first, then down. *Serré, développé.* The moves picked up speed, and Remi imagined the frothy layers of Giselle's white-and-blue skirt swirling around her legs. More *arabesques*, this time with attitude. Faster. Higher.

The music lifted her and she spun. Pirouette after pirouette. *Piqué tours en dedans*, the air flying through her hair as she whipped around.

"Again," she said to her reflection.

Remi stretched her head from side to side, rolling her shoulders before hitting play and putting everything she had into that first step. Over and over and over.

She'd dreamed about these steps, about this ballet.

She'd been a member of the corps then, on the verge of stepping up to a soloist position. Her obsession with Giselle was in spite of not knowing if she had the skill to pull off such an iconic role but wanting it so bad that her teeth ached from the hunger of it. It was the role she'd thought might show her parents what she was capable of, that ballet wasn't only rigidity and form. That when used correctly, the training could set her free instead of binding her.

"Again." She restarted the music.

This time she stopped thinking and let the notes take her over. It was like falling into a trance, as though someone else controlled her body and she was only a vessel for the story. The steps fueled her. They penetrated her bones, fortifying her. They became her and she became them.

The last part of the piece, a series of *piqué* turns, was like flying. The world rushed past, but Remi's head was clear, her mind unburdened for what felt like the first time in months.

The sound of someone clapping startled her. She whirled around, hand at her throat, to find Wes Evans standing in the doorway of the studio.

"That was a hell of a show," he said. He leaned against the doorframe, hands shoved into the pockets of his jeans, his dark hair wild and windswept.

She glanced at her reflection in the floor-to-ceiling mirrors. Speaking of windswept…

Remi tightened her ponytail. "Can I help you?"

"You already did."

What was *that* supposed to mean? She hit the pause button on her phone. The sudden silence amplified the beating of her heart.

Of course your heart is beating hard. You just danced your butt off. It has absolutely nothing to do with him.

"Seriously, you're…magnificent." He stepped into the room and let the door swing shut behind him.

If she thought he'd looked incredible before, then this was about to blow her expectations out of the water. Tight indigo jeans, chunky black boots, and a fitted black leather jacket. All that darkness made his eyes look like chips of aquamarine.

She wasn't sure how to respond. Having someone like him—someone who knew good ballet—catch her unawares was daunting as hell. She'd sooner have him walk in on her naked.

Great work. Now she was thinking about where *that* might lead.

Stop it. Now.

"Thank you," she said, her cheeks burning. "Are you here with Frankie? There's no parents-and-kids class this morning."

"Actually, I called to see when you'd be teaching next and I was told you were scheduled for this morning. I was hoping to catch you before your class. When I mentioned that I was here recently, your boss seemed to remember the story about the guy who got roped into joining your parents-and-kids class."

Remi's cheeks burned. So Mish had confirmed that they'd talked about him—*great*. "And you hustled over early to talk to me?"

"It's almost eight." His lip quirked. "I'm usually at work by this hour."

"Well, if you think turning up will convince me to go on a date with you, then think again," she said, choosing to shield herself with a hint of snark.

"*Giselle* is an interesting choice," he commented as though she hadn't shot him down.

The Anaconda isn't used to rejection.

Oh God. Now she *really* needed to stop letting her mind wander.

"Why? It's one of the most beloved ballets of all time." She busied herself with untying her pointe shoes.

"*Interesting* was the wrong word." He stopped in front of her, his shadow blanketing her. "Ambitious is more what I meant."

Ambitious. In other words, beyond her skill level. She knew it, of course, but the assessment stung a little.

"I know many a ballerina who'd give their leg for the role of Giselle," he added.

"I imagine the *piques* would be a little difficult with only one leg."

He grinned. "Figure of speech."

He was right, of course. Giselle was one of the most sought-after roles in existence. To be the perfect Giselle—to do the legend justice—a dancer would need to have near perfect technique, grace to rival the prima ballerinas of the past, *and* they'd have to be an actress too. Giselle was known for its combination of mime and dance, something that could trip up even the most perfect technical dancers.

Which was exactly why Remi loved it. It required heart and feeling, passion. Not just a series of immaculately executed steps.

"And how did I do?" She wrapped the ribbons around her pointe shoes, fighting the dread building in her stomach.

If his assessment was too negative, then it might crush what was left of her spirit. But if it was too positive, then she wouldn't believe him.

Pathetic.

"I believe I said it before." Wes reached his hand down to her. "Magnificent."

She hesitated a second before accepting the gesture, bracing herself for the singing electricity that zipped between them. It came right on cue. Dammit.

"High praise from a VIP like yourself." She stowed her shoes away in her bag and then stuffed her feet into her sneakers.

"VIP?" He cocked a brow.

"Well, being the son of a Broadway star and an accomplished ballerina, you must have some weight in the industry. Hence, very important person."

His eyes raked over her, and for the first time since they'd met, she saw something sharp. Edgy. His jaw ticked.

"I guess you could say that," he replied. "Although you make it sound like I'm a bull being assessed for breeding."

Her lip quirked. "Is this where I get to check the goods?"

"I don't know about you, but I like to at least have a meal first."

"Wow, a real live gentleman. Didn't think those existed anymore."

Remi was suddenly aware they'd drifted close to one another, as though some invisible force were pushing them together. Each sentence traded was like a degree added to her body temperature. She pressed her hand to her cheek.

"Hot?" he asked.

"You tell me."

The taunt slipped out without her permission. Dammit, she wasn't supposed to be baiting this guy. He was already getting under her skin, and that was a strictly guy-free zone. Falling was not an option.

Wes cocked his head, a sly smile playing on his lips. This time she couldn't complain, since she'd invited the devil to look. "I don't think any word could do you justice, Remi."

"Cheat."

"Women like you transcend words."

Okay, wow. So he hadn't said anything new, but the intensity of his voice—the slight growling edge, almost argumentative, passionate—sent a tingle through her. It'd been a long time since anyone had surprised her.

Dating had taught her a few things. Namely, that men were consistent creatures. They used the same lines, the same moves. The same tried and tested methods of seduction, if they bothered at all. And they grossly overestimated their impact.

But then there was the rare man like Wes. He didn't need to use lines or techniques to make her pause. He didn't need to shove his way into her attention. He didn't need to *try*.

This man is dangerous, and you know it.

Wes watched with curiosity as a kaleidoscope of emotions flashed in Remi's eyes. A few minutes earlier, he'd witnessed something amazing—a dancer who let herself go beyond perfection. Ballet attracted a certain type of person. Competitive, ambitious, type-A people who enjoyed a little self-punishment and a whole lot of discipline. The ones who successfully harnessed that while engaging their creative side often rose to the top, riding the balance of two things that, on the surface, seemed in direct opposition.

Remi danced like her soul was on fire.

That's when he knew she was the one. His centerpiece. The perfect person to tell the *Out of Bounds* story.

"You're slick, Wes Evans. I'll give you that," she said, hoisting her bag over one shoulder. "I'm sure it gives you a good hit rate with the ladies."

"But not with you?"

He'd give her the chance to explain away her attraction, but he could see it plain as day. Pink dotted her cheeks and she had this little tic, repeatedly fiddling with her clothing. Itchy hands. She was trying to keep them busy. Not to mention that her eyes were wide as saucers.

She swallowed. "I didn't say that."

"You knocked me down before."

"And yet here you are."

He laughed. "Here I am."

"Come to ask me out again?"

He *had* been about to do that. Ever since their chance meeting he'd had a head full of Aussie blond. Long legs, fair skin. Big, soulful brown eyes.

But then he'd seen her dancing and everything he thought he wanted had been blown to hell.

"I want you to audition for me," he said.

Her mouth popped open into a small O shape. "What?"

"An audition. It's where an artist demonstrates their ability and skill in the hope of attaining a job," he teased.

"I know what an audition is," she ground out. "Just not why you're inviting me to one."

"You're talented. I'm looking for talent." A smirk tugged at his lips. "Seems like a mutually beneficial arrangement to me."

She sucked on her lower lip, denting it with her teeth. Most dancers would have been thrilled by a personal invitation to audition for a show, especially from someone as established at him. But Remi was at war with herself—her could see it in the way her eyes flicked back and forth, as though she was weighing the pros and cons.

"I'm not looking to go back to the stage," she said eventually.

He'd have believed it more if she hadn't used a voice that sounded as though it belonged to a cyborg. Rehearsed, that was the tone. As though she practiced saying it over and over in the hopes she might one day believe herself.

"Why not?"

She crossed her arms and looked him square in the eye, jerking her chin as if to gesture to the room around them. "I already have a job."

"Dance isn't a job. It's a calling."

"That your way of telling me you're not paying?" She snorted. "Not interested. Not even a little bit."

"Oh, you're interested," he said with a laugh. "That much I can tell."

She rolled her eyes. "So you're a mind reader as well as a director?"

Defensive, but no denial. Interesting. "I don't need to read your mind when your body language is loud and clear."

Her arms fell to her sides at the same time a little noise of exasperation escaped her. "Yeah right."

"Huff and puff all you like, I know what I can see."

"Maybe I'll blow your house down, Wes. You'd better watch out." The bravado was all a front.

Growing up in his parents' elite social circles had taught him a few things about reading between the lines. That was the thing about rich people—they often didn't say what they were thinking. The dance world had its share of politics, social climbing, and the like. He'd learned at a young age that taking things at face value was a mistake. That trusting people who claimed to care about you was a mistake. That not protecting yourself from people who wanted to use you was a mistake.

Now, with a gorgeous woman trying her hardest to reject him, he was glad he'd honed that skill. Otherwise, he might've walked away, and doing that would have been an epic mistake.

"A big bad wolf masquerading in pointe shoes, huh?" He grinned. "It's a contradiction, and I happen to like those."

"I'm not auditioning," she said, hoisting her bag over one shoulder. "I've put that part of my life behind me."

Old wounds. A voice telling her to be afraid. No dancer of that caliber ever really let go of their love for the stage. He simply had to figure out why she was avoiding it and do what he could to help her break through that barrier.

"Then have a drink with me," he said. He wasn't going to convince her today, that much was clear. But he'd be damned if he let her go now that he knew she was it.

Her lips twitched. "Was that your plan all along? Flatter me with talk of auditions and then pretend like you were downgrading to drinks?"

"All I know is that I'm going hate myself if I walk out that door without a yes in some capacity," he said. "And I'm not the kind of guy who knowingly does things he'll regret."

"You're charming." She bit down on her lip, stifling a laugh. "Too charming."

"No such thing." He held his phone out. After what felt like the world's longest pause, she took it from him and put her number in. "Saturday night. I'll message you the details."

When she handed his phone back, her fingertips grazed his hand and the brush of contact was like an open flame. "I have to go. I've got class now. Unless you're planning to stay for this one too?"

"I'll save it for the weekend."

"Are you going to show me your moves?" She cocked her head, a glimmer of mischief in her eyes. "I can't wait."

As she walked out of the studio, her long, golden ponytail swishing against her back, Wes's eyes feasted on her. She had the perfect ballerina's body—long and lean, strong. Legs that went for days and a silky, fluid movement that turned ordinary body mechanics into art.

He swiped his thumb across the screen of his phone and dialed Sadie's number. "I've found our ballerina," he said. "She just doesn't know it yet."

Chapter 5

Don't go into the dating jungle unarmed...
By Eva Love (*Spill the Tea* love and relationship reporter)

On the *Spill the Tea* Love and Relationships team, we're all about giving you the tools to level up your love life, which is why we've been so fascinated by the app that's taking Manhattan by storm!

The Bad Bachelors website and app are designed for the women of New York to have more transparency about the men they're dating. Going on a date? Simply look up your bachelor's name to see what his previous dates have said about him.

From the Bad Bachelors site: "How do reviews work? Well, it's no different than leaving a review for your favorite restaurant on Yelp. Bad Bachelors uses a five-star rating system and allows users to share more detail in the review section. We're in the business of helping you make informed choices, and we rely on our users to get quality data. So, next time you date, don't forget to rate."

With more apps than ever to aid you in finding the man of your dreams—or the man of your evening—dating has become a whole new battlefield. Some app developers have realized that women are looking for safer, less invasive ways to date, resulting in the rise of female-centric apps like Bumble. In a sea of dick pics and crappy "hey, baby" pick-up lines, technology is starting to give women more control.

Bad Bachelors has already been lauded by many women as the key to improving their dating experience, helping them avoid dating disasters with "nice guys" who turn out to be anything but.

But is there a dark side to Bad Bachelors? One user recently wrote to us that she was no longer using the app after her brother was targeted by an ex-girlfriend who convinced her friends to review him poorly, dragging his rating down and causing the woman he was currently seeing to break things off.

Is it possible that this idea is good in theory but not in practice? We're curious to hear YOUR experiences.

FOR A BRIEF MOMENT, WES WONDERED IF IT WOULD BE possible to commit murder with anything on the table in front of him. The forks and knives had already been cleared away, but the dessert spoons remained. They would be slow, sure. But *persistence* was Wes's middle name.

Or maybe he could use one of the fancy champagne flutes his mother insisted on wheeling out for a "simple" dinner. Not that she drank alcohol, mind you. But still, appearances must be upheld, even if it was only a family gathering.

Sometimes he wondered if his mother was convinced that the media had spy cameras in her Park Avenue apartment. That would explain why she swanned around the house in a Chanel suit despite everyone else wearing jeans.

"I still think you should hold a press conference," his mother said. A strand of pearls as fat as Christmas ornaments hung around her slender neck. "It's unacceptable."

"A press conference?" Wes looked up at the ceiling and prayed for strength. This night was sucking every last bit of patience out of him. "What the hell am I supposed to say?"

"That it's abhorrent for media outlets to discuss your…" She wrinkled her nose as though smelling something particularly unsavory. "Personal parts."

"Everyone knows he's got a big dick, so what?" All heads snapped in the direction of his brother-in-law, Mike. "Who cares?"

At the head of the table, Wes and Chantel's father reached for a large decanter of whiskey and poured himself a glass that was on the generous side of three fingers. Wes signaled him to pour another. No words were exchanged as a heavy crystal glass filled with amber liquid was passed over.

That was his family in a nutshell. Adele bitching at everyone while the drinks were poured and looks exchanged. Tonight he would take advantage of his apartment being stumbling distance from his parents' and try to Band-Aid the family awkwardness with some Johnnie Walker Blue Label.

"It's *is* a big deal," Adele spluttered. "This is bringing unwanted attention to the school and—"

"Ah, so *that's* why you're worried," Wes said. "Not because you think it might affect me or my show."

All his parents gave a shit about was their ballet school, and especially that people might shy away from it if Wes's show failed. Without their high standing as a feeder school for the New York City Ballet, they'd lose the prestige that his mother clutched tighter than the pearls around her neck.

"All I'm saying is that you should *do* something about

it instead of letting the rest of the world think they can say what they like." She adjusted the cuff on her jacket, her voice as icy as the shade of blue Italian wool it was made out of. "Take control of the narrative."

"Isn't all publicity good publicity?" Mike asked. "If people are talking about him, then they'll talk about the show."

Adele sipped her water and waited while their personal chef delivered the dessert course. God forbid they discuss something personal in front of the "staff." Usually Wes was able to brush aside his mother's rigid and old-fashioned stance on things, but tonight he was one snide remark away from cracking.

The clink of china plates being placed on the table filled the awkward pause. As the door to the kitchen swung shut behind the chef, Adele reached for her dessert fork and took her standard "one bite only" from the chocolate mousse cake in front of her.

She sniffed. "If they're saying such disgusting things about him on this Bad Bachelors app, then imagine what they'll be saying about the show."

"How are those two things even related?" Wes knocked back a long gulp of the whiskey. Smooth heat warmed the back of his throat and he sucked in a breath. "The reviews are a joke and everyone knows it. I'm not worried about how it will affect the show because it won't. People take that shit for what it is—mindless gossip."

"You never know," Mike said, forking a chunk of cake into his mouth. "People might come along for a chance to glimpse the Anaconda in his natural habitat."

"Ew!" Chantel whacked her husband's arm with the back of her hand.

"What?" He grinned. "It's true."

"I don't care what brings people to the show so long as we fill every seat on opening night," Wes said. "They won't be thinking about some tabloid rag the second the lights go down."

"Most shows aren't successful, Wes," Adele said. For a second, she looked genuinely concerned rather than judgmental. "Even the most talented people fail on Broadway."

"I won't fail."

"You're unprepared." She shook her head as though dealing with a difficult child. "You can't waltz into this business and think that everything will turn out fine."

"I've got one of the best choreographers in the country, I've got a unique concept, and I've got backing from a big investor." Wes ticked the items off on his fingers. "And I'm ready to finalize the cast, no thanks to you."

Adele's lips pursed and the air was thick with silence. Even Mike raised a brow. It was a rare occurrence for anyone to challenge the Evans matriarch with witnesses. No doubt Wes would experience the brunt of his mother's retaliatory anger at a later point.

"I'm confident," he added.

"You're cocky," Adele said. "And you don't give any thought to how this affects those around you."

"You mean how this affects *you*."

After dinner was over, Wes walked with Chantel, Mike, and the girls, since they all lived in the next block. A year or two ago, he'd seen that as a point of pride—his family was close. But this adventure had started to reveal the deep cracks and dark truths about the Evans family. To the outside world, they looked perfect. On the inside, however, the bonds were rotting away.

Chantel had seen it a long time ago, facing their mother's wrath when she'd walked away from a position with the New York City Ballet to focus on her health— both mental and physical. Wes had always been the peacekeeper in the family, the one who smoothed over the arguments and tension. But now he was experiencing firsthand what his sister had gone through all those years ago, and it had shattered any illusions he had about his family. Especially about his mother, whom he'd once admired more than anyone else.

"Can you believe her?" Chantel fumed as they walked out into the street. Mike walked ahead, Frankie on his shoulders and Daisy asleep in her stroller. "She was a dragon tonight."

"I knew leaving the family company would cause problems."

A hint of a smile tugged at one corner of her mouth. "She's pissed at you for once."

"Don't look so smug about it."

"Why wouldn't I? You've been the golden child since the day we popped out of her womb, and I've always been the rebellious twin who never played by her rules. I have to take what I can get."

"Brat." Wes slung his arm around her shoulders. "She's wrong about my show though. It's not going to fail. I've done my research. I've got a good team. I'm going into this with my eyes open."

"I know. She wants it to fail so you'll come back under her wing."

"You mean under her thumb."

Shit had well and truly hit the fan when he'd announced that he was resigning from his role as chief operating officer at Evans Ballet School. Ever since he'd graduated from college, he'd been working with his parents, pouring everything he had into their dream, thinking it was his dream as well. One day, it'd hit him like a bolt of lightning—nothing about his life was his own.

Not his status, nor his reputation, nor his work. It was all a product of the family he'd been born into. What had he really achieved for himself? Nothing.

It was precisely why *Out of Bounds* was so important. Delivering a successful show would prove that he had what it took to succeed on his own. It would be a true test, especially since his mother had made it clear that she wouldn't be supporting him in any way. There were whispers that in addition to *not* supporting him, she was actively telling people to stay away as well.

Fine by him. He wanted it that way, so when *Out of Bounds* became a smash hit, he would know it was in spite of his parents and not because of them. Nothing— not even his mother's controlling approach to her family—was going to slow him down.

"I don't think I've ever seen you so nervous before a date." Darcy nursed an Old Fashioned, toying with the toothpick that had a cherry speared on one end. "You haven't asked for reinforcements in a long time."

"I don't need reinforcements. I just…" Remi sucked in a breath, wishing the butterflies that'd taken up residence in her stomach would bugger off somewhere else. "This guy is different. He's dangerous."

Why the hell had she said yes in the first place? The second he'd walked into her studio, all bright-blue eyes and cocky swagger, she'd lost her head. And the way he spoke, so smooth and intense and goddamn sexy—how was a woman supposed to stand a chance?

"And what exactly do you mean by dangerous?" Darcy's fiancé, Reed, sat across from them at the high table in the middle of the bar where Remi was due to meet Wes in less than ten minutes.

"I mean he's…" She huffed. "The kind of guy who makes me lose my words."

"Never a good sign," Darcy agreed.

Reed rolled his eyes. "I don't remember you having that problem," he said to Darcy. "You were always quick with a smart-ass comeback."

Darcy laughed, her silver tongue ring catching the light. "Damn straight. Maybe you weren't good enough to make me lose my words."

"Don't taunt me," he said, wrapping an arm around her shoulders. "Or I'll make you pay for it later."

"Get a room, you two." Remi pretended to stick her finger down her throat.

"I wanted to, but someone begged us to come for a

drink," he drawled. The guy had a dry sense of humor, and the mischievous twinkle in his dark eyes told her that he was quite happy to be there.

"So he gets you a bit tongue-tied. Big deal." Darcy asked, ignoring her fiancé, "You sure, it's nothing to do with the Bad Bachelors reviews?"

"Ugh, is that thing *still* around." Reed put his glass down, his nose wrinkling. "I thought—" He stopped abruptly and grunted. "I can't believe someone hasn't sued them yet."

"I don't know what to think about the reviews," she said. "I read a bunch this afternoon in the hopes they might give me a reason not to come tonight."

She had the sensation of hurtling down a river toward a waterfall, ready to fly over the edge into the abyss below. It was exhilarating, terrifying. Wes had dangled the biggest possible carrot in front of her—an audition. She hadn't even known what for at the time he'd asked, but a little digging later had revealed that he had some unique, modern dance show in the works. Something out of the norm.

They'd shared some crazy chemistry in the dance studio, but that wasn't the only reason she'd put on a pair of heels and headed out of her apartment tonight. The lure of an open door into the world that had rejected her was tempting.

You're not here for an audition opportunity. You're here for a date.

But part of her knew that was bullshit.

She hadn't told her friends about the audition. About a year ago, she'd made a big declaration about how she didn't need to chase the traditional prima-ballerina dream to be happy. Her stomach clenched, the assault of memories sending her off-kilter.

But what about Mish and the barre studio?

She shoved the guilt aside, because it was more than likely tonight wouldn't go anywhere. Even if she did decide to audition—and that was a big *if*—there was no guarantee she'd get a callback anyway. So guilt was premature.

Across the bar, Wes walked in off the street. Even if she hadn't been waiting for him to arrive, she would have noticed him. And she would most definitely have let her gaze linger. He wasn't the kind of guy who allowed a passing glance; he demanded attention—demanded a good ten seconds of open admiration. Minimum.

His dark hair was wavy and windswept, and he wore a white henley that hugged every sculpted muscle. The sleeves were pushed up to his elbows. No jacket. The heads of three women sipping cocktails snapped in his direction as he walked past, but Wes didn't seem to notice.

"That's my cue," Remi said, downing the rest of her pinot grigio in one long gulp. "Wish me luck."

"Charm that snake!" Darcy raised her glass and laughed when Reed rolled his eyes.

Remi smoothed her hands down her dress as she headed over to where Wes waited by the bar. She hadn't been sure what look to go for—professional or sexy? The little black Isabel Marant number had cost a pretty penny at Barney's, even with a hefty discount. But it walked the fine line between smart and sensual with ease. The short hem exposed her legs—a.k.a. her best feature—and the long sleeves and subtle ruffle at the base of her neck kept her covered up, even if the fabric was sheer enough to let a little skin peek through. She finished the look with a pair of nude patent leather pumps that faked an extra few inches of her best feature.

So far this dress was three for three at successful dates.

So which is it—sexy or professional? She definitely seemed to be leaning toward sexy.

For the first time in ages, Remi wasn't sure what she wanted. The two possible outcomes—taking Wes to bed or taking him up on his offer—were mutually exclusive. This was a fork in the road, saying yes to one absolutely meant saying no to the other.

In the dance world, sex between coworkers should be approached with extreme caution, something she'd learned the hard way. And if she had the chance to reclaim the career she'd lost, then no way in hell was she going to make that mistake again.

"Wow." Wes's smile broadened as she got closer, his gaze sweeping over her. "That's a hell of a dress."

"Thanks." She slid onto the stool next to him and crossed her legs, causing her hem to rise higher up her thighs.

So, we're not going for the professional look then?

They each ordered a drink, and Wes put his card down to start a tab. "Chantel tells me you're from Melbourne originally."

"That's right." She nodded.

"You're a long way from home."

"This is my home now." Remi forced a smile, trying not to think of the day she'd left with tears in her eyes and stitches on her heart. "Melbourne is a beautiful place, but New York is like living in my childhood dream. I watched *Breakfast at Tiffany's* on repeat when I was young, and I always wanted to come here."

Only she'd assumed it would be a place to grow her career, rather than to hide from her past.

"Do you miss Australia?" he asked.

"I miss some things about it, like soft licorice and meat pies and lamingtons. I miss the beaches too. Oh, and the summer in Melbourne is dry. Much easier than dealing with the sticky heat here." She paused as the bartender passed over their drinks. The wine was cool and fresh on her lips, and her pink lipstick left behind a faint print on the glass. "But Manhattan is a fairy tale. It's Beauty and the Beast all rolled into one."

"That's very poetic." His strong hands toyed with the glass containing his scotch, his thumb rubbing over the intricate designs cut into the crystal.

A lot could be learned about a man when he drank— did he savor it or gulp it all down in haste? Did he go for quality or quantity? Did he drink for enjoyment or because he wanted to impress? She tended to go for guys who were into spirits. If they had a cocktail, it was simple and classic—usually a Negroni, a Manhattan, or an Old Fashioned. Occasionally a gin and tonic, although those guys sometimes verged too much into hipster territory.

The amber liquid glowed in the intimate lighting of the bar, and it sloshed against the edges of the glass as he brought it up to his lips.

He's definitely a savoring, lingering kind of guy. Good with his mouth.

"Was it a big change coming here?"

"Yes and no. I mean, obviously we all speak English, but at the same time, it often feels like I'm speaking another language." She toyed with the hem of her dress, and his eyes tracked her every movement.

The muscles in his neck worked as he swallowed. *Good boy.*

"One time, I was going through security at JFK on my way to Mexico, and I forgot my flip-flops. Only we don't call them flip-flops in Australia. The poor security woman was mortified when I loudly proclaimed that I'd left my thongs at home and that I wasn't going to be able to walk around the beach without them. She must have thought I was going to one of those kinky sex retreats."

Wes's eye sparkled and the sound of his laugh was like a shot of pure arousal to her system. As much as she loved broad shoulders and a hard set of abs on a guy, there was nothing sexier than the sound of a genuine belly-deep laugh.

"Needless to say, I shocked the large family behind me." She cringed. "Not to mention the guy I got stuck next to on the plane, who'd also heard the whole thing and tried to hit on me."

"Okay, so thongs are flip-flops. Good to know." He nodded. "Any other Aussie-isms I should know?"

"An entrée for us is the starter, not the main course. We call Sprite *lemonade*. *Grog* is alcohol. *Pissed* means you're drunk. And we call Speedos *budgie smugglers*... well, we say it for a laugh anyway."

"Budgie smugglers?" Wes raised a brow.

"Yeah, because it looks like you've stuffed a budgie down there." She bit down on her lower lip and stifled a laugh. "Or, in some cases, I guess they should be called parrot smugglers."

Wes chuckled. "Why on earth did you want to leave a place like that?"

"It was time for a change."

"And you left ballet behind?" He cocked his head. "Weren't you part of a company?"

"Yeah." She bobbed her head. "I was with the Melbourne Ballet Company...but it didn't work out the way I wanted it to. And I love Australia, but it feels so far from the rest of the world." She traced the rim of her wineglass with the tip of her finger. "And there's a lot of world to see."

"So you're an adventurer?"

"An adventurer in the making." She tilted her head. "My parents wanted me to experience more than the little slice where I grew up. They're big travelers."

"And you came here all by yourself?"

"Yep, me and a suitcase." The truth hovered on her tongue. Something about Wes's easygoing smile made her want to talk. It wasn't often she went on a date where she wasn't bombarded by someone talking *at* her instead of to her. And he seemed genuinely interested. "I'm independent like that."

Independence wasn't a choice for Remi. Her parents, while loving, never wanted to coddle or nurture her quite like the parents of the other kids in school. And then, when her ex had abandoned her and she'd suffered one of life's greatest losses, she'd gone out on her own. Forged a new life. New connections. A fresh start.

But the lesson she'd learned from it remained: She was responsible for her own happiness, and that meant protecting every boundary she put in place.

Never get tied down.

Never expect anything.

And most of all, never let people make you vulnerable.

Chapter 6

"If you asked me to recall what we talked about,
I would have no idea. Talking is not required with
Wes."

—LooneyToonie

WES WATCHED THE GORGEOUS WOMAN IN FRONT OF HIM,
her face lit up like Times Square as she talked about her
life in Australia. Growing up in his parents' circle meant
he mostly socialized with people who were too Botoxed
to show such joy. Whenever his parents held an event,
all the people they invited were like boring cardboard
cutouts, stiff and emotionally stifled.

It was no wonder his sister and Sadie had never fit
into that scene. And for years, Wes had put up with the
constant matchmaking attempts, always struggling to
come up with a fresh excuse as to why he didn't want to
date some mini-Adele his mother had picked out for him.

She would hate Remi. Would hate that, with her
endless legs and mussed "just woke up" blond hair, she
looked like pure sex. Adele would also hate that she joked
about budgie smugglers and thongs, and that she laughed
loud enough for everyone around them to hear.

But Wes was smitten. The accent certainly helped—there was something about the lazy lilt of the Aussie accent, the way she pronounced "er" as "ah," and that she apologized for "yabbering on," which he could only assume meant that she talked a lot.

He would have been perfectly happy to listen to her talk all day.

"Tell me about your show," she said all of a sudden.

They were a few drinks deep and her cheeks were flushed pink from the wine. Her hair had started to escape the contraption holding it up, letting soft strands of gold float down to frame her face. The bar was packed now, the pouring rain driving people to seek shelter and a drink to warm their insides, which meant Remi had scooted closer to him and their knees brushed each other's as they shifted on their stools.

"It's called *Out of Bounds*, and it's a show with no separation between audience and stage." He sipped his Oban single malt and relished the warmth in the back of his throat. "It's modern dance, a mix of ballet and contemporary. But I've also cast a dancer who's immensely talented even though she's never received any formal training. She does lyrical hip-hop and animation, which you don't see a lot of on Broadway."

"So it *is* a Broadway show?"

"Well, it's Off-Off-Broadway," he clarified. "We're hoping to take the show wider, but at the moment, it's being produced independently. We're relying on funding from a few key investors. The plan is to generate enough interest to move it to an Off-Broadway theater for a second run, and then hopefully, we'll build buzz to take it further."

"Why start in New York?" Remi asked. "I've heard from a lot of people that Broadway is the hardest to crack because it costs so much to produce a show here. Why not start overseas?"

It was a good question. Even London's West End was cheaper than the astronomical costs of Broadway. It might have been smarter to start in another country and work back to New York.

But that wouldn't give Wes the same satisfaction. Fact was, he had something to prove. To himself, to his parents. To the people here who thought he would fail. To those who thought he'd let his surname carry him.

"This is my home," he said. "It's where I grew up watching my dad perform and watching my parents build their ballet school. This is where I want to succeed."

"Lofty ambitions." She nodded. "I can certainly appreciate that."

"What's the point of aiming for something if you don't pick the biggest challenge? I don't want a show to thrive where it's easy. I want to know I've cracked the hardest market in the world." The familiar tingle of excitement and anticipation burned in his veins. *This* was his passion in life—creating, striving. He needed to be knee-deep in a challenge to feel alive. Setting the bar low would only leave him feeling like he hadn't tried hard enough. And that was unacceptable.

"Isn't that a very New York attitude to have, thinking that we're better than everyone else?" He laughed. "There's something about Broadway. It's like a drug. Once you get a taste of the bright lights, nothing else compares."

Remi placed her empty wineglass on the bar and

adjusted the hem on her dress. It kept creeping up her thighs, taunting him with a few inches of bare skin but not high enough for him to get a glimpse at what she wore underneath. "*Some* things are still exciting."

Hell yes they were.

"Why did you ask me to meet you here tonight?" She leaned on the bar, her hand dangling over the edge a hairbreadth from his leg. A delicate gold chain hung around her wrist, the links catching the light and winking at him as if they could see the dirty thoughts running through his head. "Is this a date, or were you going to ask me to audition for you again?"

"You make it sound like those two things can't be one and the same."

Her eyes turned from smoky to wary. "Do you normally date people who audition for you?"

"No. Never, actually."

He usually avoided mixing business and pleasure because it had become hard to tell whether the "pleasure" was real or if it was the other person using him as a stepping-stone. And since starting work on *Out of Bounds*, he hadn't even thought about sex until the moment he'd stepped into Remi's studio. With the intoxication of chasing his dreams keeping him high on life, dating and sex had taken a back seat. But apparently the unintentional celibacy had left him with a dormant appetite, one that she'd easily resurrected.

"So why am I different?" she asked.

That was a damned good question.

"I'm a gut-feeling kind of guy," he replied with a shrug. "I know when something feels right."

"And you're seriously telling me that someone as connected as you is looking for dancers in barre studios?" She shook her head. "Isn't that scraping the bottom of the barrel? Surely you would have people clamoring to audition."

"If you were simply a barre teacher, then I wouldn't have asked you," he said. "But I know what talent looks like. I know how it moves and how to spot it even when the person who owns it tries her damnedest to write it off. I've been around dancers my whole life, and you're it."

"'It'?"

"That rare person who was truly born to do what they love."

Remi's eyes searched his face, as if looking for some minuscule hint that he might be trying to deceive her.

"You know all the right things to say, Wes," she whispered. "But I've heard all those lines before."

"They're not lines."

"I've heard *that* one too."

"What do I have to gain by lying to you?" He sipped his drink.

"There are unscrupulous men in the world who use the lure of stardom to get girls into bed."

Wes set his glass of scotch down on the bar with a clunk. "Excuse me if this sounds cocky, but I've never had trouble in that area. I don't need to lure anyone with false promises."

"That *does* sound a little cocky."

He leaned forward, bracing his arm on the bar and closing the space between them. "Something tells me you would have come without me dangling a carrot."

"I take it back. It's not cocky—it's arrogant." The twitch of her lips belied the stern tone of her voice.

"I've been called worse." He brushed a strand of hair from her cheek. "And I notice you're not in a hurry to deny it."

"I'm not." She matched his moves, leaning in and planting a hand on his thigh. Her touch was confident and sure—this was a girl who knew what she wanted and had no qualms in taking it. So why on earth was she resisting him? "I would be more than happy for this date to go somewhere more intimate, so we could get to know each other better. But the second I cross that line, that's it. I can't be both business and pleasure, Wes. I won't do it."

Her statement sounded more like a question, like she was asking him to choose: ballerina or bedfellow? "Which one do you want more?"

She leaned back and drained the rest of her wine, the action exposing the long column of her neck. "I don't know," she said after a pause. "I told myself I was done with auditions."

"Why?"

Her gaze drifted across the bar, over the room teeming with well-heeled Manhattanites, over the clusters of people deep in intimate conversation and the chic modern art on the walls. "Do you ever get that feeling that some things aren't meant to be? That your life is on a course out of your control?"

"No, I don't." Wes had been luckier than most with his upbringing, but that came with its own pressures and limitations. "There's a reason I don't have dancers lining up to audition."

Remi cocked her head. "Why's that?"

"My mother doesn't want me doing this show. I've had a few dancers turn down the chance to audition because they're worried they'll be cut out of her social circle, that they'll lose any advantage a relationship with her might have." It was the one time people *weren't* faking interest in him in order to get access to his parents.

Remi blinked. "Why would she do that?"

"Because she wants me to come back to the family business. She thinks the idea for the show is weird, and she's furious that I've gone out on my own, instead of doing the traditional thing, because it might damage her reputation."

"Do you think she's trying to sabotage you?"

"*Sabotage* is a strong word." He rolled his empty glass between his hands. "All the dancers I know, bar a small handful, are too afraid to join me. I had a lead dancer lined up and she pulled out last week because my mother helped her get a contract with the Cincinnati Ballet."

"So if by some chance my audition is successful, I'd be shooting myself in the foot when it comes to the rest of the ballet world in New York?"

"Probably the whole country, if I'm being honest. But that's only a problem if the show fails," he replied with a grin. "And I don't intend to let that happen."

Remi bit down on her lip, emotions rolling and shifting like a kaleidoscope over her face. Her temptation was palpable, like a something he could grasp with both hands. It was tangible and real. He almost had her.

"If I say yes, then I'll walk out of this bar immediately," she said. "No good-night kiss. No taking this someplace else."

"Deal." Without hesitation, he stuck his hand out and her eyes tracked the movement. He couldn't tell if she was relieved or disappointed. "If you agree to audition, then we'll pretend this was a business meeting and nothing more."

"Promise?"

"You have my word, Remi. And you don't know me yet, but I take that very seriously."

An excited smile lit her whole face, making her deep-brown eyes sparkle. "Okay."

"Okay?"

"I'll audition." She clasped his hand, and he had to force himself to ignore the energy that sparked at her touch.

It would be hard burying that feeling, but he'd do it. *Out of Bounds* was his number-one priority. And Remi, while intoxicatingly gorgeous and sexy, was too valuable for him to blow the opportunity to see what she was made of. His gut told him they were a match made in Broadway heaven. Sex could wait; his show couldn't.

———

Remi stood in front of the small theater that Wes was using for the auditions, holding her jacket closed to ward off the blustering fall wind. She'd awoken to miserable, gray skies and the screech of branches thrashing against her window like some omen from the gods—*Stay inside. Don't go to the audition.*

"That's your inner coward talking," she said to herself.

Knowing that didn't help her feet feeling like lead balloons. With each step toward the theater's entrance, she'd get another flash of memory. It was like being haunted by the ghost of her failed dreams.

Her first audition in New York had been a complete disaster. It was for a smaller ballet company and should have been an opportunity to boost her confidence, not to mention possible leverage with some of the larger companies later on. But she'd tripped in the first part of the audition class, which had made her so nervous that she'd forgotten her steps and made a mess of things. Remi *never* forgot her steps. She might have a terrible memory for birthdays and anniversaries, but when it came to choreography, her mind was a steel trap.

But on that day, everything had come to a head— her regret over screwing things up back in Australia, her anger at Alex for using her, and her grief over the life she'd lost.

Emotion was good for dance; it could be cultivated and shaped, manipulated to pull something special out of a performance. But the type of emotion she'd experienced that day—that molten self-loathing and doubt— was a disaster waiting to happen. The company director had been as stunned as she was when the music stopped. Needless to say, she hadn't been successful.

The second audition hadn't been quite so dramatic, but it was a total flop nonetheless. Still shaken from the first failure, she'd pushed herself to get right back out there. But perhaps she should have waited until her bruised ego had healed, because the doubt monsters sank their claws in, and she hadn't been able to shake them. Nerves had caused her to give a soft performance where she couldn't feel the music properly and her limbs were like petrified wood. She'd wanted to shout that she was capable of so much more, especially when a look of disappointment streaked across the director's face, telling Remi the woman had had high hopes that weren't met.

"That was then," Remi said, craning her neck to look up at the theater's entrance.

She'd purposely avoided telling Annie or Darcy about the audition to make sure that, if this happened to be failure number three, then at least she could lick her wounds in private. Her friends would no doubt be supportive, but sometimes it was easier to deal with the difficult stuff alone.

Sucking in a breath, she marched up the stairs, her ballet bag bumping against her hip and the breeze ruffling her ponytail. The second she'd walked out on Wes at the bar three nights ago, she'd slipped back into her old way of doing things. Getting up at the butt crack of dawn to go for a run, monitoring everything that went into her mouth. Her old audition routine had come back to her the second she'd started the music, like the steps had been lying there, dormant, waiting patiently for her to call on them.

She nudged the door open with her shoulder and shut it quietly behind her. Music floated into the foyer where a young woman sat at a trestle table, playing on her phone as her dark hair hung in a curtain around her face. An audition sheet was displayed in front of her. Only a few names were printed.

It certainly wasn't what she'd expected. Normally, an audition for a show like this would be teeming with dancers. They'd clog the foyer and street, sizing one another up and mentally comparing turnouts and posture and figures. Those who did the circuits together might swap notes or critique one another, but the Manhattan dance scene could be cutthroat. Getting into the right company could mean the difference between having a foothold in the ballet elite versus squandering your good years in the back of the corps at a small company that wasn't going anywhere.

"Hello?" Remi ventured, her voice feeling too loud in the quiet foyer.

The young woman looked up and offered a smile. "Here for the *Out of Bounds* audition?"

Was she supposed to mention that Wes had invited her? Give some hint that she was here on his request? She decided against it. No matter how long she stayed away from home, there was some deeply rooted cultural quirk that prevented her from doing anything that might appear as though she were big-noting herself.

"Yes." She nodded. "I'm Remi Drysdale."

"Put your details down here." The woman pushed the sheet of paper forward and indicated the next blank line.

Remi didn't recognize any of the other names on the sheet, but that wasn't entirely surprising—she was hardly up-to-date with stuff like that. It should have been ignorant bliss. But Remi's imagination was on the manic side of active, and by the time she'd signed her name, she'd convinced herself the other dancers auditioning were world-class professionals that would make Wes wonder why in the hell he'd asked her to come in the first place.

Unfortunately, catching the tail end of another dancer's audition didn't do anything to quash that fear.

Most auditions she'd attended were run like a class to ensure they could see all dancers within the allotted time. But smaller productions often had solo auditions.

In the center of the stage, a willowy brunette performed a textbook-perfect arabesque with exquisite extension. Then the dancer performed a *bourrée* across the floor, her arms moving like delicate wisps of smoke, almost as if she were some ethereal being instead of a mere mortal.

"Shit," Remi muttered under her breath. What little confidence she'd mustered plummeted through the floor.

Wes probably pulled the whole "you defy words" schtick on all the dancers he met. If it was true that his mother was trying to cut him off at the knees by luring prospects away, then the guy was likely doing whatever he could to get bodies into the theater.

But you felt that connection. You can't fake that kind of chemistry.

Yet he'd picked his side without hesitation, forgoing sex for her to be here today. Surely that meant something.

Maybe he wants you for a bit part. A filler role. Someone in the background.

Had she let his supposed attraction go to her head? Had she read too far into the seductive words and heated glances?

Her thoughts continued to swirl while she changed into her pointe shoes and warmed up. When brunette dancer finished her audition, Wes and the woman next to him asked her several questions, and it was clear they all knew one another. By the time the room grew silent, Remi's body was ready but her head was as calm as a bag of squirming kittens.

Relax. You can do this.

Even her inner voice couldn't pep talk her way out of this mess. Oh God, it was going to be a complete disaster. The third time might be the final nail in the coffin.

"Remi?"

Wes's voice snatched her attention back to the present, and she responded with an automatic smile. Her mask. This wasn't the time to be flying full-throttle into a doubt spiral. He'd seen her, so she had to go through with it.

"Hi." The rest of her words evaporated before she could wrap her lips around them. She was a hundred times more nervous now than she had been at the bar.

"I'd like to introduce you to my partner, Sadie. She's also our choreographer." Wes motioned to the woman beside him who had funky blue and purple hair. She had a gold spike through one ear and wore a shredded pair of fingerless gloves.

His partner? Remi's stomach flip-flopped. *Partner* was such a broad term—it could mean anything from colleague to fuck buddy to future wife.

He wouldn't have been propositioning you at a bar if he was with someone else. Calm the hell down.

"Great to meet you." Sadie stuck out her hand and smiled warmly. "Wes told me he found you teaching barre fitness."

"That's right. Wes might be one of my best students yet," she joked. When in doubt, try to be funny. That was her motto.

Judging by the crinkle around Sadie's eyes, it landed well too. "Okay, I approve," she said to Wes. "I like this one."

"You haven't seen me dance yet." The self-deprecating comment slipped out before she could stop it. Stupid subconscious.

"That's what you're here for." Wes motioned to the stage. "Why don't you show us what you've got? We'll do the pointe piece first and then the contemporary piece second."

Remi nodded and sucked in a fortifying breath as she headed down the aisle, stopping to hand a USB loaded with her audition music to the guy in the makeshift sound booth down by the stage. She shrugged out of her sweater and left it on one of the seats in the front row before ascending the steps.

You can do this. Pretend you're in the empty studio at work and no one is watching. No one is judging. Just dance.

The lights blinded her, fracturing and splintering and bathing everything in a haze of silver and gold. The neat rows of seats blurred in front of her as her focus narrowed to her accelerating heartbeat. It pounded in her chest, echoing through her whole body right down to where her toes nudged against the toe box of her pointe shoes.

Don't lose it. Not now. Not when you finally have another chance.

She found the center of the stage and took her opening position—supporting leg planted, her right knee bent, foot bowing out over her pointe shoe. Her head was down, shoulder blades flexed, her arms outstretched with elbows bent in a crane-like position. She waited there, holding herself rigid.

One step after the other. You know how to do this.

Can you, though? The negative voice had gained

strength, chewing on the adrenaline pumping through her veins. She never used to be like this—fearful, doubtful. She never used to be frightened of the stage. For years, it'd been her home, her safe place. Her arena. And now it was like coming back to a mean ex-boyfriend. She wanted to prove she was the better person, that she didn't harbor any ill feelings. That she'd moved past the nastiness that'd knocked her sideways.

The music started and Remi took a breath, allowing it to flow through her limbs. Softening her. Her body moved with it, sucked it in. When she looked up, she caught Wes's eye. His expectation was like a knife to her chest.

Not now.

The steps were designed for a non-class audition, where the dancer wasn't being led by an instructor and had to provide their own choreography. It highlighted her best moves, yet had enough variety to show a company or production her range of jumps, turns, and extensions.

It was like beautiful math. Carefully calculated and thorough. It followed the rules.

Remi *jeté*d across the floor, ensuring that each jump was high, that her feet were perfectly pointed, that her landings were as soft as feathers. She ran through the checklist in her head, ticking off every item as she danced. Shoulders down, core strong, hands light. She followed the music, letting it guide her through the steps.

The ending contained a series of turns—*piques* and *pirouettes* and *fouettés*—that she made look as easy and effortless as possible. Silence cut into the studio as the music shut off at the requisite point for general audition lengths. There was no applause. Nothing but the creak and groan of the old building. She was almost afraid to look up.

But when she did, she knew it hadn't been enough. He looked...confused. Sadie's expression was more neutral as she scribbled something on a piece of paper and handed it to Wes. Ugh, that didn't look like a good sign.

You have another piece. You can win them over.

But Wes placed a hand on Sadie's shoulder and then he was on his feet, striding down the steps of the aisle and then up the ones leading to the stage. Was this it? Was he going to let her down with a gentle no...or a brutal one?

Tears pricked the backs of her eyes. What had she done wrong? She'd remembered all the steps, hadn't missed a single beat of the music. It was a good deal better than the previous two auditions, but still, Wes had that look on his face. The crease between his brows told her this wasn't going to be good news. She hadn't wowed him.

"Can we talk for a second?" he asked as he strode over, his dark hair gleaming under the stage lighting.

The man looked so at ease with himself. His gait was fluid and laid-back, his shoulders steady and straight. It would be easy to mistake him as a chill, friendly guy who liked to laugh, but Remi could clearly see he was the king of his domain. So confident he didn't need to beat his chest about it like other macho douchebags. He commanded attention with only his walk.

"Sure." She hoped to hell her voice didn't sound as wobbly out loud as it did in her head.

He motioned for her to follow him to one side of the stage, where they paused in the wings. Here, the light was shrouded, and the darkness hinted at intimacy and a whole bunch of things that *shouldn't* have been in her head right now.

Focus, you idiot.

"I know you're a great dancer, Remi," he started.

Oh God, this is it. Don't cry. Don't make a bloody fool of yourself!

"But I feel like I'm watching you dance by numbers. It was…too perfect."

"Too perfect?" It wasn't a concept that existed in ballerina world. Nothing could ever be *too* perfect.

"For the contemporary piece, I'm going to choose your music and I want you to just go with it."

Wait, what?

She blinked. "That's pretty much the opposite of everything I was ever taught about auditions."

He nodded. "I understand. To turn up unprepared is an insult to the people auditioning you. I've heard it all."

"But you still want me to do it?" She licked her lips and found them parched. "I don't know if I can."

"Of course you can."

"I don't want to mess up." The words popped out of their own accord and she cringed. Now was not the time to be vulnerable.

"Can you trust me?" he asked.

She looked up at him, biting down hard on the inside of her cheek. He wanted her to wing it. Was he crazy?

In any other aspect of her life, she would have done it. In fact, when it came to trips, gift buying, and going out on the town, she was totally Team Wing It. But with ballet? Hell no. There was nothing spontaneous about her chosen art form. She liked the discipline, enjoyed the way it gave her routine and progression. Winging it? No way. Even her warm-ups were heavily curated.

"I want to trust you, Wes. I do." For once in her life, she wanted to be that articulate person who could carefully frame an argument. But words—like her dancing skills—continued to fail her. "You're asking me to do something that I don't have control over."

"I know, but *Out of Bounds* is all about doing the old things in a new way. It's about breaking preconceived notions of what ballet and dance are." He speared her with a look. "And based on what you showed me...I can't hire you."

The rejection stung like a whip slashing her skin. "I understand."

"But I *want* to hire you. What I saw that day in your studio was on another plane." He touched her shoulder, his thumb skimming over the skin bared by the thin straps of her leotard. "I *know* you're an incredible dancer. But I don't want this traditional, overworked crap. Give me something passionate, get angry or sad or melancholy. Just give me something. If I want a ballet zombie, I know where to find them, but I need more than that."

He was asking her to be vulnerable in a way she hadn't in years. In a way she never allowed herself. Because structured choreography was something she could hide behind. It was a mask, a role. A barrier between her and the people judging her work that allowed her to say, *They're not rejecting me*, even if they were. But Wes wanted her raw and unfiltered. Stripped bare.

She swallowed past the boulder in her throat. "Fine. I'll wing it."

Chapter 7

"The guy drops so many panties he should invest in Victoria's Secret shares...eventually those panties won't be yours."

—EllieTwoStep

WES RETRACED HIS STEPS BACK ACROSS THE STAGE, THE sound of his dress shoes echoing in the quiet theater. The second Sadie had slipped him a note that said "thumbs down," he knew he'd have to intervene. Remi was the star of their show; he would bet everything he had on that. But what he'd seen a few minutes earlier...

It was clear she'd been trained by people like his parents. People who thought perfection was the standard to aim for. Their dancers could never be too disciplined, too practiced, or too well trained. They wanted obedience, dedication.

He wanted passion that would ignite a room.

And Remi hadn't given him that. The performance wasn't bad by any stretch, because technically he couldn't fault her. But it was boring. He'd caught Sadie looking down at her notes from the previous audition, and that was not what he wanted.

On his way back to his chair, he stopped by the sound booth and handed over his phone with a song ready to play. The second Wes's ass hit the chair next to Sadie, the music started.

He could see the fear in Remi's large eyes, even from this distance. She missed the first few beats of the music and Sadie shot him a *what the hell is going on?* look.

"Give her a chance," he said.

Remi stood in the middle of the stage as if she'd turned to stone while the music played on. Beat after beat floated past her. Wes's chest clenched as he willed her to show them some of the magic he'd seen that day in the studio. But he got nothing.

Just as he was about to call down to the sound tech to shut the music off, her hand started to move by her thigh. It was as though she wanted to conduct the music. Or maybe learn it. The movement traveled up her arm and down through her torso, spreading through her body like life itself.

Then she bent down and untied her pointe shoes, carefully nudging them to the edge of the stage and out of her way.

Yes.

Her body changed then, losing the rigidity from earlier and turning liquid. Each joint moved gracefully but with power. This time, she wasn't simply following the music— she was consuming it. Forcing it to dance with her.

She reared back on one leg, the other high and bent in front of her, arms bowing back behind her head. It was like something had been unchained inside her, a wire snipped that allowed her to move freely and organically.

She twirled and jumped, rolling from one move to the next as though it was the most natural thing in the world.

Yes!

Sadie glanced at him, a brow raised. "I don't know what you said to her, but it's clearly working."

The song continued to pump through the speakers, fueling Remi. She used the whole stage. Filled it with her presence. She took his advice by the throat. Demanded his attention. Sure, the choreography was unbalanced and there were a few uneasy transitions here and there. But as far as improvisation went, it was damn good.

"I told her to wing it," he said with a shrug.

"If this is how she wings it…" Sadie shook her head, an awestruck expression on her face. "I can do a lot with her."

"I know. She's exactly what we wanted."

Since the song wasn't cut to fit the general audition requirements, it played on and so Remi danced on. By the end, her chest rose and fell with quickened breath, and her cheeks were flushed pink with exertion. Unchoreographed dancing tended to do that; when people let the music take them over, there was no thought to proper breathing or pacing.

She knew she'd done well. Wes could see it in the glimmer in her eyes as she collected her pointe shoes from the front of the stage and glanced between Sadie and him.

"Ask her anything you want," he said to Sadie. "I have everything I need to know."

"Me too." A wide grin stretched over her face. "Your mother is going to be jealous we discovered this one."

The following twenty-four hours had been the roller coaster to end all roller coasters. Remi's world hadn't simply been turned upside down; it had been flipped inside out and pounded into an entirely new shape.

Wes had called her within thirty minutes of her leaving the theater to let her know he wanted to cast her for his show. Then Mish had announced Remi, along with her counterpart, Aisha, as the instructors for the Park Slope studio in such a lovely and thoughtful way that Remi still hadn't worked up the courage to tell her about the show. Would it be possible for her to do both jobs?

She sighed. Not likely. Even if she could make the schedule work—which would require traveling from the East Harlem location where the show would be rehearsing all the way down to Park Slope in fifteen minutes—*not possible*—there was no way her body would be able to take it. Rehearsals and performances were both mentally and physically grueling.

But what the hell was she supposed to say to Mish? *Thanks for the opportunity but I got a better offer*? Ugh. Why did everything have to get so complicated?

Remi's laptop made a familiar ringing sound and the Skype icon flashed on screen. Seven p.m. New York time would make it late morning in Melbourne. She scooted over to the couch, the remains of a piece of buttered toast in her hand, and hit the Answer button. Then she stuffed the last bit of toast into her mouth.

"Hemprfph," she said, waving at the camera.

"Have we caught you at dinnertime?" The smiling faces of her parents filled the screen. They were dressed in identical baby-puke green outfits, and her mother had a strand of wooden beads around her neck. Her wild hair was wiry and stuck out in all directions. And her father was as bald as ever, but these days, he had a shaggy, salt-and-pepper beard covering half his face.

"No, just eating a piece of toast," she said, and then she cringed. *Shit*. She hadn't done the mental preparation for a family call.

"Toast?" Her mother frowned. "You know wheat is terrible for you. So inflammatory."

Good thing she hadn't said buttered toast, or else she'd have a lecture about the effects of cattle and dairy farming on the environment. Her parents were vegan, and Remi had always found it interesting that they were so concerned by the "restrictive nature" of her studying ballet while being quite happy to follow a lifestyle that removed entire food groups from their diet.

"How are you?" her dad asked, ignoring his wife's concern. He'd always been the more easygoing of the pair.

"Good." Remi curled her feet up underneath her and pulled a pillow into her lap. She'd always cuddled their dog, Gruber, whenever they had "family chats" and ever since the move to New York, her hands felt empty whenever they called. "I'm dancing again."

So much for keeping that information to herself. Remi was convinced her parents had some kind of truth radar installed in their Skype camera, because she never could keep anything from them. Growing up in a household where lies were considered the highest form of disrespect—above and beyond disobeying any other rules—Remi hadn't developed much of a filter.

"Dancing?" her mother asked, the skin between her eyebrows forming a deep crease. "Or doing ballet?"

"Ballet." It felt like she was confessing to a substance addiction. Their judgment radiated through her laptop screen. "I got a part in a small show. It's an independent show, very artistic. Kind of quirky."

She knew how to play to her mother's likes, because that seemed to ease a little of the concern in her expression. "Since when is ballet quirky?"

"This is a modern ballet. It's not like what I used to do."

In fact, it was exactly something she would have turned her nose up at a few years ago.

"So you won't be working yourself until you fall in a heap, then?" her mother asked. "You won't cry yourself to sleep because you didn't get the part you wanted? You won't be mindless from the exhaustion?"

"Opal." Her father frowned, his bushy beard bobbing up and down. "Stop it."

"I already got the part." Remi knew she should have bitten back the words, but dammit, she wanted her parents to say *well done* for once. To be proud, even if they didn't agree with her career choices.

"You know what I mean," her mother said. She toyed with the strand of beads around her neck. "Ballet is so hard on you. They demand everything and what do you get in return?"

"The chance to follow my dream." The second she said it, she knew it was true. It *was* still her dream. The buzzing feeling in her heart hadn't gone away simply because she'd been too frightened to try again the last few years.

"I thought you'd moved on." Opal sighed.

"I thought I had too," she whispered. "But I haven't."

After a few beats of silence, Opal said, "Promise me you'll look after yourself. Okay, possum?"

Her childhood nickname caused a smile to burst onto her face. "I will."

"I mean it. You need to fuel your body properly." Her mother looked at her pointedly.

"Got it. No more toast."

"Lots of vegetables, drink your water. I have this great meditation app that helps relieve the mind during periods of stress. I'll send you the name of it."

"An app, huh?" Remi teased. "Don't tell me you've entered modern civilization after all?"

She'd had to beg them to get Skype when she'd moved. There was something about seeing their faces—no matter how pixilated and blurry from the crappy internet in their off-the-beaten-track location—that made her feel a little closer to home.

"All right, all right. That's enough out of you," Opal grumbled. "And you should keep some citrine close by. It'll help with any negative energies."

There was Buckley's chance that she'd start carrying around a chunk of rock, thinking that it might help anything. No matter what her mother said, Remi didn't believe that an inanimate object would impact any "negative energies" but she managed to keep her mouth shut. More than likely, a parcel would turn up in a week or two with a piece of the damn thing anyway. When some people moved away from home, their mothers sent them treats from home, like Caramello Koalas, Vegemite, and Tim Tams. But not Opal Drysdale.

A care package from Remi's mother was likely to include something to ease whatever chakra she thought her daughter was having trouble with, a handwritten mantra for her to read aloud, and some healthy, organic snacks that tasted like the bottom of a shoe.

"Now you're doing this show, does that mean you have to quit your job at the studio?" her father asked.

"I think it does." Remi sighed and pushed a strand of hair from her forehead. "I thought I might be able to do both, but I remember how strenuous the performance schedules were back home. This is a much smaller production, but the timelines are tight."

Wes had explained to her that because the show was independently funded, they had limited time for rehearsals because each day in the theater before the show opened was a day when they weren't recouping their money. It sounded like the rest of the cast had already been working together for over a week, and she was coming in late because their original soloist had pulled out at the last minute. Hence, Remi was behind schedule.

You know you can pick up choreography quickly, and Wes has already promised to work with you day and night until you nail it.

Day and night. The thought sent a tremor through her.

"So…I need to resign," she added. Guilt was already weighing her down. Knowing that she was leaving Mish hanging right after the opening of the studio made her feel like a horrible friend.

"You don't look too happy about that," Opal said.

"I feel bad that I'm leaving my boss in the lurch."

A smile tugged at Opal's lips. "We might not always agree with each other's choices, but you have to live your life. If this is your dream, then you won't be happy unless you chase it."

And with that, she had her mother's blessing. It felt like a weight had been lifted off Remi's shoulders. It wasn't that she needed her parents' permission to do anything; they weren't that kind of family. But Remi had always wanted to make them happy, to do them proud. And while she might not get that, exactly, hearing her mother say she understood her—even in that indirect way—was the boost Remi needed to deal with the Mish situation.

Two feet in. Black or white. Yes or no. That's how you live your life.

Either Remi was going to chase this dream, or she was going to give it up for good. This would be her last chance. If she got through this show in one piece, then she would know she'd gone down the right path at this fork in the road.

"So, what are the chances of you flying to New York to see me perform?" Remi asked with a cheeky smile.

"Well, you know how we feel about those big cities." Her father stroked his beard. "It's not really our thing."

"Never hurts to ask."

Remi wasn't disappointed. If there was one thing she'd learned in her life, it was that she could only rely on herself. Her parents had taught her to be independent, and life had taught her that she couldn't always expect external reinforcement and encouragement.

Wes had given her this opportunity, but that's all that she would ask of him. Now it was up to her to work hard and dance her heart out if she had any chance of getting back on track with her career.

On Wednesday morning, Wes arrived at the studio space he and Sadie had rented because the Attic wasn't available for another week and a half. That was theater for you—two steps forward, one step back. Like a demented cha-cha.

"Morning, sunshine," Sadie sang as she flung the door open before he even had the chance to knock. A handwritten sign telling the cast to come up to the first floor was taped to the door he'd just come through. "This place is a bit of a dump, and it's drafty as hell."

"Yeah, but the price was right." He followed her inside and up a flight of narrow stairs.

This studio was small, but it would comfortably fit his lean cast. It had a barre along one wall with mirrors behind it. A vacuum cleaner sat upright in one corner, evidence that Sadie had already done her best to clean the place up. But the lighting was crappy, and a scraggly crack ran through the plaster on one of the walls. If only his mother could see him now. Compared to the light, airy studios at Evans Ballet School, with their specially engineered floors and luxurious changing rooms, this place was practically a crack den.

"What are the plans for today?" he asked, shoving his hands into the pockets of his leather jacket.

"Warm-up, obviously. I'm going to give them extra time because it's cool in here and the last thing we need now is an injury."

Wes bobbed his head. "Good."

"Then we'll do a class for an hour, barre work and

floor work. That will give me a bit of extra time to assess where Remi is at. After that, we'll take it from the top. I want the opening nailed by the end of the day."

It was ambitious. The opening of *Out of Bounds* was explosive, the choreography intricate. It would be hard to mimic the theater environment in a studio setting, as some audience members would be sitting on chairs on the stage during performances, and the dancers would be sprinkled through both the traditional stage area and in the aisles.

"I like the ambition," he said. "Do they have any chairs here for us to practice on?"

"Unfortunately, no." Sadie toyed with the single long feather dangling from her ear. The colors matched her blue and purple hair. "But I've got some tape to mark out where the chairs would be. Might not be such a bad thing, give Remi a chance to find her feet before we tell her that she needs to dance *en pointe* on a chair without kicking the head off someone who's paid to come and watch her."

"She'll be fine. More than fine," he said. "I have a good feeling about her."

Sadie snorted. "I bet you do."

"What?"

"I see the way you look at her. It's been a while since you were infatuated with someone." She grinned. "But I know that look."

Their conversation halted as the sound of footsteps echoed in the stairwell. The cast wasn't due for another half an hour, so he could guess who it was. As a slim woman rounded the corner, dressed in all black, her dark hair slicked back into a small bun, Wes sighed. Lilah.

No doubt she'd come to talk rather than simply to get a jump on her warm-up.

"Sadie, Wes." She nodded. "Can I have a moment?" she asked him.

"Sure." He looked around for somewhere to afford them a little privacy, and Sadie nodded toward a door in the back corner. It led to a pokey kitchenette.

He'd known this conversation was coming. In fact, he'd been preparing for it, trying to figure out how to sweet-talk his dancer and soothe her ego enough that she wouldn't walk out on him. Because Remi might be his shining star, but it wasn't a one-woman show.

"So your email said you've found a new lead," Lilah said as the door swung softly shut behind her.

"That's right. I'm going to introduce her today."

"Can I get some feedback on why I wasn't considered for the role after Ashleigh left?" Her lips pressed into a line so flat and straight it was like someone had run a marker across her face.

He'd seen Lilah use that expression ever since she was thirteen years old, when she was an accomplished young dancer but not a prodigy. His mother had been determined to train her hard, see what she was made of. Lilah had blossomed under his mother's tutelage and guidance, growing into a talented artist with poise, grace, and strength in equal measure. She worked incredibly hard—sometimes too hard, in Wes's opinion. She could train the life out of a piece, drain that sparkle by concentrating too much instead of letting herself feel the music.

Still, when he'd been struggling for dancers to join his production, Lilah had stuck her neck out for him.

She'd gone against his mother's advice and auditioned for Wes. And he'd given her a role in the ensemble.

She wasn't right for the lead.

"You *were* considered, Lilah. I thought long and hard about it." Wes raked a hand through his hair, pushing the strands back, although they immediately sprang forward, stubborn as ever. "You're an exceptional dancer. But I had something very specific in mind for the lead role."

"Something very specific in that you weren't looking for a trained dancer?" Her voice was ice cold.

"Who told you that?" Christ, if his mother was interfering again, he was going to lose it.

"You know what ballerinas are like," she said with a shrug. "They love gossip."

He wasn't going to add fuel to the flames by trying to push Lilah to spill her source—her source who was clearly making shit up. "You'll have the opportunity to meet Remi today. She *is* trained, and she was previously with the Melbourne Ballet Company."

"But she hasn't worked in New York? In America?" Lilah turned up her nose. "Do the Australian companies even compare with what we have here? I mean, where did you find her?"

If he let it be known that he'd found her working in a barre fitness studio, the cast would be up in arms. Dancers took their craft very seriously, and many of them looked at the trend of ballet-inspired workouts as a way to capitalize on their art form.

"It was a chance meeting," he said carefully. "Now, I understand you're disappointed. But I want you to know that I picked you to be in this show because I believe in your talent. The lead role required something specific, but this isn't the last show I will do. And the lead role will need an alternate."

Lilah's expression softened. "Right."

"We have a small cast, and any injuries or illness will leave a hole. I'm going to be pairing people up for the major pieces, so we're covered if something goes wrong."

"And you're saying if I stop complaining, you'll let me be the lead alternate?" A smile tugged at her lips.

"I'm saying if you work hard *and* stop complaining, I'll consider it." He shot her a look. "I expect you to play well with others, okay?"

"Fine." She made a small huffing noise in the back of her throat. "But I didn't agree to face your mother's wrath so I could be shoved into the back line and forgotten about."

"Trust me, Lilah," he said with a sigh, "you make it impossible for anyone to forget you."

"Your mother once told me perseverance was the only way to succeed in this career. I won't get anything by keeping my mouth shut."

He couldn't argue with that. Ballet took discipline and hard work, but what a lot of people didn't see was that dancers required a good deal of mental fortitude as well. Not only to get through the seemingly impossible physical demands, but also to deal with the constant competition and rejection.

Lilah would forge ahead of dancers with more talent simply because she had an iron will. Now, all Wes had to do was ensure that Lilah didn't decide to use that will against him.

Chapter 8

"Once you've been with a guy like Wes, most other men will come up short. Literally and figuratively."

—TheSnakeCharmer

"MISH, I'M *SO* SORRY." REMI BIT HER LIP AS SHE PAUSED at the address Wes had texted her for their rehearsal. She'd promised herself that she wouldn't set foot into the studio without first telling Mish she was resigning. "I only found out yesterday."

And since she'd been hemming and hawing about what to say, she'd left it until the very last minute to keep that promise.

"I can't believe you didn't tell me, Remi." The pause on the other end of the line seemed to stretch on forever, and Remi bounced on the balls of her feet. "I just... I get it. This is what you want to do with your life. But if you were auditioning, you should have told me."

"I know. I kept telling myself it wasn't going anywhere." Guilt clutched at her heart like a fist. "It was self-preservation...and it was completely selfish."

Mish swore under her breath. "It's lucky I've signed

someone on for Midtown who's looking for extra hours. You've really left me in the lurch."

Two dancers streamed past Remi, bags bumping against their hips as they jogged up the stairs immediately inside the doorway. The door sat open long enough for Remi to watch them disappear up to the first floor.

"I don't have any excuses, Mish. I know I screwed up, and I can't even tell you how much I regret doing that."

Mish sighed, the sharp sound cut off by a tiny meow close to the phone's speaker. "Just make the most of it, okay? If you're going to do this, then don't be half-assed about it. And when you get famous, remember I gave you a job when you were struggling to get by on tips."

"I won't forget it, I promise."

"Fine. I'm still mad at you."

Remi swallowed and bobbed her head. "You should be."

"All right, I'd better go. Looks like I need to start calling around to fill these hours." Mish ended the call without giving Remi a chance to say goodbye.

She'd send a card and a giant box of chocolates by way of an apology when she got home. Deep down, she knew Mish would forgive her; they were friends as well as boss and employee. But Remi had some serious groveling to do. *Hard-core* groveling.

Then, she suddenly felt light as a butterfly. The studio was on West 127th Street, which might have been the farthest Remi had ever traveled up Manhattan. The street looked a little run down, and she'd almost walked right past the building.

Stifling an excited grin, she pushed the door open

and started up the stairs. The previous evening had filled her with a strange sense of déjà vu as she'd run through her old routine. Classical music had blared through her speakers as she'd sat cross-legged on her floor stitching elastic and ribbons into her new pointe shoes, softening the toe box with her hands and darning the platform until she knew it would support her the way she wanted.

Voices floated down from the studio, and Remi's heart thudded in her chest. What would her castmates be like? Would they welcome her with open arms? Would they ask questions she didn't want to answer? Excitement turned to unbridled panic as she climbed the last few steps.

All you have to do is make sure you don't repeat your mistakes. That's it. Just dance. Easy peasy.

For some dancers, auditioning and the stress of not knowing whether they'd gotten their desired part was the tough bit. But Remi knew the world beyond auditions was fraught with opportunity for failure.

"Ah, here she is." Wes's voice stopped Remi in her tracks. She stood in the doorway leading to the studio, several pairs of curious eyes glued to her. "The final piece of our puzzle. Everybody, I'd like you to meet Remi Drysdale."

There were a few waves, and some noticeably crossed arms. One woman in particular looked like she was trying to burn a hole through Remi's head with the power of her narrowed eyes.

"Hi," Remi said, hitching her bag higher up on her shoulder.

"We're waiting on a few more people, but Sadie will introduce you around," Wes said as he walked over.

He wore a pair of black sweats with Converse sneakers and a Yankees hoodie that shouldn't have looked appealing in the slightest. Only, the fabric of the pants clung to his muscled thighs and sat snugly over his crotch. Holy moly…

Eyes up. Now.

"Come and see me after your warm-up and we'll go through the paperwork." He squinted for a second, studying her. Thankfully, he didn't ask why she'd suddenly turned into a human furnace.

"Sure."

In her nervousness, Remi instantly forgot the names of everyone Sadie introduced her to. She remembered what it was like when she'd first joined the company back home. Everything was overwhelming, but she would settle in. She would develop relationships with the other dancers. After all, they were all professionals.

By the time Sadie had walked her around the room, the final members of the cast had arrived, and they all spread out across the room, warming up their muscles and tendons with TheraBands and lacrosse balls. Almost all were classically trained ballet dancers, from what Remi could tell, but they also had a female hip-hop dancer who'd joined them to warm up, though she wouldn't be taking part in the class immediately after. She seemed friendly but looked a little out of place in her bright-orange sweatpants and chunky sneakers.

"Everyone take a spot at the barre, please." Sadie clapped her hands together and then grinned at Wes, who was standing on the other side of the room. "Ahh, makes me feel like I have a class full of eager students again."

She ran them through a standard warm-up of *pliés*, *tendus*, *rond de jambes*, and *port de bras*. The exercises increased from slow and gentle to more demanding.

"That's it, two *demi-pliés* in fifth." She walked around the room, stopping to help the dancers correct their technique and turnout as they needed it. "And up, two, three, four. Take a slight bend and then down, two, three, four. Now forward, sweep the hands around and back up. Rise, two, three, four. Legs together!"

Remi let the instructions wash over her, falling into the music as she had done time and time again. It was shocking how quickly it all came back—the way her legs moved, the way her hands formed softly curved shapes as she swept them through each position. It was like she'd never left.

Her body became malleable. Ready for more.

They moved to the center to work on their jumps and *allégros* and Remi felt Wes's eyes on her the whole time. It was like the morning he'd walked into her class, only now their roles were reversed—*she* was the one performing for him. Here, in the small studio, his eyes cutting through everyone else to lock onto her...the intimacy settled like a hum in her bloodstream.

When the class was finished, Sadie asked everyone to change into their pointe shoes for some *adage*, but Wes called Remi over. She grabbed her things and followed him to a door in the back of the room, aware that people were watching them. Well, one person in particular— the brunette who'd been staring at her earlier.

"Is it all coming back?" he asked, dropping into a seat at a small table in what appeared to be a mini-kitchen.

"It is." She took the seat across from him. "I don't know how I stayed away so long. Teaching barre was great, but it's not the same."

"Well, we're glad to have you on board." He leaned back in his chair, interlacing his hands behind his head. The action stretched his chest and shoulders out, and Remi had to force herself not to drool.

Down, girl.

"I've, uh, got all the paperwork you asked for in your email." She dug the file out of her backpack and cringed. "But you have to promise not to laugh."

He raised a brow. "Well, *now* you've got me intrigued."

"I have a…rather unconventional name." *Unconventional* was putting it mildly. There weren't a lot of people who knew it either. It was a piece of information handed out on a strictly need to know basis.

"Remi?" An adorable crinkle formed between his brows. "Unless that's not your real name."

Best to get it over with. She slid the file across the table and he flipped it open. A second later, his mouth twitched.

"I said no laughing," she warned.

"Reminiscent Sunburst Drysdale." He looked up, doing his utmost to keep a straight face. It was a valiant attempt. "Hippie parents?"

"Got it in one." Heat crept into her cheeks. No matter how many years passed, she still hated her full name with the fire of a thousand suns. Or should that be the fire of a thousand sunbursts? But her parents would have been devastated if she'd changed it. "I grew up being force-fed hemp seeds and kale. My parents are… unique."

"Sounds like it would have made for an interesting childhood."

She snorted. "If you think spending weekends doing macramé is interesting, sure."

"Don't tell me, ballet was your rebellion."

"My grandmother used to take me to classes and recitals. She was the one who pushed me to pursue it as a career." The loss stabbed her in the chest as painfully now as it had the day she'd passed away. "My parents aren't fans of the whole discipline and giving-up-your-life thing."

"I see." He nodded. "Well, I'm glad you've got a rebellious streak then."

Something about his tone made excitement unfurl low in her belly.

"This is your chance to ask any questions before I throw you to the wolves." He grinned. "I've told Sadie to take it easy on you today, but that's it. One day's grace period is more than I give most people."

"And why are you being so generous with me?" Was that a hint of flirtation in her voice?

What happened to keeping things strictly business, huh? Cut that out. Now.

He chuckled and the sound slid down her spine. "I don't want to scare you off."

"You won't," she replied. "I don't scare easily."

"Must be because you grew up in a country where everything wants to kill you." He flipped her folder closed and leaned forward on his forearms.

The action closed the distance between them, and she reveled in the details of him up close. A slender ring of dark gray lined his blue irises, and a tiny dimple formed in his cheek when he smiled. Details that were like the final dusting of sprinkles on a perfectly iced cupcake.

"No questions," she said. "I'm ready to throw myself into work."

This was her chance to make all the painful rejections and mistakes worth it. The chance to prove to all the people who'd abandoned her back home that she could push on and rise above the rumors and the gossip and the judgment.

Remi would *not* screw up this opportunity.

Is the Anaconda flying solo?

By Felicity Morgan (*Spill the Tea* society and culture reporter)

Rumor has it that Wesley Evans and his upcoming Off-Off-Broadway debut have stalled due to a lack of financing. Now, we know that Evans isn't hard up for cash. His mother and father are entertainment industry royals, and the family boasts real estate in some of the most prestigious buildings in the city. Their ballet school was also recently named one of the top dance education institutions in the country, beating out the Joffrey Ballet School for the first time ever.

With connections like that, why would Evans require funding for his project? Should we take this as a hint that his parents aren't supportive of this creative venture?

A source close to the *Spill the Tea*'s society and culture team has revealed that Evans recently stormed out of the offices of prominent Broadway investor Leonardo Marchetti. The property mogul touted as a "guardian angel of the arts" has invested in some pretty outrageous shows in the past (anyone remember that quirky *My Brother Joyce*, which involved the singing dog?) but it appears that Evans has failed to impress.

Despite announcing that details for the show would be available sometime this month, Evans's website remains curiously devoid of information. His social media reveals little else, having gone quiet in the past week.

Some speculate that the rise of his name in association with the Bad Bachelors website might have something to do with it. The website, which allows New York women to rate and review their dates, has slowly taken over Evans's online presence.

Since Marchetti has previously spoken about the "filth" infiltrating the entertainment industry, perhaps Evans's association with the Bad Bachelors website and his dirty little nickname—the "Anaconda"—were enough for him to turn down a funding request.

Or maybe Evans's show simply isn't any good. We'll have to wait and see.

Spill the Tea has reached out to Evans's office but has yet to receive a response.

Wes picked up his water bottle and squeezed, crumpling the plastic in his fist. When he couldn't squeeze it any harder, her threw it across the room, where it hit the wall of his office and bounced back across the floor, stopping at his foot. He was about to crush the damn thing under his boot when the door flung open.

Mike didn't ask permission to enter. Ever. The big

guy took a seat on the other side of Wes's desk. "What happened?"

"With what?" Wes drove his fingers through his hair, resisting the urge to throw something else. "The fuckups are growing so fast I can't keep up."

His brother-in-law grunted. "Chantel sent me that article about the funding withdrawal. Did Leonardo back out?"

Wes snorted. "Yeah, I guess you could put it like that."

Marchetti was one of the biggest players on Broadway. The guy *loved* theater and dance, and since he had more money than God, he chose to pour a decent chunk of his wealth into fledgling productions.

On their first meeting, Leonardo had been a ball of energy. The older man was loud and slightly flamboyant, with a shock of white hair that he meticulously styled and an endless collection of pinstripe suits in every imaginable color. He'd claimed that Wes's idea was a goldmine waiting to happen and had promptly agreed to invest in the show. Contracts needed to be drawn up, but there was a verbal agreement.

That was until Wes had gone in for a meeting, where he was due to present the current status of the show— the theater location, casting, and an updated running budget. Only that had all been waylaid when Leonardo announced he was pulling out. He hadn't even bothered to take a seat in the boardroom where Wes had set up his laptop. He'd simply walked in, firebombed their deal, and walked back out.

There was a chance Wes could fight it and claim he'd proceeded based on Marchetti's verbal agreement, but that would sap the money he had already allocated to *Out of Bounds*. And if he didn't win, then the show would die for good.

"What happened?" Mike asked again.

"He said that he couldn't have his name attached to someone who swings his dick all over town." Wes rolled his eyes. "That he wanted to keep Broadway filled with old-fashioned values like what my parents have. And the fact that women I've dated are writing about me on the internet is out of line with what he represents. Then he told me he wanted to clean up the minds of New York like Giuliani cleaned up the streets."

"He's running for office." Mike smacked a palm to his forehead. "Fucking hell."

"He didn't say that." Wes spun on his chair and looked out over the city. Central Park stretched out in front of him like a great green blanket. The view normally calmed him, set his mood straight. But not today. "But it sure as hell sounded like a campaign slogan."

"So that's it? He's out?"

"Definitely out." Wes swung back around and slapped his hand down on his desk, the sound cutting through the air. "Goddammit, everything was going so well too."

A loss of funding wasn't simply a minor setback; it could cause the whole show to go under. Last week, Wes had thought of the Bad Bachelors site as a blip on the radar, an annoyance at most. But now it had cost him something dear. Something important.

Frustration ripped through him, and he clenched his fists so hard his knuckles turned white.

"Does this mean you'll consider taking some of my money?" Mike asked. He leaned back in the leather chair and interlaced his fingers behind his head. Wes knew that pose—it was the power-play pose.

"Shut up, Wall Street. I don't want your shitty banking money."

Mike snorted. "Why do you have to be so pigheaded about it? I have the money, and I'm happy to help."

It would have been the easy option. But Mike's money belonged to his family—to Wes's sister, to Frankie and Daisy. They were well-off, but most of their wealth was tied up in investments or in college funds for the girls. And while he was certain the show would be a success, there was no way he'd *ever* risk putting his nieces at a disadvantage.

Besides, having that kind of thing hanging over his head could affect the way the show was produced. He didn't want anything to influence him to take the safe route with *Out of Bounds*.

"Save it." Wes held up a hand. "Take the girls to Paris or something."

"You're as bad as your sister, you know." Mike grunted. "Bullheaded and stubborn, the lot of you."

"Hey, you married into this family. No sympathy. You knew damn well what you were setting yourself up for."

"That's what I get for marrying my high school sweetheart." They fell quiet for a few seconds until Mike cleared his throat. He wasn't going to let this go. "Is this Bad Bachelors thing really so bad?"

Wes glanced at his laptop. The Bad Bachelors website was open on his screen, the overtly feminine pink banner featured a set of plump, shiny lips with a manicured finger held up in a *shhh* motion.

Wes's page on the site contained a press photo that had been taken during a work trip to Amsterdam, where he'd gone to visit the Dutch National Ballet. Underneath was a set of five stars with the figure *89%* listed next to it. According to what he could find out, the site now required men to sign up themselves, but his profile appeared to have been created very early on. There was no way for him to delete it that he could see. Not without contacting the Bad Bachelors admin, anyway.

Threatening legal action was certainly an option, but Wes was reluctant to go down that path with his public image already overrun with less-than-ideal messages. If he poured fuel onto that fire by trying to get the reviews removed, would it make the situation better or worse? He really wasn't sure. Besides, rule number one of the internet was that it never forgot anything. There were already screen captures of his reviews and quotes featured in articles. Deleting his profile now wouldn't solve this problem.

"Here." Wes turned the laptop around. "See for yourself."

Mike leaned forward, his eyes widening and a smirk developing on his face. "Wow."

"Don't look so smug, man," Wes said. "We haven't checked if you're listed on there."

Mike chuckled. "Unlikely. I've been a one-woman guy since I was in my teens. So I can crow all I like without fear of repercussions on this one."

"Bastard," Wes muttered under his breath.

He leaned back in his chair while Mike continued reading the reviews on the site. Wes didn't have pages and pages of them like some guys did. He dated a bit, but no more than the average single guy. And lately, he was all work and no play, which meant most of the reviews were from women who'd dated him *before* the site was even created.

Curiosity had compelled him to look around Bad Bachelors in an effort to justify his anger at Marchetti. And he *did* feel justified. The reviews were nothing. Nonsense. All they confirmed was that he'd dated women and liked sex.

Certainly nothing terrible enough to warrant backing out of a business deal.

"Jesus." Mike's booming laugh ripped through the quiet office. "These reviews are fucking hilarious."

"This isn't a joke. It's affecting my work." Even to his own ears, it sounded stupid to be upset over something so trivial—after all, everyone knew the internet was full of stupid shit like that. Wes knew he should be able to rise above it. But Marchetti pulling out had put a major dent in his plans.

"They're comparing you to a foot-long, saying you need an expert snake charmer..." His brother-in-law scrolled down, mouth open in shock. "How does this website even exist? It's a miracle they haven't had the pants sued off them."

"Maybe they haven't attacked the right person."

"You know, now that I think about it, there was some big deal about a guy being New York's 'most notorious' bachelor a few months ago." Mike tapped a finger to his chin. "Maybe it had something to do with this site."

"Doesn't ring a bell."

Mike reached over the desk and grabbed the cordless mouse. "Give me a sec."

A few minutes later, he turned the laptop back to face Wes.

"This guy." He tapped on the screen where a picture of a guy in a sharp suit stared back at him. "Reed McMahon. Used to be some hotshot PR guy. They called him the 'image fixer.' This site pretty much destroyed his career…at least that's what I heard."

Wes studied the picture. "I don't recognize him."

"I knew a guy who hired him a few years back after his ex-wife doctored photos of him and sent them to the guy's clients."

"What does that have to do with anything?"

"Check out the last article on the Bad Bachelors site about him."

Wes scrolled down the page. "It says he's getting married. So what?"

"And they reiterated their policies about reviews and announced some changes to how they're managing the site."

"Okay." Wes stretched the word out. "Am I missing something?"

"You think the crazy person who decides this kind of website is a good idea retracts their opinion of someone publically without a reason?"

Hmm, Mike had a point. "You think he threatened them?"

"I think *something* happened." He rubbed his hand along his jaw. "And that makes me think this guy would be worth talking to."

"What good will that do? The damage with Marchetti is already done and, frankly, after our meeting the other day, I'd be more than happy to show him how wrong he is."

"If it were me, I'd reach out to this Reed guy and see what he knows about Bad Bachelors. At the very least, he might have some tips on how to manage any bad press. I'll see if the guy at work has a contact number." Mike folded his hands in his lap. "What are you going to do about the show in the meantime?"

That was the million-dollar question.

"*Out of Bounds* is going ahead, funding or no funding." Wes drummed his fingers on the top of his desk, letting fury bubble away inside him. "I don't care if I have to scrape every last penny together myself."

"Oh yeah? And how are you going to do that?"

"No idea. Sell my apartment and my car. Move back in with Mom and Dad."

Mike snorted. "I give it two weeks before a homicide is committed."

"Who's your money on?"

"I'll plead the Fifth on that one, thanks."

Wes nodded. "Smart man."

Maybe it had been naive, but Wes had thought himself above engaging with this kind of gutter-dwelling gossip. Hell, his family had dealt with it often enough—gossip rags had announced his parent's divorce a few times, and they'd even tried to claim Chantel had an eating disorder. "Scum," his mother had called them. Vultures who preyed on people in their weakest moments. Not worth the air they breathed.

There was a chance, though, that his silence was the reason this whole damn thing hadn't gone away. He'd allowed the story space to grow by not providing an alternate narrative. Still, wouldn't talking about it add more noise to the fray? He didn't agree with his mother that a press conference was the right way to deal with it. Wouldn't that make him look defensive?

But maybe Mike was right. Chatting to Reed McMahon might give him an idea how to tackle all the noise from Bad Bachelors. Even outside his experience with the site, the guy dealt with this kind of thing for his job. He should be able to give Wes some advice.

"Let me know if you can get a number for that PR guy. I'll talk to him," he said eventually. "And if Marchetti wants to get his panties in a bunch over such a stupid, shitty little thing, then let him. The show *will* go on…no matter what."

Chapter 9

"Women who say size doesn't matter are lying to themselves. Nobody in their right mind would choose a pickle over a foot-long."

—DancingQueen

REMI'S BODY ACHED IN A WAY THAT ONLY OTHER DANCERS would understand. It was like winter had settled into her bones and made a home there. There was a unique point beyond pain and fatigue where ballerinas dwelled. Everything creaked. Without having danced at her usual pace for the past few years, all her hard skin and time-earned calluses had disappeared, leaving her feet soft and vulnerable. Open to blisters. It would take a while to build that hardness back up again.

Even an evening foot bath with Epsom salts hadn't helped.

And that was only day one. Which meant for the time being, she would have to wear her Ouch Pouches and push through. The inside of her lip was shredded from gritting her teeth through it, but she knew her body would adjust.

Sighing, she tilted her neck from side to side and

then swung her arms in circles, trying to loosen up. This choreography would *not* beat her.

"Feeling a little stiff?" One of the other dancers approached her. Her name was something starting with L... Lilah?

"First day back is always a painful one." Remi sat on the floor, legs stretched out in front of her while she bent forward.

"I was sure I hadn't seen you around before." Lilah's dark eyes studied her. It was like being peeled apart layer by layer. "Has it been a while since you were part of a production?"

Remi wasn't sure how much Wes would want her to say. Or how much *she* wanted to say. "It has. I was with a company back in Australia, but I decided to take a break when I came to New York."

"Seems like the opposite of what most ballerinas do when they come to New York." Lilah sat next to her and crossed one ankle over the opposite thigh, twisting to open up her hip. "You're in the best city for dance in the whole world."

Like she didn't know that. Remi tried not to bristle; it wasn't like Lilah meant to insult her. Being objective, in her position, she probably would have been surprised too.

"Sometimes it takes walking away to realize you have a true passion for something." Remi drew one foot to the inside of her thigh and stretched back down again.

She eased into the position, her muscles already starting to loosen. Thank God she'd been teaching barre classes the last few years. Her feet might not have been prepared for full days *en pointe*, but at least her flexibility was still there.

"Right." Lilah nodded. "So how did you come to audition for Wesley?"

Remi bit down on her lip to stifle a smile. Wesley. His full name seemed so formal and stiff. Not like the sweet joker she knew. "Totally by chance. He saw me dancing and invited me to audition. I was thrilled, obviously."

The other dancer continued to study her, not looking entirely convinced of Remi's story. "Well, you must have impressed him. There was a lot of competition for your part, you know. The original lead has gone on to dance with the Cincinnati Ballet. I heard they're talking about giving her one of the little swan roles in *Swan Lake*."

"Dance of the Little Swans" was a notoriously difficult piece of choreography due to the quick pace and linked hands of the four dancers, meaning any slight misstep or missed beat was instantly visible. Not to mention the sixteen *pas de chats* in a row.

It was a role that would only be handed out to incredibly talented dancers.

This is not the time to start indulging your imposter syndrome. Wes put you in this role because you earned it. He cares too much about the show to do it for any other reason.

And, given what she'd witnessed in rehearsals yesterday, the cast was brimming with talent. So he would have had plenty of choice within that small group alone for the lead role.

"I'm very grateful that Wes gave me the opportunity," Remi said, keeping her voice smooth in the hopes she might be able to keep the doubt where it belonged—hidden. "I'm going to give it my best shot."

Lilah nodded. "I'm sure you will."

Something about her tone filled Remi with a sense of unease. She'd watched Lilah in the rehearsals yesterday. Like everyone else here, she was talented. But there was a hardness to her, a glinting edge to her words. To the way she danced. And, Remi suspected, to her personality as well.

In Remi's experience, most dancers stuck together. Delivering a performance worthy of a standing ovation was *always* a team effort. The lead dancers couldn't deliver a story without the character performers, without choreographers and costume designers and shoemakers. Everyone had to be on the same side for a performance to work.

At least that's what Remi believed. But every so often, she'd encounter a dancer whose ambition was such a driving force in their lives that they had no problem stomping on relationships to get ahead. They were the minority, thankfully. But something told her that Lilah was one of those people. Maybe it was intuition.

Or you know what it could also be? Paranoia.

"Wes assigned me to be your alternate," Lilah said as they continued to stretch.

Of course he did. Freaking great.

"Well done." Remi forced herself to smile. She would *not* engage in any feather ruffling so early into rehearsals. "I'm glad we're going to be working together."

"Me too," Lilah replied, but the smile didn't quite reach her eyes.

After the warm-up and classes were completed, Sadie picked up right where they left off yesterday.

"We're going to run through the opening scene

with the seat sequence." Sadie brushed her blue and purple hair away from her face. "One of the features of this show is that the audience is mixed in with the cast. So we have two rows of seven seats each on the stage, facing the rest of the audience. Obviously, these aren't the same as what's going to be in the theater, and we've had to beg, borrow, and steal to get them here for practice."

The mismatched chairs were set up in a replica of that arrangement, with a few extra chairs facing them to represent the traditional audience area.

"We're selling tickets for the chairs marked with an X," Wes said.

Remi's eyes snapped over to the side of the room.

She'd been so in the zone, she hadn't even noticed his arrival. He leaned against the wall, a crisp, white shirt rolled up at the sleeves and open at the collar. Fitted jeans hugged his thighs and dark stubble coated his jaw. She could almost feel the scratch against her fingertips. Remi swallowed and found her mouth dry.

"Since we went over all the choreography yesterday. Today we're going to practice with a stunt double." Wes pulled a dummy off the ground. "This is Alfred."

The dummy, which was dressed in a fancy, old-timey costume including a frilly cravat, stared at them with blank eyes.

"Once we move into the theater next week, Sadie and I will start sitting in the seats, so we can simulate what it will be like on opening night."

Remi wasn't even ready to think about that yet. She'd stumbled through the choreography yesterday, trying to master the intricate set of moves, which involved a few kicks past where a real live person would be sitting.

She'd mentally dubbed that spot the "death seat."

Don't look scared. You don't want to give them any more reason to think you shouldn't be here.

Wes set the dummy down one chair from the end. "Let's run through the section where you're already on the chairs."

He motioned to Remi and held out his hand. Clearing her throat, she walked over to Wes, trying to get into dance mode, which was bloody hard with him standing there looking like Prince Charming. With his strong jaw and those blue, blue eyes, he could have been lifted right out of a fairy tale. She braced herself for a white-hot sizzle of attraction as she slid her palm into his, and *boy*, did it deliver. Touching Wes was like letting someone hit her with a Taser.

Sex Taser…was that a thing?

Stop it.

She wrapped her fingers around his and stepped up onto the chair. It was such a benign piece of furniture when you were sitting on it, but standing on a chair—in pointe shoes, no less—was all kinds of terrifying.

Who said that you should never work with children or animals? Maybe props should have been included too.

"Face forward," Sadie said. "Bring your right foot down below the line of the chair. Swish right, then left, then kick out to your right. Repeat on the other side. Then we'll turn to face the person sitting next to you, up into *arabesque*. Hold, two, three. Then you come down off the chair."

Sadie mimicked the steps, making it look easy as pie. *That's because she's on the ground.*

"Think you can do it without taking Alfred's head off?" Wes grinned up at her.

Maybe if you stop blinding me with that sexy smile, buddy.

"Sure." She nodded.

"I'll count you in," Sadie said. "Three, two, one. Swish, swish, kick."

Remi's toe box made a soft *clunk* when it hit the dummy's plastic arm. Dammit.

The whole room was watching her. The dancers were in various positions—some standing and some of the floor. But they were all waiting to see Remi in action. Yesterday, she'd managed to hide in the back for most of the day, catching up on what she'd missed so far.

The choreography was unique, as was the soundtrack, which consisted of a mix of contemporary music and bass-heavy dubstep. Sadie was a creative genius, and Remi was thrilled to be working with her. But something was holding her back—stopping her from fully embracing *Out of Bounds* and throwing herself into it.

She kept telling herself it was her feet. She needed a few more days for them to adjust to the grueling schedule. But what if a few more days didn't help? The risk of what she was doing suddenly weighed on her as if she were carrying all of New York on her shoulders.

And sure, she put her pointe shoes on regularly and pirouetted around the barre studio. But it wasn't the same. If something hurt there, the shoes came off. Here, she didn't have that luxury.

"Remi?" Wes's voice brought the room crashing

back to her—the uneven surface beneath her feet, the pairs of eyes curiously staring her down, the thundering of her heart against her rib cage. It echoed through her whole body, turning her vision blurry. Making it feel as though a fist were closing around her throat.

Not now, please. Not now.

She'd had one panic attack in her whole life. But she'd never forgotten what it felt like—the strange hot and tingly sensation in her face, the tilting of the room in front of her, the way her hearing seemed to turn inward, amplifying her breath and the rush of blood in her ears.

"Remi?"

"I'm fine," she said, but the panic had strangled her words. She steadied herself against the back of the chair, her fingers biting into the wooden frame. "It's just my… allergies. I need a drink."

"Of course." Holding out his hand again, he helped her down. "Lilah and Melinda, why don't we get you up while Remi takes a quick break? We can try the sequence with the two of you on the chairs, and Ace, Angelo, and Marsha in front."

Remi pressed her hands to her chest as she hurried to the kitchen. Her stomach seemed to be doing Sadie's moves over and over. She planted her palm against the door to the kitchen and stumbled inside.

Get it together. You gave up a paying job for this. If you don't make it work, then you're back at square one.

Chapter 10

"I always wonder if I made a mistake ending our
one and only date without convincing him to come
back to my place—but he didn't want to mix
business and pleasure."

—MOMAFan

WAS IT POSSIBLE HE'D MADE A MISTAKE? WES STOOD AT
the back of the studio, arms folded, watching his cast work
through a new piece of choreography. He'd expected
Remi to find her feet and show off her brilliance. But it
was day three, and she was…drowning.

The choreography on the chair seemed out of her
grasp. Sure, working with props wasn't the easiest
thing, but his other dancers were getting it. During the
break for lunch, Lilah had taken some time to practice
Remi's moves—no doubt trying to ensure he'd see her
as the natural fit for alternate—and she'd nailed it on
her first try.

If he had any hopes of hooking another investor,
then he needed to ensure Remi was up to the task. Hell,
without her, there might not be a show at all. Because
as much as Lilah nailed the moves, she lacked the special

quality he'd seen in Remi. It was fine to keep Lilah as a backup option, but not as the star of the show.

Where was that woman he'd seen in the barre studio now?

Obviously, something was holding her back. He'd caught a glimpse of it the day of her auditions, of the fear and drive for perfection that strangled her talent. But time was running out. Next week, they would move to the theater, and then it was three weeks till opening night.

Three weeks to find more money or bankrupt yourself. And for what?

He couldn't really answer that now. Because if he did, then his gut might tell him that he was pouring everything into this show and his chances of it being successful were *not* looking good. But Wes wasn't going down without a fight. After getting his hands on Reed McMahon's email address, he'd contacted the guy to ask for help. They were meeting the following day.

In the meantime, he needed to help Remi find her feet. Maybe it was time for a little cast bonding.

The workday was coming to a close and the dancers looked tired, all except for Marsha—his hip-hop dancer—who had boundless energy and was currently trying teach a few of the ballerinas the basics of popping and locking.

"We're going for dinner," Wes announced. It was something his mother used to do with the teachers at their ballet school. At the start of every year, she'd treat them to a dinner so they could all get to know one another.

We're a team, she used to say. *A family. And family breaks bread together.*

He wasn't necessarily fond of the religious connotation, but the principle was a good one. Getting the cast to spend time together in a casual setting would ensure they connected and helped one another during what was going to be a strenuous schedule.

"While this show is in production, we'll be spending a lot of time together," he said. "So we should get to know one another a little better. Let's meet back here at seven thirty."

He knew a lot of the dancers lived in Manhattan, a few of them in roomed together in the Village. Lilah lived close to him and Sadie on the Upper East Side. He walked over to Remi.

"You're welcome to shower and get changed at my place, if you like," he said. "It'll save you a long trip on the subway."

Remi's lithe figure was encased in the typical dancer's uniform of a leotard, tights, and leg warmers. Many of the other dancers wore footless or convertible tights, where they could roll the legs up over their leotards. Some preferred leggings. But Remi looked like she was still dancing at a school with her black-and-pink outfit, including a gauzy skirt over her leotard that made her look a little out of place.

Reminiscent Sunburst Drysdale.

His lip twitched. That was a hell of a name. Maybe he was crazy, but it suited her…and he liked it. She wasn't quite what he'd expected. There was a hidden vulnerability to her, a soft center beneath her bombshell persona. A perfect blend of sexy and sweet.

"Thanks." She pulled a pair of jeans on over her

tights and stuffed her feet into a pair of white sneakers. "That's very generous of you."

Generous was one way of looking at it. But as Remi bent over to tie the laces on her sneakers, soft denim stretching over her ass, Wes thought maybe it was a form of torture. How exactly was he going to have this woman in his apartment *without* picturing what she looked like naked under the running water in his roomy double shower?

"See you soon," Sadie said as she and Lilah headed out of the studio behind the rest of the cast. Lilah gave a small wave.

Remi grabbed her things. "Shall we?"

Outside, the weather had turned from crisp and clean to gray and miserable. Heavy, dark clouds hovered overhead and a fine mist of rain settled over them.

"Damn, I forgot my brolly." Remi dug around in her bag.

"Brolly?"

"Umbrella." She gestured to the rain. "I hate this misty crap. You think it'll be okay and then two seconds later you're soaked through."

Wes pulled a black umbrella out of his satchel and popped it open. "There's room for two under this one."

She sidled closer to him, her arm brushing against his. Even with his leather jacket and her lightweight coat, he could still feel the heat of her. Or maybe it was his body reacting by jacking up his internal temperature. That seemed to happen a lot around her. As did other things.

Distraction required. You will not walk around Manhattan with a boner like some hormone-riddled teenage boy.

"Wesley Evans, always prepared to rescue the damsel in distress," she teased. Her cheeks were flushed pink, though whether it was from rehearsals or something else, he had no idea. The rain misted her cheeks and nose, making her skin look slightly glossy. It amplified the subtle smattering of freckles there.

God she was pretty. *So* damn pretty.

As they headed to the garage where his car was parked, the rain came teeming down. Remi snuggled in closer, her footsteps falling in time with his. Under the dark shroud of the umbrella, it felt like they existed in their own little bubble. This time, they weren't working together. They weren't putting on a show for the sake of what others might see.

"Why do you think I'm trying to rescue you?" he asked.

She tilted her face up, her lips full and ripe and so close it would only take the slightest tilt of his head to capture them. To see if she tasted as good as she looked.

"Well, you plucked me out of obscurity to be in your show." Something uncertain flickered across her face. "And then you've so kindly offered up your shower and your umbrella."

So kindly. Like he got nothing out of it.

You don't. Because you won't be joining her in the shower, just like you're not going to kiss her now.

But damn it, he wanted to. Even though she'd set her boundaries and he really should set his. It wouldn't be wise to get involved with someone from the cast, since it could create rifts with the other members. Create an illusion of unfairness. People might even call into question why he'd chosen Remi to be his lead. He couldn't have that. More importantly, he needed to uphold his decision not to get involved with people who needed or wanted anything from him.

Not that it stopped his body from reacting to her. With each innocent brush of her arm, his cock grew harder. His hands twitched around the handle of the umbrella, fingers tingling with the need to trace her long lines and gentle curves.

"You mean I'm doing my job by picking the best dancer for my show and being a decent human being by offering some shelter from the rain? Not exactly a high bar to jump over."

She smirked. "You'd be surprised."

"You've dated some jerks?"

"Yeah." She bobbed her head. "But I figured out what I like, so at least I know what to look for now."

"And what have you found? Have you got a type?"

He had no idea why he was asking that. A, it was none of his goddamn business, and B, he wasn't sure he wanted to know about the guys she'd dated. For some reason it made an ugly, uncomfortable feeling surge through his veins. It was basal, primal. And it made him want to hold her closer, as if he might tell the rest of the world to back off.

"Do you mean whether I like bad boys or nice guys? Clean shaven or stubble?" She laughed and leaned into him as she avoided a puddle on the sidewalk. "I don't know. I guess I don't really have the whole perfect-man checklist like some women do. I want good chemistry, someone who makes me laugh."

"So not a six pack, then?"

"Sure, a hot body is always nice. No different from how men love a bit of T and A."

Wes raised a brow.

"But I need to feel the chemistry. I know I like a guy when I get that prickle under my skin. It's like a thought I can't shake. I want someone who makes me forget about everyone but him."

She wanted consuming love. Or lust.

"What about you? Have you got a list of future-wife requirements?" She paused. "I mean, other than a Victoria's Secret modeling deal."

He snorted. "I dated *one* model."

And really, *dating* could only be used in the loosest of terms. It'd been a whirlwind adventure of travel and sex. A vacation from his real life, but the whole paparazzi thing was a total turnoff. For how well known he was, Wes generally didn't date people in the public eye, preferring to keep his private life just that. Hence, the Bad Bachelors thing pissing him off so much.

"Hardly enough to know if they're really your type," she teased.

"I guess I want someone who's independent," he said.

A.k.a. someone who didn't want anything from him other than good company and good sex. He'd dated enough users to have learned his lesson there. He'd had an independent partner once, or so he'd thought. Emily was the kind of woman who filled a room with her presence; it would linger like perfume even when she'd gone. To say he'd been infatuated was an understatement. For a hot minute, he'd dubbed her "the one."

Turns out, he was in a one-sided relationship.

"Independent." Remi nodded, clearly pleased with his response.

"You look surprised. Did you expect me to give a cup size?"

"No, I didn't. But I guess I've dated too many macho types who wanted me to play the doting partner." Her lips twisted, the joking expression morphing into something darker. "Guys who wanted me to feel like I wasn't at their level."

There was definitely a story there.

"Guys or guy," he asked.

Her lips tilted up and she shot him a knowing look. "Guy. I didn't go back for seconds."

He understood that logic. Fool me once, shame on you. Fool me twice…

"I learned my lesson," she added.

There was no need to guess what that lesson was: *Keep people at a distance.* It explained a lot—notably, her ultimatum and why she had trouble showing vulnerability when she danced unless someone pushed her.

That would need to change. And he was more than happy to help her out.

"I was hoping to get you alone so I could ask a favor, but this conversation has taken a turn."

She looked at him, curiosity alight in her deep-brown eyes. "You can't say that and then not tell me what you were going to ask."

"I've got a cocktail party to attend on Thursday night. It's an industry thing. There will be a lot of potential investors there." He tilted his head slightly, studying her for a reaction. "I'm hoping that having a gorgeous ballerina on my arm might bring me luck."

"You want me to be your date?" She blinked.

"In a work capacity," he clarified. "All aboveboard, I promise."

She nodded slowly, and he couldn't tell if she was relieved or disappointed. "Of course. I'd love to come. I don't know how much I'll be able to help, but if you think it might make a difference, I'll be there with bells on."

He nodded, feeling far more pleased with himself than he should have.

By the time they made it to the restaurant, Remi felt as though her limbs were aching from the push and pull between her and Wes. At his place, showering in his bathroom and breathing in the scent of his shower gel—which smelled so good Remi was certain it couldn't be legal—she'd been unable to ease the tangle of feelings battling for supremacy. Perhaps she shouldn't have gone with him. It'd been bad enough arriving at the parking garage to find a pristine, white Maserati, but then he'd taken her to his apartment on the Upper East Side and she'd almost turned straight back around.

She'd had flashbacks of sneaking away from her company friends to be with Alex in his blinged-out Como Tower apartment in Prahran. Wes and Alex had so much in common it terrified her—swank homes, expensive toys, upper-crust education, family pedigree… All the things she never had. All the things that had led him to dump her because they'd been found out, and rather than acting like a man and stepping up to be a father to their child, he'd told her to "get rid of it."

Remi swallowed and shook the bad memories away.

"We've got a table for you in the back corner." The server led them through the small, crowded restaurant. The air was heavy with the scent of spices and herbs, and Remi's mouthed watered.

The crew piled into the table in a jumble of limbs and coats and scarves. Wes, ever the gentleman, pulled a seat out for her and then took the spot right next to it.

He's slick. Too slick.

Her *pas de deux* partner, Angelo, sat on her other side. "How's it goin', Aussie?" In his thick Bronx accent, it sounded more like "ossie."

"You've got to pronounce it like the *s*'s are *z*'s," she said with a grin. "Ozzie, not ossie."

"All right, *mate*." Angelo chuckled. "Strewth!"

"Nobody says that." Remi rolled her eyes. "We don't say *crikey* either."

"You mean the Crocodile Hunter lied to us?" Angelo pressed a hand to his chest. "That's a bloody outrage."

It was officially the worst attempt at an Australian accent she'd ever heard. "Stop it. My ears will start bleeding."

Angelo chuckled. "Can't have that. The boss would have my head if I damaged the shining star of the show."

Across the table, Remi caught Lilah's eye, but the other woman immediately turned away, as though she hadn't been listening to their conversation.

"Glad you've got your priorities right." Wes leaned forward to give Angelo a mock-stern look and, in the process, pressed against her arm. "We're going to keep this show injury free. Bleeding ears included."

The table was tight, and when the food was delivered, they knocked elbows reaching for the bowls of potato curry and veggie samosas. Under the table, Wes's knee bumped against hers. The innocent brush of contact sent awareness zipping through her veins, giving her stomach a fluttering fizziness. She didn't move away.

It'd been so long since such a benign action had stirred any excitement. Since she'd come to New York, sex had been about fun. Fulfilling a physical need. If she met a cute guy at a bar and they were both into it, she'd allow herself to have a good time. But never with someone who had any real connection to her. Never with someone where the relationship mattered.

Wes was her boss. Her lifeline. She shouldn't be playing with fire. Again.

"I did ask you here tonight for a reason," Wes said suddenly. A hush spread over the table as all eyes turned in his direction. "You might have seen an article online that speculated we'd lost funding from Leonardo Marchetti."

"I saw it today," Lilah said, and a few people at the table nodded.

"I had hoped to shield the cast from this side of things, but at the same time, I want to be transparent. We're a small production, and I consider us to be like a family. Secrets won't do us any good." He sighed. "The truth is, we *did* lose our big investor."

"Why did he pull out?" Remi asked.

A stormy look flared quick and bright, like a flash

of lightning. "Have you heard of a website called Bad Bachelors?"

Had she ever? The damn thing was practically her wingman—or was that wing*woman*?—in the dating scene. But she wasn't about to confess that she'd read all about Wes and his "attributes."

There was a murmur of recognition through the cast, but Wes was looking straight at her as though he wanted to know her answer in particular.

"Uh, yeah." She nodded. "I've heard of it."

"So the guy we had lined up to invest in the show is a big player, but he's conservative. He didn't like the idea of working with someone who was splashed all over the internet." His lips tightened. "Let's just say the content of the reviews are…not very wholesome."

Remi swallowed. "That's not good."

"The thing is, I would normally write it off as gossip," he said, raking a hand through his dark hair as he turned back to face the rest of the table. "I'm used to people making shit up to sell advertising."

Somehow, Remi wasn't entirely convinced that the reviews were making stuff up. And they were mostly positive reviews, unlike when her friend Darcy had started seeing Reed. *Those* were some reviews to be worried about.

"Are they really saying such bad things?" she asked, feigning innocence.

You are going straight to hell, Reminiscent.

Damn, she knew it was bad when *she* started calling herself by her full name.

"No, not really. To be honest, I had a skim through,

but I didn't read them in too much detail. It's weird." He shook his head. "Makes me feel like I'm a product on Amazon or something."

Remi blinked. She'd never really looked at it like that before.

"Who cares about some bullshit website?" Angelo said with a shake of his head. "So what?"

"The public cares," he said. "But I don't want you to worry. I've already got plans in place to hook another investor. We're doing great work with this show, and now that we have Remi on board, we've got a full product to showcase to anyone who's interested in investing."

Gee, no pressure or anything. She swallowed.

"If you have any concerns, you all have my cell number, but I didn't want you to think I was hiding anything from you." He smiled, though there was a stiffness to his expression. "This production means everything to me, and you have my word I will do everything to make it the success it deserves—and that you all deserve it—to be."

Well damn if her heart didn't pirouette in her chest. She'd missed that passion, that drive and ambition in her life the last few years. She'd missed the hunger that fueled people in this industry.

Without thinking, she pressed a hand to Wes's arm before snatching it back, suddenly conscious that everyone was looking at her. "I know we can do it. *Out of Bounds* is incredible, and I'm so honored to be part of this talented cast."

His eyes swept over her, and it was like being lowered

into a warm bath. And with that, everyone went back to their meal. Across the table, Lilah watched her, a curious expression on her face. Remi shrugged off the uneasiness and made a point of chatting to everyone at the table, trying to ignore the tugging feeling that drew her to Wes.

She owed it to everyone here to give this show her all. Most of all, she owed it to herself.

Chapter 11

"When Wes looks at you, it's like you're the only person in the room. My advice: don't get addicted to that."

—ExMarksTheSpot

REMI'S HEAD WAS GOING TO POP WITH ALL THAT WAS clanging around inside it. But getting to know the cast at dinner had been much needed. Comforting. Despite her initial reservations, the other dancers were friendly and welcoming. Well, for the most part.

Maybe if you weren't so in your own head all the time, you might be able to learn these freaking steps.

Remi rose up and down in *relevé* a few times, coaxing her feet into warming up. The studio was cold, since the heaters had been turned off when they left. After dinner, she'd begged Sadie to borrow the key so she could practice in solitude. It was late, which meant the other dancers would have headed home for some much-needed rest. And while she needed that too, what she needed more was time alone with the choreography.

The steps were messing with her head. They pushed all the boundaries of what she'd been taught, what she knew. Then there was the element of the chair and the person who would be sitting right next to where she was dancing—right in kicking range.

"Stop freaking out," she said, bouncing on the balls of her feet. "You've never kicked anyone before."

Not even with some of the more athletic, acrobatic *pas de deuxs*. Her partners had always felt safe in the knowledge that they wouldn't get a pointe shoe to the face.

She glanced at the dummy in his velvety suit and cravat. "I promise I'll try my best not to hurt you, Alfred."

She swallowed and sucked in a long breath. Practice makes perfect. That's what her teachers had said to her over and over as she was training. If a step didn't work out, you did it again and again and again. And then when you thought it was perfect, you kept doing it again and again and again.

"Three, two, one," she said, counting down for herself. "*Relevé, relevé, retiré.*"

Her arms floated out and in with each movement, like bird's wings. Then she leaned forward and gripped the back of the chair, stepping up with one foot. Then two.

"Swish, swish, kick," she muttered, going over the steps in her head as she moved. "Swish, swish, ki—"

Her foot struck Alfred straight in the nose.

"Shit." She climbed down and brushed her hands down the front of her gauzy training skirt. "Three, two, one…"

This time, she got a few more beats through the routine before bringing her foot down on top of Alfred's head. A jittery feeling stirred in her stomach. Like the beginnings of panic.

She gritted her teeth. "Keep. Going."

Swish, swish, kick. *Smack!*

Tears pricked the backs of her eyes, frustration and fear mixing like a toxic swirl in her gut. She gave her dancing bag a frustrated jab and blew a loose strand of her hair from her face. Then she counted down from the top again.

Swish, swish, kick. Swish, swish, *smack*.

"Bloody hell," she muttered. "Why can't you get this?"

"Maybe because you're trying too hard."

Remi's head snapped up.

Wes stood in the doorway, arms crossed over his chest. How long had he been watching her? She'd been so deep in concentration that she hadn't noticed him come in.

So much for solitude and avoiding the source of her distraction.

"Did Sadie tell you I was coming to rehearse?" she said, climbing down from the chair.

He nodded.

"And what's this about trying too hard? I thought you'd be grateful that I'm doing my best not to give your paying customers a broken nose."

"That's part of your problem," he said, walking down to the stage. "Your mind is going straight to the worst-case scenario."

"The worst-case scenario is that I fall off the chair and break my neck. I thought the bloody nose was a good middling scenario." She couldn't keep the jagged edge of frustration out of her voice. "You could have told me I was auditioning for a part in Cirque du Soleil when I came to see you."

"I know you've been out of rehearsal mode for a long time, but it'll get easier."

They both knew it wouldn't. Ballet never got easier, exactly—it just became part of you. The pain became part of you. The music became part of you. The choreography became part of you. But like most things in a perfectionist's life, easy was never an option.

"Do you think I believe a word coming out of your mouth right now?" A rough laugh vibrated in the back of her throat.

"Not even a little bit." Wes walked over, the sound of his dress shoes echoing in the silent studio.

She was suddenly aware of how alone they were. How hidden from the rest of the world. In his apartment, light had spilled in through the windows. They'd had a timer on the clock, a reservation they couldn't miss. In the restaurant, she'd been protected by the company of her fellow dancers.

But now there was nothing to provide a line in the sand.

Wes walked straight over to Alfred and pulled him out of the "death seat."

"What the hell are you doing?" she asked, aghast.

"Getting a front row seat." He dropped down into the chair and looked up her, motioning for her to continue. "Don't let me interrupt you."

"You're crazy if you think I'm going to risk giving my boss a concussion." She folded her arms across her bust. Goose bumps rippled across her skin. Was it nerves or excitement?

"Stop making excuses."

She glared at him. "I'm putting your safety first."

"Not you're not, Reminiscent Sunburst. You're procrastinating and doing a shitty job of it."

She balled her hands by her sides. Of course he was pushing her buttons, poking her until she got riled up enough to have her "I'll show you" moment.

"If I ruin that pretty face of yours, it'll be a crying shame," she said, taking her position. "How on earth will you ever get another date?"

"You never know. It might give me some character." He grinned, completely unperturbed by her sarcastic tone. The guy was like Teflon with that stuff—the jabs glanced right off him. "Either that or you'll have to take pity on me and be my date. You know, since you ruined my beautiful face and all."

Dammit. Why did this man get under her skin like that? Normally, she was the witty one, the one with the silver tongue. That's what men loved about her—the sharp sense of humor, the snappy comebacks. But Wes's words sashayed around her, taunting her.

"Never."

"So coldhearted." He leaned back in his chair, legs spread slightly apart. The pose was unabashedly male, and Remi shifted her gaze away from him, turning back to face the empty rows of seats representing the audience.

The last thing she needed was the "Anaconda" staring back at her while she tried to nail these steps.

"Three, two, one." She counted herself in and rose up into *relevé*.

Her toes protested, but she gritted her teeth. She couldn't let Wes see she was struggling. Not when he'd placed so much faith in her.

She stepped up onto the chair, her floaty, chiffon skirt swirling around her thighs. *Swish, swish, kick*. Her foot sailed over his lap, missing him easily and she tried not to be distracted by the blue eyes trained intently on her. *Swish, swish, kick.* She turned, stepping into an *arabesque*, facing him, her back leg extended away from the chairs. Her ankle wobbled, the chair uneven enough that if she didn't rise up in exactly the right spot, she couldn't get a flat surface to balance on.

She wobbled again and fell forward, her hand coming down on Wes's shoulder.

"Whoa." He grabbed her easily, steadying her so she could bring her other foot down to the chair.

Humiliation burned in her cheeks. The other dancers seemed so much more at ease, so much more professional. They weren't scared by the strangeness of the moves or the challenge of working with these props.

"I wanted to practice alone tonight," she bit out. She was annoyed at herself for feeling so far behind, rather than at him for turning up unannounced. After all, he had every right to be there. "I'll get it, I promise."

"I know you will." He stood, his hands still on her.

Her chest rose and fell, the deep breaths threatening more emotion that she desperately tamped down. Wes moved in front of her, his other hand coming up to smooth over her hip. He settled it on the other side of her waist.

"I'm going to hold you," he said. "Go back into *arabesque*."

Swallowing, she rose onto pointe and stretched into the position. Her back leg extended behind her, pulling up to create a perfect, elongated shape. Her arms floated in front, one slightly higher than the other as she looked out over her fingertips, concentrating on the crack in the beige wall on the other side of the studio.

She held the position, feeling safe with his hands holding her steady. It'd been so long since she'd had a partner to give her a safety net. To make sure she didn't fall.

Remi didn't dare look down, fearing that staring into Wes's eyes might bring the most painful memories rushing back. She'd fallen in love once before in this very predicament—frightened of a new challenge, but with a strong, charming man holding her steady.

They'd been alone in the company studio, practicing. Her, an understudy for a *coryphée* role that had a small *pas de deux* component, and him, the handsome soloist on the rise. Remi's usual partner was difficult, temperamental. He'd tried to push her too fast, his steps always seemed a quarter of a beat too early, making it look like she couldn't keep up.

But Alex had been there for her. His career was taking off with rumors that he would be tapped for a senior artist position the following year. Yet he'd made time for her, stayed late to help her walk through the steps. He'd seemed so much older, wiser. And she'd been smitten.

God, how she'd been smitten.

She squeezed her eyes shut, forcing the memory to stop playing in her head before she made even more of a fool of herself. Bringing her leg down, she turned toward Wes, ready to ask him to move out of the way. But his hands splayed across her waist, smoothing the fitted material of her long-sleeved top.

His touch burned through the fabric, sending sparks showering over her. The frayed edges of her nerves left her open, susceptible. They made her an easy target, like a rabbit caught in the glare of headlights. Ready to be flattened. Her breath hitched in the back of her throat, her heart slamming against her rib cage.

This wasn't the effects of a memory.

It was the very real chemistry she'd walked away from the night they'd met at the bar. The kind of chemistry that was often imitated, rarely experienced. She knew choreographed chemistry, orchestrated chemistry. But this…this would burn her alive if she let it.

"Did you prove your point?" Her voice wobbled. Traitorous thing.

"What do you think my point was?" he asked.

Gone were the easy, humorous crinkles that normally bracketed his blue eyes. Gone was the cheeky smirk that lifted his lips, the one that always made her tummy flutter. Instead, he stared at her intently. Studying. Assessing. Like he could see a hell of a lot more than she wanted him to.

"To show me I can conquer my fears and all that. Was it meant to be a teachable moment?" She hated herself for trying to tarnish the flickering connection between them by being a sarcastic bitch. But Remi didn't do vulnerable. She didn't do open. Not anymore.

"I'm here to help you," he said, frustration giving his tone a sharp edge. "Call it a 'teachable moment' if you like. Call it whatever the hell you want. But the reason I'm here is because I want this show to be a resounding success, and in order for that to happen, I need to make sure you slay whatever demon is lurking in your head."

Yeah, he saw *way* too much.

"No demons," she lied. "Just a fear of props."

"Bullshit. We both know there's more to it than that."

He was still touching her, and she was still letting him. His strong hands made her waist look fragile. Made *her* look fragile.

You don't want to be bloody fragile. You want to be a strong, badass ballerina who doesn't need a man to save her.

But she was failing miserably.

"Help me down?" she asked, forcing a smile. She needed to break this spell. ASAP.

"Only if you stop feeding me bullshit," he replied. "I know you probably come from a place where keeping your mouth shut is the only way to get ahead. I've been there too. But I can't help you if you're acting like I'm the enemy."

"What if you can't help me at all?" she whispered.

He tightened his hands around her and helped her down from the chair, the change in angle casting shadows across his face. Remi wasn't short by any means, but Wes towered over her. He leaned forward, his dark hair flopping across his forehead. Without thinking, she reached up and brushed it back.

"I will keep pushing, Remi. I will poke and shove and I will make you angry enough to get out of your own head." He pinned her with his stare. "I won't let this show fail."

Disappointment stabbed at her chest. Of course it was all about the show—she was doing the same stupid thing that she'd done before. Misinterpreting signs. Reading too much into things. Hearing what she wanted to hear.

Wasn't that what Alex had said to her? *If you thought I loved you, it was because you wanted to think that. Not because I meant it.*

"I won't let *you* fail." Wes's voice had turned rough. Gritty.

Don't fall for it. Don't fall for him.

He was saying whatever was required to get her invested in her part. That was all.

"I appreciate that," she said, choosing her words carefully. They were standing far too close together. So close that the scent of cologne and rain on his skin coiled around her, warming her from the inside out. But no matter how much she shouted at her brain to get things moving, her body refused to take a step back.

"You have to stop being so…" He shook his head. "Frightened. You're acting like a little lost lamb and that's *not* who you are."

"No, I'm not a lost lamb."

"You have to get passionate." He poked her gently in the chest, and she blinked. Shock morphing to anger as a veil of red washed over her vision.

"Did you just *poke* me?"

"Get angry, Remi. Get furious."

"Stop it!" She planted her hands on his chest and shoved him back.

"You can't be a performer if you keep everything bottled up. You have to let it out." His voice was loud now, and it echoed through the studio, bouncing off the walls and rattling around inside her brain. "Do something crazy for once."

Crazy? He wanted to see crazy?

"Fine!" she yelled at him.

Then she flung her arms around his neck.

Wes stumbled back with the force of Remi's embrace, his arms automatically enveloping her as though he'd done it a thousand times before.

Only in your head.

But it wasn't in his head now. She reared up on her pointe shoes and mashed her lips to his, hard. Demanding. Hot breath puffed across his cheek as she angled her head, trying to deepen the kiss. It only took him a second to recover and for his brain to finally kick into gear. Slipping his hand up to the back of her head, he grabbed her ponytail and tugged her head back, taking control.

A surprised gasp shot out of her mouth, but it melted into a soft moan as he coaxed her lips open, teasing his tongue against hers. She tasted sweet—like the coconut drink she'd had at dinner. And something else. Something earthy and sensual that made all the blood in his body migrate south.

"So sweet," he murmured against her lips.

Her hands fisted in his shirt, the gentle knocking of her pointe shoes against the floor telling him she was still on her toes. The last thing they needed was for her to hurt her feet, but he wasn't about to stop now. No way. He'd had the first taste of heaven, and he was going to drown himself in it.

This is important. She is important. Don't fuck things up. Stop. Now.

But his body was running full tilt in one direction, and he was powerless to change the course of action. Sliding his hands up the backs of her thighs, he cupped her ass and lifted. Remi's long legs wrapped around his waist, settling her heat right where his cock pressed hard up against his fly. The contact was pure pleasure. Pure agony. And when she writhed against him, hands in his hair, nails scraping against his scalp, he thought he might explode.

"Remi," he gasped into her mouth.

He marched them across the room until her back hit the wall. All he could think about was sandwiching her between him and something hard. Somewhere he could grind his cock against the sweet, hot juncture of her thighs.

With the wall helping to support her, he could roam with one hand. Along the curve of her waist, over the flat plane of her stomach, and up to the gentle swell of her breast. Her nipple beaded against his thumb, and he rubbed back and forth. If she had a bra on, there wasn't much to it.

"Yes." Her head rolled back and made a soft *clunk* against the wall.

Wes brought his lips to her neck, sucking on the smooth, pale skin. A hint of perspiration danced on his lips, a slight saltiness that made him think of hot, sweaty nights and hands fisted in bedsheets. He needed more of her. More taste, more touch, more scent. More everything.

He hooked his finger over the edge of her top, pulling. The fabric gave, stretching under his command to expose her breasts. No bra.

A wicked grin lit his mouth the second before he bowed his head, taking a nipple between his lips and sucking. The bud tightened against his tongue.

"Wes!" Her voice was high. Taut, like a muscle pulled to extremes.

Gently, he used his teeth, and a shudder ripped through her body as she bowed against him. The woman was a wildfire. A bright, open flame. Her hips rolled against him, rubbing up and down against his erection.

His cock was so hard he had no idea how the zipper of his pants was still intact.

"My God," she panted. "You feel so…"

Her words dissolved into sounds. He tugged at the top again. Too hard. The fabric split under his fingers, but neither one of them cared enough to stop. If necessary, he'd tear every scrap of fabric from her to get what he wanted—her, naked and open. Legs spread for him.

You're not supposed to go here. Stop.

But he couldn't. A gate had been opened, and he'd run through at full speed.

The show had consumed his life in the past months, leaving no time for pleasure. And then, Remi had come along, taunting him with her long legs and sexy accent. With her brilliant smile and cheeky personality.

But she wasn't cheeky now. She'd morphed into an all-out sex bomb. Her hands cupped his faced and pulled him back up to her lips, showing him what she liked. Where she liked it. The confidence was hotter than any of it.

"Is that what you want?" His left hand toyed with her other breast.

"Yes. That." Her breath was hot against his face. The sound rang in his ears on an endless loop. It was like his ability to perceive sensory information had been shrunk to her. Only her. "Harder."

He pinched the swollen bud and she gasped.

"Again." Her sweet, smooth voice had turned dark. Smoky. He complied and was rewarded with a low, guttural sound that completely undid him.

"Christ, you're so hot." He buried his face in the crook of her neck. "This is what I was talking about. This is you. You're passionate, Remi. You're brimming with it."

Her body froze under his hands. "What?"

Wes looked up, and it was like someone had flipped a switch. The dark, smoldering heat had vanished from her eyes. Her lips—which had been wrapped around a delicious O shape—were now tightly pursed.

She unlocked her legs from behind his back and, bracing her hands against his biceps, lowered herself to the ground. "Is this a joke to you?"

What the hell had just happened? Wes shook his head and tried to retrace his steps. "Why would it be a joke?"

"Because of what you said earlier. About me needing to get passionate." For a second, he wondered if actual flames might shoot out of her mouth. "Did you kiss me to prove a point?"

"What? No." He shook his head.

"Is this what you do with all your struggling dancers, huh? You 'show' them how to feel it." Underneath the spitfire anger, there was something else. An echo of a deeper emotion—fear. "Well, I don't need a personal demonstration, thank you very much. I can figure it out on my own."

He narrowed his eyes at her. "If you think I go around kissing my dancers to prove a point, then you're sorely mistaken."

"So you've never kissed another dancer you've worked with, huh?" The tremor of hope in her voice was like a slash across his chest.

She wanted him to reassure her. But he wouldn't lie.

"I've been with other dancers," he conceded. "But not while we were working together."

In fact, he'd turned down quite a few women when he'd feared the sex might have something to do with his position at the Evans Ballet School. No way would he allow *anyone* to think getting into his bed might advance their career. Or that he might abuse his position of power.

But this was different. She already had the best part in the show.

Yeah, keep telling yourself that. You know it's not okay.

"They say it's natural for people working together to develop phantom feelings." She nodded slowly, almost as if she was speaking to herself.

"There's nothing phantom about this, Remi." He planted a palm against the wall beside her head and leaned forward. "And it has nothing to do with us working together. You and I both know that."

"Do we?"

"Are you telling me you didn't feel something that first day we met?" He laughed. The attraction had hit him like a ton of bricks, and they'd shared this amazing, sparkly chemistry all the way through her class. "I *know* you did. You came to meet me at a bar for crying out loud. You were ready to come home with me."

"And I told you I can't be both business and pleasure." She swallowed.

"Sounds like you're the one who needs to get that straight," he said, "since *you* kissed me."

"You're right." She planted her hands on his chest and he willed them to curl into the fabric of his sweater. To pull him forward. But instead, she gently eased herself out from between him and the wall. "I don't know what came over me tonight."

"You're fighting it." He watched her walk across the studio, mesmerized by the swish of her gauzy skirt over her pert ass. "You're fighting this attraction harder than you're fighting your fears about dancing."

She whirled around, holding the broken neckline of her top together in one hand. Hurt glittered in her eyes. This was a woman who felt everything down to the marrow of her bones. Yet she let her fear stifle the life out of her. "Do you think I'm not making enough of an effort, Wes? Is that it?"

"I'm not saying that at all." He held up his hands in surrender. "I'm just pointing out that maybe you need to let go a bit more. Stop being so rigid."

Yeah right. Saying that to a type-A ballerina was like throwing marshmallows at an oncoming tsunami.

"I don't want to mess this up." Her big, brown eyes bored into him. "You have a lot riding on this show, and so do I. We should focus on that."

She was right, of course. Totally right. But it didn't stop his body from roaring in protest.

She grabbed her bag and her coat from where they sat in a heap.

"So that's it?" he said. "End of discussion?"

"Thank you for stopping me from repeating a

mistake." Her voice had lost some of its sting now. The more he got to know Remi, the more he realized her fiery side was only ever a defense mechanism. When she felt like she'd gotten things back under control, the flames disappeared. "I needed that."

He stood in the middle of the room as she walked out, his head still spinning from their argument and his cock still aching from her searing kisses. Talk about a messed-up combination of feelings. Angry and horny weren't exactly a match made in heaven.

But then again, no other woman managed to get under his skin the way she did.

The sounds of the old building started to filter back in as he stood there, debating what to do. Part of him wanted to go after her, to argue her into submission and throw her over his shoulder, caveman-style. But the other part of him—the one still thankfully attached to his brain—kept him rooted to the spot.

She needed time to cool off. And he needed his lead ballerina to have her head in the game.

Chapter 12

"A guy who knows how to dance is always good in bed. Let's just say Wes's moves could earn him a Tony."

—TheatreFan

WES HAD RESOLVED TO PUT ALL THOUGHTS OF REMI AND her unobtainable body out of his mind, despite the fact that last night's kiss played on repeat in his head. As much as he wanted to revel in that sexy memory, he currently had bigger fish to fry. Attending the cocktail party on Thursday night for the American Ballet Theatre was part of his strategy for hooking a new investor. But it was only one piece of the puzzle. First on his list was meeting someone who'd been where he was.

Reed McMahon.

Clearly the website had a history of making life difficult for people. So he needed to speak to someone who'd been through it before.

Wes headed to Birch Coffee, where he was due to meet Reed. He'd been somewhat surprised at Reed's ready agreement to a meeting, given he now seemed to have moved on with his life. From what could be gleaned online, Reed had quit a fairly lucrative career in PR to go into teaching. But beyond that, it was all a mystery. Articles about him had been plentiful up until a few months ago. Then, nothing.

Wes walked into Birch Coffee and ordered himself a latte. Then he found a small spot in the back of the café to wait. Not even a minute after Wes sat down, Reed walked in. He put up his hand in a friendly salute and the other man went to the bar first, to get himself a drink, before meeting Wes at the table.

"Nice to meet you." Wes stuck out his hand. "I appreciate you agreeing to this."

"No problem." Reed lowered himself onto a wooden stool. He was dressed casually, a navy sweater over a blue-and-white-checked shirt. Jeans. Sneakers. Nothing like the slick photos Wes had seen online. "I understand you have a little review problem."

Or a *big* review problem. "Yeah. Bad Bachelors. You're familiar, I hear."

"Very." He rolled his eyes as he brought his coffee cup to his lips and sipped. "It's a name I hoped I'd never have to hear again."

"I have no idea if you can help me. I'm at my wit's end about it, and I hear you're somewhat of a PR whiz."

"Was," Reed corrected. "Not anymore."

"Did you manage to do anything about the reviews when they were causing you problems?"

Reed snorted. "I left my job after it caused me hell and sent my reputation down the toilet."

"That's not an option for me."

"My situation with Bad Bachelors was unique."

Reed rolled his coffee cup between his hands. "I wanted to get it shut down, but in the end I couldn't."

Cryptic much? "Couldn't?"

"I chose not to." He sighed. "I disagree wholeheartedly with the site and how people are using it. It's a cesspool, frankly. The owner is aware that some of the reviews aren't legitimate, but they're not moderating it correctly."

It sounded a hell of a lot like Reed knew who was behind Bad Bachelors. "How do you know *that*?"

"Inside information. And no, I can't share." He sipped his coffee. "The best thing I can advise is to not engage. Don't respond to anything online because it only feeds the beast. You need to focus your efforts on raising good press to drown out the noise. What are the crux of the reviews?"

How was he supposed to answer that without coming across like a conceited jerk? "The reviews are mostly positive," he said. "It's not the content so much as their existence."

Reed's lip twitched like he was trying to hide a smirk. "Got it."

"But I'm trying to get my show off the ground, and the investors are taking issue with the fact that my sex life is all over the internet." His knuckles tightened around the cup, the cardboard giving under his grip. He put it down before he crushed the damn thing and covered himself in coffee. "I wasn't aware I needed to get people to sign an NDA before we slept together."

"Preaching to the choir, man." Reed shook his head. "Honestly, I would try to move on. If you were my client back when I was working in the industry, I would have advised a few interviews, especially if your reviews are mostly positive. If people bring it up, you can simply brush over it and keep the focus on your show. Hell, you might even get some more people coming along out of curiosity's sake."

"Only if we can find the right investors," Wes said. "Otherwise, I'm going to be funding it one hundred percent myself, which is risky."

"Very risky." Reed nodded. "From what I know about Broadway, that's not a good move."

"Like I said, I'm not going to quit." He braced his hands on his knees, frustration coursing through him. "You really didn't find *anything* about Bad Bachelors that might help me? I thought you of all people would understand my predicament."

"I do." Reed nodded. "But it's a tough situation."

"How? You're engaged now, right? It's not like you have to worry about it anymore."

Reed looked at Wes long and hard, like he was trying to figure something out. He seemed torn, which meant he *definitely* knew more than he was letting on.

"Look," he said. "I understand why you're pissed off. Believe me, I was ready to burn down the world if it meant getting that site wiped off the map. But there was a cost I wasn't willing to pay."

"A cost that was higher than giving up your job? Your life?"

"Sometimes you change what you want out of life."

Wes bit back his frustration. "That tells me nothing."

"I'm sorry, I can't say any more than that. My advice stands, don't engage. And don't bother trying to get the reviews taken down, they won't do it." Reed shot him a sympathetic look and stood. "I do hope you manage to get your show off the ground."

Wes leaned back against the wall of the café as Reed bid him farewell and left the bustling establishment. For a moment, he wanted to let the white noise wash over him. He wanted to pretend he wasn't dragging *Out of Bounds* through thick sludge. At every turn, there was another hurdle. Another setback.

Most people might stop and wonder if it was all worth it at this point. But not Wes. He'd fought too hard already. The more walls that popped up in front of him, the harder he would push until he had what he wanted.

He mulled over Reed's words. *There was a cost I wasn't willing to pay.*

What the hell did that mean? Reed seemed to have given up everything—a job he loved, the prestige of working for one of Manhattan's top PR firms. Undoubtedly he'd given up an insane salary and lavish lifestyle. Though on reflection, it wasn't all that dissimilar to what Wes had given up for *Out Of Bounds*. He'd forgone his cushy job and padded paycheck. He'd given up a part of his relationship with his parents. He'd given up sleep and free time and all his savings.

Sometimes you change what you want out of life.

Love. All the bad press had stopped when he'd gotten engaged. Maybe that had something to do with it.

Wes shook his head. Love made people do crazy things, that was for damn sure. And perhaps it made him cold, but he couldn't imagine giving up his dream for someone. Because what was the point of a relationship if he wasn't otherwise creatively fulfilled in life?

It had to be something else. Surely.

Remi leaned back on her couch and bit down on her lip as she lowered her foot into a bucket of ice water. No matter how many times she did it—and no matter how much she knew it would help—there was no dulling the shock of that freezing temperature on sore muscles.

Her sweatpants were pushed up to her knees and her hair was pulled up into a greasy bun on top of her head.

"Great idea to have a night in." Darcy carried over the boxes of steaming pizza that were currently making Remi's mouth water and placed them on the coffee table. "People at the library have been crazy this week. Must be a full moon or something."

This week, Remi, Annie, and Darcy had moved their catch-up to Thursday, since Remi was going to be at the cocktail party with Wes tomorrow night. And the thought of trying to stuff her battered feet into a pair of heels two nights in a row was too much to bear. Plus, she'd barely slept a wink since The Kiss.

It was never a good sign when your mistakes required a title.

"Ugh, tell me about it." Annie had a pitcher of margaritas that she'd made up and three wineglasses. Since Remi's apartment was basically a glorified shoebox, the options for glassware were limited to cheap white-wine glasses and chunky water glasses that she'd bought at IKEA. "My boss was in a foul mood all week and literally everything that could go wrong with this project is going wrong. I mean, the client expects that defects found in UAT can be fixed with a click of our fingers, but it was their fault for providing shitty requirements."

Remi shot Darcy a confused look and got a shrug in return. Neither of them really understood what Annie did at work.

"Enough about our work problems," Darcy said, flipping open the top pizza box. The scent of melted cheese and garlic wafted into the air. "How's the dream career going?"

Remi had been dreading this moment. She *should* have been over the moon, but instead, she wanted to cry. Rehearsals continued to plague her confidence— even though she'd finally managed to master the *swish, swish, kick* without taking Alfred's head off. They'd also taken measurements for the costume designer today, and Remi had been horrified to see that her numbers were well over what they used to be.

It appeared that was the downside to the ladies' supper club.

She eyed the pizza with disdain. "It's okay."

"Okay?" Darcy settled onto the couch and sat cross-legged. "What's going on? I thought you'd be ecstatic."

Where did she begin? Or, more importantly, how much did she actually want to say? It wasn't that she didn't trust Annie or Darcy—far from it. But they both had jobs they loved, jobs they were good at. And for all the troubles they'd had in their lives—Darcy finding out her fiancée had been cheating on her and Annie experiencing the breakdown of a relationship at the same time her mother was diagnosed with cancer—none of it ever seemed related to work.

"I guess I'm feeling guilty about abandoning Mish," she said. It was certainly true, but it also felt like safer topic of discussion.

"That's understandable." Annie sat next to Darcy.

The two of them were like chalk and cheese. Darcy had a full sleeve of tattoos on one arm and a pierced tongue, and tended to dress in all-black outfits. Annie, on the other hand, was sleek and feminine. Her shiny, brown hair was always perfectly smooth, and you'd never catch her looking rumpled or frazzled.

But the two had been friends since childhood.

"But I'm sure she gets it," Annie continued, pouring everyone a drink. "Sometimes when an opportunity lands at your feet, you have to take it. Would you rather grow old and wonder what might have been?"

Would she have preferred ignorant bliss over the knowledge that she didn't have what it took to succeed in her dream career? Maybe.

Stop it. You will get the choreography, and you will make this work.

"Has she found someone to replace you?" Darcy asked. She leaned forward and grabbed her margarita, taking a sip.

"Yeah, at least for now." Remi shifted on her seat. "But she didn't seem that keen to talk when I rang her yesterday."

Considering she and Mish had spoken on an almost daily basis for the last year and a half, it was strange to have that gap in her life.

"She was still pretty pissed." Remi grabbed a piece of pizza and almost moaned at the melty, gooey goodness. Just one slice and then she'd eat the quinoa salad she'd prepared before the girls had arrived. "Not that I blame her at all. She's got every right to be furious at me."

"And how's the other stuff?" Darcy asked. "Is it like riding a bike?"

"Kind of. My feet have taken a beating, but I know they'll adjust and the calluses will come back, and I won't get as many blisters then."

Annie wrinkled her nose. "For such a beautiful art form, it sure doesn't look so glamorous underneath it all."

"I once had a teacher tell me that a ballerina's feet were like a warrior's hands." She pulled her foot out of the ice bath and dropped it down onto the towel she'd laid out earlier. Then she put her other foot into the bucket and cringed again at the shock. "Every battle scar and ugly bit is the product of conquering new ground."

"I like that." Darcy grinned. "Makes you sound fierce."

"And what's it like working with the Anaconda?" Annie's eyes twinkled. "Any glimpses of the beast?"

Remi rolled her eyes. "Yeah, he walks around the studio with it slung over his shoulder."

Darcy snorted, her margarita almost sloshing over the edge of the glass. "Now *that's* an image."

"Seriously, though. I need to live vicariously through you, since Darcy isn't any good to me anymore." Annie smirked and Darcy rolled her eyes, swapping her drink for a slice of pizza.

"Sorry my engagement is so boring," she retorted through a mouthful of pepperoni.

"What's he like?" Annie probed.

"Charming." It was the first word that popped into her head when it came to Wes. "And driven and talented."

"Not to mention gorgeous," Darcy added. "I saw him when we met Remi for a drink before her date-that-wasn't-a-date. I prefer my own tall, dark, and handsome man, but I can still appreciate some fine human construction."

Memories of their kiss rushed through Remi, firing up all the places he'd touched as if she were suddenly in the dimly lit studio again. The way he'd taken charge of kissing her—stunned only for a nanosecond when she'd thrown her arms around him before he jumped into the driver's seat. And the way he'd carried her across the room and pinned her to the wall…

"You're looking a little flushed, Remi." Annie shot Darcy a knowing look. "Kind of weird for a girl with her foot in a bucket of ice water."

"Did something happen?" Darcy's blue eyes widened.

"Nothing happened." The second the words came out of her mouth, she knew the denial was too quick. Too obvious. "Maybe something happened."

"What kind of something?" Annie leaned forward to grab her drink. "First base, second base?"

"Or did you hit a home run?" Darcy laughed.

Remi chewed on the crust of her pizza slice. "What is this? High school?"

"Just answer the question, Drysdale."

God. How was she supposed to fit a kiss like that into such neat little boxes? Some kisses could be classified—good or bad, tongue or no tongue, sloppy or too much teeth. But this was the kind of kiss that would usually lead to a night of hot, headboard-banging, scream-your-lungs-out sex.

That was until he had to say something stupid.

You should be grateful, or else you'd be nursing a hell of a freak-out right now instead of mild self-recrimination.

"It was just a kiss," she said, taking her other foot out of the ice bath and dabbing it with her towel.

"It wasn't *just* anything by the look on your face," Darcy said. "You've got that 'I've been thinking about it for days but I really wish I hadn't' expression."

Got it in one.

"It *was* just a kiss. An ill-advised one at that." She stood and picked up the bucket. "I'm not planning a repeat."

She walked over to the kitchen, which was behind the sofa where her friends sat, and tipped the water down the drain. Ice cubes clinked against the metal sink, drowning out Annie's response.

"I've never seen you get so angsty over a kiss before." Darcy turned and draped her arms over the sofa, watching as Remi set the bucket down and started spooning her salad into a bowl.

"I'm grumpy because you guys get to eat pizza and I have to be healthy," she replied.

"Bullshit." Annie shook her head. "You like this guy."

"I like all the guys I kiss. Otherwise, why would I kiss them?" She stuck her head into the fridge and dug around for some feta in the hopes it would make her salad taste less like a dish sponge. It also had the added benefit of hiding her reaction from her friends. "We were rehearsing and we got caught up in a moment of passion. That's it."

Keep telling yourself that.

"There's a big difference between liking a guy enough to make out with him and liking him enough to be annoyed that you did," Annie said knowingly. "What do you think, Darcy?"

"I concur."

"Don't gang up on me," Remi said as she carried her dinner back to the coffee table. It looked so bland and beige next to the delicious, crispy pizza. "I'm fragile at the moment."

"Ha, fragile." Darcy chuckled. "I know a lot of fragile people, Remi, and you aren't one of them. Believe me, you're stronger than the lot of us put together."

"And the fact that you're giving this whole ballet thing another shot is testament to that," Annie added. For all their teasing, she knew the two women had her back. With her being so far away from home, they were her surrogate family. Her best friends and sisters all wrapped into one.

"I do like him," she admitted. "He's exactly my catnip—sexy, he's got moves, he's confident without being a jerk. The problem is, if I want to move forward in this career, then he's one of *them*."

"Them?" Annie cocked her head.

"The haves," she said. "And I am the have-nots. In other words, I rely on people like him to help me get ahead. The last thing I want is anyone saying I'm trying to sleep my way to the top or that he would be the kind of guy to take advantage of me. It would hurt us both."

It was the greatest insult anyone could hurl at her. Remi loved sex, but not as a negotiating tactic. Not as payment for a favor. She would *never* use her body like that, despite what people had said last time. The whispers had cut worse than outright accusations because they'd come from those she'd thought had known her better.

Annie and Darcy knew the full story behind why she'd left Australia. Originally, she hadn't wanted to tell them, instead stating that she'd always planned to come to New York, and after she broke up with her boyfriend, it'd seemed like the perfect opportunity. Not exactly a lie.

But the day Darcy found her sobbing in the bathroom, it had all come out—the affair, the pregnancy. The miscarriage. Everything.

"Jealousy makes people say stupid things," Annie said with a sigh. "I could totally see that."

"Well, we're having funding issues with the show anyway. Maybe if it all falls in a heap, I'll let myself indulge."

"Funding issues?" Darcy asked.

"Yeah, seems one of the investors wasn't so happy about Wes's, uh…reputation, to put it delicately."

Annie raised a brow. "And to put it not so delicately?"

"He didn't like the fact that Wes's sex life was splashed all over the internet. No so much because of *what* they said, but the fact that people were talking about it." Remi waded her fork through the quinoa, trying to dig out a chunk of feta.

"Talk about flipping gender norms," Annie said. "Not that I'm happy Wes is having difficulties, but it's usually women who get judged for their sex lives."

"Well, Bad Bachelors has certainly got a hand in it."

Remi shook her head. "I thought it was such a great idea at first, but after seeing what Reed went through and now Wes, I'm not so sure."

Darcy shot Annie a strange look.

"What?" Remi asked.

"Nothing." Annie picked up her drink. "So what's Wes's plan for the show? Has he got another investor lined up?"

"Apparently there's going to be some important, rich people at this cocktail party tomorrow night." She chewed, her mind whirling at the details he'd emailed earlier that day. Not just the invite for the event, but the fact that he was sending her to see a friend of his who was a personal shopper at Saks. On him. "I'm going with him to lure some wallets open."

"Going with him as a date?" Darcy asked.

"No, it's not a date." Remi put her salad down, her appetite waning. "Definitely not a date."

Chapter 13

"Good girl's guide to dating, rule #1: start slow. You don't need a Ferrari for your first car. Wes is for advanced players only."

—GoodieTwoShoes

THERE HADN'T BEEN TOO MANY OPPORTUNITIES IN Remi's life for her to truly feel like a princess. Sure, in the early days of her career, she'd had exciting moments. Glamorous moments. But nothing like spending the afternoon with a personal shopper at Saks Fifth Avenue, playing in the VIP area where everyone had a small dog poking out of a handbag that cost more than any car she'd ever driven. But with Wes's connections, no one had called her out for being an intruder despite her anticipating a *Pretty Woman* moment the second she'd set foot in their gleaming, well-lit dressing room.

Instead, they'd served her Veuve Clicquot and macarons, and invited her to use any of the bottles of Chanel perfume that were meant for their clients.

Chanel. Veuve. Your bill is covered in full.

What parallel dimension have I fallen into?

Remi watched the city crawl by through the limousine's window as she smoothed her hands down the front of her new dress. The silvery-white fabric was decorated with tiny beads and seed pearls that caught the light, twinkling like the Manhattan skyline. She should have been pinching herself. Getting dressed up and going to a cocktail party was her favorite hobby. Instead, she felt more away from home than ever.

Perhaps it was the pressure. She wasn't here to enjoy herself. She was here to be paraded around. Shown off. Wes wanted her to charm people the way she'd supposedly charmed him. But that was before he'd had any expectations and before *she* had something to lose.

Panic clawed up the back of her throat and her fists bunched against her thighs. What if tonight was a complete disaster and she made a fool of him? Of herself? Would he let her go as easily as her ex had?

This is totally different. It's work, not personal. You're still the ballerina he chose for his show.

Not personal? Had she suddenly forgotten that they'd shared a mind-melting kiss only days ago?

Do not think about the kiss. Do not think about the kiss. Do not think about the kiss.

Shit. She was *definitely* thinking about it. And worse still, the show would only go ahead if they could secure another investor.

"We're going to stop here for a minute, Ms. Drysdale." The driver caught her gaze in the rearview mirror. His shiny, black cap and crisp, white shirt seemed so formal. Stuffy.

Remi swallowed. "Okay."

She dug her hand into the absurdly tiny clutch the personal shopper had picked out for her—an abstract, black creation that looked like a gleaming chunk of onyx more than it did a bag—and found her mirror. The makeup artist at the MAC Cosmetics counter had done a lovely job, making her already big eyes seem even bigger with smoky purple shadows and a set of thick, fluttery false lashes.

You're being ridiculous. You love makeup, you love shoes and fancy dresses and tiny bags. This is your jam. Stop being such a wuss.

Before she could send herself further into a negative-thought spiral, the door opened. Remi held her breath as Wes climbed in, the visual of him blanking out the worries in her head. The man wore a tuxedo so well it was borderline criminal. The black jacket fit him like a dream, accentuating his broad shoulders. The pants were even better still, hugging his muscular thighs and making his already-long legs look longer. And though his hair was loosely styled, it was still touchable enough that her fingers twitched with the instinct to reach out.

He slid over the back seat to sit next to her, and she was hit with a heady mix of amber and citrus, a contrast of notes rich and crisp. A hint of him underneath.

Legs together, eyes up. This is a work function.

Yeah right, like she had *that* kind of willpower.

"You look incredible." He leaned in and pressed a kiss to her cheek, his burgeoning stubble giving her skin the slightest friction. But it may as well have been a stun gun. A ripple of excitement shot down the length of her spine, and she shivered.

"Are you cold?" He frowned. "I'll get the driver to turn the heat up."

"You brought a bit of a breeze in with you." *Liar, liar, pants on fire.* "I'm fine, promise."

His eyes lingered appreciatively on where the dress split over her thigh. The neckline was delicate and modest, her back reasonably covered, and the hem swept across the floor, even in her stilt-like heels. If she was standing, the slit wouldn't even be noticeable. But in the back of the limo, it gave a generous glimpse of skin and Wes didn't look away.

"So." She clapped her hands together and forced herself to act like they were nothing more than two friends. "Tell me the who's who of the Upper East Side. What do I need to know for tonight?"

And like that, the tension evaporated. Wes leaned back and buckled himself in, his expression easy and light. This was Business Wes. Director Wes. And he slipped back into that mode with ease. Maybe too much ease.

So what? You're the one setting the boundaries. Why would that be a problem?

Dammit. Why did her head and her lady parts have to disagree about everything? They were like *The Odd Couple*.

Did you really just refer to your brain and your vagina as The Odd Couple?

"It's the American Ballet Theatre's holiday preview, so everyone from the company will be there. Everyone important, anyway." He drummed his fingers against his thigh. Remi watched the silent, even beat, trying not to remember how those strong, long-fingered hands had slipped up her body and torn the fabric of her top right off the elastic. "All the big donors will be there, and they usually have a few government representatives. Anyone in charge of arts funding. Heads of all the major ballet schools too, along with their wunderkinds."

"Does that mean your parents will be there?"

He looked at her intently for a moment. "Yes."

That was it. In the short time she'd known Wes, there were only a few topics on which he had little to say. His parents were at the top of that list.

"Sadie is going to meet us there," he added, moving the conversation quickly on. "I could only get a few tickets tonight, so it'll be the three of us from *Out of Bounds*."

Remi had to hold in a sigh of relief. At least that was one stressor off her head for the night. No other cast members meant not having to worry about them watching her with Wes. She had this horrible feeling that, as much as she tried to ignore their chemistry, her attraction to him was seeping out of every pore like a bloody pheromone.

They rounded the corner at Fifth Avenue and Ninety-First and the Guggenheim slowly came into view. The building's unique round design had always appealed to Remi. It was of another time. Old and yet futuristic. A contradiction. The smooth whiteness of the curved surface felt endless, like if you followed the building all the way around, you might end up somewhere else entirely.

The traffic slowed as they approached the museum and several other cars ahead stopped to let people in fancy ball gowns and tuxedos out. Important ballet people. It wasn't a group she ever thought she'd join again.

"How could you have been so stupid?" Melody said, her hands rubbing up and down her face. "After all the help I gave you, all the advice. You were going places, Remi. Shit, you could have gone anywhere. Why did you throw that all away?"

"I didn't think anyone would find out." Tears streamed down her face, the ache in her chest worse than any muscular pain she'd ever experienced after a grueling rehearsal. Worse than the blisters and the broken toenails and the hairline fracture in her wrist. She pressed a hand to her stomach, instinct making her protective. "It was supposed to be a secret."

"Well, you're even dumber than I thought. You know how people gossip here. They live for it. And you." She jabbed Remi in the chest. Hard. "Those rich bitches want to see people like you and me fail. They don't think we belong and they want us out. And you handed them your head on a silver platter, didn't you? All because you couldn't keep your legs shut."

"Stop." The sobs turned to heaving shudders. But Melody was right. How could she have risked all this? Her future, all those hours of hard work. All the sacrifices. All the fights with her parents.

"You knew she wanted him. You knew that her word would always be worth more than yours. More than any of ours."

"Why should she get to say who belongs with who?" Her eyes stung as her mascara ran, turning her vision blurry and blackened. "We can decide for ourselves."

"He decided, all right." Melody picked Remi's duffel bag up from the floor and held it out. "He chose his career over you. You should have done the same."

"Remi?" Wes's hand landed softly on her shoulder. "Have you changed your mind?"

She blinked as a horn blared behind them. A chilly fall breeze blew into the limo through the open door as Wes waited on the sidewalk, his hand outstretched.

"No, of course not." She slid her palm against his and allowed him to help her out of the car. "Just preparing myself."

"You'll be fine," he said. "Or how do you Aussies say it? She'll be right?"

Wes's terrible attempt at an Australian accent brought a smile to her lips. It was amazing how he did that—cut through her stress and doubt. Grounded her. "She'll be right, *mate*."

"Mate. Of course." He grinned. "How could I forget?"

Remi's feet protested the height of her new shoes as she steadied herself on the pavement. The personal shopper had insisted on a pair of open-toed sandals until Remi had proven to her that ballerina's feet were the most ungraceful part of their bodies and the lady had promptly produced a pair of pumps with a pointed toe. Elegant, yes. But they would be even more murderous than her pointe shoes.

"Clearly you need to watch *Crocodile Dundee* a few more times," she said, slipping her arm through his so they could walk in together. "Homework. I want you to report back on Monday."

"Don't challenge me, Reminiscent." His grin turned wolfish.

"Watch me, Wesley."

He laughed, and the deep, rich sound spread through

her body like a bushfire. No matter how many times she reinforced her boundaries, he seemed to smash through them without even trying.

They were stopped at the entrance by a security guard in a black suit who wanted to check their tickets. As Wes fished the thick, embossed cardboard out of the inside pocket of his tuxedo jacket, Remi looked up. The feeling of being watched trickled through her, sending ice skittering down her spine.

After scanning the museum's entry, she found the source of that uneasy, prickling sensation. Lilah. Judging by her arched, black brow, the surprise was mutual. Their gazes locked and Lilah's lips tilted up into a cold smile.

Crap.

At one point, Wes would have breezed into an event like this without a care in the world. He would have stopped to talk at least three or four times before making it to the rotunda, where the event was being held. A drink would have been pressed into his hand, palms slapped onto his back. Because he was one of them.

Or at least he used to be.

Right now, he was grateful to have Remi on his arm. The woman was a knockout in a leotard and leg warmers. But in a dress that fit her like a second skin, fabric shimmering like the scales of a mythical creature, she was otherworldly. Which meant all eyes were on her. And he was perfectly happy with that.

He nodded to a waiter and the young man came right

over so Wes could pluck a champagne flute from the gleaming, silver tray. "Here," he said to Remi, handing the glass over. "You'll need this."

"Fortification?" She raised a brow and accepted the flute, bringing it straight to her lips. "I think you might be right about that."

The people who'd once felt like "his" people were now distant. Walking into the Ronald O. Perelman Rotunda was like returning home a pariah. Eyes that would have once found his now avoided him. People who would have come to his side now slid past.

Had his mother been doing the rounds? Or was this more to do with the Bad Bachelors reviews? In the conservative ballet world, such exposure would be frowned upon. But he wasn't going to give anyone the satisfaction of seeing him squirm.

"Do you get the impression everyone is staring at us?" she asked.

"It's hard not to stare at you in that dress." He placed his hand at the small of her back, thanking the gods that it wasn't skin-to-skin contact. Feeling the heat and life pulsing through her, feeling the smooth dip at her back, might've had "unsociable" consequences.

As it was, he was having a hell of a time restraining himself. He respected Remi's wishes, of course, but that didn't mean that he hadn't thought about their kiss. About what he'd wanted to do next. About backing her up against a wall right now and delving a hand between her legs.

"Such a smooth talker," she said under her breath. "You make it look so easy."

He raised an eyebrow. "It's not supposed to be?"

"Not everyone goes through life always knowing the right thing to say, always having a line on hand." She stared out into the crowd, champagne flute hovering by her lips.

"You think it's a line?"

"Do you always return a statement with a question?" She turned, something murky and uncertain simmering in the depths of her eyes. Tonight, with all that sexy, smudgy makeup, they looked so big and so richly brown.

"I don't censor myself. I say what I think, and if that happens to be a question, I ask it." He scanned the room. Most of the faces were familiar—dancers who'd trained with his parents and had gone on to work with the American Ballet Theatre. Friends of his parents. Everywhere he turned, there were ties to them. "Out of the two of us, it's more the opposite. You're the one who doesn't say what you think."

"Excuse me?" She blinked. "Since when?"

"The other night." He lowered his voice, leaned in to her, and let the scent of flowers on her skin wash through him. Normally he hated the oversweet, synthetic scent of perfume, but it seemed to melt on her. Become part of her. "When you kissed me."

"*You* started it," she hissed.

"You want to watch the replay on that, Remi? I helped you down from the chair as any friend would."

"Friend," she scoffed. "Puh-lease."

"I helped you and my hands were at ten and two. I wasn't pushing you. Not like that." His voice was practically a growl—the mélange of anxiety about tonight, anger about his family trouble, and frustration at the fact that he wanted her so fucking bad all working him up. "I didn't lean in. You did. Now I'm not complaining, but at least own your actions."

Her mouth popped open into a surprised O shape, the gloss on her lips glinting in the light. "My, my. Who knew Mr. Genial had claws?"

"Mr. Genial?" He rolled his eyes. "Wow."

"What's wrong with being nice?"

"It's boring." He narrowed his eyes. "And don't try to change the subject."

"This really isn't the place to be discussing this," she said primly.

Right, so *now* she wanted to act all prim and proper. The other night she'd been an open flame, scorching hot. Her tongue and lips and hands all burning him to ash. Each night he'd been haunted by that kiss, temptation twisting in his mind. Creating scenarios he knew he couldn't act on.

"We *are* going to talk about it," he said. "You're hot one minute, cold the next. I want to respect your 'no mixing business and pleasure' thing, but you're giving me some confusing signals."

She pursed her lips.

"No response, huh? That's what I thought." Did it make him a bastard to feel so incredibly smug that he'd backed her into a corner? Probably. But dammit, the whole *Mr. Genial* thing stung. Maybe he *was* too nice. Chantel always said as much when they were growing up. He let his parents lead him around, let himself be molded by expectation. Let people use him.

"I've offended you, haven't I?" She laid a palm on his arm. "I didn't mean to."

"In what world is 'Mr. Genial' a compliment?" he grumbled.

"Oh, come on. It's not like it's stopped you from getting anywhere in the dating scene." She huffed. "You might not be a bastard playboy, but you've had your share of beautiful women."

"And how do you know that?"

Her expression turned sheepish. "I may have looked you up."

"Where?" If she said the name of that fucking website—

"Bad Bachelors."

He let a growl rumble in the back of his throat. "Not you too."

"What's so bad about it?"

"Other than what I said at dinner the other night? I thought the whole point of dating was to figure out if a person was right for you without any preconceptions. But maybe that's just me."

"Dating is tough. I guess some people feel like any form of safeguarding is better than nothing," she explained, though her tone wasn't exactly rock solid. "It's not always safe for women out in the big, bad dating jungle. And I don't mean emotionally."

"I understand that."

"If you're not the kind of guy who hurts women, it probably wouldn't occur to you," she said. "I know that's obviously not what people are talking about when they're reviewing you, but it might explain *why* it was created."

Possibly. But even if that was the case, Bad Bachelors was flawed in many ways.

"I don't care that people want to write reviews, but it would be better if the site wasn't completely open to the public." He sighed. "I don't give a shit what people say, but I don't want it affecting my work. Besides, why did you care about my dating history?"

"I was researching." The defensive words were belied by the guilty way she pulled her bottom lip between her teeth. "I wanted to know who I was working with."

"Then why didn't you look at *Dance Magazine*? Or *Pointe* magazine? Or the *New York Times*?" Countless legitimate publications had covered the Evans Ballet School. If she were really concerned with due diligence, she wouldn't have been looking at a gutter-dwelling gossip site.

An uneasy sensation settled in his gut. What if her reason for looking him up on Bad Bachelors was more nefarious? He thought their kiss held real passion. He thought the tension between them was organic. Without ulterior motives.

But it wouldn't be the first time someone had courted his attention for their own personal gain. Remi didn't have an entrée into the world here. Was it possible her initial refusal was nothing more than a tactic to tempt him further?

You're being paranoid. Remi hasn't shown any signs of wanting to use you. This isn't the same as it was with Emily.

"The app is convenient." It sounded like even *she* didn't believe that.

"That's a weak excuse, and you know it." He pulled her closer, not wanting to give her the idea that she could walk away from this conversation. Who the hell cared if it was an "appropriate" place to talk about it? He was done with being appropriate. He was done with letting things go. With being the unruffled Mr. Genial. "So tell me, Remi. What did you learn about me? I want to know."

Her huge eyes turned up to him. "Nothing."

"Bullshit."

One thing he liked about her was that she gave as good as she got. Even in the face of struggling with the choreography, she held her own. She held her own with him too. This time, however, she didn't have anything to say, but the slow creep of a rose-colored flush across her cheeks told him her dirty little secret.

"What did you learn?" he asked again.

The muscles worked in her neck as she swallowed, her earrings dangling against the soft curls of her hair winked at him as she turned back to watch the room. "I learned that you like to date. No real relationships to speak of. Unless those people chose not to write a review."

Only one. But that was *long* before Bad Bachelors.

"And?"

"You seem proficient in the bedroom."

"Proficient?" He chuckled. "You can make it sound as unsexy as you like, but I know you're not blushing because you read about how 'proficient' I am."

"I'm not blushing."

"Have I lived up to the hype? Was our kiss worthy of my *sordid* reputation?"

She pressed her lips together, but the subtle flare of her nostrils told him she was trying hard to control her breathing. "I've forgotten about it already."

"Liar."

"Would it help you sleep at night if I stroked your ego?"

"I want the truth." He shrugged. "That's all."

"I told you, I forgot all about it. It's like it never happened." She folded her arms across her chest as best she could with a champagne flute in her hand. It was empty, so he took it from her and then she dropped her hands by her sides. A second later, she huffed and recrossed them. "Why do you care so much?"

"You seem fidgety," he commented, resisting the urge to let a smirk break free.

"Now you're answering a question with an unrelated statement." Another waiter passed them and offered her a drink, but she declined with a stiff smile.

"Just making a comment. And in answer to your question…I'm simply curious. I don't know why you'd need to lie about it."

"You should be proud that all these women are singing your praises," she said, but her tone was blistering.

"Do I detect a note of jealousy there, Miss Reminiscent Sunburst Drysdale?"

She snapped her head toward him. "Call me that again and I will stick a pointe shoe where the sun doesn't shine."

His surprised laugh bounced around the room, bowling over the relatively quiet chatter from the rest of the guests. Several people turned in his direction, curious eyes flicking back and forth between him and Remi.

But the retort shriveled up on his tongue the second he saw Lilah and her date, a guy he recognized as one of his mother's students, walking toward them. Crap. She must have come as someone's plus-one. He pretended to pick a piece of lint from the shoulder of his jacket, as he whispered to Remi, "This conversation isn't over."

"Oh yes it is," she said. The smile on her face was polite. Forcefully so.

She could think that as much as she liked. But if she'd been digging into his personal life via Bad Bachelors, then he wanted to know why.

Halfway through the party, Remi felt as though she'd run a marathon. Wes had left her alone for a moment to insert himself into a group of men, one of whom was a possible investor. Her feet protested the too-stiff, too-high stilettos and her butt still ached from a mishap in rehearsals where she'd slipped coming down off one of the chairs. Lilah had been quick to inform her that it was a good thing she had some "extra padding" there to cushion her fall.

Professional jealousy, that's all it is.

Still, it hadn't stopped Remi checking out her figure in the fully mirrored changing room at Saks earlier that day. Sure, New York had been a little too kind to her what with all the tasty pretzels and hot dogs and those damn little Italian pastries that Darcy always brought over after visiting her mother.

But Remi had decided that she liked the way her boobs and hips had filled out. And her butt too. So screw Lilah's comment and the extra inches on her costume fitting file. Wes didn't seem to mind the "extra padding" either when he'd grab fistfuls of it during their kiss.

Retreat! Unsafe thoughts ahead.

She'd be better off worrying that Lilah was going to

go crazy on her, *Black Swan*-style, as the show drew near. But thankfully, Wes had deftly managed her questions—with her ever-so-subtle insinuation that they were sleeping together—by explaining that Remi didn't have any contacts in the dance world here, hence why he'd asked her to accompany him. He'd placated her ego by implying that Lilah didn't need his help in that area, which had stung a little. But again, it wasn't untrue.

"You must be Remi."

At the sound of her name, she turned around and found herself face-to-face with a stunning older woman who reminded Remi a hell of a lot of her ballet mistress back home. The woman was tall and willowy, and Remi knew instantly she was a ballerina. The movement in her hands and her head all pointed to years of training.

"That's right. I don't think we've met before."

The woman smiled and shook her head, a pair of exquisite earrings tinkling with the movement. Unlike some of the fancy costume jewelry Remi had looked at in Saks, the little chandeliers dangling from the woman's ears were the real deal. Diamonds paired with what looked to be sapphires.

"I'm Adele Evans." She held out her hand. "Wesley's mother."

"Oh." She could see it plain as day now. They had the same piercing-blue eyes and flawless facial structure. "It's a pleasure to meet you. He speaks very highly of you."

Adele laughed. "No, he doesn't."

Remi cringed. What on earth was she supposed to say to *that*? Despite her parents' faults and their way of pushing their opinions onto her, they never had anything bad to say about one another. She'd grown up in a loving, though nontraditional family unit and couldn't imagine a life where parents and children were at such odds as Wes and his family were.

"We have a complex relationship," she said, her expression difficult to read.

She nodded. "Family isn't always easy."

"Exactly. Especially not when you have a family with such combustible, creative personalities as ours."

Remi knew a little of Wes's strained relationship with his mother, and so she'd conjured up an image of the formidable Mrs. Evans. But this unfiltered, honest woman didn't fit the picture in her head at all.

"I hear you're the star of my son's show," she said. "But I am wondering how on earth he managed to find such a gem right under my nose without my knowledge."

"I didn't train here," she said. "I only came to New York a few years ago."

"From Australia, right?" Adele studied her. "I recognize the accent."

"You've been?"

"I spent some time performing at the Sydney Opera House when I was much younger." Something wistful and longing passed over Adele's face, like a wisp of smoke. Then it was gone. Her striking blue eyes were back to being shrewd. "Wonderful country. I saw a woman named Giuliana Michaels perform a variation from *Sleeping Beauty* that was impeccable."

Remi nodded. It was hard not to picture Giuliana's

angry face—her lips mashed into a thin line as she ordered Remi to leave. No doubt it would have been a good decade or two since the time when Adele had watched her perform. "Mrs. Michaels was the artistic associate when I was in the corps de ballet at the Melbourne Ballet Company."

"Then you must be very good. I understand she didn't suffer fools."

"No, she did not." She also didn't suffer anyone who dared take something—some*one*—her precious daughter, Ariana, wanted.

"Tell me. How did Wesley come to find you?" Adele cocked her head, eyes sparkling as though she was fully interested in what Remi had to say. And yet there seemed none of the judgment or derision she'd expected.

"I was working in a barre studio, and he brought his niece along."

Wes had told her she shouldn't feel the need to lie about how they'd met. He stood by his decision, regardless of their unusual meeting.

"Frankie? That little devil." Adele winked.

"Of course, she's your granddaughter." Remi shook her head, laughing. "Yes, Frankie. Chantel brings her to our parents-and-children class once a week. But he was filling in."

"And he could tell you were a trained ballerina?"

She smiled at the memory, at the way her breath had caught in her throat when she'd spotted him leaning against the doorframe, eyes wide and drinking her in. "He saw me practicing."

"He's always had a good eye for talent. He used to

sit in on our open days and tell me who he thought we should invite into our school."

Remi could imagine him as a kid with dark, floppy hair and bright, impish eyes, watching people dance and analyzing their technique.

"Had you decided not to work with a company in New York?" Adele asked.

Remi tried to swallow past the lump in her throat. "I was taking a break."

"I know a lot of ballerinas, dear. Taking a break is not a thing."

It wasn't. Dancers pushed through all kinds of pain. Fought against fatigue on a daily basis. They pushed harder and aimed higher than regular people. They wanted more.

They wanted…everything.

"I once saw a girl fracture her wrist after a fall and make a sling out of a pair of old ballet tights so she could complete a rehearsal." Adele winked. "You either dance, or you don't. There is no taking breaks."

This was the rigidity and single-mindedness her parents didn't understand. To them, it was a strange idea to push yourself until the breaking point simply to see how long it would take. To always be hungry for more, never satisfied with what you had. They'd tried to advise meditation, gratitude journals, daily mantras of positivity. Tell yourself that you're happy where you are, her mother had said. But that wasn't what Remi needed. In fact, she loved that ballet was the opposite of that. The eternally restless itch of ambition, always prickling under her skin… It made her feel alive.

"I made a mistake back in Australia. It ended my career there and so I came here," she said. The truth tumbled out, like a demon seizing its chance to escape. "I bombed my first two auditions and became so worried that, if I failed a third time, I might never dance again."

"Ah." Adele nodded. "That makes more sense."

"I was young and stupid."

"We all were at one time. Believe me." She flagged down a passing waiter and collected two champagne flutes, handing one to Remi in a similar way to how Wes had done earlier. She saw a lot of him in his mother, as much as he would hate to hear it. "To being young and stupid."

"Hear, hear." Remi raised her glass to Adele's and the sweet, little chime rang in her ears.

"I wish my son would realize that he's not too old to still be in that category," she said. There was a sharpness to her tone, but it wasn't nasty. More…concerned. "But my saying it over and over won't have any effect. He needs to see that for himself."

She wanted to ask Adele what she meant exactly, but something told her that wasn't a wound she should pick at. "I wouldn't listen to anyone back then either. So I can't judge."

"Hmm." Adele nodded. "Have you thought about what you might do after Wes's show, if it goes ahead? You could find yourself with some open doors should the right person support you."

Now was Adele talking about herself or Wes? "I hadn't really thought about it to be honest. This has all happened so fast."

Adele set her champagne down and opened the small,

sparkling purse that she'd kept tucked under one arm. She fished out a thick, cream business card with subtle embossing and soft, gold font. *Adele Evans, Founder, Evans Ballet School.*

"You should think about it. And then you should call me. I have a lot of contacts here and I'm always looking to help talented dancers."

"But you haven't seen me dance," she said.

"I know my son," Adele replied. "If he sees something in you, it's because it's there." She laid a hand on Remi's shoulder for a second and then she picked up her champagne and made her way back into the crowd.

Adele Evans would have the number of every major ballet company on speed dial. A good word from her would go far. *Very* far. Far enough, perhaps, that she might be able to walk into a company role, do better than the corps de ballet. New York was home to some of the best dancers in the world, and she could be among them. She could have her dream back.

What would Wes say?

The question popped into her head unbidden. Why did it matter what he thought? She wasn't beholden to him. Sure, she owed him her loyalty during *Out of Bounds* because he'd given her a chance. But beyond that? If she wanted to pursue a connection with Adele, it wouldn't be any of his business.

But despite the logic being sound, a little part of her shifted uncomfortably at the thought. He *would* be upset…and for some minute and misguided reason, that didn't sit well.

Chapter 14

"Wes and I stopped dating shortly after I found out who he was related to. My decision, not his. I've got one intimidating stage mother already. I don't want a second."

—FutureTonyWinner

Wes saw Remi talking to his mother out of the corner of his eye. Instinct told him to head over and ensure that she wasn't messing with Remi's head. But the man standing across from him was nibbling at the bait.

"I understand you already had another investor lined up," Bert Soole said. The older man was a longtime investor in the arts—word had it he supported everything from ballet to Broadway to funding a scholarship for young classical musicians. "I take it that hasn't worked out."

"Unfortunately not." Wes brought the glass of scotch to his lips and sipped, stalling. How much had Bert heard? He didn't want to get caught in a lie, but he didn't want to volunteer any detrimental information, either.

"And why might that be?"

"Creative differences," Wes replied. "This show pushes the boundaries and so do I. It won't be to everybody's taste."

"Sounds like a risky investment." Bert smiled. Wes would have put him in his late sixties or possibly early seventies, with a full head of snow-white hair and sharp gray eyes. The kind of eyes that said no detail was too small. "I tend to like those. What's the point of living if you only ever play it safe?"

"That's how I approach my work," Wes said, internally sighing with relief.

"Can I ask why you haven't approached your family to invest? I understand that your mother and father have nothing to do with this piece of work—at least that's what she tells me."

Of *course* that's what she'd said. "Would it be redundant to say 'creative differences' again?"

Bert chuckled. "You're a man who knows what you want."

"I do. I'm also willing to fund the entire thing myself if that's what it takes. But I'd prefer not to sell everything I own." It was a gamble to put it out there so bluntly, but something told him that Bert would respect the drive.

Would his ability to read people pay off now?

Bert eyed him for a moment, his silvery brows knitting above a round nose. "If you're willing to put everything on the line for this show, then it tells me you have the commitment level I look for when I sign my money away."

Wes nodded all the while fighting the urge to fist pump. "How about I introduce you to our lead ballerina?

I'm sure she'd be thrilled to hear from the person who's going to help bring this show to New York."

"Well, due diligence needs to be done. My lawyers will need to weigh in." He winked. "But please, I'd love to meet her."

As they walked over to Remi, Bert talked about his son, who'd studied in the Juilliard music program and had passed away at twenty-three from a rare form of leukemia. Bert and his wife hadn't been able to conceive any more children, so they'd funneled their considerable wealth into giving other kids the chance their son never had.

Remi stood alone at the side of the room, a tense look on her face. Even with her lips pressed into a line and her hands toying nervously with some beading on her dress, she outshone everyone and everything around her. His mother had gone, but Wes was dying to know what she'd said. However, that was a conversation for a later point in the evening. For now, he needed Remi to shine.

She turned and caught his eye, the tension melting away into a charming smile. Though he knew her well enough by now to recognize her mask when he saw it. Not that Bert would know any different. She played her part beautifully, charming the older man with stories of her home country and her adventures as a newcomer to Manhattan.

"I ended up all the way in Queens before I realized I'd gone the wrong way," she said, pressing her hand to Bert's arm and laughing. The genuine sound ran along his spine, gathering steam until his body was alive with it. "I swear, my roommate was ready to fit me with a tracking device, I got lost so frequently."

"Isn't that the greatest thing, getting lost in New

York?" Bert looked wistful. "It's been a long time since I experienced it."

"I bet it's changed."

Bert chuckled. "Well, it was a very different place when I came. It was rough, dirty. But there was still the bright lights and the shows and the music."

"What else is there to live for?" Remi smiled, but this time he saw her facade crack. It was the barest muscle movement, little more than an involuntary tic.

"I hope you'll come by the theater," Wes said. "We'd be honored to have you."

"I will. This week." Bert bid them both good night and waved to someone walking past, who stopped and pressed a hand into his.

Remi sucked in a breath. "Do you think we have his support?"

"I don't want to count my chickens," Wes said. "But I have a good feeling about it."

To be fair, that good feeling had showed up last time too. No point getting ahead of himself.

"I need you to shine when he comes to visit," Wes said. "We've got to reel him in."

She nodded. "I know."

Silence settled between them like an uncomfortable, prickly barrier. Once again, they were outside the crowd, looking in. He wondered if Remi would admit that his mother had spoken to her, or if he would have to ask. As the seconds ticked by, it became clear it was the latter.

"What did my mother want?"

She looked at him, her expression difficult to read. "Ah, so you *did* see that."

"I see everything," he said, keeping his voice light.

"She introduced herself, wanted to know how you found me."

"I'll bet she did."

"Then she gave me her business card and told me I could find myself with some open doors should the 'right person' provide their support."

His jaw clenched, his back teeth grinding together. He would have bet his last ten dollars she'd said something similar to his original lead ballerina, Ashleigh. And then he'd lost her. "And how do you feel about that?"

Remi looked up at him, her brows crinkled. "I'm curious, sure. But I won't be pursuing anything else until we know what's happening with *Out of Bounds*. I'm not going anywhere, Wes."

He wanted to believe it, but this industry had taught him that *loyalty* didn't always mean the same thing from one person to the next. "Even if things get tough?"

"Things are already tough," she pointed out. "You're worried about funding, I'm struggling to catch up with the rest of the cast…and I'm still here. That's not going to change unless you kick me out."

It eased some of the pressure in his chest to hear her promise to stay, and not just because he was worried about his show. "I'm not going to kick you out."

"Then it seems we're in agreement. The show will go on, regardless of the challenges." She shifted next to him, leaning to one side and rotating her other ankle.

"Sore feet?" he asked.

"Your personal shopper friend is a sadist in a pretty

dress," she said with a grimace. "I'd almost bet my pointe shoes do less damage to my feet than these damn things."

The shoes did look killer. They were the kind of shoes that he would love to tell her to leave on while he stripped that glittering dress from her body. Knowing what he did now—that she was firm and strong, that her breasts were the perfect handful, that when she moaned he felt it through his entire body—fantasizing was colored with the sharp edge of reality.

"We can head home a little early," he said. "My head is feeling like your feet."

"Tough crowd?"

They turned and headed toward the rotunda's exit. "Yeah. People either wanted to discuss my sex life, or they gave me a wide berth."

"I'm sorry that the Bad Bachelors thing is causing you so much trouble." She shot him a sheepish look as they wove through the crowd on their way to the building's exit. "And that I looked you up."

"I understand the curiosity."

They walked through the entrance of the building, Remi's heels clicking with each step. It was like a beetle scratching at his skin, taunting him. Inviting him to react. Instead, Wes pulled out his phone and ordered them a ride from the car service he used for events.

The night had grown cold, the breeze blowing over from the park whipping past them and disturbing Remi's hair. When she shivered, he slipped out of his tuxedo jacket and placed it around her shoulders.

"I *do* feel bad," she said as they stood on the sidewalk. "It's information that should be private. I know it can cause a lot of damage too. My friend's fiancée had trouble with Bad Bachelors. It affected his work and his sick father. He ended up quitting his job because people wouldn't take him seriously anymore. They said all kinds of bad things about him."

Wes's ears pricked up. For some reason, that sounded a hell of a lot like Reed McMahon's situation. "I'm assuming this was before they got engaged."

"Yeah." Remi nodded and pulled his jacket tighter around her slim frame. "She didn't even want to date him at first because of what the reviews said about him. He was supposed to be the 'worst of the worst.' But they're really happy together now."

"His name isn't Reed McMahon, is it?"

Remi blinked. "Yeah, it is. How on earth did you guess that?"

"I had a coffee with him recently because I wanted some advice on how to deal with the press issues."

"It's a small world, isn't it?" She frowned as if trying to figure something out. "How did you connect with him?"

"Through a colleague of my brother-in-law."

A sleek, black car pulled up in front of them, and the driver got out to open the back door. Wes gestured for Remi to go in ahead of him, waiting until she'd slid across the seat.

"Did he give you any helpful tips?" Remi shrugged out of the jacket and slipped off her shoes, tucking her feet away under the length of her dress.

"You don't need to hide them, Remi. I've seen plenty of ballerinas' feet."

A pink tinge spread over her cheeks. "They're not very attractive."

She relaxed and leaned back against the car's seat. No, they weren't "attractive" feet. Remi's were looking pretty battered—two toes were bandaged up, and she had a nasty blister on another. The nail on her right big toe was purple, showing a bruise on the nail bed. The joints in her toes were swollen in a way that made them look mildly arthritic.

"Anything that's worth doing will leave a scar," he said. They were his mother's words, and they had no business inserting themselves into his head. "And no, Reed wasn't particularly helpful."

"Oh." She frowned. "That's a shame."

"He was super cryptic. Said there was a cost he wasn't willing to pay when he went after the people behind Bad Bachelors." Wes drummed his fingers against the car seat. "Makes me wonder if he knows who's behind it."

Remi raised a brow. "Wow. I bet a lot of people would want *that* information."

"He's locked up tight about it though. Said he wouldn't tell me or anyone else." Wes rubbed a hand over his jaw. "You don't think it has anything to do with your friend, do you?"

"Darcy?" Remi shook her head. "No way. I mean, not that I know."

"It must have been something big if he was willing to resign over it. If he knew who made the app, then he could have shut them down and stayed where he was."

"That's very strange." Remi toyed with a loose strand of hair, the golden length catching the lights of the city as it rolled past. "What on earth is a 'cost he wasn't willing to pay'? Can't be money. He's got an apartment in DUMBO that must be worth a small fortune now."

"It didn't sound like an actual cost."

"A personal one then?" Remi shook her head. "I have no idea. Maybe something to do with his dad? I'll ask Darcy if she knows anything. I never heard a peep about it after they got together. I thought he'd agreed to let the whole thing go."

"Who knows?" He shrugged.

Remi tilted her head and leaned it against the window of the car. The lights played over her skin, little flickers of orange and yellow and white that made her look luminous. He wanted nothing more than to reach out and pull her into his lap.

"Do you regret hiring me?" she asked suddenly.

Wes frowned. "Why would I regret it?"

This was her demon. He'd known a lot of ballet dancers—both male and female—over the years who'd had the perfect feet or the perfect body composition but could never quite get their heads in the game. They tortured themselves with doubt, and no amount of training or perfect genetics could overcome a mind that wasn't resilient.

Sometimes it was triggered by an event—a bad injury or messed-up audition or, worse, a botched perfor-mance. He suspected Remi fell into this category.

"I feel like…" She looked down at her lap, as if trying to find the right words. "I've lost control over my talent. It used to come when I called it and I could rely on being able to perform, but now it feels like this slippery, intangible thing that deserts me when I need it most."

It was the difference between the first time when he'd caught her dancing alone and how she looked during rehearsals. The difference between her first audition piece and when he'd asked her to improvise. There was a switch that seemed stuck. A setting in her brain that needed rewiring.

"What caused it?" he asked.

She laughed. "I don't know if I'm ready to tell you that."

"So it was a guy then?" He chuckled at the surprise on her face. "Lucky guess."

"Either that or I'm embarrassingly easy to read." She leaned back and turned her head toward him. Her blond hair was starting to escape the confines of her updo, and it played over the black leather seat like wisps of golden cotton candy. "Could go either way."

"Who was he?"

"One of the soloists from my company." She chewed on her lip. "He was their pride and joy. We used to call him 'the chosen one' because he could do no wrong. Everyone loved him. Dating him was like…doing thirty-two *fouettes*. It was thrilling and sweaty and exhausting. When it was right, it was magic, but on the off days, it went to Hot Mess City in a second. And if I could have left it at one night, I would have been fine. But I was stupid and I got involved when I shouldn't have."

"The company directors frowned on it?"

"Well, they tend to in general anyway. Two dancers on the rise can make waves if they leave together. It's a big risk for the company." She paused. "But my situation with Alex went a bit beyond that. The artistic associate had a daughter who was madly in love with him. She flipped when she found out we were sleeping together, told Mother Dearest, and then all hell broke loose."

"They kicked you both out?" he asked, and when the look of pain flickered across her face like a wavering flame, he realized. "They kicked *you* out."

"Yeah, just me. Female dancers are a dime a dozen, apparently." She sucked in a breath, her hands pressing against the tight bodice of her dress. "They gave him a choice. He could keep seeing me and exit the company, or he could choose his career. Guess what he chose?"

He made a derisive sound. "Bastard."

"Yep." She turned to look out the window as they approached the Brooklyn Bridge. "So you see why I have that rule about mixing business and pleasure."

"But you still want thirty-two *fouettes*?" Thrilling, hot, sweaty. He wanted to give her that until he'd scrubbed the memory of this other guy from her brain.

"Maybe, but what I need is a barre. A guy who's solid and stable. That way I have something to hold on to if my feet go out from under me."

A strange, uncomfortable feeling zipped through him. Jealousy. He had no right to such an emotion. But it didn't stop that fast and furious unfurling of hot, primal sensation in his gut. "Don't tell me those are the kinds of guys you've been looking up on Bad Bachelors?"

"I haven't used it much lately." The light flickered in the car, making her expression difficult to read.

"But you still looked me up?"

"Yeah."

"Just me?"

She bit down on her lip. For someone who had trouble digging into the passion onstage, her emotions never seemed far from the surface everywhere else. He loved that—it made him feel like he knew her.

And right now it *also* made him feel pretty fucking pleased that he was the only man she'd been looking up.

Don't be proud of that. One, it means nothing. Two, the reviews are a nuisance and you should be cursing their existence.

"We never finished that conversation before," he said.

She shivered and wrapped her arms around herself. "And we're not going to. You know why now."

"No one can fire you from my show," he said.

"*You* can. That's exactly the point." She looked as though she wanted to say more, but she didn't. "Look, I know you're attracted to me and I'm attracted to you. I'm not going to deny that, because we're both well-behaved adults."

Wes raised a brow.

"*Mostly* well-behaved adults," she corrected herself. "Just because I want something doesn't mean I can have it. I know you're used to getting what you want, but I'm not."

She was right. Wes might be the affable, charming guy who never seemed to ruffle feathers—Mr. Genial, as she'd called him, even if he hated that label—but he went after his goals with a drive and single-mindedness that those with lesser ambitions didn't understand. He wasn't going to let other people dictate what he could and couldn't do.

Remi needed to do the same.

"I want you to meet me at the theater on Sunday,"

he said, flashing her a secretive smile. "I know it's supposed to be your day off, but I promise I won't work you too hard."

"What on earth are you scheming up?" she asked, cocking her head.

"Just meet me there."

Would she trust him? Her eyes seemed to shift from black to golden brown as the streetlights bounced around inside the car. He could almost hear the cogs turning in her brain.

"Okay," she said eventually. "Sunday."

Good. Now that he knew what Remi's demons were, all he had to do was get her to face them.

Chapter 15

"If you're looking for an excuse not to date Wes...
then this review is not for you."

—MaddyAve

THE MEETING WITH WES PROVIDED A POINT OF FIXATION for Remi over the weekend. Luckily, she'd scheduled in some girl time on Sunday morning, which would hopefully prevent her from the insanity of wrangling her libido into submission.

"What's it like waking up to this every day?" Remi stood in the center of the place Darcy shared with Reed and soaked in the view.

There wasn't anything super flashy about the interior of their Water Street apartment. The furniture was modern and clean looking, if a little minimalist for Remi's taste. The kitchen was compact but functional, with what looked to be nice quality fittings.

The view, however, was on another level. Since the apartment was on the corner of the building, the living room had two walls of floor-to-ceiling windows, which framed the East River, the Brooklyn Bridge, and the Manhattan skyline to perfection. It looked like a goddamn tourism ad. And now, having seen it in both daytime, when the sun bounced off the pale floorboards, and at night, when the city was coated in a sparkling blanket of lights, Remi could say she was officially jealous.

"Not very difficult, I'll be honest." Darcy chuckled from behind the kitchen island, where she whipped up some pasta sauce to go with the "zoodles" Remi had picked up from Whole Foods. "Although ask me again in winter, when I've been trekking to and from the library in the snow."

"Yeah, but the view at Christmas will be *amazing*." Remi sighed dreamily and wandered over to the kitchen. The scent of the pasta sauce bubbling away filled the room with a delicious aroma.

"Ugh, Christmas. The other C-word." Annie rolled her eyes. "Darcy, please don't tell me that, now you're all loved up, you're going to turn into one of those sappy Hallmark-watching types this year."

"I have a feeling Reed will be allergic to Hallmark movies." Darcy grinned. "But I might indulge."

"Yes!" Remi pumped her fist in the air. "Another member for Team Jingle Bells."

Annie wrinkled her nose. "You're disgusting, both of you."

"Come on. I spent most of my life eating a full roast lunch and sweating my butt off in cute Christmas sweaters while it was unbearably hot outside. White Christmases should *not* be taken for granted."

Annie shook her head. "It's not the holiday I have a problem with, it's all the saccharine advertising and the cheesy movies that networks shove down our throats."

"You hate anything romantic," Remi said with a huff. "Flowers, Valentine's Day—"

"Not a real holiday," Annie interjected, taking a sip of her wine.

"Ice skating at Bryant Park"—she ticked the items off on her fingers—"the color pink, anything with hearts on it, romcoms."

"*Especially* romcoms." Annie shuddered. "Sandra Bullock has a lot to answer for, you know. Kate Hudson too."

Darcy snorted. "Did I used to sound like that?"

"Yes," Remi and Annie said in unison.

"But now you're all smitten with your wonderful fiancé," Remi said with a smile. "And we couldn't be happier for you. Speaking of which…"

"If you ask me again about the wedding date, I will drown you in this pot of sauce." Darcy shot her warning look.

"Actually, I had a funny story to tell." Remi sipped her water, which Annie had thoughtfully poured into a wineglass so she could pretend it was alcoholic. "So, Wes has been having some issues with securing an investor for the show because of the Bad Bachelors reviews."

"Right." Darcy pottered around the kitchen.

"We had one guy pull out last minute, and now he's finally got someone else to give us a chance, although it's not a done deal as yet." She tried not to think about *that* scary thing hanging over her head. "But in the meantime, he was doing a bit of research on the app and decided that he wanted to talk to someone who had a similar experience."

Darcy stilled in front of the stove. "And?"

"He met with Reed." Remi shook her head. "Strange coincidence, right?"

The apartment went quiet, and Remi could almost hear her own pulse. For some reason, her intuition tingled. She'd expected Darcy to find it funny or, at the very least, have a *huh, isn't that weird?* kind of moment. But her friend was rigid as a statue. Even Annie looked at her strangely.

Remi frowned. "What?"

"What did Reed say?" Darcy asked. She turned the burner down on the stove and came over to the island, her expression strained.

What the hell is going on?

"He said he couldn't help Wes other than to give him some general PR advice." Then she remembered that cryptic line. "He said the cost of doing something about Bad Bachelors was more than he was willing to pay."

Darcy's face paled, and her eyes flicked to Annie.

"Do you know what he meant?" Remi asked, her gaze swinging between her two friends. Annie remained impassive, but Darcy looked distinctly uncomfortable. "Are you hiding something from me?"

Silence. It was so intense the lack of sound seemed to vibrate in Remi's ears. Her friends were never quiet. Not like this.

"Will someone please tell me what's going on?" Remi threw her hands in the air. "Did you have something to do with Bad Bachelors?"

Darcy swallowed. "I didn't."

"Then what 'cost' was so great that Reed didn't

pursue them? The damn website nearly ruined his career." She shook her head.

"So you think the site is appalling but you're still using it?" Annie asked.

"I stopped as soon as I realized how much trouble it was causing. I deleted it off my phone." She swallowed. The uneasy feeling in her stomach grew, blowing up like a bubble and pressing on her heart and lungs. She did *not* like where this conversation was going. "That stuff is private. Hell, it's defamation in some cases."

"Well, technically it would be libel because it's in written form," Darcy said.

"Okay, fine. Whatever." Why did she get the impression that she was being lied to right now? "Can you please look me in the face and tell me that you don't know what Reed was talking about?"

They'd been friends for four years, lived together for most of that time. Remi knew when Darcy was holding back, and as they'd become closer, that had happened less and less. Remi had worked hard to gain her friend's trust and to be the person who could give it to her straight but also be there with the pint of ice cream and a shoulder to cry on when it was needed.

Darcy's eyes met hers. "I can't tell you that."

"So you *do* know?"

Silence.

"Why didn't you say anything when I told you it was causing problems for Wes's production? That it could cause problems for this one chance I have to get my career back?"

Guilt flashed across Darcy's face like a streak of

lightning. "Annie, I'm not doing this anymore. Either you fess up, or I will."

Remi snapped her head in Annie's direction and her friend didn't react. As always, she maintained her composure, even in the face of Remi's shocked expression.

"I created Bad Bachelors," she said eventually. "It's my site, my app."

Remi's mind spun like a hamster was using her brain as a running wheel. Annie was behind Bad Bachelors. Which meant Annie was the person Reed had been tracking down while he and Darcy worked together.

"So he wouldn't expose Annie because of you?" Remi turned to Darcy. "You were the cost he didn't want to pay?"

She nodded. "Yeah."

"You've known about this for months and you both kept it from me?" It was like she'd swallowed a stone. "You've been lying to me this whole time."

These women were the closest thing she had to family in New York. God, in the entire hemisphere. There had been countless times when they'd called on each other for advice, when they'd cried and laughed together. They were like sisters. Like blood.

"Don't blame Darcy," Annie said, a guilty tone weighing down her words. "It's my fault. When Reed found me out, he made me promise to tell her or else he would do it. It's the only reason I told her. I didn't want *anyone* to know what I was doing. But he gave me no choice—I had to tell her, but I asked her to keep my secret."

"Including from me?"

"Yes." She nodded.

"You both lied to me." It felt like the bottom had fallen out from under her. "For months."

"I'm sorry." Darcy wrapped her arms around herself. That's how she often dealt with her problems—she turned inward, like an armadillo. Annie was the strong, silent type. And Remi...well, she was their opposite.

"Congratulations. I feel really stupid." Tears pricked the backs of her eyes. "And all those times we laughed over the reviews and when I told you about Wes, when I told you what was happening with the show..."

Was she an idiot? Had they been dropping hints that she couldn't see because she was stuck in her own damn head? Or had they worked hard to keep her out of the loop?

Three's a crowd.

Wasn't that what Ariana had said to her back home? She hadn't wanted to be the third wheel with Remi and Alex, so she'd eliminated the competition. And Alex had chosen the other side, like Darcy had done now. Sure, Annie might have begged her to stay quiet, but Darcy was responsible for her own actions.

Looks like Remi was on the outside. Again.

The sauce hissed on the stove and bubbled over the side of the pot. Darcy swore and ran to it, trying to save it from burning. But it splattered all over the sleek, black stovetop.

"You could have trusted me, Annie." Remi bit her lip, determined not to make herself look like even more of a blubbering fool.

"I swear it wasn't personal. I didn't want anyone to know." Annie rubbed her hands over her face. "If people found out it was me..."

"What, you might lose your job?" Remi couldn't keep the sarcasm out of her voice. "Seems like you're not too worried about it when it's other people in the firing line."

"It'd be more than that," she said solemnly. "People would come after me. The Bad Bachelors email gets death threats on a daily basis now. And emails from people who say I should kill myself for what I'm doing."

Remi blanched. "Really?"

"I've upset a lot of people." The way she said it was so matter-of-fact. The tone was the same one she used to tell them that she'd picked up milk on the way home from the office.

But that was Annie. It was how she coped with life's pressures, by hanging on to control at all times.

Maybe you need to be a bit more like that instead of always letting the nasty, little voices get the better of you.

"And you still think this site should exist, even if good people are having their most private moments splashed all over the internet?" Remi shook her head. "I know we all laughed at first. And I'll admit it: I used the site. But there's a dark underbelly to this."

"Trust me, I've thought long and hard about this. But yes, I *do* think it should exist. Along with the death threats, I also get emails from women who've finally regained the confidence to date again because of Bad Bachelors." There was a passion in Annie's eyes, like a spark of electricity. "I get emails from women who tell me they've been attacked on dates, who've been drugged and taken advantage of, and they tell me they wish something like this had existed sooner so they could have protected themselves."

"Then why didn't you tell me?"

"Because the more people who know I'm behind it, the more likely it is that someone will slip up and pass that information on."

"So if you had to start over, you'd lie to me again." Remi's voice wobbled.

Annie looked to the ground and took a deep breath. "Yeah, I would."

"Guys, can we take it down a notch?" Darcy pleaded with them. "Let's take a breath and think about what we're saying."

"No." Remi shook her head. "I understand you're passionate about this, Annie, but I can't be friends with someone who doesn't trust me."

"Remi, stop." Darcy came around to the other side of the island, but Remi had already pushed off her stool and was gathering her things.

"No. I won't." She slipped her bag over her shoulder and went to fetch her shoes and coat. "You chose sides too, Darcy."

"It wasn't my secret to tell." Her eyebrows knitted above her pert nose.

"I get it." Remi slipped her coat on and buttoned the front as best she could with shaking fingers. "You two have known each other since you were kids."

Darcy closed her eyes. "It wasn't like that."

"It's my fault," Annie said, frowning and wringing her hands. "I put her in that position because I was worried about what might happen if it got out."

On some level, she understood Annie's fears. And knowing the kind of nasty emails she'd received made

Remi feel sick. Nobody should have their life threatened. But they'd talked about the site countless times over the last few months. Annie had even shared reviews with her, all the while making out like she was just another woman using the site.

But she wasn't. Annie reached out for her but Remi shook her head.

"I need to cool down," she said. "If I stay, I'm going to end up saying something I regret."

It was times like this she wished her parents were here. She pushed out of Darcy's apartment and took the elevator down to the main floor, checking her phone as she went. It was still early in Australia. Too early to call.

The tears that had been pricking her eyes threatened again as she stepped out into the afternoon air. The sky was thick with gray clouds, rain sputtering as though it wasn't sure whether it wanted to pour down or not. The day mirrored her—miserable, indecisive.

She needed to shake off Annie's revelation for the time being and give herself a chance to mull things over. To decide what she wanted to do with that information.

Because now *she* had to pick a side—protect the friend who'd lied to her or hand the information over to Wes knowing he'd use it to save their show and, in the process, bring Annie down.

———

Wes walked through the lobby of the Attic theater, his hands stuffed into the pockets of his leather jacket. Today was the first day they had access to the place where *Out of*

Bounds would be showcased. He'd met with the theater's event coordinator yesterday afternoon to finalize the paperwork. The money came out of his personal account, since the production had already used all of his business funds. Hopefully that would be filled back up this week, once they convinced Bert Soole to support them.

But money wasn't the main thing on Wes's mind. He'd been thinking about Remi ever since Friday night. Like he'd conjured her into existence, she walked through the theater's main doors into the foyer.

Black leggings made her legs look even longer and leaner, which sent his mind back to the night of the charity ball and how he'd tried so damned hard to ignore the flash of smooth, creamy thigh revealed by the slit of her dress. If he'd had any hopes that seeing her all bundled up, a denim jacket over the top of a chunky sweater and her cheeks pink from the crisp air, might make her less appealing, then he was wrong. Dead wrong.

You know why she doesn't want to take this further. Thank God one of you has their priorities straight.

"Ready to let all your frustrations out?" he asked.

She made a worried *hmm* sound. "What on *earth* do you have planned for me?"

"A little tension reliever." He chuckled when she shot him a warning look. "Don't worry, it's all aboveboard. You have my word."

He led them into the theater, and she followed him up onto the stage. It was eerily quiet without the hustle and bustle of the rest of the crew and his production team. Usually he was being pulled in every direction at once, and he loved it. Back at the Evans Ballet School, every day was like the one before it, a perpetual Groundhog Day of white walls and an inbox that made his eyes glaze over. No one demanded anything real of him, and his work never made an impact. He was a figurehead, no better than a hood ornament on a fancy car, without the ability to influence how the business was run—or how they could change and grow, because his parents didn't believe those words had positive connotations.

But here, in the thick of *Out of Bounds*, he was excited. Alive.

"Right." He clapped his hands together and the sound echoed through the theater like a gunshot. "We're going to help you deal with this stage fright once and for all."

"I don't have stage fright," Remi said. "I haven't performed yet, so how can it be stage fright?"

"I actually think you'll be fine performing in front of a regular audience," he said. "It's your peers who're the problem. Let's call it *professional stage fright*, for lack of a better term."

"Professional stage fright?" She raised a brow. "Tell me, Doc, how did you diagnose that?"

"I *know* you're a brilliant dancer. I saw it with my own eyes." He stepped closer to her and tapped the center of her chest. "This part is working just fine. But this"—he brushed the side of her temple with his thumb, her nostrils flaring at the gentle touch—"is letting you down."

"All my problems are in my head. Gee, why didn't I think of that on my own?" She rolled her eyes.

"Be as sarcastic as you want." He grinned, which only seemed to irritate her further. "You know I'm right. The second you started working with the cast, all your confidence evaporated. And then you tell me a story about how you were shunned by your peers at your last company. You're steering clear of me because you don't want a repeat of the past, yet you're allowing the past to be right here with you. It's weighing you down. Killing your dancing mojo."

"Ugh, you sound like my parents. Is this the part where you tell me I need to eat more kale and sleep with a dream catcher over my bed?"

She was in full-defensive mode. Her eyes looked anywhere but him, and her little scoffing laugh was all bluster. But this woman wore her heart on her sleeve, whether she wanted to or not. And Wes cataloged her tells, memorizing every single one.

"I don't know why you distrust me so much, Remi."

She reached behind her head and fiddled with the elastic holding her ponytail in place. Stalling. "You intimidate me."

He blinked. At least she was being honest with him now. That *had* to be a step in the right direction even if it wasn't the step he'd expected.

"Why?"

She finally made eye contact, spearing him with her luminous brown gaze. "Because you're *it* in this town. You come from dance royalty, you've got this hot new show, and from everything I've read about you online, you're some kind of super-hung sex god, and it's…a lot. You're practically perfect, and it kind of scares the hell out of me."

Family connections. Opportunity. His body. Why did it always come down to those three things?

"A practically perfect, super-hung sex god." He shook his head. "That's quite a pedestal."

"To be fair, you were on it before we met." She wrapped her arms around herself as if she wanted the chunky sweater to swallow her whole. "I didn't put you there."

"You're not intimidated by me; you're intimidated by my reputation. You were perfectly fine flirting your ass off during that barre class," he pointed out.

"Let's call that blissful ignorance," she said. "I would have preferred not to know the nitty-gritty about your uh…" Her eyes dipped down for a minute, and her face turned tomato red. "Finer points."

"My finer points?" He couldn't resist smirking. "Care to elaborate?"

"Nope. Now, can we get on with whatever little experiment you want to conduct, so we can both get back to our respective weekends? I'd rather forget that I even opened this can of worms."

"Fine." He motioned for her to follow him to the edge of the stage. "Now I know you're going to think this is some hippie bullshit, but I've seen a lot of dancers let their heads get the best of them over the years. That's *not* going to happen with you. But I need you to go with what I'm asking, okay?"

"I'm not usually in the habit of saying yes before I know what I'm being asked." She smirked. "If you want me to cluck like a chicken, it ain't gonna happen."

"I want you to teach me your opening sequence."

She frowned. "What?"

"We're going to pretend you're the choreographer,

and I'm the dancer. You're going to teach me *your* part of the opening sequence, and I'm going to dance it." He shrugged out of his jacket and tossed it down onto the front row of seats. Then he toed off his shoes and socks. "It's a little role play. A power switch."

She looked distinctly unconvinced but she removed her jacket and sweater anyway. "If you think it'll help."

"I do." He winked. "And I did promise you I'd show you my moves."

He'd seen his mother use this with one of her mentees. The theory was that if the dancer was put in a position of power—that is, being the teacher instead of the student—they could embody the confidence they perceived people in that position to have. By getting them to go through the steps in a low-stress situation, they were strengthening the neural pathways that would help them come performance time.

She stripped down to her leggings and a tank top that molded tightly to her curves.

Focus, Evans. Try thinking with your head instead of your dick for once.

"Should I leave my sneakers on, or do you want to see me in pointe?" she asked.

"Sneakers are fine. We're going to be doing this in *demi-pointe*."

"Got it." She turned to face the rows of seats. "Let's start in first."

He walked up beside her, mimicking her position. "Okay."

"We're going to rise up into a *relevé*." She sprang up onto her toes, almost achieving a proper pointe stance even in her Converse high-tops. "Then back down to first. *Relevé* again and back down to first."

She demonstrated the movement, up and down, with precision. When he followed suit, she nodded. "Then we go up into *retiré*, back down to first, and repeat the sequence."

Her body moved effortlessly, free of the tension he'd noticed crowding her shoulders and stiffening her joints. She seemed almost…buoyant. He copied her, doing a pretty mediocre job of it but getting the timing right. For all the time he'd spent in the industry, he was never destined to be a dancer himself.

"Then we go back to the chairs." She walked toward the back of the stage counting the steps. "Step up, turn. Swish, swish, kick." Her foot sailed past Alfred's head without incident. "Turn again. Swish, swish, kick. Turn, *arabesque* with both hands in front, third position."

She brought her leg down and gracefully hopped off the chair, having perfectly executed her steps. Sure, she wasn't in pointe shoes, but the movements were there— and she didn't kick the dummy.

"From the top." It looked like she was grasping the teacher role with both hands.

They ran through the sequence a few times without music. Occasionally she'd stop to correct his technique—or lack thereof—and show him the proper way of executing the steps. Now she had him on the chair, helping him with his arabesque.

"You need better rotation here." She reached up and touched his thigh, helping him find the correct position. "Otherwise, your foot will be pointing the wrong way."

Wes steadied himself with one hand on the back of the chair.

"Don't dip forward." She pressed her other hand against his stomach. "Pull in your abdominal muscles and lift the chest. You're not a plane coming in for landing."

He snorted. "If I'd known you'd be such a hard-ass, I wouldn't have told you to role-play."

She ignored the dig. "If you're not flexible enough to have the back leg up so high, then bring it down a little so you can maintain the correct technique."

Her hands worked along his body, pulling and pushing him into shape. It was a perfectly normal thing for a ballet teacher to do, because it was critical for the dancers to feel their bodies in the right position. It gave them context. Allowed their bodies to learn.

But the way her fingers skimmed over him, skating over his stomach and thighs, felt far too good.

All the blood in Wes's body headed south, and a black pair of sweatpants wasn't going to hide shit. He dropped his leg and hopped down off the chair, his bare feet hitting the stage with a slap.

"Demonstrate it for me," he said.

"The arabesque?"

"The whole piece," he said. "Talk through the steps."

"Okay." She nodded and went to the front of the stage. Thankfully, she hadn't looked down and realized that he was sporting a hard-on.

That was the whole issue with Remi—around her, he seemed unable to separate professionalism and pleasure.

The two were so entwined, wrapped up to the point he had no hope of entangling one from the other. He wanted her.

And no matter how hard he tried to focus on his show, he couldn't shake it.

Chapter 16

> "Wes is the kind of guy who turned me into a total
> yes-woman, as in: yes please, yes more, and oh
> God yes."
>
> —CinnamonTwirl

REMI KNEW *EXACTLY* WHAT WES WAS DOING. AT LEAST
she did now, even if it hadn't been clear right at the start.
The thing was…it was working. For the first time since
she'd joined *Out of Bounds*, she felt confident.

But that could disappear the second the cast comes in tomorrow.

Maybe she'd pretend to be instructing someone else,
rather than performing. She had to admit, it lightened
the pressure in her head. Even now, as she worked
through the piece, calling out the steps as she went, the
negative voices remained at bay. At this point, she was
desperate for any solution, because their potential investor was coming in on Wednesday. If she messed up,
everyone would pay the price. Not just herself, and not
just Wes. But the entire cast.

She couldn't let them down.

By the time she finished running through the first
sequence, sweat trickled down her back. It was a lively

opening, like the dance equivalent of fireworks, meant to entrance the audience and have them riveted from the first beat.

And she hadn't made a single mistake.

"Wow." Wes clapped his hands together, an unrestrained smile on his face.

"Just wow?" she teased, feeling pretty darn good about herself. "Am I defying words again?"

That was the strange thing about ballet—when the magic was there, you felt it to your very core. It rippled through you, fueling your blood and shimmering with each breath. But when it was gone, sometimes the best thing to do was stop looking.

"*That* is why I wanted you for this show." His eyes were alight, the pale blue of his irises glowing. "That, right there. I knew you'd be perfect."

She swallowed. "Let's see if I can replicate it when Bert comes to watch."

"Stop." He walked over to her, his hands landing on her shoulders. "If you don't tell that voice in your head to shut the hell up, then you're going to get stuck in this vicious cycle."

"You think I don't know that?" she said softly. All she'd ever wanted was to have that confidence onstage that she seemed to embody without issue everywhere else. Give her stilettos and a miniskirt, and she was fine. Put her in pointe shoes and *poof!* It was gone.

"I want us to be a success story." He squeezed her shoulders, his fingertips pressing into her bare skin. "I want us to be a sensation. Together. Anything I can do to help you, just say the words."

Kiss me.

No, that was a terrible idea.

"This helped," she said, shaking off the unrelenting whisper of desire winding its way through her body. Dammit, why did he have to be so sweet and sexy? So in tune with her? "The role reversal."

He was looking at her like he wanted to say something else. Was his head swirling with rationales and reasoning? Was he trying to come up with an excuse to break the rules?

Your rules. Not his.

God, she wanted to give in. She wanted it like ice cream and pizza and fresh-baked bread. All the things she knew were bad for her but tasted oh so good. And the more time she spent with Wes, the more reasons she found to throw caution—and her panties—to the wind. He wasn't like Alex.

How do you know that? You thought Alex wasn't that way until it was too late.

"Maybe we should do this again," she said, not knowing exactly what she meant, only that her brain was driving her to create a scenario where they were together. "I feel good working with you. It feels…right."

And it did. He'd never held back in telling her that he believed in her, no matter how much she resisted.

"It should feel right." He pushed his hand through his dark hair, parting the strands and clearing them from his chiseled cheekbones. "We're in this together."

I want you.

Oh God, she needed space. Needed a second outside the vortex sucking her in and leaving her without brain function. "Are we done, or did you have something else planned for today?"

"That was it." He stepped back.

"I'll get changed then." Her eyes darted to stage right, where the dressing rooms were located. "Don't feel like you need to wait for me."

Smooth, Drysdale. Like a freaking cactus.

She turned on her heel, her sneakers squeaking against the polished boards as she grabbed her bag and headed for the dressing rooms. She'd put her tights on under her leggings, unsure exactly what Wes had wanted when he'd told her to meet him, and now all the layers made her feel like she was burning up.

She swept past the heavy, black curtains at the side of the stage and jogged down the steps that lead to the cast and crew area. All the theaters she'd worked in were laid out like that. When she got to the door, she paused, her hand pressed against the frame while she listened. Silence. Wes wasn't following her.

She wasn't sure whether she should be relieved or disappointed.

Don't follow her, don't follow her, don't follow her.

Wes waited as long as he could. But his feet carried him through the wings and to the front of the only dressing room with a closed door. It was like having an out-of-body experience. He wasn't in control here.

Yeah, your dick is in control. Idiot.

He shouldn't be doing this. It wasn't the smart move.

The safe move. And Remi had made it clear things couldn't go any further between them. Except watching her blossom tonight had been like a shot of pure ecstasy. It was validation he knew what he was doing and proof he'd been right to hire her. When she let go, it was like watching a story come to life.

Remi could see right into him. She knew *exactly* what he wanted—how he wanted it. Her body was magic on that stage. Fucking magic.

Out of Bounds was her and she was it.

He held his fist up to the door, hesitating a moment before he let it fall with a single heavy thud.

"One second." Her voice floated through the door, along with a rustling sound, before it swung open. Light spilled into the dark hallway, backlighting her. The gold strands of her hair gleamed. "I thought you'd gone home."

"I wanted to see you for a minute before I go." His voice didn't sound like his own. It was all scratched up and rough, frayed—like how his nerves felt from the pressure of resisting her.

The hem of a floaty, pink dress hovered midthigh and dipped into a shallow a V at her chest. It was simple and pretty, sweet, and yet it made his blood pulse so hard through his veins that he had to grip the doorframe to keep steady. Her clothes from before—pink ballet tights, a pair of leggings, a T-shirt, and her sweater—were draped over the back of a chair.

"Okay." She stepped back, inviting him in.

The click of the door shutting behind him was like a gun being cocked.

Careful, Evans. This is dangerous territory.

"I wanted to say again that you were great tonight." He cleared his throat. "I know it's been a rocky journey, but Sadie's choreography is perfect for you."

"Thanks." Her fingers toyed with the hem of her dress, the silky fabric gliding between her fingers like water. He wanted to bunch it in his fists. "I'm really excited to be part of the show."

"I'm excited to have you." His cock pulsed. Shit. "As part of the show," he clarified.

Wow, way to engage awkward-teenage-boy mode. Since when did he have a hard time getting words out? Of all the things in life that could possibly trip him up, it wasn't his ability to communicate.

But Remi had him questioning everything he'd ever known. Everything he'd ever thought about himself.

"I'm excited you're excited," she whispered, a smile tugging at her lips.

"You're trying to tease me."

"Not trying." She sucked on the inside of her cheek. It was her go-to move for stifling a laugh. "Succeeding."

"You're succeeding at a whole lot of other things. The teasing is the least of my problems." His brain fired messages to every part of his body, commanding him to grab and kiss and bite and tear. To ravish and devour and pleasure.

"What are you doing here, Wes?"

The light overhead flickered, the bulb making a slight buzzing sound. Outside, wind whistled through the building. The old structure made its own music, a collection of sounds unique to this place. But right now, the only thing Wes gave a damn about was that tiny, stuttering breath coming and going from Remi's lips.

"I don't know." He stuffed his hands into his pockets. "I can't seem to make myself leave."

Against his better judgment, he stepped forward. That one small action sucked the restraint from the room, turning the air electric. It mimicked the feeling he'd experienced watching Remi take charge of the stage earlier.

Her eyes widened, the black of her pupils expanding as she backed up against the counter behind her. White-knuckled fingers curled around the painted wood, as if she wanted to steady herself. But he couldn't prevent himself taking another step. Then another. And another.

"Stop," she whispered.

He froze in his tracks, cursing under his breath. With the mirror behind her, he caught a glimpse of himself. He looked wild, his eyes dark and his shoulders tensed like a lion ready to strike.

"We've talked about this." Her voice betrayed her—that lovely, husky, desperate quality was a lit match to his desire. The flames licking at his insides burned brightly out of control.

"You want me."

"I do." Her eyes fluttered shut and she sucked in a breath. "God help me, I do. I did the very second you walked into my class, and I've been fighting it tooth and nail ever since. But that doesn't change the facts. You *know* what I'm afraid of."

"This isn't work, Remi. The second I walked in here, it became something else."

"We can't separate it, no matter how much I want to." She shook her head. "You have no idea how much I *need* this opportunity."

"As much as I do."

"Then you know why I can't screw things up by sleeping with you."

He growled, frustration and anticipation warring in his veins. "I know. I know."

Why was this so different for him? In any other situation, he'd walk away. Hell, he probably wouldn't have gotten close in the first place. They both had so much on the line. But Remi had a magnetic pull that gripped him by the balls. And it wouldn't let go.

"We made the right decision that night," he said. "You being in this show is more important than sex. What we're doing with *Out of Bounds* is more important than sex."

"But?"

"I still want you." He raked a hand through his hair, forcing himself not to reach out and touch her. But his restraint was a rubber band pulled tight. "God help me, I want you so fucking bad it makes me ache."

"I want you too, Wes," she whispered. "I can't help it."

"Should I walk away?"

She squeezed her eyes shut. "Promise me I'm not making a mistake. I don't want to ruin this."

"I'm not going to do anything that will put the show or you at risk. You're it for *Out of Bounds*. Whether or not we sleep together, the show needs you. Sex won't change that."

He wanted to see the restraint fall from her face. Wanted to see her come apart and be the raw and unfiltered her. He took another step forward and reached for the tie holding her dress together at the side of her waist.

"If you turn me down now, I will walk away and it won't come up again," he said. "No consequences. I promise."

She lifted her head, her hand coming to his, fingertips dancing over his knuckles. "Will it be insulting if I say I don't want anyone to know?"

He shook his head. "We're not at work now, so it's nobody's business. This is just for us."

"Just for us," she echoed. "I like that."

"I need to hear you say it's okay, Remi." He brushed a strand of hair behind her ear. "I don't play in the gray area."

"Yes," she breathed. "I want this. I want…"

"You want?"

"I want you to touch me." She sucked in a breath. "Please, Wes. I want to do this."

He tugged on the silky tie of her dress, pulling it easily through the loops at her waist. The fabric split open at her chest, falling away to reveal nothing but a pair of soft, silky panties and miles of gloriously naked skin.

"God, Remi." He choked the words out. Her body was incredible, supple and strong. Delicate yet powerful. A series of contradictions that made him want to drown in her. "You're…"

He ran a hand down the edge of the dress, pulling it farther to the side so he could see all of her. Her skin was smooth, her nipples hard and rosy pink. She had a smattering of freckles on her chest, and a tiny mole on her left breast. Beautiful details. "Didn't I tell you once before that you defied words?"

"Always so smooth," she teased softly.

He slipped the dress from one shoulder and then

the other, and dragged the backs of his knuckles along her neck, down her chest, and over the peaks of her breasts. A tremor rippled through her, sending a gasp knifing through the quiet air. The theater groaned in the background, echoing her.

There was no way this could be wrong.

"Stand," he said. She complied, and he hooked his fingers beneath the waistband of her panties. "Once these come off, I'm not going to hold back. I'm going to make you explode. Then I'm going to fuck you. Are you okay with that?"

Her mouth hung open, slack with desire. Eyes blackened. "Yes."

"Good." He pulled the elasticated waist of her underwear down over her hips and thighs, then down her calves until she could step out of them. "I've been dreaming about you, Remi. About having you like this."

"Here?"

"Everywhere." He helped her to sit up on the counter. "Anywhere."

"Tell me."

He splayed his hands at her thighs, pushing them open until her knees hit the counter. "I woke up this morning thinking I could taste you on my tongue and smell you on my sheets. But I had a hand full of my own cock and that was very disappointing."

"Oh God." She whimpered when he slid his palms up to her sex, his thumbs drawing her open.

"Beautiful." He stuck one thumb into his mouth and then spread the moisture over her clit, brushing her in slow, even circles. "Everything about you, Remi. Perfection, inside and out."

"Wes," she panted, her hips tilting forward. "That feels… Oh."

"I thought about you the first night I saw you. I imagined bending you over the barre and pulling that pretty pink leotard to one side so I could take you."

Remi's head lolled back and the panting turned to long, keening moans. She fisted one hand in his shirt and wrapped the other around the edge of the counter, her hips grinding in time with the slow, sensual assault of his hand.

"Get ready for me," he growled, stroking his finger up and down the seam of her sex. A subtle sheen had developed across her forehead and nose, making her glow. Damn, the woman was a goddess. "Get ready, Remi."

He slipped a finger inside her, testing her before adding a second one and curling them toward himself.

"Yes. There," she gasped.

Pleasure played like fireworks across her face, dynamic and vibrant. She hid nothing from him. Greedy, his eyes drank it in, gulping down every thrust of her hips, every pulse in her neck, every flutter of her lashes.

"So close." Her eyes clamped shut. "I'm so close."

Yes. Show me.

As if hearing his silent command, a shudder ripped through her. The sound of her gasps bounced around in his head. He wanted to remember that sound forever.

Every nerve in Wes's body was alight and burning with need. He might be the one commanding her pleasure now, but she had him captive. Like she'd reached into his chest and wrapped her fist around his heart. And no matter how much he rationalized and wrote off his infatuation as a physical thing, deep down, he knew the physical wasn't going to be enough.

The world filtered back to Remi slowly, as though someone was lifting the layers of a gauzy veil from her eyes. First, it was the beating of her heart, a sledgehammer-strength pounding against her rib cage. Then, the sound of breath whooshing out between her lips. Then her eyes fluttered open.

Oh boy, the visual was even better than she could have imagined.

Wes was looking at her like a feral animal eyeing a meal. His crystalline eyes were wild and otherworldly, his dark hair flopping over his forehead. Without thinking, she reached out and brushed it back, which earned her one hell of a crooked smile.

Hold on to your hormones, girl.

"Thought I lost you there for a minute," he said.

"No way. I'm not missing a second of this."

"You're an all-in kind of woman, aren't you?"

"Hell yeah." She trailed her hands down his chest until they snagged on the waistband of his pants. "If I decide to cross a line, I don't just walk over it. I run, full-steam ahead." She brushed her fingers down over the bulge in the front of his pants, feeling every ridge in his cock.

Slow breath. There's no need to be intimidated…

But how could she not be? The whole world knew Wes first for what he was hiding in his pants. Or not hiding, as the case was now. The outline of his erection made her suck in a breath. Holy hell, he really was as big as people said.

"You okay?" He swept her hair back over her shoulders, letting his knuckles trail across her skin.

"Yeah."

"Don't be nervous."

"I'm not," she lied.

It wasn't only the thought of whether the mechanics would work—was there such a thing as a guy who was *too* big? If she'd finally let herself give in to this temptation, to break the rules she'd set to protect herself, then a failure to launch would be a mammoth disappointment.

No pun intended.

Beyond that, her brain was already freaking out about tomorrow. How would she pretend she hadn't seen this incredible man naked? What if it affected her dancing? What if he tired of her and she lost this opportunity? This lifeline?

More importantly, what if this did nothing to quench her hunger?

What if, what if, what if…?

Dangerous words.

"You're thinking too much," he said.

"You've found my secret shame." She tugged his pants down over his hips. Slowly, slowly. She wanted to draw it out. "Neuroses and an inability to relax."

"Clearly we need to find you a solution for that," he said. "Another orgasm or two might help."

It certainly couldn't hurt. Orgasms were never a bad thing, obviously. But Remi had found that many guys thought all climaxes were created equal. Like coming was some binary thing—either you did or you didn't. End of story.

Women knew the whole truth. An orgasm was good. But the ones that made your toes curl and your back arch like you were trying to snap your body in half were gold and, unfortunately, rare.

And it appeared that Wes wasn't the kind of guy who simply relied on the power of what was in his pants. He knew how to use *all* the tools at his disposal.

Thank you, whoever is up there.

"I like the way you think," she said, pulling the fabric down all the way.

A pair of black boxer briefs hugged his waist and thighs, showcasing a perfectly sculpted body. Wes toed off his shoes and discarded his sweats. His T-shirt followed, landing in a heap on the floor.

Holy moly.

If she hadn't been intimidated before, then she sure as hell was now. The guy should have been cast in bronze and stuck in a museum. Broad shoulders balanced out well-muscled thighs, and a trim waist was defined by those V-shaped muscles that made her mouth water every damn time. Wes might not be training in the studio much these days, but he obviously did something to keep fit. A body like that did not exist without a reason.

Perfection is never an accident, as her old ballet teacher used to say.

He stood for a moment, waiting to see if she'd relieve him of his final piece of clothing. When she didn't move, he hooked his thumbs into the waistband of his briefs and peeled them from his body.

Sweet mother of…

His cock bobbed back up against his stomach, thick and hard. He was every inch as described.

"Eyes up here, sweetheart," he teased, his finger pressing under her chin and tilting her face up.

"I thought men liked it when their partners made a fuss over their size." She aimed for a sassy tone to cover the excitement and embarrassment causing her cheeks to flame. But one look at Wes told her he wasn't buying it.

"Flattery is overrated." A hand came down on either side of her hips, penning her in. "I'd rather hear you scream my name when I've got my mouth on you than have you stroke my ego."

She leaned back against the counter, resting on her palms. The way he loomed over her, casting a shadow with his frame, made her feel small and vulnerable in the best way possible. It was easy to feel like there was no world outside this room when he looked at her like that, when he took charge of the space and filled it with simmering anticipation. Under his intense stare, she could forget about tomorrow. She could forget about all the mistakes she'd made up until now. Forget that perhaps this was the biggest mistake of all.

"Too many people pumping up your ego?" She sighed when he pressed forward, his cock pressing against the inside of her thigh. "I can be mean if you want."

"You don't have a mean bone in your body." He chuckled against her neck, sending warm breath across her skin.

Then his mouth came to hers. The kiss was sudden, like need had taken hold of him with brute force. His lips were firm, his tongue breaching her mouth and demanding she return the favor.

Fisting her hands in his hair, she pulled him closer. He tasted of mint and something subtle, something slightly earthy. His hands were at her hips, at her thighs, biting into her skin as he dragged her legs around him. Entwining them.

"Condom," she gasped. As much as she hated to interrupt the moment their passion ignited, she wasn't going to let her lady parts overrule her head where *that* was concerned.

Wes broke free and found a foil packet inside his wallet. The sound of it tearing made her shiver, anticipation building at the base of her spine and spreading through her like a drug. She wanted to be full with him, wanted to feel their bodies melt into each other.

"Hurry up," she urged, and he was back between her legs in an instant. The head of his cock nudged her entrance.

"You got somewhere to be?" A lazy smile drifted across his lips as he ran his hands up her sides and over her rib cage until he cupped her breasts. "Am I keeping you from something more important?"

His thumbs flicked over her nipples at a leisurely pace. The damn man was taunting her.

"I've got an episode of *MasterChef* to watch." She tipped her nose up to him. Hot as Wes was, she wasn't going to let him think he was in charge. This wasn't work, as he'd said, which meant he wasn't her boss right now. "So if you could get to it, that would be great."

She'd expected him to laugh, but instead, he pressed her farther back, sandwiching her between his hips and the counter. "Don't make that mistake, Remi."

"What mistake?"

"Thinking because I like to laugh that I'm a pushover in bed."

"We're not in bed," she teased. "Mr. Genial."

His eyes flared. Oh, that's what he was talking about. *That* was the mistake.

"Get off the counter and turn around," he growled. "This is what happens when you push Mr. Genial to his limits."

The sound of his voice, low and rough and edgy, ripped through her. It was like pouring gasoline on a bonfire. Now she couldn't control the flames. So she obeyed. Wes stepped back and watched, his eyes catching hers in the mirror surrounded by naked bulbs. It was like a dance. He'd taken the lead and now she had to follow.

"Put your hands on the counter."

She pressed her palms down without breaking eye contact in the mirror.

"Widen your legs."

Sucking in a breath, she stepped her feet farther apart.

"Tilt that beautiful ass up to me."

Despite the fact that Remi wasn't a wallflower, there was something bold about this scenario. The mirror, the gravelly commands, the lights all around them. Knowing that hundreds of performers had been standing in this exact spot touching up their makeup or fixing their hair made it seem illicit. Naughty.

"That's it," he said softly, his hand coming to her lower back. "Perfect."

He smoothed his palm over her skin in slow circles, running over the dip at her waist and the flare of her hips. Over the curve of her butt and down the backs of her thighs. It was like he wanted to memorize her with his hands.

"Don't take your eyes off me," he said as he lined himself up behind her. "I want to see every bit of pleasure on your face. I want to see those hungry eyes while I slip inside you. I want to watch your face when I make you come again."

Oh. My. God.

"Yes," she breathed.

His fingers teased her entrance for a moment, warming her up, and then it was him. All of him. Holy moly.

"Breathe, baby." One hand smoothed up and down her spine as the other rested on her hip. "Don't tense up."

How on earth am I supposed to relax when it feels like you've got a tree trunk back there?

She squeezed her eyes shut, trying to quell the nerves bubbling up and killing her buzz.

"Look at me," he commanded.

Her head snapped up, her gaze on his, and he gave her a cheeky smile. Never before had she thought a smile might melt her into a pile of goo, but Wes's smile was it. Sexy, sweet, and crooked enough to land on the right side of perfect.

"I've got you," he whispered. "I'm not going to do anything to hurt you."

"I believe you."

Mistake. This wasn't supposed to be about trust or smiles or any of that shit. It was pure primal need. Sex. Nothing more.

Her brain attempted to come up with a counter-argument, but the second he pushed inside, the words evaporated. Everything was gone except for the feeling of fullness that sucked the air out of her lungs.

"Fuck," he muttered, his eyes fluttering shut for a second as he seated himself all the way inside her. "You feel even better than I imagined."

Remi fought the warning from her body that it was too much. After a few long breaths with them just standing there—joined and unmoving—she started to adjust. Her body molded to his, accommodating his size. Then the sharp sting turned into another kind of burning sensation. Something liquid and hot and addictive.

"Wes," she gasped, moving her hips back and forth. "Please. We've waited long enough."

He came forward on his hands, lining her back with his chest. Hot breath blew against her ear and his hair tickled her temple.

"Tell me if you need to stop or slow down, okay? I want you to feel good."

She nodded, swallowing at the sensation shooting through her at only the slightest movement of his hips. It was like every nerve ending in her body had been put through the ringer. The soft brush of his hands left flames in their wake.

Wes reached for the hair band holding her ponytail in place and pulled it free, so her hair fell around her shoulders, sending goose bumps skittering over her sensitized skin.

"More," she demanded. "Faster."

"Patience." He nipped at her ear, slowly pumping in and out of her. "If you think I'm going to rush through this, you're mistaken."

"But I need…"

What did she need? Bloody hell. She didn't even know anymore. The slow fucking, full eye contact in the mirror, him winding her hair around his fist—it was everything. He gave her hair a soft tug, causing her head to come back against his chest.

"Tell me," he growled.

"Don't hold back." She arched her back as he drove deep. "I can take it. I *want* it."

"That all?"

"I want you, Wes. Just you."

The sound that erupted from him was barely human. Knowing that she was driving him as crazy as he was driving her pushed her right to the edge. They were partners. Equals. They stirred up feelings that shouldn't be there.

"I want you too, Remi."

When he pushed back into her, the sensation was electric. The counter rattled as he thrust into her, but clinking glass didn't slow them down. Nothing mattered except them. Except pure feeling.

"Remi." Wes swore under his breath. "Touch yourself."

Yes. She reached down, her fingers working instantly to crank her pleasure up. Orgasm hit her hard and fast, her body trembling around his.

His moan cut off into a sharp grunt as he buried himself deep inside her with a final thrust.

Silence settled over them, and a thud came from inside the theater. "Do you think we frightened Alfred?" he said, burying his face into her hair.

"I'm less worried about Alfred and more worried about the entire city of Manhattan." She leaned her head back against his shoulder. "Pretty sure I came hard enough to rattle the foundations of this building."

"It was goddamn hot, let me tell you." He watched her in the mirror, cheeks flushed pink and her hair falling around her face. "Come back to my place. I want round two in a proper bed."

"Round two?" Her eyes met his in the mirror. "I like the sound of that."

Chapter 17

"Some things really are too good to be true. It's not cynical—it's a necessary protection."

—MisguidedInManhattan

THIS TIME AROUND, HAVING REMI SHOWERING IN HIS apartment was done right. Meaning he had her pinned against the tiles, his hands full of her ass while he plundered her mouth. Warm water streamed over them both, melting him into her. His cock was hard against the inside of her thigh, but he was going to stay true to his word.

Round two would happen in a proper bed. This was simply a warm-up.

Her head lolled back against the titles, exposing the length of her neck to his mouth. "I thought we were supposed to be freshening up."

He slipped his hand between her legs. "You don't feel fresh?"

A soft, little grunt escaped her lips as her hips rolled against his hand. "No, fresh is not how I would describe it."

He chuckled. Remi was right about one thing—the second she decided to cross a line, she practically flung herself over it. How had she put it? *If you're going to do the wrong thing, may as well enjoy it?*

So true.

"How about clean, then?" He sucked on the side of her neck.

"This is anything but clean." She looked up, her eyes full of mischief. "And you know it."

Water droplets clung to her lashes and the edges of her full lips, making her look like a water sprite. "Okay, you got me. Guilty as charged."

He reached for her hand and pulled it to him, guiding her fingers around his bare cock. Her nostrils flared and her eyes turned black and smoky. Damn, those eyes. They reflected everything she felt—fear, determination, desire. Whatever was so far beyond desire that she looked like sex personified. She held nothing back.

With his hand covering hers, he worked her grip up and down his length. Blood surged through his veins, making him impossibly hard.

"God, Wes." Her mouth was open, her eyes fixed on the slick up-down rhythm of their hands. Watching her watching *them* was doing unspeakable things to him. Pressure built at the base of his cock, urging him to thrust into her hand. Hard. Faster. To take what he needed.

But there was no way in hell he was going to rush tonight. For all he knew, she'd leave tomorrow morning and act like it never happened. He needed to string it out, fill his head with memories in case that's all she left behind.

He let her hand go and she continued to stroke him, flicking her thumb over the head of his erection in a way that made his balls feel tight and achy.

"Was this part of your fantasies?" She gave him a tight squeeze and he grabbed her head with both hands, slamming his lips down on hers. Her hand continued to work him, getting rougher and bolder with each stroke.

"Everything was, Remi. If you can physically do it, I imagined it." He grinned against her mouth. "And I imagined some things that were impossible too."

"Creative," she murmured.

Reluctantly, he pulled his head away from hers and reached for the tap. "Bed. Now."

"I thought you were enjoying yourself." Her lips tilted up into a smirk.

"Too much." He brought his hand down on her bare ass, and the smacking sound echoed against the tiles in the shower. "And if you keep doing that, I'm going to give you cause for a second shower."

She laughed. "Maybe I want to get you off with my hands."

"Later," he growled. "I'm not going to waste tonight on hand jobs when I can get between your legs again."

He helped her out of the shower and bundled her up in his robe. The fluffy, white fabric made her look like an angel, especially with all her glossy, sunshine hair tangling around her shoulders.

"And to think I was calling you Mr. Nice Guy. You're so demanding."

"It was Mr. Genial." He backed them into his bedroom without even bothering to dry himself off. Water ran in rivulets down his chest and she traced them with her finger. "That really pissed me off."

"Poor baby," she teased. "Such a fragile male ego you have."

"You're asking for it, Remi. I can be really fucking impolite in bed."

She threw him a haughty look. "I don't believe it for a second."

He picked her up and her surprised squeal pierced his ears. The bed squeaked as he unceremoniously dropped her and was over her in a flash, pushing the robe open. Her bare sex was gleaming, slick with need. She didn't believe him to be anything but the nice guy? Ha. He was going to fix that.

He spread her legs and dipped his head between them without any pretense. His reward was a long, deep moan from above, followed by a sharp snap of pain when her nails raked over his scalp. In the bedroom, she came undone immediately, her body turning pliant in his hands.

He nudged her clit with this tongue, listening for her cues to see where she liked it most. Learning her. And she had no problem communicating here. He drew the sensitive bud between his lips, and she arched off the bed, her back bowing as her hand held him down.

"Yes! There." Her thighs trembled against his ears and he pulled back, chuckling as she made a frustrated noise in the back of her throat. "Why did you stop?"

"Because when you come, I want to be all the way inside you." He reached into his bedside drawer and pulled a condom out. "I want to feel you squeeze me so hard I think I'm going to break."

She propped herself up on her elbows and smirked at him. "When I come? Not if?"

"It's one hundred percent *when*." He sheathed himself and stalked up the bed, settling between her legs. "I can play your body like a harp."

"Oh, is that right?" She looped her arms around his neck. "You think I'm *so* easy."

"Nah, I'm just that talented." He winked and they both dissolved in laughter.

That's how it was with her—fun. Funny. Sweet.

He grabbed her hips and rolled the two of them over, so she was straddling him. The view was everything. Her long, damp hair tumbled down over her breasts and brushed his stomach when she leaned forward. He'd met a lot of women who talked a big game until they were stripped down, but Remi was the opposite. She knew she was sexy and desirable, and she wasn't ashamed of it. He loved that about her. And together, they were comfortable. They worked.

But tomorrow it would be gone, dissolved like cotton candy on an eager tongue.

That's definitely a Future Wes problem.

Tonight, he was going to live in the moment.

"You've got a big mouth, Wes." She nipped at his chin. "You're always talking, talking, talking."

"Are you used to quiet fucking?"

She shifted her hips, allowing him to position himself at her entrance. "I don't let myself get used to anything."

"That'll have to change." He groaned when she slid herself down on him, slow and steady, her hands planted on his stomach. "You're going to be feeling me for days."

She rolled her hips, tilting back and forth until she found the right spot. He saw the moment she got there, because her eyes fluttered shut and her hands balled into fists. He pulled her down against his chest, wrapping his arms around her waist. Hot breath fanned out over his neck as she rode him, her face buried in his neck.

When her legs started to shake again, his fingers bit into her hips and he thrust faster and faster, determined to get there at the same time she did. She tipped over a few seconds before him, the tremors running through her body and into his.

The last thing he remembered was the sound of his name hoarse on her lips.

Remi wasn't sure what woke her. It might have been the cooling of the sheets in Wes's bed or the savory scent wafting in from the kitchen. It could have been the clink of bowls and cutlery or the light filtering in under the closed bedroom door.

She pushed up into a sitting position and raked her hair out of her face. At some point, she'd been covered with a crisp, white sheet, but Remi didn't even remember making it under the covers. They'd been furious in their devouring of one another—teasing and taunting and grabbing to the point they'd never even pulled the duvet cover back.

In fact, the last thing she remembered was Wes's arms around her, easing her to one side as he stayed inside her after they'd both come. And holy freaking smokes, what an orgasm. She'd had some fine lovers in her time but nothing this…primal. Wes brought her to life in a way that no one else had.

She ran her fingertips over the sheets, too smooth and unrumpled to have been involved in their lovemaking. What the hell was she doing? It was one thing to admit that she had no willpower and to indulge in her attraction. It was another thing entirely to come here and play happy lovers.

This is exactly what you did last time. You were attracted to Alex and you allowed it to make you stupid.

She'd seen things that weren't there, signs he never put out. Not to mention the fact that she was now lying to Wes. Well, by omission, anyway.

Freaking Annie. Groaning, Remi dropped her head into her hands and tried to make sense of it all. Her best friend was easily the most wanted woman in all of New York. It wasn't like the app had never come up in conversation. They'd talked about it. Messaged one another with screenshots of reviews. Used it repeatedly.

That meant there had been a whole lot of opportunity for Annie to say, *Hey, about that app. I created it.* But both her and Darcy had kept Remi out of the loop. It was the first time since she'd entered their little circle of friendship that she'd truly felt like an outsider.

It would be one thing if the app didn't affect her or anyone she knew…but it did.

Now, what was she supposed to do? It was an impossible choice—pick her friend or her career. Her pseudo family member or the guy who held the key to her dreams. She'd been on the losing end of that choice before, and now suddenly she was the one facing it.

Remi climbed off the bed and wandered into Wes's master bathroom to find her dress and underwear in a heap on the floor. She pulled her panties up over her hips and slipped her arms into the dress. Walking back into the bedroom, she wrapped the fabric ties around her body and knotted them at her waist.

She paused at the closed bedroom door that led to the rest of the apartment, pressing her hand to the wood while she mustered the courage to face him. It was messed up, but Remi was more comfortable in the throes of sex than in the moments after. With every other guy since Alex, she'd changed as soon as the deed was done and left with a saucy wink or a lingering kiss. She *always* left.

Only tonight, she'd fallen asleep entwined in his arms. This was different. *He* was different.

"Woman up," she said to herself. "You can make a swift exit and then go on like it never happened."

But the second she pushed the bedroom door open, her heart melted. His dining table was set for two, a bottle of wine open with two glasses waiting. Wes was in the kitchen, concentrating on measuring out some soy sauce into a sizzling pan on the stove. The guy even had an apron on. Seriously, who the hell was he?

It was like someone had polled a bunch of women and created the perfect man. Handsome face, incredible body, a giving lover, and a whiz in the kitchen judging by the scent.

"You're so perfect it's kind of ridiculous," she said.

He whipped his head around, the surprised expression morphing into a sexy smile. "For someone who had enough orgasms to put her to sleep, you sure are full of insults."

She padded over to him, her bare feet making soft

slapping sounds against the floorboards. "Maybe you should try harder to be less intimidating."

"It's all in your head, Remi." He slipped a finger behind the waist tie and pulled her closer.

"You can't possibly be ready to go again." She laughed and pressed a hand to his crotch, as though this was totally normal behavior, and found him hard again. "Bloody hell. You're a machine."

"A sex machine."

"That's not normal." She couldn't help but rub her hand up and down. Call her shallow, but she was all kinds of excited knowing he was so eager for her. "I have serious concerns for your health and well-being."

"What do I do, Doc?" He drew her against him, walking them away from the stove until he hit the other set of cupboards behind him. Her hips swirled against his, eliciting the bite of his fingers at her waist. "How do I rectify this issue?"

"I don't know if anything can be done. You might have to amputate."

"Whoa." He grabbed her by the shoulders, his brow crinkled. "You *never* joke about that kind of thing. You trying to give me a heart attack or something?"

She laughed and draped her arms over his shoulders. "At least that might slow you down."

"There will be no further discussion of cutting off my manhood, thank you very much." He looked her in the eyes and she felt it right down to her toes, making them curl against the polished boards. How did he do that to her? It was such a small thing and yet it was... everything. "Now, can I interest you in my specialty?"

"You ask me now, after I've had your specialty twice tonight?" She bit down on her lip when he rolled his eyes.

"I'm trying to be romantic here and you've got your mind in the gutter." He didn't look annoyed in the slightest. "I might be a machine, but even machines need fuel."

Dinner. It seemed a whole lot scarier than the touching and kissing and panting. The smart move would be to bail now, before things got weird. Before they started talking and doing that kind of stuff she generally avoided.

But the truth was she was really freaking hungry.

"It smells amazing," she admitted.

"It's my go-to—honey, soy, and ginger stir-fry with whatever vegetables I happen to have in my fridge." He released her. "Tonight that's carrots, snap peas, and red peppers."

Most guys wouldn't have worried about dinner. A good guy might have offered to call the local Chinese takeout place. Wes had made her something healthy and delicious like it was nothing.

"Why are you so sweet?" she asked, folding her arms across her chest. "Have you got some kind of trick up your sleeve?"

He chuckled. "Yeah, I want to feed you so we can go back to bed afterward."

"You don't need to feed me to do that."

"Maybe I enjoy your company. Is that so hard to believe?" He grabbed a wooden spoon and stirred the vegetables around the wok, lifting the scent of ginger and garlic into the air. Remi's mouth watered. "And, despite what you might have read, I don't fuck around for the sake of it. If I sleep with someone, it's because I like them."

The scariest thing of all was that Remi *wanted* to believe him. Normally when a guy tossed her a line like that, she'd smile and nod all the while thinking, *yeah right.* It never affected her, because she refused to put herself in a situation where she'd get attached. Like the time she had a friends-with-benefits arrangement with a guy who lived in Las Vegas. He'd only ever come to New York for one or two nights at a time. It was fun. *Only* fun.

That was the kind of thing she needed in her life. Something low maintenance and low commitment that required the minimum attention. Like a cactus.

Cactus sex, good. Homemade stir-fries and real conversation sex, bad.

"In case that wasn't clear enough, I like you," he added.

No, no, no.

Her head had clearly gotten the memo, but the uneven, too-fast thump of her heart showed that not all major body parts were on the same page. And that was a problem.

"This is the part where you give me some verbal indication of whether or not that feeling is reciprocated." He shot her a crooked smile. "So I don't stand here like an idiot twiddling my thumbs."

Her first instinct was to make some kind of joke that revolved around an inappropriate use of the word *twiddle.*

"I like you too," she said.

Wrong answer! Abort mission. I repeat, abort mission.

But her damned feet didn't move. It was like someone had superglued her to the ground. Instead, she wrung her hands and tried not to grin like an idiot at this impossibly perfect guy who'd cast a spell on her.

"You sure it's not the endorphins speaking?" she asked. "Sex makes the brain do funny things."

"I know the difference between lust and like." He dipped the spoon into the sauce simmering away on the stove and blew on the steam curling upward before bringing it to her lips. "And I haven't wanted to cook a meal for someone in a long time."

She let him pass the spoon between her lips and sighed when the flavors exploded on her tongue. Seemed the bedroom wasn't the only area where Wes had some serious skills.

"Suddenly I'm very hungry," she said.

"So that means you're not going to run away when I turn my back?" he teased.

She shook her head. "You've convinced me to stay."

He pulled two bowls down from an overhead cupboard and set them next to the stove so he could serve their dinner. Remi went to her ballet bag and fished out her phone. Five missed calls and twice as many texts. Both Darcy and Annie had been trying to get ahold of her.

She would have to deal with that issue soon. Remi looked back at Wes as he carried their bowls to the table, his sweats hanging low on his hips and his white T-shirt clinging to his muscled chest. Her mouth was watering, and it had nothing to do with the stir-fry.

Annie and Darcy could wait. The whole Bad Bachelors thing could wait. Another day wasn't going to make a lick of difference. For once, she wanted to forget her issues and indulge in things that made her feel good, like the old Remi used to.

"I feel like I know nothing about you," she said, taking a seat.

Wes sat across from her, filled their water glasses, and set the bottle down. "After all we've done tonight, you feel like you don't know anything about me?"

"Well, I now know *some* things." She laughed. "But I spilled my whole sordid past in the limo after the cocktail party and I haven't got anything in return."

"Ah, so it's an eye for an eye with you." He speared a piece of carrot on his fork. "What do you want to know? I'm an open book."

For some reason she didn't quite believe it. Wes came across easy and breezy, the funny guy with the quick smile and charming quips. But something told her that was all surface-level stuff. The veneer.

"What are you afraid of in life?"

Wes blinked. "You sure you don't have a background in investigative journalism. Geez, talk about jumping in with the hard hitters."

Never once had she asked a date anything meaningful like that. Usually it was all *What would you take to a desert island?* and *Where would you go if money was no object?* kind of questions. But something deep inside her wanted to connect with Wes. Wanted to know him beyond what he presented to the world. Maybe she'd been starved for connection for too long.

Or maybe it's that the whole "I like you" thing really means something.

More likely, it was that she'd opened up to him and she wanted to know whether he would do the same for her.

"I'm afraid people use me," he said. He reached for his water and took a gulp.

"People or person?"

His lip quirked. "What did you say last week? You didn't go back for seconds?"

"Something like that."

"Well, this was the same. I dated a girl in my early twenties who was a dancer—contemporary mostly, but she did ballet as well." He paused. "I thought she was it…and after three years, I asked her to move in with me, and she told me she couldn't keep living a lie. She said the only reason she'd stayed with me so long was because she was worried about losing the connection to my family if she broke up with me."

Ouch. Remi cringed. "That's brutal."

"When you have a powerful family, people sometimes pretend to be interested because they want something from you."

"Is that why you wanted to know what your mother said to me?"

"I was worried she was going to warn you away from the show. But yeah…I guess I wanted to see your reaction as well."

The words revealed a lot, even if his facial expression remained neutral. It wasn't hard to see why people wanted a piece of him. Although she couldn't imagine needing to pretend anything with Wes—everything he stirred in her was the real deal. Which was exactly why it'd been hard to keep her distance.

"I'm only after you for legitimate reasons," she said with a wink.

"Oh yeah?" His eyes roamed her hungrily. "What's that?"

"I had to see if the Anaconda was real." She couldn't even get through the sentence without breaking off into laughter. "Sorry, I couldn't resist."

"Laugh all you want, Remi. I'm going to make you pay for that later."

Remi reached for her drink, unable to wipe the smile off her face. She couldn't remember the last time she'd felt the excited frisson of a real connection. All she had to do was make sure she kept that feeling in check. This thing with Wes was still a bad decision and she couldn't afford to let it get out of hand. Indulging did *not* mean throwing all caution to the wind. They would have to keep it quiet, and she would still have to keep her heart under lock and key.

Chapter 18

"I think there's a lot more to Wes beneath the surface, and I can't say I got there in the short time we dated. Beware the charming smile—it's a locked door."

—StillDating

REMI WAS THE KIND OF PERSON WHO NEEDED TO WORK problems out of her system with some kind of physical activity. Action kept her mind calm enough to look at things with an objective eye—as much as was possible— and rehearsals for *Out of Bounds* had been kicking her butt on a daily basis.

That's why she'd decided to accept Annie's offer for a drink only two days after their blowup. Plus, she was hoping it would stop her friend from calling every couple of hours. She'd had to turn her phone off earlier that day because the notifications were driving her nuts. But that was Annie in a nutshell—the woman was like a dog with a bone when she wanted something.

Remi walked into the Williamsburg bar where they'd agreed to meet. She'd left the theater early for a remedial massage in the hopes it might help with some of the tightness in her calves that was causing issues with her jumps. There was nothing like the punishing touch of her massage therapist, Isla, to get things working the way they were supposed to.

Since this bar was only a few blocks away, Annie had offered to meet her there. It was unusual she was even out of work at this hour. Normally, Darcy and Remi had to pry her away from her laptop during the week. But she must have left early, because she was already perched on a stool with a cocktail in front of her when Remi arrived. Her shoulder-length, brown hair hung in a curtain across her face as she tapped furiously at her phone.

"Hey," Remi said as she walked over and slung her bag over the back of the barstool next to Annie.

"Oh, hey." Annie offered a tentative smile. "Thanks for agreeing to meet me."

"You didn't leave me a lot of choice," she replied as she took a seat. "People were starting to wonder if my phone was possessed."

"Sorry about that." Annie tucked her hair behind her ear, exposing a neat, single pearl stud. "I couldn't concentrate on work and I wanted to set things straight. I feel really bad about how things went down on Sunday."

Remi studied her friend for a moment. It was hard to believe this was the woman behind Bad Bachelors. In her white silk blouse and black pencil skirt, freckles dusting her nose where a pair of chunky black glasses sat, she looked totally unassuming. Gorgeous, but unassuming.

It made her want to laugh. The bar had several groups of men scattered around it—a couple of suits in one corner, a cluster of hipsters in another. A lone man with blond, surfer-style hair and beads around his neck chilled out at the end of a bar, nursing a beer. How many of them would want to know Annie's identity? That she was the "Dating Information Warrior" who created a platform for all their dirty laundry to be aired.

"I know I was wrong to keep secrets from you and especially for dragging Darcy into it," Annie said, pausing to take a delicate sip of her drink. "It's fine that you're pissed at me, but please don't be mad at her. She's sick over it and it's not her fault. *I* put her in that position."

Remi didn't want to soften, but the loyalty that Darcy and Annie had for each other was admirable. It was funny now though, looking back on Darcy's relationship with Reed knowing that Annie was partially responsible for the wedge that'd been driven between them before they worked everything out.

"I'm not pissed," Remi said. "I'm hurt."

In her family, lies were the worst sin you could commit. Her mother had always said that if she could own up to her actions, then nothing would ever get between them. Which was exactly why her gut was churning over keeping this from Wes.

"You have every right to be." Annie traced the wooden bar, her fingers catching on a small indentation. "I was so terrified of people finding out I figured the best course of action was silence. The only reason Darcy found out was because Reed tracked me down."

"How did he manage that?"

She laughed, but the sound was laced with bitterness. "I made a mistake. I was so blinded by worry that he was going to chew Darcy up and spit her out that I did something I shouldn't have. I attacked him and someone he cared about, and in the process, I left myself open. It was a stupid move."

Remi wasn't sure exactly what that meant, but ultimately, it didn't matter. What was done was done.

They paused as the bartender approached them and Remi ordered a diet Coke. Bert was coming to watch the *Out of Bounds* cast tomorrow, and she needed to be on her A game. But part of that had to include clearing her head of this issue with Annie.

"Are you going to talk to me about it now?" Remi asked.

Annie's eyes darted around. The bar wasn't yet busy, and nobody was within earshot. But she had that wild, paranoid look of someone who knew they had a reason to hide. "I need to know you're not going to pass any of this along."

That was a tall order, considering how Remi had found out. Her mind shifted to Wes, to the playful smile and his warm hands and the passion with which he approached everything in life.

By keeping this secret from him, they were starting something based on a lie.

Starting something? You slept with him once. You don't owe him anything.

But she did. She owed him for opening a door to the career she'd so desperately missed. And she owed him for believing in her when she didn't even believe in herself. Unfortunately, there were only two options at her disposal—lie to Wes and protect Annie or hand Annie over and lose a friendship.

Dammit. She was screwed no matter which way she turned.

"I won't say anything," she said reluctantly. No matter how hurt she was, there was too much history between them to decimate that relationship.

Without Darcy and Annie, Remi might never have found her feet in New York. They'd helped her acclimatize to her new home, given her companionship, and been an ear in her moments of overwhelming homesickness. Her first few months in New York were a dark time, and the two women had been her light.

"Thank you." Annie reached across the bar and grabbed Remi's hand. "I know I don't deserve it."

"Tell me what happened." Remi plucked the wedge of lemon from the rim of her drink and gave it a squeeze. "From the beginning."

"The site has…" Annie shook her head. "It's taken on a life of its own. It was never meant to get this big."

"Why did you start it?"

"Blind fury, I guess." She tucked her hair back behind her ear, even though it hadn't moved an inch since the last time she'd done it. "Obviously I was crushed after…"

The engagement that wasn't to be. Remi remembered it well, and it had given her the chance to support Annie in the same way Annie had supported her in the wake of her breakup and miscarriage.

"But I had this strange delayed reaction. I was fine for a while. Then Darcy's wedding fell through. More and more, I saw these beautiful, smart, talented women get bulldozed by relationships. They'd get swallowed up and broken down by men who treated them like they were disposable." Her eyes shimmered.

Annie didn't appear sad. Rather, fury burned brightly in her pursed lips and clenched hands. She wasn't the type of girl to lay down and accept defeat. To simply take whatever life threw at her. Hell no, she'd come out swinging. Always.

"And it occurred to me that some of the guys had a pattern—search, seduce, destroy." She ticked the items off her fingers. "They'd find women who caught their eye. Then they'd build them up and say all the right things only to walk away after getting what they wanted. The women who weren't getting hurt were the ones who knew that, either because they'd learned that lesson, or because they didn't place importance in traditional relationship goals."

It was true. Annie's assessment covered Remi's relationship with Alex to a T. He'd approached her after a day of rehearsals, and she'd been too star struck to decline his offer of a coffee. Over a few months, they'd met often, and he'd tell her how talented she was and how far she would go with the company. That one day, he knew they would be dancing together as principals.

It was the dream she'd clutched to her chest ever since she was a little girl. The ultimate ballet fantasy.

Then once the sex produced problems, he'd dropped her like a hot potato.

Ever since, Remi had approached sex from a very different angle. It was something to be enjoyed, a way to blow off steam. But it meant nothing...until Wes.

"And that's even before you get into the more insidious

behavior. The really nasty, damaging stuff like pigging and stealthing." Annie shook her head, looking as though she might be sick. "Did you know there are groups of men who get a woman to agree to have sex with them and remove the condom in stealth without her permission exposing her to unwanted pregnancy and STDs? *This* is what women are facing in the dating world today. It's dangerous, and we need a way to warn one another."

Remi had no idea how to respond. It *was* a disgusting and unsafe world in some corners of the dating jungle.

"I wondered if there was a way to let people know *before* they got into a relationship what might be in store for them," Annie said. "I know not all men are bad. And I don't, despite what a lot of people have said, hate them."

She paused as a gentleman walked past, his eyes lingering with appreciation on them both. Annie took the break in conversation as a chance to order another drink.

"So the problem we have," Annie continued, "is that the ones who hurt you the most are able to do it because they know how to act like the good guys. I wanted to create something to shift that power. I figure, if women won't spend thirty dollars on a lipstick without checking the reviews, then why should they open their hearts up to men without the same reassurance that they're making a good decision?"

It was a damn good point. And Remi had embraced Bad Bachelors in the beginning, using it to avoid men who might be tempted to call after a steamy night— possibly the opposite of how it was used by most women, but it worked for her. It offered some protection in a landscape where women were vulnerable.

"I understand that." Remi bobbed her head. "But people aren't products. How can you classify something as complex as a human with five stars? And even then, positive reviews don't always have a positive outcome for the person."

Wes was the perfect example of that.

"Sex is…" Remi shook her head, trying to find the right words. "Complicated."

"I know." Annie toyed with the stem of her cocktail glass. "And early on, before it blew up, I had moments where I wondered if I'd done this appalling thing. Was I taking everything the internet made terrible about human interaction and fueling it?"

"People are vicious behind their computer screens," Remi said. She'd seen it plenty of times reading the comments on a YouTube video or at the bottom of an article or blog post. Reviews for products like books or makeup could be just as bad; people bled snark and judgment onto their keyboards in a way that would *never* happen face-to-face.

"That worried me at first." She sighed. "Then I got an email from a woman who was divorced. She'd managed to walk away from an abusive relationship after putting up with constant gaslighting and physical abuse. She told me that she never thought she'd be able to date again. She was too scared of meeting someone like her ex-husband and getting trapped a second time."

Remi's chest squeezed. "That's awful."

"She said the app really helped her find the confidence to try again. A guy she worked with asked her out, and he had good reviews. So she went on a few dates with him. Now the relationship didn't work out, because they didn't have much in common, but she said that she would never have been able to take that step if it wasn't for the app giving her some confidence that she knew what she was getting herself into." Annie bit down on her lip. "I'll admit it, Bad Bachelors started as a coping mechanism. But you, me, and Darcy had *all* experienced pain, and I wanted to see if there was a way to help others avoid it."

"And what about the good guys who get caught up in it?" Remi asked.

"I ended up changing the way it works, so men have to connect their Facebook accounts. It was the only way I could stop myself from getting sued." Her hand came up to her ear and she twisted the pearl stud around. "But anyone whose profile was created before that would still be on there. I couldn't delete everything and start from scratch. I can only make sure the site is built to weed out the crap. The algorithm looks for indicators of fake reviews, and I read every email claiming a review is fake. But I won't shut the site down, not when I know it does good things for a lot of women."

"If you believe in it so much, then why don't you come forward?"

Annie swiveled on her barstool and looked out into the bar. It was getting busier now, more groups of people had come in and the noise level was rising. The sound of laughter and conversation was mixed with the rattling of ice cubes in the bartender's cocktail shaker. The scene was vibrant and warm. Fun. Nothing like the dark shadows of their conversation.

"Could you imagine what would happen to me?" Annie looked at her. "I'd be outed within hours. I have no doubt that some of the people who send me threats would be crazy enough to show up on my doorstep. I'm doing something that makes people angry. The truth tends to have that affect."

Remi wasn't sure how to feel. She understood Annie's motivations and her fears, she understood the desire to do something good for her gender. And hearing her stories about the women she'd helped certainly made her believe there was some good coming from Bad Bachelors. But the system Annie had created was also primed for abuse, it brought private information into the public—things which should exist for two people behind closed doors were suddenly detailed for the world to see.

"So you're going to keep Bad Bachelors alive?" she asked. She lowered her voice, because there were people coming closer to them now, crowding them.

"I am." She nodded. "The site is important. It's helping people. I know some men might get caught in the crosshairs, like Wes, but it's helping more people than it's hurting."

Remi wasn't so sure about that.

"I know it's a burden to have this information," Annie said. "That was another reason I didn't want people to know. It's a tough secret to keep and I understand I'm asking a lot. But you know me, Remi. I believe in the good that this site does even if it didn't start out that way."

"I'm sure you do believe it."

"So we're still friends?" Annie's eyes were wide and

pleading. And it wasn't a ploy to ensure her secret was safe. They *were* friends. Real friends.

"Of course." Remi sighed. "I don't agree with everything you've done, but I understand."

She rolled her shoulders back. Everything hurt—her body, her head, her heart. Annie was right—this secret was a burden. But she'd committed to keeping it, so that meant sucking it up and moving on.

Wes let himself into the theater while it was still dark outside, well before anyone else was due to arrive. He flicked on the lights, juggling his laptop bag and takeout coffee cup in his free hand. The closer they got to opening night, the more there was to do. He'd met with the bank yesterday, to discuss loans for the show should things fall through with Bert. The outcome was bleak. Even leveraging himself to the hilt, things would be tight. He'd need to take a loan against his apartment to make it happen, not to mention making a quick sale on his car. With everything balancing on a knife's edge, it was critical today went well.

He headed down the steps and set himself up in the front row, digging his laptop out of his bag and settling in to answer some emails. He had information to pull together for the marketing and PR intern who was helping them with the show. The graphic designer had also sent through the artwork for the show's poster and social media banners, which required his sign-off. Once everyone arrived this morning, Wes would rev the cast up and get them wired to give Bert Soole the best possible showing.

If today didn't go well, this hurtling train would be headed straight into a brick wall.

At the sound of footsteps behind him, Wes turned to see Lilah walking down the aisle. She had her hands tucked into the pockets of her jacket, her sports bag bumping against her hip.

"You're here early," he said. "Are you hoping for some extra warm-up time?"

"Yeah." She didn't quite meet his eye.

Wes immediately went on high alert. Something about her body language seemed off—like a tension in her muscles that wasn't the same as what came from hours of rehearsals and training. She dropped her bag a few seats away but made no move to change out of her boots and into her ballet shoes.

"What do you want to say?" he asked.

She looked up, her lips popping open into a shape of surprise. "How did you know I wanted to talk?"

"I've known you a long time, Lilah. You're not exactly covert with your feelings." She never had been. At least, not to Wes. "What's bothering you? Are you concerned about the investor visit today?"

"It's not that." She shook her head. Lilah crackled her knuckles, the popping sound like miniature gunshots in the quiet theater.

"Do I have to drag it out of you?" he asked, folding his laptop closed so she knew she had his full attention.

"I heard you," she said. Her face didn't reveal much, but her voice wavered with something dark—hurt, maybe. Or shame.

He frowned. "You heard me what?"

"I heard you with Remi. In the dressing rooms." She paused. "I came here on Sunday to make sure I had the address right and I found the entrance unlocked. When I came in I heard…"

Everything ground to a halt—his breath, his heart. His mind. For a few seconds, there was nothing but blank disbelief.

"You're sleeping with her," she finally said, shaking her head. "I knew it must be something like that. I kept watching her dance, watching her make these silly mistakes and fumble over things she shouldn't, and I had no idea why you chose her over me."

Questions crowded his mind, fighting to be the first one out of his mouth. How was it that every single time he thought he'd taken a step forward, something would slam into him without warning? There was always another hurdle.

"Are you going to deny it?" she asked, her lips pursed.

"No." He shook his head. "We're all adults here, so I feel no need to explain myself or my choices when it comes to something private like that."

"How is it private if you're doing it here?" Her voice was edged with hurt. It was obvious Lilah thought the sex was a component in him hiring Remi and that she had been denied an opportunity which was given to someone she didn't deem worthy.

"You're right. It was absolutely inappropriate." He wouldn't argue on that point—it'd been reckless. Desire had swept him up and encouraged him to forget about the right way of doing things. He wasn't going to apologize for sleeping with Remi, only for where it had taken place. "I didn't realize anyone was here, and even still, we should have taken it elsewhere."

"I didn't think your show would have a casting couch, Wes. I really didn't." She shook her head. "Is that what's required to get ahead in this industry?"

"No, of course not. My being with Remi has nothing to do with *Out of Bounds*."

"Then what do I need to do? I work *so* hard. I push myself to the point of exhaustion, hoping that I'll make it. People keep telling me to give more, to try again." Her eyes glimmered and a tear dropped onto her cheek, snaking down the side of her face and clinging to the edge of her lip. "I auditioned because I believe in this show. I believed you could help me with my career. And then I find out I'm stuck in the corps because you don't want to fuck me?"

He cringed. This situation needed to be handled delicately. Remi was the better choice for the lead role regardless of his attraction to her. Sure, she had more baggage than a family going on vacation. And yes, she'd been a bit rusty at the start. But she'd bounced back quicker than most people would have in her situation. It was testament not only to her skill but to her perseverance and work ethic. In addition, she had that sparkle, that x factor. They'd simply needed to unearth it. Together.

"Lilah, let me be clear. I hired Remi for her talent. She's an incredible dancer, and I stand by my choice." He took a second to force air into his lungs, to keep his voice steady. "I know she's had a few issues with the choreography, but I have been working with her behind the scenes, as has Sadie. The fact that I put you in the corps does not mean I don't see your potential. But the fact is, I feel you're both in the right roles for this production."

Lilah's nostrils flared and her cheeks were pink, but she stayed silent.

"Now, my relationship with her has nothing to do with the show. It was not a factor in her audition or any decisions I made about this show."

"Then why have you kept it a secret?" Her distrust was palpable.

The night Remi had come back to his place, they'd had dinner, gone back to bed, and lost themselves in each other until after midnight. Then he'd driven her home because she didn't have her gear for the following morning. The drive home had given him time to think.

They'd set no boundaries, made no promises other than to keep it quiet. He understood her reasoning, and he agreed. What they did after hours was none of anyone's business.

You've made it their business by not being discreet.

It was an epic slipup.

He tried to find the right words, to find the balance between honesty and diffusing the situation. "It's something that happened recently, and we don't have a label for it. I also don't make a habit of talking about my sex life. Everyone else seems to do enough of that."

"Right."

"Why did you wait until now to confront me?"

"I needed to sort it out in my head first." Lilah's eyes lowered and she sucked on her bottom lip. "You know, your mother once told me that only people who seize every opportunity like it's their last will survive in this industry. And I've done that. I've been to audition after audition after audition. I avoid going out with my friends so I can train or so I can stay away from bad food. I have sacrificed everything I can think to sacrifice."

"Being a professional dancer means dealing with a lot of rejection, Lilah. You know that. Some people take longer to blossom than others." He rubbed his hands down his thighs, nerves making his palms sweaty. "You're only twenty-three. You have time to find your feet."

"No one is giving me a chance," she said through gritted teeth.

Wes wanted to point out that he wasn't *so* desperate for dancers that he hired her simply because she knew how to tie her pointe shoes. He had given her chance. Obviously, it wasn't the chance she thought she deserved.

"*I'm* giving you a chance," he said. "After this, you'll have more professional work under your belt and you know I'll sing your praises."

"It's not enough." She shook her head. "I want the lead role."

A cold, icy unease settled in the pit of his stomach. "*Out of Bounds* already has a lead dancer."

"You're in charge of the show, so you can change that." Her voice was wire tight, high pitched. "You can put *me* in that role. I'm her alternate. I know the choreography."

The tone of her voice told him that she wasn't asking or suggesting.

"I'm not firing Remi," he said, trying not to lose his cool. But his control was slipping, the muscles in his jaw tensed and his fingers curled.

"You're going to make me say it, aren't you?" she said. She bounced on her toes, her arms wrapped around herself.

"Say what, Lilah?" The words came out sharp-edged with frustration.

"Given the problems you've had finding investors for this show due to how public your sex life is, I'm sure people would be interested in knowing that you're sleeping with a cast member." The threat was wobbly and uncertain. She didn't want to be threatening him, from what he could see, so she must have believed it to be her only option.

"Don't do this, Lilah." He drew a breath to ground himself. Flying off the handle would not help the situation. "You can't retrieve a threat once you've made it."

Her eyes were big and round, and red rimmed. "I have to. This career is the only thing I've ever wanted, and it's clear that hard work isn't enough."

He shut his eyes for a moment, trying to quell the anger rising up hot and fast, ready to erupt. "If you're going to do it, then don't be a fucking chicken about it. Spell it out for me."

"I want you to get rid of Remi and put me in her role or else I'll go the press and tell them you're hiring women in order to sleep with them."

"You mean, you'll go to the press and lie," he bit out. "Because that's what it is. I would *never* abuse my power to lure someone into bed."

Guilt flashed across Lilah's face, but it was gone in an instant. "I guess that will be for the public to decide."

Behind them, the door to the theater banged open

and the sound of tinkling laughter swept through the space. He could pick out Remi's voice immediately, the way her words ended in that familiar, soft *ah* sound contrasted against her *pas de deux* partner Angelo's harder Bronx accent.

"I'm not going to screw up our chance today," Lilah said. "I know we need the investor's support. But I want an answer tomorrow."

"How kind of you," he drawled.

She stared at him for a moment, as if she had something more to say but Angelo's booming laughter made them both jump. She grabbed her things and headed away, her footsteps silent. Maybe he should have lied, but it wasn't in him.

Firing your lead dancer isn't in you either.

Fuck. What was he supposed to do? His gut told him this problem wouldn't go away if he simply ignored it. Part of him wondered if the news of him sleeping with Remi would be such a big deal. Sure, within company ranks, it could cause problems. Jealousy and the breakdown of relationships could really mess with a production schedule, not to mention a lover's quarrel could affect onstage performance. But this was *his* show. His rules.

Still, as much as he knew being with a dancer in his show wasn't a problem on the surface, how would the rest of the world see it? Would he be able to shake the stigma of his "casting couch" in light of the abhorrent behavior rife in the entertainment industry? So many men in power *did* abuse their positions.

Regardless of the fact that it was consensual and unrelated to their work, and that there would be no one to corroborate Lilah's story, it could very well ruin everything. Even if Remi came out to confirm that their relationship hadn't started on nefarious grounds, her career could be devastated as well as his. If she went on to audition for another company, they might look at her as the girl who tried to sleep her way to the top. And who would want to work for him?

He needed to make a decision: betray Remi and save his show—and potentially her career—or risk it all. Whichever way he went, it would be the best of a truly rotten bunch.

Exhaustion tugged at the edges of Remi's mind. Her brain wanted to explode from being so full. Her stress over the Annie situation and guilt about not telling Wes was swirling behind every thought. The knowledge that the future of the show was riding on her performance for Bert Soole's visit today had her wound tighter than a clock. And then there was the little distraction of what to do about Wes.

Or the *big* distraction as the case was.

"Yo, Remi." Angelo's deep voice shook her out of her thoughts. "I feel like I'm dancin' with a sack of potatoes here."

"Sorry, sorry," she muttered. She removed herself from his grip and shook her arms out. "I was early on that turn."

She stepped back into place, waiting for the warmth of Angelo at her back to tell her when to go. When his hands came to her waist, she bent her knees and sprang up, feet beating back and forth until she landed soft as a feather. Then she stepped forward, prepared, and launched into a triple pirouette, dipping low into an *arabesque penché* as Angelo slowly rotated them around.

"Much better!" Sadie called from the front row. "But I want to see it again. Softer with your hands, Angelo. I don't want to see your fingers digging into her. Make it look easy."

"Isn't that always the fuckin' motto?" Angelo said with a good-natured roll of his eyes. "Make it look easy. I'd love to see a weight lifter make it look easy."

"Hey." Remi nudged him with her elbow. "Who you calling fat?"

"You're not fat, baby." He pinched her thigh. "You're full of muscle."

With his longish black hair, full sleeve of tattoos, and a piercing through his left brow, Angelo looked nothing like the men she'd danced with growing up. But that was the beauty of *Out of Bounds*—Wes had assembled a cast of people who were unique. Their dancers were like a band of talented misfits, those that didn't fit the bunhead mold.

Sadie started the track again. Though many of the moves were traditional in nature, the soundtrack they'd chosen was anything but. A heavy-bass dubstep beat burst from the speakers and Remi got into position again.

"One, two, three." Sadie clapped her hands together with each beat, her eyes tracking them as they moved across the stage. "That's it, Remi. Higher! Two, three, and again."

Sweat ran down the back of her spine, making the already-clingy fabric of her black leotard adhere to her skin. Her pointe shoes knocked against the floor, allowing her to glide in *bourrée en couru*, the small, fluttering steps taking her across the stage, with Angelo leaping soundlessly behind her. She caught the flash of movement, counted his *grand jetés*. One, two, three.

"Turn, turn, and down," Sadie called the steps out, using her hands to emphasize the beats. "Yes, soft arms. Perfect, Remi!"

Today it felt right. Like the steps had finally been imprinted on her mind. Her muscles were strong and pliable, her feet curved and steady. The music flowed through her veins in that magical way that'd she'd missed with all her heart.

Yes.

She looked up, her gaze cast high into the audience over her extended right arm. Hands and wrists soft, eyes steady. She swept down over her pointed leg, and then around following the curve of music. When she came back up, she saw Wes standing in the front, watching her. His arms were folded tight over his chest, his blues eyes wide and penetrating.

Angelo came up behind her, wrapped his arms around her waist, and pressed his face to her neck.

Sadie clapped. "Love that feeling, Angelo!"

Then he swept her up and back, her spine curved over his shoulder as she let her head and arms fall behind her. When he brought her down, she was turned to face her partner—away from Wes's intense stare—her leg came up. Angelo hooked his arm under her knee and then she was in the air again, flying. Floating. Turning.

The emotional up-and-down movement of the dance mimicked the thoughts dipping and soaring in her head. Confused as she might be, this feeling was like returning to family after years of being away. It was like the blast of warm air after coming in from the cold. The stage was solid beneath her feet when Angelo brought her down and tears pricked at the backs of her eyes. It felt so good to be home.

"That was magnificent!" Sadie hopped up onto the stage and rushed over to them, her blue and purple hair glimmering under the stage lights. "You two…ugh. So damn good. That was the best I've seen you do it."

Remi pressed her hands to her lips, the feeling of relief sweeping through her like a summer storm—heavy and thick, like the air right before it broke.

"No tears, baby. You've nailed it." Angelo slung an arm around her neck. "Man, that was better than sex."

Sadie threw her head back and laughed. "How would your boyfriend feel about you saying that, huh?"

"Oh, he knows." Angelo grinned. "Ballet will *always* come before sex."

Remi's eyes drifted to where Wes stood, unmoving. She waited a moment for him to chime in, to support Sadie's encouragement and share in their celebratory moment. But he hung back, looking on like an outsider.

A strange, old feeling gripped Remi's heart.

Don't be paranoid. There's a lot riding on today. He's probably stressed out of his mind.

She'd come to realize that Wes locked a lot of those feelings up, shielding the cast from the stresses he shouldered as director. He was like the head of their strange, misfit family, the protective leader not wanting anyone to see him worry.

But the tension in his face, the brittle way his folded arms barred his chest, put a barrier between them.

It's nothing to do with you. Just dance your heart out today and let that be enough.

Chapter 19

"I dated Wes not long after he'd broken up with his teenage sweetheart, so I guess you could say I was the rebound girl. I liked him a lot, but he wouldn't open up. And no relationship can thrive on good sex alone."

—NeverTheSlamDunk

REMI STEPPED BACK INTO DOWNWARD DOG, FEELING THE pull in her calves and hamstrings as she pressed her heels into her yoga mat. Most ballerinas at her company back home had done Pilates or yoga every day to maintain flexibility and to work out the kinks created by hours of rehearsals. For some reason, that habit had stuck with her even when she wasn't dancing.

It'd been a stress reliever. The only way to quiet her mind and give her reprieve from the tears that'd come fast and frequent back then.

Now it was her time to reflect on the day. And oh, what a day it had been.

Remi grinned into the curtain of blond hair that pooled on the mat in front of her. It was like something had finally clicked. When nerves had overtaken her upon seeing Bert Soole walk into the theater, she'd leaned on Wes's trick, pretending she was demonstrating for a student—no pressure, no expectation. It'd freed her mind of the too-loud doubt monsters and allowed her to simply fall into the music.

She'd nailed it, and the thunderous applause from the older man was better than any standing ovation she'd ever received.

Remi moved through her yoga poses until she came to corpse pose, laying on her back with her eyes closed. She took a few breaths and then pushed up into her final seated position to finish the session.

It was like she'd thrown herself back into the past. She felt good. *So* good. Like she'd recaptured the joy from before her life had gone to hell.

She stood and rolled up her mat, tucking it under one arm as she went to the kitchen to get a glass of water. Her mail sat in a small heap on the kitchen counter, a yellow parcel postmarked from Australia drawing her eye. The only people from back home who sent her anything were her parents.

Remi already knew what would be inside. She tore at the thick tape sealing the flap of the envelope and dug her hand inside. Her fingers brushed something soft and luxurious, a small velvet pouch that contained clinking items.

The drawstring cord was soft beneath her fingers, and it looked handwoven. Twine in shades of purple, blue, and a soft, buttery yellow were braided tightly, so the colors almost blended into one. Inside the pouch were three stones—purple, blue, and yellow, to match the twine. Her mother had included a handwritten note.

My little sunburst,

I know you think I'm a crazy old lady who believes rocks are magical, but I'm thinking of you now, and this is all I can do to help since I know nothing about your ballet world.

Amethyst—will help you be calm and balanced before your big show.

Citrine—will help you manifest your biggest and brightest goals.

Fluorite—will ward off negative energy, and this blue just looks pretty too.

Carry them around, and even if you don't believe they'll do anything, let them remind you that I am thinking of you always.

Love, Opal

A smile curved Remi's lips. Her mother never signed her letters, emails, or messages by any maternal name. It was always *Opal.* Because she was, before anything else, herself. Not a mother or a wife or a sister or a daughter. Just Opal.

For a long time, it had made Remi wonder if Opal hadn't wanted to be a mother. The kids she'd danced with had the type of helicopter parents who were at every class, every rehearsal, every recital, and every competition. They stood close by, always taking notes, ready to retie a ribbon or tame unruly hair, ready to cheer a win and commiserate a loss.

Remi's grandmother had been that person for her,

but still the questions came. Where's your mother? What time are your parents arriving? Who's in the audience for you today?

But this was how Opal showed her love, in something that had personal meaning to her. In something tangible that Remi could rub between her fingers. She plucked the piece of polished amethyst from the pouch and rolled it in her palm, enjoying the cool weight against her warm skin.

As Remi walked back out of the kitchen, her phone pinged across the room. A text.

WES: I'm in your neck of the woods. Can I come by?

She swallowed, her heart immediately kicking up a notch. They'd barely spoken today, or since the night they'd spent together. He'd been occupied with their investor, introducing the man to Sadie, their marketing intern, and several of the dancers, but not her.

You met him at the cocktail party. Wes was simply trying to be fair.

REMI: Sure. Buzz the intercom and I'll let you up.
WES: Be there in 5.

Remi raced through the apartment and had the speediest of showers, allowing herself only enough time to wash the day from her skin and to scent her body with something sweet.

"You'd shower for anyone that was coming over,"

she said to her reflection in the foggy bathroom mirror. "No one wants to smell your sweat."

But those reasonable words did little to ease the excited flutter in her stomach. A flutter that told her she was speaking utter crap. She *knew* that Wes wasn't like anyone else coming to visit, that she'd showered and lathered herself in strawberry-scented body gel because she hoped he'd get close enough to notice it.

She changed into something soft and subtle, worn jeans with busted knees and a waistband that sat low on her hips, with a fitted gray T-shirt that made her boobs look good. The intercom buzzed as she was blasting her hair dry.

Remi raced over to the receiver and skidded to a stop. "Hello?"

"It's me."

Desire unfurled in her stomach at his deep baritone, so smooth and warm and rich. Like a well-aged whiskey. *It's me.* There was an intimacy in the lack of identification. Like him coming to her apartment was a regular thing. *Their* thing.

"Come on up." She released the lock and smoothed her hands down the front of her top.

A few minutes later, there was a knock. Sucking in a breath, she steadied herself as she wrapped a hand around the knob and pulled the door open. He might be coming to talk about work, not necessarily to ravish her against the living-room wall.

"Hi."

His hair was damp, blackened by the rain, and he'd pushed it back from his face. The dark leather jacket was spattered with dots, and indigo jeans clung to his long, muscular legs. All that darkness made his blue eyes look glowing and otherworldly. He could have been the intoxicating, moody antihero of a movie.

Remi stepped back and motioned for him to come inside, her eyes stuck on him as he shrugged out of his jacket.

"I hope I wasn't interrupting anything," he said, hanging it on the coat stand by her door. It looked out of place next to her rose-colored wool coat and the rainbow-checked scarf.

"Not at all. I was going through my evening routine. Yoga, ice buckets. You know the drill." Suddenly she wasn't sure what to do with her hands. "Can I get you a coffee?"

"I'm fine."

The silence stretched on, not quite awkward but not totally comfortable either. Like their relationship. They were in that weird no-man's land between casual sex and something that couldn't be confined to a label.

"Do you collect gemstones?" he asked, looking at where her mother's gift sat on the counter.

"Ah, no. These were an 'I'm thinking of you' present from home." She picked up the piece of citrine and handed it to him. "Hippie parents, remember?"

"Pretty." He turned the stone over, examining it from all angles. "What's this one supposed to do?"

"Help manifest my dreams and goals." She laughed. "It must have worked, because it arrived today and I kicked butt onstage. Good timing, right?"

"Hmm." He nodded.

For once, Wes wasn't full of words and smiles; he seemed uneasy. Withdrawn.

"What did Bert say after you two left this afternoon?" she prodded.

"He loved it." Wes put the stone back on the table and finally met her eyes. "Said it was one of the most creative pieces of work he's seen in a long time. He loved the soundtrack, thought the combination of Marsha's hip-hop piece with your *grand pas de deux* was unique and exciting. He loved that it's not all pointe work, that we've got some barefoot contemporary as well."

"That's wonderful." She grabbed his shoulders and squeezed. "So he said yes? We've got the go-ahead?"

Wes enclosed her hands in his. "He said yes."

Relief tore through her. She'd done enough to help them get the show across the line, and she hadn't let Wes or her castmates down. "Oh my God, that's such a good feeling." A laugh burst from her lips. "I'm glad you came to tell me. I've been on tenterhooks since you walked out of the theater. Everyone was."

The atmosphere had been electric. Sadie couldn't concentrate, the dancers had been jittering with nervous energy. But they knew it had gone well, the collective feeling was buoyed, and they were quick to congratulate one another on giving good performances, considering rehearsals were still under way. That was the magic of an audience. Seeing the delight on someone's face as they watched could breathe life into the dancers.

"Why aren't you bouncing off the walls, Wes? You should be pirouetting all over the place." She laughed. "We did it!"

Without warning, he crashed his lips down to hers, making her stumble back against the couch. All the excitement that'd been burning bright a second ago turned from sunshine to flame. His hands were in her hair, his lips coaxing hers open. He tasted of mint and rain, smelled as heavy and dark as a thunderstorm.

"God, you smell good." He moaned into her neck, his hand coming up under her T-shirt to palm her breast. "Like a goddam strawberry sundae."

Her head dropped back as he feasted on her skin, his stubble scratching with each searing kiss. She fisted her hands in his shirt, trying to keep her balance as he pinned her to the back of the couch.

Her brain scrambled, sifting through the mixed messages. One minute, Wes was distant and closed off; the next, he was on her, his touch burning her up. Should they be doing this again? Usually Remi went into something with rules and a plan firmly in place. One night, maybe two or three. No commitment.

But the way he was kissing her now—like it was the key to shared survival—overrode sensible thought.

"Wes," she sighed as he pushed his other hand underneath her T-shirt and felt around the back, growling in frustration. "Front closure," she gasped.

He fumbled with the clasp of her bra, finally wrenching it open with a satisfying snap. Then they were skin to skin, his palms at her breasts, thumbs brushing her nipples. Turning her on so hard she had to shut her eyes, giving her brain the ability to focus only on what mattered. Her hands were damp from the rain in his hair, but she wouldn't let go as he lowered his head to her chest.

"Yes." The word hissed out between her front teeth as he sucked on her.

He planted his hands on her hips and hoisted her up onto the back of the couch, roughly nudging her legs apart with his thighs so he could get closer. She hung on because there was no other option. This wasn't the slow, sensual seduction she'd experienced at his place on the weekend. Nor was it the sexy, ever-so-dirty doggy style they'd had in the dressing room. This was something else entirely.

He bit softly down on her nipple, and she cried out, tugged his hair so hard it made him grunt. This was furious sex. A primal connection edged with feral passion. Wild and out of control, risky and yet perfectly natural, like all moments had led her to this point.

His hand cupped her through her jeans, the heel of his palm grinding against her sex. It wasn't enough. "Undress me," she whispered. "I want to feel it properly."

Goddammit. What the hell was he doing right now?

Wes tore at her clothes, yanking her T-shirt up over her head and shoving the open bra from her shoulders. She pushed off the couch and her shaking hands worked at the buttons on her jeans. Soon, they were sliding down her hips, and he tugged her panties down too, worried that if he didn't take her quickly enough, all this perfection might evaporate into a puff of smoke and bad dreams.

You're supposed to be firing her.

But he didn't want to. Not after watching her today when she'd proved him so right his heart had hammered against his rib cage. Watching her had been like taking a peek into her soul—it was raw. Honest. Emotional. All the things he'd seen from the very start. She was like a bottle of champagne that had been shaken and uncorked, fizzing and wonderful.

Her hands were at the hem of his T-shirt, yanking the fabric up and trapping his arms above his head. Her nails scratched his stomach as she grasped for the fly of his jeans, leaving a small, pink line across his skin. The slight flash of pain only served to amplify everything else—the scent of strawberries on her skin and the intoxicating blackness of her eyes. She yanked the jeans over his hips, taking his underwear with them, until they both stood naked in her living room.

"Bedroom. Now." She turned to direct him, but he grabbed her, pulling her close so that they were lined up front to front. Her breasts pressed against his chest, her pebbled nipples brushing over him in a way that made fire shoot through his veins.

"Are you on the pill?" he asked, pressing his forehead to hers. "I'm clean."

"I am…but…" Her eyes fluttered shut, the breath whooshing out of her mouth. "We shouldn't…"

He cupped her face, his thumbs brushing her cheekbones. "It's fine. You're right. Let's be safe."

A shaky smile pulled at her lips, the furious pace slowing to something gentler. Softer. "Sorry. I want to be careful."

"Of course." He pressed his lips to hers, showing

her that he belonged to her for tonight. However she wanted him, he was hers. "So do I."

She led him to the bedroom, her fingers interlaced with his, and this time they stepped slowly. Outside, a siren wailed, getting louder and louder before fading as an emergency vehicle raced past. She flicked on the lamp at her bedside table, and a pinkish glow illuminated the room. His eyes immediately snagged on her bed—on the gold headboard that was begging to have wrists tied to it.

"I've never brought anyone back here before," she said.

Aside from the bed and side table, a simple chest of drawers was the only furniture in the room. Atop it was her ballet bag, the flap open so he could see a pair of pointe shoes sticking out. Another two pairs sat next to it, along with a pile of pink ribbon and scissors and a bottle of glue. Tools of her trade.

She wound her arms around his neck and pressed up onto her toes so she could line her mouth up to his. "I'm glad you're here."

Guilt stabbed him in the gut. They should be talking, not having sex. A huge black cloud loomed over them, and Wes had no idea what he was going to do. But all he wanted right now was to drown in this amazing woman, to entwine himself with her. He wanted to fall asleep with her hands pressed to his chest and his nose buried in her hair because she made him feel whole and good and like everything would be okay.

He stroked a hand up and down her back, tracing her spine with his fingertips as they kissed. Slow this time. Gentle and exploratory. Remi stepped back and pulled Wes with her, guiding him toward the bed. She let go only long enough to draw the covers back and grab a condom before her hand returned to his—fingers encircling his wrist—as she silently asked him to follow.

You shouldn't be doing this.

But he had no hope of stopping. His brain was outnumbered by every other part of him—the primal parts and the soft, emotional parts he didn't often call on. With her head against the crisp, white pillow, she looked like an angel reclining into a cloud. Gold hair cushioned her head, and her wide, brown eyes sucked him in.

"You're about to say something corny," she said with a wicked smile. *That* was what hooked him every damn time with her. The little contradiction—hardness beneath the soft, burning heat beneath the cool, still surface. Layers of her.

"Am I now?" He lowered himself over her, settling between her legs.

"Uh-huh. Usually you look at me like you're starving, but tonight you've gone all soft."

He rocked against her, brushing his very hard cock over her inner thigh. "I think you might be mistaken."

"Well, there's definitely no softness here." Her hand reached up to touch his face. "But here…well, that's a whole other story."

Shit. It terrified him to think she could read him so easily. While he'd always prided himself on having that same skill, part of the reason he'd cultivated it was so he could control how others saw him. He was never able to let the stress of working with his family show to anyone at the Evans Ballet School. Airing dirty laundry was high up on his mother's list of punishable offenses.

"You want me to look rougher?" He shook the unsettling thoughts from his head and leaned back, reaching down to grab himself. Playing a role was easier than trying to decipher what this all meant. "You want me to look like I'm a wolf and you're Little Red Riding Hood?"

He ran his fisted hand up and down his length, eyeing the condom still gripped between her fingers. It'd been stupid to suggest they didn't use it, but he'd been so damn caught up in her. In them. It felt like they had years between them instead of weeks.

Her lashes fluttered as she watched the movement of his fist, her lips falling open. Words forgotten.

"Cat got your tongue?" he teased, holding his other hand out.

She handed over the condom and watched as he tore the packet open. Then he tossed it aside and rolled the rubber along his cock, taking his time to draw out the anticipation. When he was protected, he leaned back down and planted a hand on either side of her head.

"It's hard to watch you and talk at the same time," she said, an embarrassed half smile quirking the corner of her lips. "I'm usually good at multitasking too."

"I don't want you doing that now." He lowered his head to hers, touching his lips to her nose. "I want you focused on how good I make you feel. How good *we* feel."

Dammit, what the hell was wrong with him? *We. Us.* They weren't words he should have been using.

"That won't be hard." She rolled her hips up against him, encouraging him to press harder between her legs. "I always feel like that when you're around, despite my better judgment."

The words were like a sledgehammer to his solar plexus. How did she slay him like that? It'd taken her a while to trust that his intentions were good. That he truly meant what he said. And now he had her, nothing between them, and he didn't deserve it.

Nothing between you? Yeah right.

He couldn't deal with that right now. His brain had only so much space, and tonight, he wanted to fill it with the best things. With how he *wanted* to act, instead of how he was being forced to act. With the fantasy that they could be together, even though he was certain he'd lose her.

The finality of it rattled him.

"Stop staring at me like you're trying to figure me out," she said, grabbing the sides of his face. "Just kiss me."

So he did. He sank down into her, his hands sliding under her body so he could hold her tight as he moved his hips against hers. When it felt right, he pushed forward, burying himself inside her, rewarded with her sharp gasp so close to his ear that he felt it right down to his toes.

He rocked back and forth, her pelvis tilting up to let him slide in deep. Each thrust gave him something new to revel over—the feel of her silky hair brushing his hands, the hot breath against his neck, the flutter of her sooty lashes. Every damn detail was more beautiful than the last.

"I like you," she whispered into his ear as her thighs clenched around his hips. He smothered her words with a kiss, pushing into her harder and faster, chasing the wave of her pleasure. The second her soft, little mews turned to gasping cries, he followed her over the edge.

———————

Later, Wes cleaned himself up and came back to the bed. Remi immediately scooted over and curled into his side, her head resting on his chest while her hand toyed with the elastic of his boxer briefs.

"Sorry about before," she said. "I didn't want to ruin the mood with the whole condom thing."

"You were right to say it. I lost my head." He smoothed his hand over her hair, taming the little wisps of spun gold that glowed in the lamplight. Outside, the sky had turned an even darker shade of indigo.

"I guess I should feel proud that I can make the great Wes Evans lose his head."

He frowned. "I know my sex life seems to be some kind of torrid zoo exhibit at the moment, but when I'm with you, I don't think about any of that. There's no one else."

It was like the "before" of his life didn't even exist. Remi had the power to blank the past from his mind, to erase the memory of all the fun but mindless sex he'd had through his twenties. She even hushed the more meaningful aspects of his past, the bits that were like faded bruises.

"You're a lot more serious than you let on," she said, looking up at him. Her lashes cast shadows onto her cheeks, her eyes dark and unreadable in the low lighting.

"I am," he admitted. It was so easy to play the removed Mr. Genial that he hadn't even realized he'd been doing it until Remi called him out. But he could be real with her, let his fears and the less desirable parts of him show—his frustration, anger, doubt.

Maybe she would understand the situation with Lilah.

Are you kidding? The second you say anything to her this—whatever it is—will be over quicker than you can say you're sorry.

He should say something now. Be an adult and bear the consequences of his actions, rather than mentally dithering over it. He let out a breath and opened his mouth, but the curl of Remi's fists against his chest cut off the words before he could speak them.

"I was pregnant."

He blinked. "What?"

"When I left the Melbourne Ballet Company after they kicked me out. I was pregnant." She swallowed, her eyes squeezing shut. "I told Alex. It was his, and I knew it could end my career—not every dancer bounces back after pregnancy. But I loved him and he...told me to get rid of the baby."

Wes clenched his back teeth, sucking in the sadness of her voice and turning it into something darker. "He told you to have an abortion?"

She nodded. "I think he was frightened of what people might say. I was young. Still an adult, of course, but we had our whole lives ahead of us and a baby didn't fit in. That's when I figured out he really *had* been planning to keep our relationship under wraps the whole time."

"Did the company know?"

She shook her head. "No, I don't think so. But they gave him a choice and he said he was willing to commit to the company instead of me, knowing that I was carrying his child..."

"Bastard." Wes shook his head.

"He told me that if I said a word about the pregnancy to anyone, he'd say I tricked him into it." She bit down on her lip. "It wasn't like that. I was on the pill and I'd gotten sick. The antibiotics must have stopped it from working. I didn't realize. But it definitely wasn't on purpose."

"Oh, Remi." He pulled her closer, wrapped his arms around her head, and pressed his face to her hair. "I'm so sorry."

"I wanted to let you know that's why…about before. I kind of freaked out. It's not that I don't trust you." She pressed her lips to his chest. "I need you to know that. I *do* trust you."

Shit. Every second he spent in this bed was another inch deeper into the hole he'd dug. He needed to think about how to handle this situation with her. There were too many moving parts, too many feelings involved. He wanted to blurt out that he wanted her more than anything.

But that's not true is it? Because you want Out of Bounds *more than you want her. It's your dream. The launch of your new career, one you've built by yourself. For yourself.*

But having that would now mean giving up what'd started to feel with her. It wasn't anything tangible yet, more the potential for something to blossom and grow. The potential for something lasting.

"I'm sorry you had to go through that," he said, shutting his eyes and hoping that he could somehow fix this colossal mess.

"My parents told me to stay with them, to have the baby and forget about ballet." She swallowed. "I agreed. Then a few weeks later…she was gone. Anabella, that's what I was going to call her. I don't know how I knew she was a girl, but I did."

"Christ." As if his heart needed another blade run through it.

"That was my sign," she said. "I knew then that I needed to start over. It was like the universe was telling me to try again. And it took a while, but here I am. Thanks to you."

He was officially the biggest asshole on the face of the earth. Well, second only to the guy who'd knocked her up and then walked away. He had to fix this. Not tonight, when Remi was so raw and open. Tonight, he needed to comfort her. But he couldn't drag this out any longer. Tomorrow, he needed a solution.

Chapter 20

"Here's the thing you need to know about Wes Evans: he's got a short attention span and plenty of options."

—HeyThereDeLilah

WES STOOD AT THE CORNER OF SEVENTY-EIGHTH AND Park Avenue, bouncing up and down to get his muscles warm in the crisp, early-morning air. The only part of him that was warm were his hands, since he had a coffee cup in each.

This was Manhattan at his favorite time of day— before the city had truly woken. But today he found no comfort in the solitude. After a few minutes of waiting while his mind turned over and over like an engine failing to start, he saw a familiar flash of blue and purple.

"The last time I was awake at this hour I was still drunk from the night before," Sadie grumbled as she came up next to him, grabbing for the coffee cup in his right hand. She wore a hot-pink sweater that hung down to midthigh over a pair of leggings that were printed with a galaxy design.

"I'm surprised putting that sweater on didn't wake you up. I'm pretty sure satellites can see you from space."

"Some people aren't born to blend in, baby." She grinned and sipped her drink. "So what's the cause for the early-morning wake-up call? I thought everything was on track."

Yeah, until he fucked it up. Literally and figuratively.

"So we have a problem…"

"What the hell has happened now?" She shook her head. "Don't tell me Bert pulled out. I swear to God—"

"It's not that."

"Then what? Did our theater burn down? Did Remi break a leg?" Her eyes widened. "It's not that, is it?"

"No, she's fine." How the hell was he supposed to say it without sounding like the biggest chump on planet earth?

There is no way because you are *a chump*.

"Then what? Spit it out for crying out loud, you're killing me."

"I slept with Remi." He put the coffee cup to his lips and sucked the warm liquid down his throat. But even liquid gold from his favorite café wasn't going to make this situation any easier.

"Okay," she sounded the word out slowly. "How is that currently affecting the show?"

Her confusion over why that point was important was how people *should* react to such news. But he knew that Sadie was as open-minded as they came; it's why he'd approached her to choreograph for him in the first place.

"You didn't get her pregnant, did you?"

Wes cringed at her question, given what he'd learned last night. "No, it's not that. But someone found out."

"Who?"

"Lilah." He sighed. "And she came to me about it, thinking that's why Remi got the lead spot over her."

"Is she delusional?" Sadie shook her head. "I told you that one was going to be trouble."

She had. Sadie had wanted to pass on putting Lilah in the production, knowing that she could have a difficult temperament. But she'd conceded that Lilah would make a good corps member, since her contemporary ballet skills were strong…though not strong enough to be the lead.

"I was there at Remi's audition. It was a joint decision to put her in that role," Sadie said. "I'll back you on that one hundred percent. Lilah's claim has no substance. Especially since you didn't sleep together until after Remi was hired."

"I know that, but she's threatening to go public." They walked along Seventy-Eighth toward Central Park. "Given how everyone's been talking about my Bad Bachelor reviews, she's certain the media would be interested. And with everything else that's happened in the entertainment industry…they'd believe her too. Why wouldn't they?"

It made Wes furious to be lumped with the sleazy men who took advantage of young creatives, who used their powerful positions to coerce women into bed. Or did even worse. He abhorred that evil side of the industry, and there was no way he would ever contribute to it. His attraction to Remi was reciprocated and their sex was consensual. But he knew that even if Lilah's claim had nothing to back it up, her merely saying the words would be enough to cast a shadow of doubt over him, Remi, and any of their future work.

"That. Little. Shit." Sadie's face had turned pink, her eyes all but shooting fire.

"She wants me to give her Remi's role in exchange for her silence."

"Do you really think she'd go through with it?"

He rubbed his free hand over his face, hoping it might ease the throbbing in his head. "I have no idea, honestly."

"Have you told Remi?"

He shook his head. "Not yet."

They walked the next block in silence while Wes fumbled through shitty solution after shitty solution, none of which allowed him to retain both the show and his relationship with Remi.

"But you're going to, right? You have to tell her." She looked up at him suddenly. "You're not thinking of firing her, are you?"

"Remi? I don't want to fire her. But in my panic-induced scramble…yeah, I thought about it for a second. Isn't it better to lose one dancer and save the whole show?" He sighed. "I went to her place last night, but I couldn't do it."

"You were right about her, you know. She's perfect for this role." Sadie shook her head. "We won't have a chance of going wider with Lilah as the lead. She's not ready and she doesn't have the same depth."

"I agree. And I'm not going to put this show on unless I'm happy with it." He laughed when Sadie elbowed him.

"Unless *we're* happy with it. We've got one chance—if we don't open with a bang, then why bother?"

Aside from all the growing feelings he had toward Remi, the facts were the facts. She was the better dancer. Without her, the show would struggle to succeed. Maybe it was better to risk Bert pulling funding and to weather the stench of a scandal than to give in to Lilah and let her drive the show into the ground.

You're not going to throw all that money and hard work down the drain. The show will go on.

"Are we going to lose it?" Sadie asked as they hit Central Park.

A pair of men jogged past, way too energetic for the early hour. Wes scowled. He couldn't remember how long it'd been since he'd sprung out of bed without some kind of worry on his mind. Not since the show started, anyway.

This is what you want. The pressure and stress are part and parcel.

"I won't give up," he said. It was the only honest answer. "Part of me wonders, even if Lilah does spill this information, are people really going to care that much? It's just sex."

Even as he said the words, he knew people *would* care. They should care, frankly. The creative industries were rife with unconscionable behavior, people in power abusing their positions, and young people being taken advantage of—whether it was physically, financially, or otherwise.

But if both he and Remi came forward to say nothing unethical was going on, would people believe them? Would her career weather that storm? Would his?

Sadie looped her arm through his. "Have you thought about talking to your mother? I know she and Lilah were close at one point. Maybe she might be able to talk some sense into her."

Wes scoffed. "You're suggesting I talk to the woman who's been trying to drag this production down from day one? What's that going to achieve other than giving her something to gloat about?"

Sadie shrugged. "You know I've never been her biggest fan, but she's been dealing with temperamental creative types since before you were born. I mean, you never really gave her the chance to be involved in your show, did you?"

He mulled for a moment as they walked through the park, his gaze catching on the vibrant blaze of orange, yellow, and red leaves made even brighter as the sun came up. Everything glowed. It was like the trees were giving their grand finale, knowing the end was inevitable. But they wouldn't go quietly into winter. They wouldn't surrender their color until the last leaf fell.

"No, I didn't," he admitted. Their boots crunched on the path, grinding the fallen leaves into the earth. "Why would I when she told me I was throwing away my family legacy?"

"Hmm." Sadie bobbed her head. "Fair enough."

"I'm going to fix this," he said. "I have to."

If only he could figure out the right way to tackle this problem without reinforcing Remi's fears that he would abandon her in favor of his career, like her ex had.

Remi felt lighter when she woke up. Last night with Wes had been…amazing. And not only the sex. *That* was not in question. But she'd trusted him enough to unburden herself of the past, and it was like her heart weighed less than before. Whether she'd chosen to acknowledge it or not, she'd carried the anger and guilt over how things had ended in Australia like a boulder around her neck.

Wes had left not long after midnight, leaving her with a heated kiss that held the promise of more to come. And she'd grinned like a fool all the way back to her bed, falling into a deep, satisfied slumber that'd seen her sleep right through her alarm.

But she couldn't seem to feel stressed today, even if she was running late. Because things were finally looking up. As she headed out of the subway and down the street where the theater was located, she had the *Out of Bounds* soundtrack pumping through her headphones, her mind tracing the steps over and over. She must have looked a bit strange, her hands moving in small gestures, miniatures of what she did onstage.

She tugged her headphones out of her ears as she entered the theater. Before she made it through the door to the theater's main area, however, the sound of her name froze her to the spot. Biting down on her lip, Remi backtracked and pressed herself around the side of the ticketing booth, out of sight. The voices got louder, as did the fall of footsteps.

"I hope she's okay." It was Angelo speaking. "It's not like her to be late."

There was a pause in conversation followed by a frustrated "What?" in his hard, Bronx accent.

"Maybe I know something you don't know." The female voice held a singsong smugness. Lilah.

A cold fist wrapped around Remi's throat. She couldn't know about Remi and Wes…could she? There was no way. They'd been careful not to flirt in front of the cast, careful to be polite and professional and platonic in public.

"Spit it out." Angelo laughed. "If you're going to gossip, then at least say something."

"She's probably not here because Wes fired her."

The wind was knocked out of Remi's lungs.

"What? How do you know that?" Angelo huffed. "And when the hell is he going to tell everyone else?"

"Let's just say they've been doing *more* than rehearsing, and apparently it hasn't worked out," Lilah replied, her shoes hitting the wooden floor. "I'm assuming he'll be telling everyone when he gets in today."

"And I suppose you're going after her role."

"I *am* the alternate."

Remi held her breath, not daring to turn her head and look to see where Lilah and Angelo were going. She was certain her heart was beating loud enough for them to hear her, but after a few minutes without confrontation, she peeled herself away from the wall.

What the hell? How did Lilah know what was going on? And if Wes hadn't even shown up to the theater yet this morning, that meant he must have known something was going on last night when he'd come over.

For a moment, she couldn't move. Memories swirled thick like fog in her head. She'd been here before. Had this same swelling nausea, this same rush of blood in her ears that made it feel like someone was holding her head underwater.

No, no, no, no.

She pressed a hand to her forehead. Wes was supposed to be different. She'd resisted him as hard as she could, but he'd worked on her. Bending her with his sweet words and kind gestures, with his care and humor and sexy, crooked smile.

"Oh God," she whispered, taking a huge breath and trying not to let the smoothie she'd had for breakfast come rushing back up.

What was she supposed to do now? Who else had Lilah told? The thought of facing the cast, knowing that her affair with Wes was public knowledge and that she might be on the chopping block for it was too much. She needed to think, and she couldn't do that here.

Remi pushed open the door to the theater and darted out onto the street. The noise of the city overwhelmed her, horns blaring and voices yelling and engines rumbling. It was too much. Too loud and too bright. She walked down the street, her feet breaking into a jog as the need to escape built up like pressure in her veins.

Get out, get out, get out.

She'd done it again.

Just as she rounded the corner, ready to escape down into the subway, she caught site of a familiar face. Of all the bloody luck.

"Remi?" Wes's brow wrinkled as he took her in, his gaze sweeping from her trembling hands to the tears welling in her eyes. "What's wrong?"

"You were going to fire me?" She should have

walked on, but the words shot out of her faster than she could contemplate the consequences. "And you told the cast before you told me? What the hell?"

His face paled in a way that made Remi's heart sink. It was the pallor of guilt. "Who said that?"

"Lilah. And apparently she knows we're 'doing more than rehearsing,' according to what she told Angelo." She wanted to scream at him as much as she wanted to throw herself into his arms. "God, you must think I'm stupid. Did you really think I wouldn't find out?"

Alex's betrayal had come to her attention in a similar way—he hadn't told her, the chickenshit. She'd found out from another dancer.

He's not leaving the company, Remi. They said he could have another chance if he cut ties with you.

She blinked, trying to stem the resurgence of tears at the memory of how she'd held a hand over her belly, wondering how the father of her child could walk away without even telling her. She'd been a fool then, and she was a fool now.

"Fuck," he muttered as he raked a hand through his hair. "It's not like that. I'm *not* firing you."

"Really? But you're not denying that you told Lilah we were sleeping together. That was supposed to be between us. We agreed." Remi was suddenly aware that she was yelling at him, the tumultuous feelings roiling inside her had taken control of her voice box. "Why would you do that?"

"I didn't tell her. She found out…she overheard us in the dressing room." He took a step closer, but Remi immediately backed up. She couldn't let Wes into her space right now, not when everything was on the line. "Remi… Christ. She's trying to blackmail me."

Remi shook her head. "What?"

"She came to me and threatened to go to the media with a story about how I had a casting couch for my dancers." His lip curled in disgust. "She said the only thing I could do to keep her quiet was to fire you and let her take the lead role."

Her instinct had told her from the start that Lilah was trouble. She'd seen dancers like that before—so desperate to get ahead they would step on and over whoever they saw as competition.

"When did this happen?" Her lower lip trembled. She knew the answer and what it meant—Wes had come to her place last night with this knowledge, and he'd chosen to take her to bed instead of telling her the truth.

"Yesterday." His lips pressed into a flat line, guilt flashing in his blue eyes.

She squeezed her eyes shut. "Before you came to see me?"

"Yes." He didn't even hesitate. "I wanted to tell you."

"But what? You were so overcome with passion that you simply forgot?" Sarcasm poisoned her words. "Bullshit."

"No, I didn't forget."

"Then what? You were more interested in getting off than in treating me like a human being?" She shook her head. After he'd been so sweet, after he'd led her to think they had something special—even if only the very first inkling of something—he'd gone and ruined it all by not opening up to her. That was the worst part of all—not

that people knew about them, not that there was specu-
lation about her being fired. But that he'd had the opportunity to tell her the truth and chosen not to. Like Alex.
Like Annie. "Tell Lilah I hope she's happy. Everyone is
going to judge me now no matter what I do."

She stormed past him, but his hand caught her wrist.

"Remi, wait."

She met his eyes, refusing to look away even though
she wanted to sink through the floor.

"You promised me that sex wouldn't get in the way.
But if you could take me to bed last night knowing what
you knew, without saying a word…then it *has* gotten in
the way," she said. "Why didn't you tell me? We could
have thought about how to deal with Lilah together,
like a team."

Sure, she would have freaked. But him coming clean
and wanting to work through it together would have
at least shown he had her interests at heart. His actions,
however, revealed a lot.

"I'm sorry. I know I should have told you. I was…"
The crisp fall wind ruffled his dark hair, blowing the
thick strands around his forehead. "I didn't want to ruin
this."

"I guess it's a good thing I didn't throw your mother's
business card out, because it looks like I might need the
contact." She yanked her wrist free and headed down
into the subway, slipping her headphones over her ears
so that if he tried to call to her, she wouldn't be tempted
to turn around.

Bad Bachelor review: Wesley Evans

What can I say about the time I dated the great Wes Evans? Not much. It was like cotton candy—sweet, fun, and lacking in substance. But I get the impression that's all he's interested in. Why would someone like him need to go through the work of a proper relationship?

Here's the thing you need to know about Wes Evans: he's got a short attention span and plenty of options.

Take for instance his show, *Out of Bounds*. He's using the recognition of his family name and the notoriety of his sex life to garner publicity for it. He knows he can lean on those two things without going through the hard work like everyone else. Oh, and how do you think his lead ballerina got her role given she hasn't worked professionally in over four years? I'll give you one guess. ;) —*HeyThereDeLilah*

Remi woke on Thursday with the certainty that things couldn't possibly get any worse. But oh…they had.

Overnight, she'd had her phone turned off because Wes kept calling and texting. A touch of guilt lingered over how she'd thrown the comment about his mother back in his face. Okay…more than a touch. It was a nasty thing to say. But dammit, she was hurting. Lashing out certainly wasn't the most adult way to deal with things, but it was all she had at her disposal right now. The walls were back up because her heart needed time to recover. To fortify.

When she woke up and switched her phone back on, she saw the missed texts from Angelo asking, "What the hell is going on?" She'd also had messages from Sadie, a few other cast members, and one from Darcy asking if they could catch up soon because she wanted to make sure everything was okay.

But then another text came through from Wes.

> **WES:** Don't worry about the Bad Bachelors thing. It doesn't mean anything.

Her heart sank as she reached down to the floor and pulled her laptop up onto the bed. She'd deleted the Bad Bachelors app off her phone after the night she'd told Wes she'd looked him up, and she hadn't been on the desktop version either. The more she learned about Bad Bachelors, the less she wanted anything to do with it... especially after knowing who was behind it. She cracked one eye as she typed his name into the search bar.

The most recent review made her stomach vault. But that sick feeling turned to fury when she read the reviewer's username. *HeyThereDeLilah*.

It could easily be mistaken for a reference to the catchy song, but the capital *L* told her all she needed to know.

Remi rolled her eyes, trying to mask the desire to cry out with something stronger. Angrier. Of course, it was one more thing Wes hadn't told her. Or else it was another of Lilah's lies. How could she tell the difference? Neither of them told the truth.

She shoved the laptop away and brought her fingertips to her temples. *Out of Bounds* was supposed to be going live in two weeks. They'd cut it right down to the wire in terms of funding, but Wes had pulled it off. Most people would have bailed earlier, but he'd put his own money on the line. Used what he had to secure the theater and ensure things kept moving. He'd risked his own finances for the show. Logically, she knew that meant him hiring her was nothing like what Lilah had implied.

But would other people see that? Remi wasn't sure she could face the possibility of people looking at her the way they had when her affair with Alex had hit gossip circles. People always questioned the woman—was she opening her legs to get ahead? Was she trying to sleep her way to a better position?

She'd been seen as manipulative, as relying on her sexual prowess, which could only mean she didn't have the talent to back it up. If she had any hope of stepping onstage opening night, two things would need to happen: one, damage control with the cast and the media and two, she would need to officially end things with Wes. No more sexy, late-night visits. No more sneaking off after rehearsals. They were done.

Could they keep people focused on what mattered? Remi had no idea.

She reached for her phone and scrolled through the messages she'd missed overnight. One from Annie stood out.

ANNIE: Hey, I'm taking tomorrow off. Think you can sneak away for a coffee?

Remi glanced at the clock beside her bed. It was 9:00

a.m. The cast would already be powering through their warm-up class with Sadie. But Remi wasn't setting foot into that theater until she had her plan sorted. No way was she getting blindsided again.

REMI: Sure. Meet at Bluestone Lane? Financial Dist.
ANNIE: Give me 30 min. I'll see you there.

Remi took her time getting ready, and when she left her building, the sun shone down so brightly that she had to shed her denim jacket. The weather was in that strange up-and-down portion of the season, when the city couldn't quite decide if it was cold or hot. She slung the jacket over her arm and headed toward Flatbush Avenue in the direction of the Seventh Avenue subway station, her headphones over her ears. Blowing off rehearsals for a second day in a row was an offense that would incur serious reprimanding. So much could change in the course of forty-eight hours. Steps could be tweaked, technique could be developed, something might click and everything would suddenly work. Two days could mean her castmates surging ahead of her after she'd worked so hard to catch up in the first place.

Doesn't matter. You don't go back without a plan.

Her phone buzzed.

WES: Are you coming in today?

She shoved the phone back into her bag and headed down into the subway. It would take at least one more day for her feelings to simmer down to a level where she could talk to him without either wanting to burst into tears, or toss a drink in his face. The worst thing was, however, it wasn't anger. She was mourning him. Though they hadn't defined the boundaries of their relationship, she knew they had something special. Like when she executed a perfect triple pirouette, she got that tingly, magical feeling when she was with him. The feeling that told her right from the start to be careful.

But she hadn't listened. She'd been lured in by the possibility of them, what they could be, when she should have been focusing on her golden opportunity.

Remi got off at Wall Street and headed to Bluestone Lane. This one was her favorite of the Bluestone cafés because of the brightly tiled counter and friendly staff.

"Good morning. What can I get you?" The familiar Aussie accent washed over her, making her feel a little less alone.

"I'll have the flat white and an avo smash. Some feta too." She dug into her wallet and pulled out a few wrinkled bills. Four years in this damn country and she still had to check every bill she handed out because they all looked so similar, unlike the colorful money from back home.

"Good choice." The woman rang up her order, and Remi handed the money over. "Did you stay up to watch the grand final last night?"

"Grand final?"

The woman laughed. "How many years have you been here now? You've forgotten all about our national treasure."

Remi laughed. "Ah, the footy. No, I wasn't keen to stay up that late to watch it. Did you?"

"Sure did. The Dockers were playing." She clamped a hand over her heart.

"And they lost." The barista looked over the espresso machine with an evil grin. "Carn the blues!"

"Well, I'm going to be a terrible Australian and admit that I'm not a big footy fan." She pretended to duck. "Don't throw anything at me."

The woman chuckled, shooting her a mock-angry look. "I bet you hate Vegemite too. Traitor."

Remi laughed and found a seat by the window to wait for Annie. There was something comforting about listening to the two people behind the counter discuss at length the virtues of Vegemite. For the first time since she'd moved, Remi wondered if maybe the time had come for her to go back home.

Maybe you should go home. Pack it all in and commit to a life of eating kale and hemp seeds. Foster some animals and forget about human interaction altogether.

Remi reached into the pocket of her jogger pants, her fingers feeling for the smooth edges of the citrine crystal her mother had sent her. She drew the stone into her palm and closed her hand around it, wondering what she was supposed to feel. Where was the voodoo her mother believed in? The stone was surprisingly cool, given where she had it stashed, and it felt heavier than it looked for its size.

Carry them around, and even if you don't believe they'll do anything, let them remind you that I am thinking of you always.

Remi swallowed, finding a lump in the back of her throat. Her parents might not have understood her dreams, they might not have wanted the life for her that she wanted for herself, but they loved her. That was never in doubt.

Opal had been devastated when Remi moved away, but she'd never stopped Remi from doing anything. She wouldn't come for a show or even a tourist visit. But if Remi said, "Mum, I really need you," she knew Opal would hop on the first plane out.

Remi squeezed the stone and dropped it back into her pocket as Annie pushed open the door to the café. She stopped by the front counter to place her order and then took a seat next to Remi.

"Hey, I'm glad you were able to get out of rehearsals for a bit," Annie said. "How's it all going?"

To Remi's complete embarrassment, her eyes welled up. She blinked the tears away, refusing to break down in public, and told Annie everything that'd happened and showed her the review.

"Wow." Annie blinked when Remi finally took a pause. "I don't even know what to say."

Remi sipped her coffee, which had turned lukewarm. She picked at the avocado on toast, her appetite waning. "Neither do I."

"Why would this woman do something so horrible?"

"Being a professional dancer isn't like other careers. You can follow the rules, put in the hours, give it everything that you have, and still end up going nowhere." She sucked in a breath. "Desperation to succeed makes people do some strange things. I don't think this is a personal attack because she hates me; she simply wants what I have."

"And forcibly taking it by lying is going to result in a long and successful career?" Annie shook her head. "Those kind of antics might work in the short term, but the second the next project comes along and people realize it's not talent that's gotten her there, she'll get dumped. It's a shortsighted approach."

"True." Remi bobbed her head. "Although I wonder if the review on Bad Bachelors is an indication that Wes let her go."

"Are you going to speak to him?" Annie asked.

"I have to. But not until I know exactly how I want to approach this whole thing." Remi bit into her toast, but it tasted of sawdust, so she pushed the plate away. "And the first thing I need to do is get that review taken down. If any of the media outlets that have been following Wes and his show see it…I can only imagine what's going to happen."

Annie remained quiet while she read the review on Remi's phone, her perfectly shaped brows knitting together. "I can't take it down, Remi. You know that."

"Why not?"

"Because it doesn't break the terms and conditions of the site. There are no threats, there's no inappropriate or graphic language. There's nothing that indicates her statement about dating him is a lie." Annie shook her head. "And if I look at her profile, she's rated other men before this happened, so it's a genuine, active account."

"She's telling the world that we're sleeping together." Remi forced herself to speak slowly and at a moderate volume when really she wanted to scream and curse. How could Annie not see what a huge problem this was?

"She didn't actually say that, and she hasn't named you." Annie tucked her hair behind her ear. "I'm sorry. My hands are tied."

"No, they're not. It's your bloody site."

Annie's eyes darted around. Thankfully, the café was between rushes of customers and the people behind the counter were busy chatting. "Yes, but I have these rules for a reason. I can't go deleting reviews when they're not doing anything wrong. It would undermine the reviews system."

"I'm your friend, Annie. I'm a *real* person who is being affected by this. My career is on the line." She sucked in a breath, heat flooding her cheeks. "I found out your secret. I haven't told a soul because I value our friendship."

"And I'm grateful for that," Annie said, a deep crease forming between her brows. "I really am, Remi. But if this review suddenly disappears without warning, then why would people use my site? Worse still, it might indicate that we're connected and I already had to fight off one guy who got too close. I can't have any trail lead back to me."

"So you're not going to help me?"

"Don't make me choose, Remi. Please."

She stood, grabbing her bag and slinging it over one shoulder. "You already have."

Remi felt like she was sitting inside one of those spinning rides in a children's playground, watching everything around her turn and turn until it was nothing but a murky blur.

How had she screwed everything up so badly?

Chapter 21

"New York dating has taught me one important lesson: know when to walk away. That point should come before your life is a steaming pile of rubble."

—LostInManhattan

WES STOOD IN THE PRIVATE LANDING OF THE PARK Avenue building where his parents lived. It was one of those gaudy places with gold-trimmed this and wood-paneled that. Where chandeliers came in groups of two or three. It had the whole "more is more" aesthetic that he hated about a lot of the buildings in this section of New York.

But anything—even having his retinas permanently damaged by all this flash and finery—was better than sitting in the theater, watching *Out of Bounds* take its last wheezing breath. After he'd seen Remi yesterday, he'd stormed into the theater ready to have it out with Lilah.

It hadn't taken long to get it out of her that she'd told a few people about him and Remi and predicted the lead ballerina's soon-to-be-announced dismissal. She'd cried angrily when he'd fired her, accusing him of holding her back. Threatening to tell the world what an asshole he was. Fine by him. He'd get his lawyers involved if she decided to slander him. It's what he should have done in the first place, instead of being so worried about trying to keep her quiet.

But Wes didn't have it in him to placate her. Besides, what was the point? Without Remi or Lilah, they wouldn't be able to launch in two weeks. None of the other corps dancers were right for the part and learning the whole show in two weeks would be tight even for the strongest members. And the theater was booked right after their initial run for another production, so to create more rehearsal time would mean cutting into how long the show could run.

He *might* be able to pull off opening night if he found someone immediately. But the fact was…he didn't want anyone else.

And if Lilah decided to go out with a false story about his casting-couch mentality, he'd have to deal with it then. Sadie would back him; the people he'd worked with at the Evans Ballet School would back him. It was a risk he needed to take. Because when *Out of Bounds* played in his head, he only saw Remi. And, as much as he wanted to deny it, a large portion of what was in his head revolved around her. Period. She'd become entrenched in his life. He was enamored with her. And now he was on the verge of losing it all. The very least he could do was to show her that the lead role was hers. Unconditionally.

Which was pretty much the only thing that could have brought him here voluntarily.

The door to the gallery opened and his mother stood there, a strand of pearls at her neck and her makeup and hair done as though she was about to head to a formal event.

"Wes." She smiled. "Can I get Marie to fix you a drink?"

"I'm fine. Thanks."

His eyes swept over the room. Not a picture frame was out of place, not a speck of dust marred any of the furniture. It was like a museum. A memory flashed, him chasing Chantel around the room and knocking a vase over. His mother had flipped. Years later, he'd learned how much the vase had cost. Why would anyone spend so much on something so pointless? It wasn't like they even kept flowers in it.

"I, uh…" He dropped down onto the floral couch, running his hands over the familiar embroidered fabric. "I wanted to talk."

Adele raised a brow. "About?"

Where the hell was he supposed to start? It felt like everything had turned to shit so quickly, but, in reality, things had been amiss from the beginning.

"I want to clear the air," he said. "And I want your advice."

The quiet clink of cutlery sounded in the next room, where Marie was no doubt setting up for lunch. Adele looked him over, her blue eyes shrewd and knowing. It was one thing that always frustrated him about his mother—as much as he quietly admired it: without fail, she could figure people out. Even him, who was so good controlling what people saw.

"What happened?" she asked. "Something's gone wrong with the show, hasn't it?"

He waited for her to look pleased. Or smug. Or, at the very least, to have some kind of I-told-you-so air about her. But she didn't.

"The show is fine. It's all the people *in* the show that's the problem."

"People usually are the reason for problems." Adele smiled. "Especially in smaller productions, where one person makes up a larger percentage of the total."

She had a point. At a big company, there were plenty of people to choose from. But he could only pay so many dancers, and, as it was, they were accepting the minimum for a chance to be part of the production. Losing one dancer would halt things. A corps member wasn't so bad, because they always had alternates. But losing the lead *and* the only other person who knew her choreography was a catastrophe.

"I did warn you this could happen," she added.

Wes gritted his teeth, biting back the defensive reply. Unleashing his frustrations on his mother wasn't going to do anything expect make the wedge between them even bigger. And despite knowing that his family was far from perfect, he didn't want the damage to be permanent.

"Opening night is in two weeks," he said. "And I've messed it up."

He told her everything, from start to finish—though details of his time with Remi were kept to a minimum. Adele listened without expression, giving him no indication of what she thought. Maybe he was proving her right?

She leaned back in her chair, her neat nails drumming against the arm of the wingback where she sat across from him. "I guess if you're going to mess something up you may as well do it properly."

"Great advice," he said, rolling his eyes.

"Do you have any idea why I didn't want you to go down this path?" she asked.

Here we go. Let's relive all the ways she thinks I'm failing at life.

"I was cast in a show like that once. It was this strange independent ballet with a director who was one of those mad-genius types. Great ideas but usually too high out of his mind to properly execute them."

Wes blinked. He had no idea that his mother had ever performed in anything outside her illustrious career with the New York City Ballet.

"I left the company after I'd been a soloist for two years, certain that they were going to keep putting other girls ahead of me. I was disillusioned. So I left, got cast in this show, and within three weeks, I realized it was the biggest mistake of my entire life." Her lips twisted into a sheepish smile. "The only reason we are here now is because the ballet master had a soft spot for me. Not enough to promote me early, mind you. But he said if I came back and did my time, they would pretend like it never happened."

Wow. There were not many people who would be afforded *that* kind of second chance.

"So I went back, I kept my mouth shut, and I worked the hardest I have ever worked in my whole life." She toyed with the pearls at her neck. "But I know that if I hadn't gotten out of that show when I did, my career would not have recovered."

"And that's what you thought would happen to me?" Wes asked, frowning. "Although for the record, I'm not some high-as-a-kite director. I *believe* in this show."

"I know, but you're trying to fund it yourself knowing that such a small percentage of these shows actually succeed. You're happy to send yourself broke on one opportunity." His mother shook her head. "Of course, you must know your father and I would bail you out."

"I don't know that. I certainly don't assume that you'll foot the bill for my mistakes."

Something glimmered in Adele's eyes. Was it respect? She made it so difficult to tell. "Well, for the record, I would."

"Even if you think I'm throwing away everything you built for me?"

"I could have worded that differently," she admitted. "I was angry that you decided to leave without giving us a say."

"It's my life. My career. You *don't* have a say." He would not budge on that. Of course, he wanted his parents to be proud. Who didn't want that?

"You could have warned me, Wes. How does it look when you suddenly walk out without explanation?"

"I handed my work over. I wouldn't leave the company struggling." But he'd been so caught up by this idea, so wrapped up in his lightbulb moment about what was wrong with his life that he hadn't given much thought to talking things through with his parents. Perhaps it was because he knew they would try to convince him to stay, and he didn't want to risk that. "And why should I care what people say? God, I'm so sick of people talking. Wouldn't the world be a hell of a lot better if people would shut the fuck up for once?"

The clinking in the next room came to an abrupt halt and he cursed under his breath. Everything was getting to him right now, and it wouldn't stop until he'd righted things with Remi.

Don't you mean until you've righted things with the show?

"You should *want* people to talk, Wes," his mother said. "Talk helps our work. But we want them saying the right things. Not speculating over our dysfunctional family."

He'd never heard his mother call them that before. "You think we're dysfunctional?"

She lifted her shoulders in a shrug. "I've got a daughter who couldn't run fast enough away from her pointe shoes and a son who walked out of the family business without a word. I think my grandchildren are frightened of me too."

He looked at his mother then. *Really* looked at her. She still had the grace of someone who danced often, even though her feet gave her pain and she could only wear flat shoes these days. Like him, Adele was a master of presentation. To others she was charming and poised, elegant. Intelligent. To their family…well, she hadn't been the kind of mother who'd embraced that role. She'd never planned on having children, and being surprised with twins must have been tough. It was almost like she'd never quite figured out how to mesh being a mother with her dreams.

"You think Frankie is frightened of you?" he asked.

"I don't know. She asked me the other day why I don't look like the grandmothers in her picture book. She called me a pretty dragon."

Wes snorted. "Oh, Frankie."

"She's going to give her mother nightmares one day." Adele smiled ruefully. "Kind of reminds me of how I was as a young girl. My father cursed me all the time."

"I would have thought you were the perfect child from how you used to tell Chantel and I that we were always running amok."

"You were." She folded her hands neatly in her lap. "I wondered sometimes if you wished I were like the mothers in books too."

At times, he had. But Adele wasn't one to cuddle or coddle her children; she never patted them on the head for a job well done. She was hard in a lot of ways. Demanding, strict, and had expectations that felt as high as the moon. She was with her children exactly how she was with her students.

"I love you, you know," she said. "I don't always agree with what you're doing and I know I don't say it often. Or enough, perhaps. But I do."

"I love you too." He supposed that other parents and children might've hugged at this pointed, or at least reached out for physical connection. But that wasn't her way, and he'd learned to accept what she gave. "Why did you steal Ashleigh away?"

Adele sighed. "I didn't. She came to me because she had similar fears about the show as I had. Cincinnati Ballet had contacted her, asking for an audition. She wanted me to put in a good word, and I think she's wonderful, so I did. I knew it might affect your show and I felt bad about that, but I did what was best."

"For her," he said. "Not for me. Not for your son."

"You found Remi, didn't you?"

Wes couldn't argue that logic. "So you didn't push her?" he asked.

"No. But I should have told you what was going on," she conceded. "I was still mad at you. It was petty for me to have kept it to myself."

"And did you tell other people not to audition for me?"

She shook her head. "For anyone who asked, I told them they needed to weigh the pros and cons. A big company might mean slower progress, more competition. However, the opportunities are broader and there's more career prestige. But I never told anyone not to audition."

After their blazing fight when he'd quit, Wes had assumed the worst of his mother. And he shouldn't have. "So can you help me save this weird, ill-advised show?"

"Is that the thing you want to save?" she asked.

"Why else would I be here?"

"The whole time you were telling me about your problems, I kept hearing her name: Remi, Remi, Remi." She flicked her hand back and forth in time with the words. "She's beautiful. I can understand why you want to save things with her."

"And you think that's separate from saving the show?"

"No woman wants to feel like she's being pursued for what they can give you, Wes. Women want to be pursued because you're so compelled to be with them that you have no other choice than to fight as hard as you can." She paused, studying him. "I know losing Emily was tough. And I suppose your father and I haven't been the best influences when it comes to putting relation-ships before other things in life."

"I admire how ambitious you both are. I want that for myself. I want to build something important and meaningful and creative."

"And I want you to have everything." His mother's voice was unusually soft. "But sometimes that's not possible."

Remi *might* come back to the show if he convinced her that he could manage the press. But he knew deep down that it would be as a ballerina only. Not as *his* ballerina.

"I know."

He had a choice to make. Choose the show and convince her to come back so they could prepare for opening night, knowing they would only be together in a work capacity. Or give up the show to prove that he wanted her for all the right reasons.

The Anaconda and the Casting Couch...

By Peta McKinnis (*Spill the Tea* society and culture reporter)

Sounds like some kind of twisted fairy tale, right? But this story isn't taking place in a faraway castle. Oh, no, we've got more drama right here in New York City than the Brothers Grimm could ever have dreamed up.

We've been following Wes Evans's breakaway from the Evans Ballet School with interest. Information about Evans's show, which we now know to be called *Out of Bounds*, came out last week with the release of an intriguing poster and the following blurb:

Some things can't be contained by boundaries. Some

experiences should be close enough to touch. Why watch the show when you can be part of it?

Given his background, this does sound like a huge step away from the kind of work the Evans Ballet School produces with their annual workshop performances. But *Spill the Tea*'s Society and Culture team is all for people pushing creative boundaries! It sounds like *Out of Bounds* is set to be a unique offering to those who've grown tired of traditional ballets.

However, while perusing the Bad Bachelors website yesterday (it's our not-so-secret guilty pleasure, no judgment!) we stumbled across a review, written by user *HeyThereDeLilah* that indicates the possibility of some unsavory practices happening behind the scenes of *Out of Bounds*.

"Take for instance [Wes Evans's] show, *Out of Bounds*. He's using the recognition of his family name and the notoriety of his sex life to garner publicity for the event... Oh, and how do you think his lead ballerina got her role given she hasn't worked professionally in over four years? I'll give you one guess. ;)"

It doesn't take too much reading between the lines to figure out what this reviewer is talking about. Could Evans be using his position of power to lure female dancers onto the casting couch? We sure hope not! But if that's the case, then the *Spill the Tea* team will be boycotting *Out of Bounds*.

While many recent articles regarding unethical behavior in the entertainment industry seem to focus on Hollywood, even the ballet world has been rocked by abuse allegations in recent times. We've reached out to Evans for comment. But let's just say, based on previous attempts, we're not holding our breath for a response.

The second Remi saw the article about Wes, it was all over. She wouldn't be going back to *Out of Bounds*, even if it was under the agreement that she and Wes were done. Because the media had swooped in for the kill. It wouldn't be long before questions were asked and larger publications started to sniff around.

Thankfully, her name wasn't mentioned in the article, but if the show went ahead in its current format, then the chances of her walking away unscathed were nil.

Unfortunately, Wes didn't have that luxury. Of course she was still furious that he'd lied to her, but that paled in comparison to the insinuation that he was taking advantage of people. Even though there would be no evidence to support any illegal—or even unethical— practices in his show, the bad stench of such suggestions could hang around forever. People might chose not to work with him in the future because of it.

And he didn't deserve that. Wes was a great director— kind and encouraging and inspiring. Exactly the same as in his personal life. But where did this leave her? Them? The show?

Remi did the only thing that might help. She texted her mother. A second later, the distinctive Skype ringtone shattered the quiet and Remi settled on the couch with her laptop.

"What's wrong, possum?" Opal's face showed up clear for a second and then broke down into a pixelated mess before landing somewhere in the middle.

Bloody hell. Where did she even start? She had no idea what she expected her mother to say, because all she would do was reinforce Opal's belief that the ballet world was destructive and toxic and negative.

"Is it ballet or a boy?" her mother asked. Even with

the slightly blurry screen, Remi could detect a knowing smile. "Both?"

"How do you always know what's wrong?" Remi rolled the piece of citrine in her hand, out of the way of the screen. For some reason, the little yellow lump of rock had comforted her since everything went to crap.

You're legit going crazy now, turning to rocks for support.

But it wasn't really that. When things went to hell in a handbasket, only her mother could help. And since a hug wasn't in the cards, a rock would have to do.

"Because I know you better than anyone." Opal smiled. "Anytime I've seen you frown since the time you were six years old, it was either ballet or a boy."

"It's both." She spilled the whole story to Opal, everything from the way Wes found her and her struggles with choreography, to Lilah's meddling and Wes's deception, to Annie's secret and all its unhappy aftermath. "What should I do?"

"I'd like to be selfish and say come home."

Remi blinked. Opal had never once asked her to come home, never even mentioned it. "Selfish?"

"When my baby is hurting, I want to hug her."

A lump lodged in the back of her throat. It was times like this that homesickness grabbed her by the throat. How easy would it be to pack her things and hop on a plane? To never come back? What did she really have tying her to New York anymore?

Nothing.

But then she'd be no better than the person she'd been four years ago, running away from her problems as if it could solve everything. And she knew now that it didn't.

For four years, she'd avoided her dreams, avoided connecting with people because she might get hurt. Working on *Out of Bounds* had shown her that she'd been living half a life. An incomplete life. And she deserved so much more.

"Would you come here?" she asked. "To New York?"

"If you need me, I'll come." Opal cocked her head, frizzy hair backlit by the light above their kitchen table. "You know that."

Remi imagined she was there right in front of her mother, like she used to be every time she had a problem. They'd sit at the crooked, little table in the kitchen, mismatched mugs of green tea in their hands, while Opal soothed all her worries.

"You've got to come clean with Wes," her mother said, breaking into Remi's thoughts. "I know I sound like a broken record, but honesty is the best policy. If, after it all comes out, you need to walk away, that's fine. But do it with a clear conscience."

"You're right." She bobbed her head. "It's been eating away at me."

"As for the dancing…can you live without it?"

"No." The response was so instant it took Remi aback. "It's been hard, but I finally feel like I have some purpose again. I feel…useful. Fulfilled."

"Then why do you need me to give you an answer?"

This was where she belonged—in New York, dancing. Feeling scared of failure because it meant she was actually striving for something instead of letting life pass her by. It hurt to be away from her family. It hurt to put herself out into the world raw and vulnerable. It hurt to face the consequences of her actions.

But she was doing something instead of being passive in her own life.

"I want you to come," Remi said. "I miss you and I'm worried if I come home…"

It would be so easy not to go back to the show. But she needed to be strong and face the cast. Face Wes.

"Talk to me after you've settled things with Wes," her mother replied. "And then if you still need me, I'll pack my bags."

Relief filtered through her system. Opal was not like most mothers, but she *was* still a mother. "I love you, Mum."

"I love you too, poss." She put her hands to the screen. "You're stronger than you think."

As she ended the call with her mother, a text came through from Wes.

> **WES:** I know you're mad at me, but I need you. I have to fix this. All cast meeting at 11am. I hope you'll come.

Remi looked at the text for what must have been the hundredth time as she walked toward the Attic.

I need you.

The words made her breath catch, made a feeling of hope stir in her chest. But she tamped it all down. This wasn't about feelings; it was about doing what was right. Wes had given her a chance when no one else would, so she would be there for him. Regardless of how anything went down, she was not going to let people think that he took advantage of her.

She had made that mistake, and now she would own up to it.

Her stomach roiled at the thought of having to come out with something so private in front of a group of people, and it dawned on her that this must be how he felt reading his reviews on Bad Bachelors. Despite the good it did, there was a whole insidious side to it. And Remi vowed that she would block the damn thing from her computer and never look at it again.

Guilt knifed through her. Wes wasn't the only one keeping secrets in this situation—Remi had hidden her connection to Bad Bachelors. And though she'd tried to convince Annie to take the review down, ultimately it didn't matter. She'd still kept it from him. So, she would come clean. At least then, when she walked away for good, it would be with nothing hanging over her head.

Shaking off the thoughts of her damaged relationships with Wes and Annie, and her fears about facing the cast, she trudged up to the theater's entrance.

"Girl, I thought you'd fallen off the face of the earth." Angelo came up behind her, a concerned expression belying his teasing tone. "What the hell is going on?"

"Not everything Lilah told you is true," Remi said, and Angelo looked at her sheepishly. "But some of it was. I think Wes is going to clear everything up today, so I won't steal his thunder."

"Are you okay?" he asked as they headed into the theater together.

"I'll survive," she replied with a shaky smile. "I always do."

Survival. It's what she'd done last time, fleeing to America after losing Anabella. A wave of grief hit her out of nowhere, the force sucking the air from her lungs and painfully squeezing her heart. Angelo steadied her, but she waved him off, making out like she'd simply tripped.

These days, she managed to keep memories at bay. The night she'd told Wes about losing her child, she'd been able to keep it together. But now, looking at the smoking ruins of what could have been, it was too much. Grief was strange like that; it fed on other parts of your life, gaining strength from unrelated darkness. Remi pressed a hand to her chest and felt the thumping of her heart.

You're doing the right thing. It doesn't matter if everyone in here is judging you, because you owe Wes this.

They walked into the theater. Wes stood on the stage, his head bent as he talked to Sadie. The rest of the cast was seated in the audience, along with Wes's sister.

Angelo ushered Remi into an aisle and she dropped down next to Melinda, one of the corps dancers. The other woman turned and smiled, curiosity painted over her pretty face though she was polite enough not to ask any questions. After a few more minutes, the rest of the cast was present. All with the exception of Lilah.

"Thank you all for coming here today. I know there have been a lot of questions about the status of *Out of Bounds* recently, so I'm hoping to get everyone on the same page." His eyes found hers across the rows of old red-and-gold-upholstered theater seats, and the connection zinged with electricity. No one else could make her feel so much with only a look. "As some of you may be aware, I had to let one of our cast members go. What happened is between me and that person. I won't talk about it or criticize that person in public, so don't bother asking me."

Remi bobbed her head slowly. Wes had integrity beyond the average person, that was for damn sure. After what Lilah had done, she deserved to be called out for her shitty behavior. But Remi knew that wasn't Wes's way. And his classy actions weren't for show either.

He'd never taken her to task in rehearsals for struggling to catch up, like some directors would have. Her well-intentioned ballet mistress in Australia never held back on giving feedback publically, even if it might dent a dancer's confidence. That was the ballet world—striving for perfection meant facing harsh truths. But Wes had used a different approach—he'd pushed her, sure. But it'd happened in private, where she could react without fearing judgment from the rest of the cast.

Then why did he lie to you? He was in your home—in your bed—all the while knowing what was at stake.

And that was the one thing she couldn't let go of. If she hadn't overheard Lilah talking to Angelo on the way into the theater, she would have walked into a shit storm totally unprepared. Totally unarmored.

By staying silent, Wes had shown where his loyalties lay: with his career. And that was fine; she should have *known* that would be the case. Because when push came to shove, people in this industry valued their careers above all else. But Remi wasn't content to be cast aside like that ever again.

Chapter 22

"I still want to believe in Happy Ever Afters. But I think fairy tales get it all wrong. We don't need a prince to save us—we need to save ourselves."

—FormerlyJaded

WES SCANNED THE CROWD OF CURIOUS FACES. HE HAD Sadie by his side, who'd turned up early with coffees in hand, ready to show her support.

And then there was Remi. The second he looked at her, it was like everyone else faded away. In spite of how badly he'd messed up by lying to her, she'd come for him.

"I do want to clear up some of the rumors that have been circulating. I am not in the habit of discussing my personal affairs in front of an audience," he said. "But I also understand where I've made mistakes. Especially those that have affected this show. I want to dispel any suggestions about there being a 'casting couch' for this show. No dancers were selected due to anything other than their talent. I have never and will never take advantage of people."

Even saying it made his stomach twist in disgust.

"However, Remi and I engaged in a relationship *after* she was chosen to be the lead in *Out of Bounds*." His gaze sought her out in the audience, and even in the dim lighting, he could see the pink coloring her cheeks. But she nodded at him, giving her silent acceptance. "This had nothing to do with her role in the show. We kept it quiet because…well, we didn't know how to label it. And we both understood there could be implications of announcing it. Unfortunately, this information has made its way into a public forum, and it's taking over the press we had started to build for *Out of Bounds*."

The *Spill the Tea* article was one of a handful that had broken that morning. How much longer would it be before larger outlets picked it up? Before someone got Lilah to speak?

"I had two decisions in front of me. We could press on and hope that the media believed me when I told them the truth. We could hope that the show was good enough to blow everything out of the water to the point where people stopped gossiping." He sucked in a huge breath, his heart and lungs crushed by regret. "But my fear is that these questions will linger, regardless of how well we do. I am loathe to allow any of you to be tainted by such rumors, especially Remi."

Her eyes widened, but she didn't speak up.

"This means, for the time being, I am halting production of *Out of Bounds*."

A confused din rose up from the audience, the cast members looking to one another with bewilderment. A few people started to ask questions, but Wes held up a hand.

"You will all be paid for the time you were contracted,

and I will do it out of my own pocket." It was going to make starting up the show at a later point difficult, but he'd be damned before he reneged on the promises he'd made to his cast. "My hope is that the noise dies down and that we can resume *Out of Bounds* at a later point. This was an incredibly tough decision to make, but I thought long and hard about it. My reputation has already been called into question, so I can only behave in the best way I know how in order to make amends.

"Remi's reputation, however, might be spared by a delay in production. Now, I could press on regardless and understand that she might want to withdraw. But the fact is, there is no *Out of Bounds* without Remi. The unique quality that she brings to this production is irreplaceable. In some companies or in other productions, people *are* replaceable. But I believe in everyone here as individuals, so I hope that explains why I'm making this decision."

In the audience, Remi's eyes glittered. She pressed a hand to her chest but sat still as a statue, like she'd been frozen by his words.

"I will not forge ahead by putting her needs and reputation second to my own goals."

He brought his hands together, fighting the urge to say everything else that bubbled away in his head. It would be too easy to shout out what he felt for her, but that would need to be a private moment between them. For now, Wes was sick of private things being made public, and he would not go into further detail about his relationship with Remi. All he could do was hope that his actions were speaking loud and clear this time.

"I need more time to speak with our investors before I know where this leaves us. For now, I'll let you all go, but you can expect information from me in the coming days as to what the next steps are." He tried to smile, but today it wouldn't happen. "I thank you in advance for your understanding and patience while we navigate this speed bump."

The cast sat for a moment, clearly shell-shocked by the news. He knew some of them would find other work in the meantime. The investors might leave and his own finances might take a hit so badly that the show could die all together.

So be it.

This was the sacrifice he had to make for Remi. Because it was true what he'd said—she *was* irreplaceable. In this show and in his life. One by one, the cast stood and headed for the exit. Chantel came to the front of the stage and looked up at him.

"I'm proud of you, Bro. That took balls." She grinned. "I know you'll get this show going. You have our support one hundred percent."

"Good, because I'll be living on baked beans and toast after it's all done," he quipped. "I'll have to sell the apartment and live in the suburbs."

Chantel shuddered. "Please don't joke about that. You know I don't go below Forty-Seventh."

Sadie squeezed his shoulder and left him to wallow in his misery. He crouched down and rested his forearms on his knees, as if inspecting the ground beneath his feet to make sure it wasn't falling away. He had no idea how long he stayed there, staring at the lines in the wood, wondering what had caused those imperfections and scratches. When he finally stood, only one person remained in the theater. Remi.

"You'd better go before they turn the power off," he joked. His footsteps echoed through the quiet building as he walked across the stage and down the steps to the red-carpeted aisle. "We're no longer tenants of this theater."

Remi waited for him to reach her, her hands knotted in front of her body. She looked every bit as beautiful as the memories flashing in his head like a movie montage—same rosy cheeks with scattered freckles, same gold hair and sunshine smile.

"Does that mean we're going to be breaking the rules again? I have a habit of doing that around you."

"Bad influence, that's what my friends say." He cleared his throat. "Thanks for coming today. I wasn't sure you would."

"I wasn't sure I would either," she replied. "But I didn't want anyone believing Lilah. You don't deserve that."

He glanced around the empty theater. Later, he'd have to come back for all the bits and pieces they'd left behind—like Alfred—but right now, he wanted to get the hell away from it all. How could things have been messed up so badly?

Because you didn't speak up. You didn't let her in when you should have been honest about what was going on. It affected her, and you kept quiet.

"I meant what I said before." He jammed his hands into his pockets. "There is no show without you."

"What if I don't want to come back?" she asked.

"Then I'll move on and find another idea." He

shrugged. "I guess we'll find out if I'm a one almost-hit wonder."

"You're not," she said softly.

"If you walk away, I'll understand." All the things he wanted to say were swirling in his head, butting up against one another in the fight to leave his lips first. "But *you* have the choice. I shouldn't have lied to you, and…God, I was so frightened that you'd cut and run."

"Were you going to fire me that night?" she asked.

"I thought about it." He cleared his throat, the shame at his moment of weakness filtering through him. "But the second you opened the door and I saw that perfect smile…I knew I couldn't do it."

"Why?" Her eyes were guarded, but she didn't look away. "Because you wanted what was best for the show?"

"I wasn't thinking about the show or about your career or mine. The second I came into your apartment it was…us. No work, no politics. It was purely selfish, because I want to keep you around. And I knew that Lilah finding out about us was everything you'd been afraid would happen."

"It was." She shook her head. "A person can forgive themselves once for making such a critical mistake, but twice? There's no excuse."

"Maybe there's one excuse," he said.

The feeling had been growing in him with terrifying urgency. The feeling that was a whole lot more than like, that was a whole lot riskier and more foreign. He and Remi fit together; they worked well. They sparked off one another. She'd trusted him to help her face her fears, and he'd trusted her to give it her all without holding back. As two individuals, they were talented. But together…together, they were beyond anything he could have imagined.

"I don't think anything justifies making the same mistake twice."

"What if I told you I lied when I said I like you?" he said.

Her blond brows shot up. "That's a hell of a way to win me over."

"What if 'like' was the word that felt safe, but it didn't quite capture what I was feeling?" He had *not* planned on doing this today, so the words came out clumsy and uncoordinated. Stumbling. Like a baby llama on pointe shoes. "I don't know what comes next because love seems crazy. We've known each other less than a month, but I'd be lying if I didn't admit that I felt something the first time I saw you. I *knew* you had something rare."

Her eyes widened. "What are you trying to say?"

"That I am handing you everything. The fate of *Out of Bounds* is yours." His chest felt like it had been run through with electricity, the sizzle of every frantic beat in his ears. "I know you were devastated by what happened last time—that you were abandoned, that you were kicked out. But this time it's different. You're in control."

"But that show is everything to you," she said. "Why wouldn't you find someone else?"

"There is no one else, Remi. You're it." He swallowed. "For the show…and for me."

Remi wondered if she'd imagined it all. If she might suddenly be jolted out of this hazy dream and find herself staring at the ceiling above her bed. But the sincerity in Wes's face wasn't something she could dream, because she wasn't sure she'd ever seen him display that mix of raw honesty and vulnerability before. Usually he covered things with a charming smile, with a quip or a wink. But now there was no creasing around his stunning blue eyes nor the beginnings of a smirk twitching on his lips, nothing that meant to soften the impact of his words.

"Are you saying…you love me?" She blinked. This wasn't something she could easily process, because it was never supposed to happen. After she'd left Australia, love wasn't something she'd planned to seek out. At least, not for a very long time.

"I don't know how to say it. Love is for people who know each other inside and out. And I feel like I'm only scratching the surface with you." He rubbed the back of his neck. "But I want to know everything about you. I want to learn all the things you like and what you dislike. I want to help you achieve your dreams, and I want to be the person who's there every day telling you how talented you are until you finally start to see it for yourself."

Remi covered her mouth with her hand, trying hard to keep the soft, little sob inside. She'd never dared hope that Wes might be falling for her the way she was for him. Last time, she'd convinced herself that she was loved back when she wasn't. And she'd been terrified of stumbling down that path again.

"Tell me I'm not out on my own here," he said,

a nervous laugh cutting through the words. "I'm not imagining that this was more than sex, right?"

She shook her head. But her lips were frozen in shock, her tongue lay heavy in her mouth while her mind whirred, scrambling to catch up. Could she believe it?

"You know how to make a guy crazy," he said, placing his hands on her shoulders and giving her a playful shake. "Talk to me. Because I'm feeling like a real idiot now spilling all this out."

"I more than like you too." The words came out in a rush as she curled her hands over his. "And I think you *do* know me, because everything you said now shows me that."

"I want to know more." He lowered his forehead to hers, and the sweetness of it all was so right, so perfectly right, that Remi finally allowed herself to relax. "I want to know every detail so minute that you'll go crazy telling me."

She laughed. "That's going to take a long time."

The charming grin was back, but this time it wasn't a cover. It was real. "I see you've discovered my plan."

"Clever. I'll need to keep an eye on you."

"Please do." His expression sobered. "But I'm serious when I say that I shouldn't have lied. Remi, I'm sorry. I was so angry that I'd risked everything like that, angry at myself for pushing you to go against your rule."

"I wanted it," she admitted. "I was scared, sure, but I caved because I wanted it. Not because you pushed me. You're hard to resist, you know."

"So you're not going to resist me now?"

A smile curved on her lips. "Not on your life."

With the show out of the way and Wes coming clean, she could make her decision from a place of clarity rather than fear. Knowing that he was willing to sacrifice his dream production to be with her...well, it told her everything she needed to know. He wasn't going to abandon her; he wasn't going to put selfishness first.

All the feelings and desires she'd pent up were running riot in her veins, that wonderful, fizzy excitement making her feel like she was about to levitate. Dance brought her joy and fulfillment, and she had Wes to thank for bringing her back to it. For pushing her boundaries and forcing her to be truthful with herself.

"I'm done resisting," she said.

"Good. But this time *I* have a rule." He brushed his thumb over the corner of her lips, parting her mouth in a way that made the blood thrum harder in her veins. And like that, their sweet moment turned sexy. "No more secrets. Between us or about us."

No more secrets...only, she *did* have one. Annie. Bad Bachelors. Saying yes to Wes now while withholding that piece of information would make her behavior no better than what he'd done. She had no idea where she stood with Annie, no idea if there was even a friendship to salvage.

But all she did know was that she wanted to be with Wes. Without guilt or secrets lurking in the corners of her mind.

"No more secrets." She sucked in a breath. "I know who runs Bad Bachelors."

Wes blinked. "What?"

"It's my friend Annie." She spilled the entire story

from how she'd used it when her friend Darcy first decided to get back into the dating scene, to how Darcy's fiancé, Reed, had found out Annie's identity and they'd all kept it a secret from her.

"So that's what he meant," Wes said. "The cost that was too great."

"It was Darcy." She sighed. "He didn't want to come between her and Annie. They've been friends since they were kids."

"And you trust me with that information?" He looked shocked.

"I don't want there to be anything between us. You know all my secrets now, all my truths." She bit her lip. "I promised Annie that I wouldn't tell, but I can't have a skeleton in the closet that might come to hurt us later. I begged her to do something, to take your reviews down."

"For the show?"

"And for you." She wrapped her arms around herself. "I couldn't stand the thought of you suffering for it. But she wouldn't listen. I don't want her to get hurt and I think she might if people know, but I can't start something with you if it's not a clean start."

"People will always talk. If it's not that site, it'll be another. At least now we're giving them something positive to say."

"You want to tell people about us?"

"Remi, I want to tell the world. I want to shout it so loud that I lose my voice over it. Everyone is going to know what a lucky son of a bitch I am."

"And the show?"

"Like I said, it's yours. If you want to bring it back,

we'll do it." He brushed his lips over hers. More the promise of a kiss than a kiss itself. "If you want to move on and talk to my mother about getting her to help you find a role somewhere else…"

Her heart and her mind were so full the answer wasn't far from her lips at all. "If I'm going back into this world, I'm doing it with you, Wes. Not anyone else."

"She could get you a place in any dance company," Wes said. His eyes were bright with hope—hope that she would say the right thing, hope that their bond was stronger than either of their desires for their careers.

And it was.

"I choose you, Wes. Before anything else, I choose you."

Epilogue

Two months later...

> "Wes is easily the most creative, inspiring person
> I've ever met. He's fiercely independent while also
> being inclusive and generous. He's attentive and
> kind and well-rounded. And yes, his reputation in
> bed precedes him for good reason. But the man is
> more than the sum of his parts, no matter how good
> those parts are."

—RemiDrysdale

SNEAKING OUT OF THE DRESSING ROOM RIGHT BEFORE THE
show was about to start was a bold move. Usually, prior
to a performance, Remi would have her headphones on,
the show's music playing as she mapped the moves out
in her mind, her body going into an almost meditative
state to quell the nerves. *Especially* on opening night.

She peered around the corner of the door that led
out from the dancer's hallway and into the foyer, her
gaze scanning the room. Since her hair and makeup
were already done, the ability to blend into the crowd

of buzzing theater goers had vanished. But this was too important a thing to miss.

"Remi!" Chantel came over and spoke in a stage whisper, her eyes narrowed. "What the hell are you doing out here?"

"You look beautiful." Frankie gazed up at her with wide-open eyes.

"Thank you, sweetheart." Remi bent down to give the little girl a hug before popping back up. "Have you got the flyers?"

Chantel nodded. "Enough for every seat in the house."

The pink sheets of paper had the *Out of Bounds* logo along with a message urging theatergoers to flood the Bad Bachelors site with reviews for the show, rather than for Wes. In the last two months, Remi and Wes had worked hard to clear the gossip surrounding him and *Out of Bounds*. He'd appeared on morning talk shows, promoting their work and dodging questions about the reviews and media frenzy over his sex life.

He and Remi appeared in public together, talking openly about their relationship and about them working together. *Pointe Magazine* had even contacted her to do a feature on her return to the ballet world, which was another dream come true.

But the Bad Bachelor reviews remained. Remi and Annie's friendship was on shaky ground. However, Annie had insisted not only on coming to opening night, but also buying tickets for her whole team in a gesture of support. They would work things out eventually. But for now, Remi had another idea for how to quash the salacious reviews.

"How are you going to hand them out without him seeing?" Remi asked.

"Don't worry about it. I've got it covered." Chantel winked. "Besides, he's not going to be coming out to the audience until the last minute. It'll already be done by then."

Remi nodded. "Okay. I'll see you after the show."

She ducked back through the door and headed down to the dressing rooms in time to find Wes giving the cast a pep talk. He shot her a relieved look when she walked through the door and shed the long, black cloak that'd covered her costume. Everything was ready to go. Her costume fit like a glove and the floaty, black skirt swished around her legs like a gauzy cloud. She'd been over the moves in her head a thousand times.

"This is our chance to make a splash," Wes said to the group. "I believe in you all and I believe in this show. Our investors do too, so let's show them their faith in us was worth the wait. More importantly, let's show the audience what the dance industry has been missing!"

There was a cheer from the group, followed by nervous chatter as everyone shed their outer layers and ran through the final preparations. Since there was no curtain on the stage and all the chairs were lined up with audience members seated, the show started in the wings.

Those who were onstage—and had paid for the privilege—looked left and right, trying to figure out what was going to happen. A grin split Remi's face wide open when her dad turned toward the wings and looked straight at her. Next to him, Opal's hair glowed like a frizzy halo under the stage lights. When they'd agreed to come and watch her—on her assurance she'd give them an experience like nothing they'd ever had before—she'd never felt more loved and accepted by them.

Tonight, both she and Wes had supporters in the audience. Chantel, Mike, and the girls would be in the front row along with Wes's parents. Darcy, Reed, and Annie were here too. Even Mish had come, saying she wouldn't miss it for the world. And Bert Soole, their angel, was there with his wife.

Boom! The first, bass-rattling beat hit and *Out of Bounds* burst to life in a riot of dancers rushing the stage and audience in dizzying color. All except for Remi, who was the only one in black.

The music filled the theater, audience members turning their heads to and fro, unsure where to look. The opening was designed to confuse. To excite.

When Remi strode back to the chair next to her father, she smiled for a second before stepping up onto the chair. *Swish, swish, kick.* Her foot sailed past his face, and he could no doubt feel the air rushing between her satin pointe shoe and his nose. *Swish, swish, kick.* She turned, rose into arabesque and held herself steady and confident. Strong. Her dad looked up at her, awestruck.

Power washed over her, like a drug filtering through her system. She commanded this audience. Held them captive. They were hers.

And she did it all for Wes.

"Wes Evans is a true artistic genius."

"Broadway hasn't seen talent like Wes Evans for a long time. *Out of Bounds* is an exercise in restrained shock, in perfect execution of an idea that takes the traditional and rips it to shreds."

"*Out of Bounds* isn't a show. It's an experience."

Wes gaped openmouthed at his laptop. The sight of his Bad Bachelors profile flooded with reviews for *Out of Bounds* was *not* what he'd expected when Chantel had texted him that morning, telling him to go online. The entire first page of reviews had nothing to do with his body or his sex life or his reputation. It was only about his show. His creation.

WES: How did this happen?
CHANTEL: Ask your girlfriend.

He looked over to where Remi slept beside him, a content smile on her lips. Her hair was a tangled heap of golden strands, like a fuzzy lion's mane. The woman slept like she was dead, tipping over into slumber with ease and staying there as long as possible. He brushed her cheeks with his knuckles and she didn't even stir.

Opening night had exhausted them both. Not enough that they hadn't fallen into bed with mouths pressed together and limbs entwined, but it was quick and furious. Not the usual slow exploration he preferred. But he'd make it up to her later.

They had a grueling schedule ahead. Two shows today and for the next few days, with a couple of evening-only days after that. It would take a toll on her body—giving her aches and fatigue. But he would be there every step of the way, cheering until his throat gave out.

Last night, she had been a vision. More beautiful and powerful than he'd ever seen her before.

"You're staring at me," she said sleepily, cracking one eye open. "I can feel it."

"Good morning." He leaned down and kissed the tip of her nose.

She rolled toward him and eyed the laptop. "Read anything interesting?"

"Only a flood of reviews on Bad Bachelors."

"What do they say? Wes Evans has a massive cock?" She laughed when he rolled his eyes. "What? You do."

He chuckled. "You know very well what they say."

She snuggled against him, resting her head on his chest and pressing a hand to his stomach. "I couldn't think of any other way to help."

"Baby, you help by dancing your heart out. You were incredible last night." He leaned down to kiss her, coaxing her lips open and sliding his tongue against hers. "My star."

"I love you," she whispered, her eyes shining.

They hadn't said it before, but the words sent a wave of comfort through him. Hearing her say those words felt so right. As right as watching Remi on his stage, and as right as waking up with her in his arms. Their lives were inexorably linked. Their dreams forever entwined. And there was no more fear about the reason Remi was here with him. She had offers flooding in from the show's preview. Interview requests and audition invitations clogged her inbox daily. Before the show launched he'd asked if she might leave *Out of Bounds*. But what he was really asking was if she'd leave him. Remi had simply frowned and shook her head. Never, she'd said. They were a team. A partnership. And that meant more to her than any possible job offer. Their relationship was number one, and everything else had to get in line.

"I love you too," he said.

Wes rolled Remi beneath him, her body automatically aligning to fit his. Their moves were in sync now, their bodies in tune.

She tilted her face up to his. "How did I get so lucky?"

"Must be those weird, little crystals you always carry around."

Remi laughed. "They're not weird."

"Miss Reminiscent Sunburst Drysdale, are you turning into a hippie?" He peppered her cheeks with kisses, and she glared at him in mock annoyance.

"And what if I am? Would you stop loving me?"

"Never, baby. You're mine until the last curtain falls."

"Good thing our show doesn't *have* curtains." She looped her arms around his neck and dragged his head down to hers. "I want this to last forever."

Keep reading for an excerpt from

Bad Bachelor

Available now from
Sourcebooks Casablanca

So bad it's good? Save that for your Liam Neeson movie marathon. Bad has no place in your love life.

With more ways than ever to meet your future Mr. Right, you'd think the women of New York would be at an advantage. But trying to find a soul mate in a world of Instagram filters and mobile dating apps is tough—expectations are high and attention spans are low.

It's all too easy for your date to check out potential matches while you're in the restroom. He could be swiping right on a dozen other ladies in the vicinity. Chances are he'll be out the door in less time than it took to read your bio.

So how can you sort the good guys from the serial bachelors? That's where the Bad Bachelors app comes to the rescue. Our app is designed for the women of New York to have their say. Going on a date? Simply search your bachelor's name to see what his previous dates have said about him.

How do reviews work? Well, it's no different from leaving a review for your favorite restaurant on Yelp. Bad Bachelors uses a five-star rating system and allows users to share more detail in the review section. We'll guide you through the process with review prompts—such as "Did he turn up on time?" and "Did he want to know more about you?"—to ensure that your review provides useful information.

We respect that our users may not feel comfortable posting reviews under their real names, so we do allow anonymous reviews. However, only verified users can add a bachelor to the Bad Bachelors database—your profile must be linked to identifying information such as a Facebook profile or phone number.

If your date moves to the bedroom, that's great! However, we ask that you keep reviews PG-13. We don't need to re-create *Fifty Shades of Grey* here.

User MidTownMolly had her best date in weeks thanks to reading a positive review of her workplace crush. "The review spurred me to ask him out, and he said yes! We went for dinner and talked nonstop until he dropped me off at home. I'm already excited for date number two."

If you date a stand-up guy and it doesn't work out, don't be afraid to let your fellow ladies know he's a potential catch. Remember, even if he didn't knock your socks off, that doesn't mean he's not happy-ever-after material for someone else.

We're in the business of helping you make informed choices and we rely on our users to get quality data. So, next time you date, don't forget to rate. Tomorrow, we'll be posting a profile spotlight on our "Bad Bachelor." This one should be avoided at all costs. I don't want to spoil anything before our post goes live, but let's just say he's our worst-rated bachelor yet!

With love,
Your Dating Information Warrior
Helping the single women of New York since 2018

Chapter 1

"Reed McMahon is a master manipulator. He knows exactly what to say and how to say it. Don't believe a word he says."

—MisguidedinManhattan

Sweat beaded along Darcy Greer's brow as she smoothed her shaking hands over the full skirt of her wedding gown, her fingertips catching on the subtle pattern embroidered into the silk. Long sleeves masked her tattoos, turning her into a picture-perfect bride. Her mother had been so pleased when she'd chosen this dress because the priest wasn't too thrilled with her ink. Truthfully, Darcy hadn't been thrilled with looking like a cake topper. But she also hadn't wanted any drama to mar her big day. Besides, it was only a dress.

I can't believe I'm doing this…

She sucked in a breath and surveyed the picturesque blue sky with clouds so white and fluffy they looked like globs of marshmallow. A flawless day, the photographer had assured her, all the better to capture this important moment.

Empty space stretched out from all sides, making her

feel small, like a blip on the surface of the earth. A smile tugged at her lips and she tilted her face up, letting her eyes flutter shut as a cool breeze drifted past.

Just breathe…

Her best friends stood before her, looking immaculate in their bridesmaid gowns. They each wore a color that matched their personality—Remi, the ballerina, in soft pink and the ever-practical Annie in a classic royal blue. These women had gotten her through the toughest times in her life. They'd made sure she was here today in one piece, finally ready to release her old life.

"All right, ladies." The photographer raised his camera, the big lens pointing in Darcy's direction, unblinking like a Cyclops's eye. "Everyone get into position. I want this first shot to be perfect."

Darcy's heart skipped a beat. This was it, her last opportunity to put a stop to this madness.

You okay? Annie mouthed.

Darcy nodded. She would be okay, she would be okay, she *would* be okay.

Pop!

The first shot hit her straight in the ribs and stung like hell. She gasped, her hands clutching at the spot where crimson bled across the white silk. The camera clicked. A moment captured.

The pain was more than she'd expected, but there was something deeply satisfying about seeing the splash of color against the ugly, white silk.

Pop! Pop! Pop!

"Wow, guys, give me a minute." Darcy backed up, dodging a green balloon sailing through the air. "And don't look so happy about being able to throw stuff at me."

She reached for a water balloon of her own and took aim, Remi's soft-pink dress in her sights. Her throw was off and the balloon burst against the ground, splashing orange paint over Remi's feet and legs.

"Now you look like a beautiful sunset," Annie said, hiking up her long skirt in one hand and reaching for a ketchup bottle filled with red paint. She ran over to Darcy and squeezed a stream of it all over the sweetheart neckline of her wedding dress. "Ah, much better!"

"I look like I'm starring in a remake of *Psycho*." Darcy glanced down at herself. Red paint dripped along her body, running in rivulets across the silk. "I need more color."

"Coming right up." Remi grabbed a small paint can and a tiny brush. "Watch me unleash my artistic side."

She splashed purple paint in a flamboyant arc, turning Darcy from a horror movie extra into something out of a modern art exhibition.

"This is wonderful, ladies." The photographer clicked and clicked, capturing Darcy's shock as Annie paint bombed her out of nowhere. "These photos will be amazing."

A high-pitched shriek pierced the air as Annie turned on Remi and the two girls battled it out with their respective weapons. Soon, the elegant dresses looked like a finger-painting lesson gone horribly wrong. Splotches of orange and green peppered Remi's blond hair.

They'd decided against using the proper paintball guns on advisement of the venue owner—safety first and all that jazz. Getting shot at close range apparently stung like a bitch. So they'd spent a painstaking hour filling up water balloons and other containers before the shoot.

Darcy picked up another ketchup bottle filled with paint and used it to make a sad face on the bottom of her gown. "I hate this goddamn dress."

Annie covered her mouth in a failed attempt to stifle her laughter but instead smeared paint across her cheek. "Sorry, Darcy. I know you only picked it to keep your mom happy."

"You're right." She frowned. "The whole damn wedding was more about her than it was about me."

Annie slung an arm around Darcy's shoulder. "Come on, this is your anti-anniversary party. Your 'thank God I got out while I could' bash. It's time to celebrate, not mope about your family issues. That dress is ugly as hell anyway."

The beginnings of a smile tugged at Darcy's lips. "It *is* ugly, isn't it?"

"Fugly even. Seriously, I didn't have the heart to say anything because you know I love your mom"—Annie wrinkled her nose—"but I wouldn't even bury my cat in that thing."

Out of nowhere, a balloon burst between them. "Hey!"

"Two for the price of one," Remi crowed, her Australian accent amplified as she raised her voice and pumped her fist in the air. "You beauty!"

"We were having a moment," Darcy said in mock protest.

"Yeah, and now it's a rainbow moment." Remi toyed with two fresh water balloons, a cheeky grin on her face.

"Do it," Annie said. "I dare you."

"Do you double dare me?" Remi walked toward them, her arms swinging in that dainty, fluid way of hers.

Annie tried to make a break for it, but Darcy wrapped her arms around her waist and held on tight. "Get her, Remi."

The balloons exploded and both girls screamed.

By the time they'd run out of things to throw at one another, Darcy was famished. The owner of the venue—which was normally an outdoor paintball arena—had kindly allowed them space to conduct the photo shoot and let them make use of the open-air cafeteria as well.

She glanced at the picnic table full of cupcakes and let her eyes settle on the top tier of what would have been her wedding cake. Apparently, you were supposed to save it for the first anniversary.

But what if the wedding never happened? Surely that was an excuse not to keep it. Except her mother had; she'd saved it when the rest of the cake had been thrown into the trash. Now, a year after Darcy *should* have been married, her mother had foisted it on her like some kind of cruel joke.

It said a lot about their relationship.

The offending lump of cake—covered in thick, Italian-style marzipan icing—sat in the middle of the table. Poking at it with her forefinger as if it were an alien species, Darcy considered her options. Eat it or toss it?

"Let me show you how to deal with this." Remi picked up the cake and signaled for the photographer to follow her. She hurled it into the air and it landed with a satisfying splat on the ground a few feet away.

"See?" she said. "No more devil cake."

Annie clapped her hands together. "Now we can get this party started."

This "party" was something that had taken a lot of convincing. Darcy had wanted to let the day come and go without ceremony or recognition. She would have been perfectly happy to sit in her sweats and eat ice cream straight out of the tub like a Bridget Jones cliché. But she was the kind of woman who could admit when she was wrong—the trash-the-dress party had proved far more entertaining than she'd first anticipated. Plus, it made for an interesting catch-up rather than their usual wine-and-vent sessions.

Every week, the three friends got together to unload their latest funny stories and problems on one another. It'd been a tradition since high school, when Darcy and Annie would meet to do their homework together. Translation: talk about boys and update their Myspace profiles or whatever else sixteen-year-old girls did before smartphones.

Remi had completed their trio when she'd moved to New York from Australia a few years ago and ended up being Darcy's roommate. These women had glued her back together—and *kept* her that way—since her wedding had been canceled the previous year.

"These look delicious," Annie announced as she pored over the tiered cake stand filled with cupcakes supplied by Remi. "I wish I could bake like you."

"I wish I could bake something without setting the oven on fire," Darcy quipped as she washed her hands at the small outdoor sink, scrubbing at the green paint under her fingernails. "But we can't all be Martha Stewart, can we?"

"Just don't tell my family that I'm using sugar and wheat flour—they'll think I'm poisoning you." She cringed. "Everything in their house is hemp-infused, plant-based bullshit."

"Well, I can't cook or bake," Annie said. "According to my mother, that means I'll make a terrible wife."

"Ugh." Darcy forced down a wave of nausea. Nothing could recall her lunch faster than the thought of motherly expectations. "Please don't use the *W* word around me. Mom's been trying to set me up with her friends' sons. Literally any and all of them. I don't think she cares who it is so long as I get a ring on my finger."

"Did you remind her what happened the last time she set you up with someone?" Annie snorted. "Or won't she take any responsibility for that?"

"She dropped off the top layer of the wedding cake as a reminder that I should be trying to find 'the one.' *And* she had the audacity to tell me she hadn't given up on me, like I'm some hundred-year-old spinster who's about to be eaten by a houseful of cats."

Annie blinked. "Right."

"If only she could see you now." Remi grinned.

The photographer hovered around them, snapping pictures of what must have been a hilarious scene: three women in full hair and makeup, wearing paint-splattered dresses and eating cupcakes. What a sight.

"Maybe she meant it as an encouragement," Remi said.

"The message couldn't have been clearer. It's been one year and she wants to know why I'm not out there trying to find a man so I can fulfill my purpose as a woman and start making babies."

"Screw that." Remi wrinkled her nose.

Annie opened the champagne with a *pop* and poured the fizzing liquid into each of the three champagne flutes. She measured precisely, ensuring each glass was equal.

"Here's to you, Darcy. Happy anti-anniversary." She handed the glasses out and held up her own. "Congratulations on dodging a bullet."

"Still feels like I got shot." She shook her head as their flutes all met in a cacophony of clinks.

"Better to have loved and lost than to have gone down the aisle with the wrong guy," Remi said, sipping her drink. "Here's to moving on."

There was a chorus of "hear, hear" from the girls as they clinked their glasses again.

"Nothing like a new fling to take your mind off the old one," Remi added, gesturing with her champagne. "Forget about relationships and have a little fun. You've earned it."

It sounded so simple when she said it like that, but Darcy was out of practice. Besides, there was this little, tiny problem that had developed since the almost-wedding. The very few times she'd gotten close to getting physical with a guy, her nerves had kicked in and she'd lost all sense of excitement. Was *sex anxiety* a thing? Because that was probably what she had.

"I don't know…" Darcy sunk her teeth into the pile of frosting on her cupcake.

"Think about it. If you quit a bad job, you would start looking for another one, right?" Annie said. "You don't stop working because you had *one* bad job."

Remi snorted. "Only you would compare a relationship to a job."

"I'm serious. Getting a job and dating aren't all that different. You have to assess each other to see if you're a good fit and then you have a trial period to see if it's going to work out."

"Do you make your dates sign a contract too?" Darcy teased.

"I'll tell you when I have enough time to go on a date." Annie sighed. "Like in the year 2045."

Remi peeled back the brightly colored paper on another cupcake. "As ridiculous as that comparison is, she has a point. One bad experience doesn't mean a lifetime without sex. It's perfectly acceptable for men to enjoy casual sex, so why not us too?"

The group murmured their agreement. Even the photographer nodded emphatically.

"Have you been with *anyone* since Ben?" Annie asked.

The girls looked at her curiously. Darcy hadn't spoken much about the demise of her engagement or her failed attempts to put herself back into the dating scene. She'd always been the most private one of the group. Growing up with a mother who was emotional to the extreme had made her develop a natural resistance to showing her feelings.

Maybe that's why you never saw it coming. You didn't ask enough questions or pay attention to the right things.

"The only kind of sex I've had in the last year has been with me, myself, and I." Darcy sighed.

"Oh, a threesome." Remi winked. "Kinky."

"And even that hasn't been too spectacular," Darcy said.

"Not for a lack of trying, mind you. I've had a few dates, but anytime the guy even tries to kiss me, I freeze up."

Annie reached out and patted her knee. "You're stressed. That's totally understandable."

"What do I have to be stressed about? I love my job, I'm healthy, I have a great family…"

Annie raised a brow.

"Okay, not *great* but they're decent human beings… most of the time." Well, barring the cake incident. "Finding your fiancé making out with someone the day before your wedding doesn't have to ruin everything. Single is the new black, right?"

"I love you, Darcy, but this #foreveralone thing is stopping right *now*." She set her drink and half-eaten dessert down on the table. "You need to break the dry spell."

After the split, getting back into the dating scene had gradually moved from the "too hard" basket to the "never, ever again" basket. Except there had been this little voice in the back of her mind lately, whispering dangerous thoughts to her, asking questions she wasn't sure how to answer, like whether she was happy being alone. Or if she'd be able to watch her beautiful friends walk down the aisle and be okay missing out on that experience herself.

Despite hating her mother's über-conservative ways, deep down, she still wanted the white-picket-fence dream—a wedding, a loving husband…even the babies.

But all that required her to date. And that meant facing up to the fact that she had no idea *how* to date. She'd given up her chance of learning those lessons when she'd fallen head over Dr. Martens at nineteen.

Now, eight years later, she was starting from scratch with no skills and no real experience to draw on.

Casual sex might sound like a piece of cake to some people, but the idea of dating was terrifying enough. As for casual sex? Darcy had never had a one-night stand. Ever.

"I wouldn't even know where to go to meet someone," she muttered. "And I deleted Tinder the second I started getting dick pics. Not to mention that I'm so out of practice even if I *could* make it past a first date. I can't flirt. I can't do witty banter. I can't play the temptress. So how am I supposed to have casual sex?"

And that wasn't even the hard part. Being able to trust someone again and not be paranoid that they were secretly living a double life, now *that* was the real challenge.

"Being celibate is so much easier."

"Hey, if that's what you want, I support you one hundred percent." Annie reached out and squeezed her shoulder.

"Say the word and we won't mention the dating thing ever again," Remi chimed in.

Darcy scratched at a fleck of dried paint on her dress. "I *do* want to get back out there," she admitted. "But I'm scared I'll pick the wrong guy again."

"Then you need to find a guy who's trustworthy," Annie said, pausing to sip her drink. "Someone who wants the same things you do."

"And how would I find a guy like that? It's not like I can trust what they write in their dating profiles."

"You could try the Bad Bachelors app," the photographer piped up. All eyes turned to the young man in the vest and bow tie. A heavy-looking camera hung from a thick strap around his neck. "I read about it the other day."

Darcy shook her head. "What on earth is the Bad Bachelors app?"

"Oh!" Remi bounced up and down in her seat. "I heard about this. Apparently, someone started this app that has all the single guys in New York listed and you can rate and review them."

"You're kidding." Darcy blinked. "So it's Yelp… for guys?"

"Or Uber? You know, go for a ride and then rate your driver," Remi said and Annie choked on a mouthful of cupcake.

Darcy shook her head and downed the rest of her champagne, immediately reaching for the bottle to refill her glass. "You're making this up."

"I swear, I'm not. Does anyone have the app?" Remi asked, but the girls shook their heads. "Give me your phone."

Within minutes, they'd downloaded the app and were browsing through profile after profile of gorgeous, single New York men. Each profile had at least one photo, a brief description, and a star rating. It looked as though the app was fairly new, but there were already a ton of reviews posted.

"These are hilarious," Remi said, swiping across the screen. "Look at this one. 'Trenton Conner, thirty-eight. Doctor. The only thing that's large about this guy is his ego and his credit limit.'"

"Let me read." Annie grabbed the phone and swiped a few times. "'Jacob Morales, thirty-nine. Technology executive. Things were going well until he rolled over and fell asleep right after sex. Then his maid came into the bedroom to shoo me out of his apartment.'"

Darcy laughed. "Oh my God."

"This one's nice." Annie held the phone in one hand and her drink in the other. "'Darren Montgomery, thirty-one. IT manager and entrepreneur. Darren is a lovely guy, very sweet and kind. Romantic. But we didn't have much in common—I hope he finds the right woman for him.' I'm going to mark this one as a favorite for you."

"Gimme." Remi grabbed the phone back. "What about this guy? 'Alexei Petrov, thirty. Investor. This guy will take you on the ride of your life…' Oh no. Looks like he might've being dating a few women at once. Next!"

Darcy pressed her fingertips to her temples. "No cheaters, please."

"Oh dear." Remi turned the phone around to show a photo of the most beautiful man Darcy had ever seen. And yes, *beautiful* was the right way to describe him. He was so perfect looking, and yet there was a hardness to him, like a marble statue—beautiful and cold and unyielding. "'Reed McMahon, thirty-two. Marketing and PR executive. Reed McMahon is a master manipulator. He knows exactly what to say and how to say it. Don't believe a word he says. He goes through women like candy.'"

Darcy wrinkled her nose. "He sounds like one to stay away from."

"Look, you can sort by highest and lowest rated." She laughed. "This guy is the lowest rated—number one on the Bad Bachelors list. Fifty women have rated him already. Serial dater, not interested in commitment, colder than an iceberg...looks like he always has a different woman on his arm."

"What about the good guys? *Are* there any decent men on that thing?" Darcy sighed. "I feel like I'm searching for a unicorn."

"We'll find the right guy." Remi's eyes sparkled at the thought of playing virtual matchmaker. "Why don't we swipe through and put a list together?"

"A list will make it easier. I like that idea," Annie said.

Remi rolled her eyes. "Of course you do."

"Say I *hypothetically* agree this is a good idea," Darcy said, drumming her fingers on the edge of the table. "What am I supposed to do? Walk up to these guys and say, 'Hey, you've got a five-star rating. Let's date'?"

"It's called recon." Annie grinned and Darcy could already see the cogs turning in her mind. "We'll go through the top-rated list and help you narrow down some options. You never know, with six degrees of separation and all that, you might have a friend in common who can introduce you. But at least you know up front that the guy is a decent person...unlike if you met someone randomly at a bar."

Darcy rolled the idea around in her head.

Maybe this wasn't such a terrible idea: a lower-risk, research-led type of dating. As a librarian, that appealed to her. She could get all the information she needed up front and avoid the dangers associated with spontaneous dating.

Besides, what harm could a little research do?

Acknowledgments

So many people influence the creation of a book. Firstly, I want to thank my parents for getting me started in dance, and for all the hours they spent sitting through my exams, rehearsals, concerts, and competitions. Thanks to my entire family for putting up with me practicing my routines in our lounge room, and especially to my mum for the many hours she spent sewing sequins onto my costumes.

Thank you to Cat Clyne for being as excited about my books as an author always hopes their editor will be, and for saying "go for it" when I asked if I could make lots of inappropriate jokes about Wes's "reputation." Thanks to Stephany Daniel for her enthusiastic and helpful emails, and to Dawn Adams for the amazing covers. Plus a massive thank-you to the entire Sourcebooks team for helping me bring this series to life. You're all a dream to work with.

Thanks to my incredible agent, Jill Marsal, for her invaluable advice, for keeping my schedule in line, and for always being quick with a supportive word.

Thanks to the Ladies Supper Club for showing me what amazing female friendships look like. Thanks to Jen and Mary for the walks that always clear my head, and to Taryn for your constant positivity and encouragement.

And lastly, thanks to my husband for supporting me on this journey from the very first step, for helping me when I get stuck with a plot problem, and for always reminding me to celebrate the wins, no matter how big or small.